CROSS
THE *LINE*

CROSS THE LINE

SIMONE SOLTANI

Berkley Romance
New York

BERKLEY ROMANCE
Published by Berkley
An imprint of Penguin Random House LLC
penguinrandomhouse.com

Copyright © 2024 by Simone Soltani
Penguin Random House supports copyright. Copyright fuels creativity,
encourages diverse voices, promotes free speech, and creates a vibrant culture.
Thank you for buying an authorized edition of this book and for complying
with copyright laws by not reproducing, scanning, or distributing any part of it
in any form without permission. You are supporting writers and allowing
Penguin Random House to continue to publish books for every reader.

BERKLEY and the BERKLEY & B colophon are registered trademarks of
Penguin Random House LLC.

Library of Congress Cataloging-in-Publication Data

Names: Soltani, Simone, author.
Title: Cross the line / Simone Soltani.
Description: First edition. | New York: Berkley Romance, 2024. |
Series: Lights out
Identifiers: LCCN 2023058307 (print) | LCCN 2023058308 (ebook) |
ISBN 9780593818145 (trade paperback) | ISBN 9780593818152 (ebook)
Subjects: LCGFT: Romance fiction. | Novels.
Classification: LCC PS3619.O43957 C76 2024 (print) |
LCC PS3619.O43957 (ebook) | DDC 813/.6—dc23/eng/20240125
LC record available at https://lccn.loc.gov/2023058307
LC ebook record available at https://lccn.loc.gov/2023058308

First published in the United Kingdom by Pan Books,
an imprint of Pan Macmillan, in 2024.

First Berkley Romance edition: July 2024

Printed in the United States of America
1st Printing

Book design by Jenni Surasky

For anyone pushing through the pain every single day.

And for Mom J. I would have let you read this one.

FORMULA 1 RACE SCHEDULE

~~Bahrain • March 3–5~~

~~Saudi Arabia • March 17–19~~

~~Australia • March 31–April 2~~

~~Azerbaijan • April 28–30~~

~~United States (Miami) • May 5–7~~

~~Italy (Imola) • May 19–21~~

Monaco • May 26–28

Spain • June 2–4

Canada • June 16–18

Austria • June 30–July 2

Great Britain • July 7–9

Hungary • July 21–23

Belgium • July 28–30

Summer Break

Netherlands • August 25–27

Italy (Monza) • September 1–3

Singapore • September 15–17

Japan • September 22–24

Qatar • October 6–8

United States (Austin) • October 20–22

Mexico • October 27–29

Brazil • November 3–5

United States (Las Vegas) • November 16–18

Abu Dhabi • November 24–26

DEV

October
Austin, Texas

I've fucked up. Boy howdy, have I fucked *all* the way up.

My race engineer is in my ear, asking questions like *What happened?* and *Are you okay?* and, most importantly, *How much damage did the car sustain?* I need to answer him—need to reassure him and the team that I'm conscious after skidding through gravel and hitting a barrier at nearly a hundred miles an hour. For now, they'll have to trust my vitals displayed on the pit wall computer screens, because I can't seem to form the words to tell them. Not because there's anything physically wrong with me. It's just that my brain is . . . not present. It's taking a day off. Fully out to goddamn lunch. And it's not because of the crash.

"Dev?" Branny's voice breaks through the fog, his concern deep and clear over the radio. "Can you hear me? Are you okay? Repeat, are you okay?"

"I'm fine," I choke out, still clutching the steering wheel. My knuckles are probably white underneath my gloves. "Car's done, though. I'm sorry, everyone. This is on me."

Like any good engineer, he'll want to question what the

problem was, but he knows better than to ask it over the team radio, where anyone in the world could be listening. It'll wait until the debrief, and then I can get my ass handed to me by our CEO, our team principal, and my lead mechanic. And I'll deserve it, because this really was on me.

This was no fault of the car, the track surface, another driver, or a force of nature. No, I committed a mortal sin while behind the wheel.

I got distracted.

It shouldn't have happened. It's *never* happened in all my years of racing, and certainly not during the five I've spent in Formula 1. I've never let my mind wander so far that I braked too late and lost the back end. I barely had time to react before coming to a bone-shuddering stop in the barriers.

"Turn the car off and come back to the pit," Branny instructs.

I do what I'm told before I ruin anything else. I can only imagine what the TV commentators will report as they discuss the possible reasons for my crash. I can practically hear them saying, *It's such a disappointment, but what matters is that he's okay.*

But I'm not okay. I'm far from it. I screwed up big-time— and I don't mean the crash.

I can't stop thinking about it, even as I pull myself out of my ruined car and step away from millions of dollars of damage. If I'm being honest with myself, things may never be okay again.

Because I kissed Willow Williams last night. And now I'm a dead man walking.

WILLOW

Seven months later, May
New York City

I've nearly set my apartment on fire. Again.

Making macarons should not be this hard. They're small and cute, and the recipe calls for super simple ingredients— it's just egg whites, almond flour, and sugar. So why, oh *why*, can't I make a single batch without completely messing up?

"Oh no, oh shit," I mumble as I snatch an oven mitt off the counter and pull out the now-smoking confection. According to the timer, they shouldn't be done for another five minutes, and yet these are nearly burnt to a crisp. Either the recipe was wrong about the baking temperature, or my oven was sent straight from hell. I'm betting on the latter.

I'm desperate to re-create the infamous Stella Margaux Bakery's classic macaron because, as of a month ago, New York City's one location closed for renovations, and I simply can't live without them. The news was enough to make me consider moving back to the West Coast, where there's a Stella's practically every hundred feet.

Then again, I might not have a choice about returning to San Diego to live with my family if I can't find a job in the next couple of months. I came to New York four years ago for college and had plans to stay for possibly the rest of my life. My education was bankrolled by my amazing parents, with the stipulation that after graduation, I'd support myself. Truthfully, they'd have no problem continuing to help me, and they absolutely have the means, but it's the principle of it all. I made a promise, and I'm going to keep it. I just didn't think it would be this difficult.

I busted my ass during undergrad with a double major in communications and sports marketing, a minor in English, and a new internship every semester. With all that experience, I thought it would be easy to find a full-time position working in the marketing department of a professional sports team—a.k.a. my dream job. But after dozens of flat-out ignored applications, zero callbacks after interviews, and endless *We'll be in touch* lies, I'm still unemployed.

It would be so much worse if I'd graduated ages ago instead of just last week, but I've been applying for positions for months now, hoping to have a job in place by the time I was handed my diploma. My brother landed one in his field months before graduation, so I figured there was no reason I couldn't do the same.

Ha. Joke's on me, because here I am with no job, a dwindling sum in my bank account, and a two hours' drive from the closest Stella Margaux's. This is not what I call *living my best life*. But damn if I'm not trying.

"What's on fire?" Chantal asks from the doorway to the kitchen, grimacing at the smell.

I sigh and move to open the window, sparing a glance back at my roommate as I do. "My hopes and dreams."

"Figured. Smells awful."

Can't argue with that.

"This is the fourth batch I've ruined today," I lament as I shuffle over to her. Seeking comfort, I rest my temple against her upper arm. It's not quite her shoulder, since I'm five foot nothing and she's a six-foot-one angel. "The first ones weren't sweet enough. The second ones were flat as crepes. The third were underbaked, and these are—"

"On fire."

"*Singed*," I correct, pulling back and giving her a warning look. I can't be too mad, though, because they *were* kind of on fire at some point. "I can't get it right and I don't know what I'm doing wrong."

"Take a break," Chantal instructs. Her tone is firm, but there's a tenderness in it. "You can try again tomorrow."

She's right, and I'll absolutely pick myself up and dust myself off for yet another attempt, just like I always do. But she knows my frustration isn't just about macarons. She knows how badly I want my life to be perfect and how upset it makes me that I'm struggling to pull it off. As my roommate since our freshman year, she's witnessed plenty of my highs and lows, and is well-versed in all my hopes and dreams. I'm lucky that her own dream job as a financial analyst—go figure—is keeping her in New York, because I don't know what I'd do without her.

"I'll order takeout so no one has to enter this disaster zone," she says, pulling her phone out of the back pocket of her denim shorts that showcase her long, deep brown legs. "And check your phone, would you? It keeps buzzing in your room, and it's driving me nuts."

I flash her a bashful smile. "Sorry. I didn't want to get distracted, so I left it in there."

She cocks a brow playfully. "You mean you didn't want to risk dropping it in the batter again."

My face flames at the mention of that specific baking attempt. "It only happened one time!"

She flips her braids over one shoulder as she strolls out of the kitchen, the delicate beads at the ends clicking together as she goes. I helped her pick them out last week, the gold and deep azure perfect for the warming temperatures and one last hurrah before she starts her new job and has to have a "professional" hairstyle. It'd be great if the world could stop telling Black girls what's appropriate when it comes to our hair, but today is not that day.

Sighing, I undo my apron and hang it on the hook by the window. The pastel pink cotton flutters in the warm breeze, silently mocking me and my failure. I don't even bother looking at the charbroiled macarons as I leave the kitchen and pad down the narrow hallway to my bedroom.

I pass Grace's open door along the way, catching a snippet of the conversation she's having on the phone. Judging from the occasional groan and the (very few) words in Cantonese I understand thanks to the lessons she's given me over the years, she's talking to her mother. She's probably assuring her that she won't miss her flight to Hong Kong tomorrow, which she's done twice before.

She gives me a finger wave as I walk by, and I blow her a kiss in return before slipping into my room next door. The sun streams in through my gauzy curtains, casting short shadows across my desk. My phone sits on the surface, wedged between a few skincare products and a mug full of glitter gel pens. The screen is dark, but when I scoop it up, a litany of texts and missed calls, all from my brother, greets me.

Most people would assume there'd been some kind of emergency, but this is just how Oakley operates. If he can't get a hold of me—or anyone, for that matter—on his first attempt, he'll keep calling and texting until they pick up. There's no subtlety with him.

I don't bother looking at any of the twenty texts. They're probably just emojis and the sentence *Pick up!!!!* over and over again. Instead, I tap his name and put the phone to my ear, flopping onto my ruffled duvet to stare out the window at the brick apartment building across the street.

"Took you long enough," Oakley grumbles when he answers.

"I was busy," I say vaguely. If I confess my baking catastrophe to him, he'll never let me live it down. "What's up?"

"Do you want to go to Monaco?"

Another thing about my brother—he doesn't beat around the bush.

I'm used to it, but the question still throws me. "Monaco?" I repeat. "Like, the country?"

"*Yes*, Willow, the country," he mocks. "Keep up."

I roll my eyes, mentally flipping him a middle finger. "God, I was just checking."

"So?" I can imagine him prompting me by circling his hand in the air, ever impatient. "You interested or not?"

"I mean, yeah," I reply, even though I'm suspicious of the offer. "Who wouldn't be? But why are you even asking?"

"Because I'm going next week and thought you might want to tag along. Plus, it's a race weekend, and—"

My snort interrupts him. "I should have known this was a motorsport thing."

When my brother was a teenager, his life revolved around kart racing, which led to a successful but short-lived career in Formula 3. In the end, he gave it up to have a "normal" life and went off to college. Personally, I wouldn't have given up the opportunity to be a professional athlete for anything. But that's the difference between Oakley and me—he had options in life. I didn't.

"*And*," Oakley barges on, "my company is hosting a huge event. I figured you might want to schmooze with athletes, then watch the race from the paddock. I've got passes, courtesy of SecDark."

Part of that "normal" college experience for Oakley involved studying cybersecurity. He was recruited during the fall semester of his senior year by one of the leading companies in the industry, SecDark Solutions, and has worked for them ever since.

The business was so successful that they'd recently branched out into sponsoring various sports teams and athletes, a Formula 1 team among them, which would explain the party and paddock passes. If I wasn't so proud of my brother for working his way up the ranks of such a flourishing company, I'd be jealous as hell.

But considering I'm being offered perks from his wins, I can't complain that he's doing better than me.

"I know you're not having the easiest time finding a job," he says before I can ask more about the event, "but this could be a good opportunity for you to network. You haven't given up on sports marketing, have you?"

Rolling onto my side, I pull my knees up to my chest. I'm more embarrassed by Oakley's gentleness than I would be if he was making fun of me for still being unemployed.

A career related to sports has always been my dream. I grew up loving baseball and basketball, loved going to games with Oakley and our father, loved the electric energy of a crowd cheering for their favorite team. I was hooked from the second Dad took my hand and led me into my first stadium. There was no going back after that. I wanted to be like the people on the field and the court. I wanted to run bases and make half-court shots. I wanted to hear my name chanted, to have it echo throughout the stands and beat in the hearts of fans.

Unfortunately, my body kept that dream from ever becoming a reality. Even though it took years and countless doctors to get a diagnosis of hypermobility, I knew early on that I was different from other kids. That I'd never get to do some of the same activities they did.

My baseball career ended after a dislocated shoulder during my first T-ball lesson, and basketball was simply out of the question thanks to all the running and sudden stops that my unstable knees couldn't handle. Being an athlete just wasn't in the cards for me.

So, after years of watching and learning from the sidelines, I figured sports marketing was the next best thing. I could still be immersed in a world that brought me joy, and I could share that joy with others. At least, I could if I got a job.

"No, I haven't given up." I sigh. "I'm still waiting to hear back from a few places."

"Then come to Monaco in the meantime," he wheedles. "Like I said, the event will be perfect for networking. Or, fuck it, just consider it a vacation on my dime. A joint graduation gift and a super early birthday present."

"All in one?" I drawl. "Wow, you're *so* kind."

"Let's be real. I'm only offering because Mom made me."

"So, I should be thanking her for this invitation and not you?"

"Semantics," he says, dismissing my comment. Then he launches back into his pitch. "Just think of all the people you'll meet. You know how many athletes and their teams will be at this party? If you don't end up with a job offer at the end of the night, I'll cliff dive off the coast."

I snicker. "You'll do that even if I do get an offer." We both inherited the adrenaline junkie gene. I just know better than to act on mine.

"Probably," he concedes. "But seriously, Wills. This is a great opportunity. And you don't even have to lift a finger. I'll handle everything."

I shift onto my back and study the ceiling, twisting the hem of my sundress between my fingers. "You promise it's worth my time?" I hedge, but excitement is already starting to bloom in my chest. "I don't want to be away for too long and miss out on an interview."

"I promise. You can fly in on Wednesday and fly back Monday morning."

Holding my breath, I mull it over. He's right. It could be an excellent networking opportunity. And who wouldn't want to spend a few days in one of the coolest places in the world? Besides, who am I to turn down a free trip?

"Okay, fine," I blurt before my brain can catch up. "Take me to Monaco."

CHAPTER 2

DEV

Monaco

I'm pretty sure everyone at this party thinks I have an STD.

For the record, I don't and never have, despite my escapades that the press loves to report on. This rumor has everything to do with my social media manager—my *former* social media manager now—who quit her job by announcing on all of my online platforms that I was the new face of at-home STD testing kit brand IYK Quick Results. Without it, I wouldn't have discovered that I had chlamydia so quickly. But don't worry, I'm being treated for it. Though, unfortunately, it's an antibiotic-resistant strain. Some guys just have all the luck.

The posts gave the company a boost, but for me? I haven't had sex in six weeks, and most of the women here won't even look at me. It's a goddamn disaster.

I know I have a case for defamation of character, but the damage is already done, and I'm not interested in hurting Jani in retaliation. Moving past it is my best option at this point. And if I'm being honest with myself, I *might* have deserved to face her wrath after everything I put her through while working for me. I wasn't the easiest client, but who the fuck wants to have every aspect of their life documented for the whole world to see? Yet Jani insisted on it day after day until I finally snapped.

Unfortunately, that made *her* snap in return. Now my reputation is in the shitter, my team is giving me the cold shoulder, and there are whispers that my sponsors believe I might not be the right person to represent them. I can't lose them—can't lose that money—because without it, I'll lose my place with Argonaut Racing.

"God, would you lighten up? You're going to scare off all the women looking like that."

Beside me, Mark innocently sips his champagne. His tux barely fits him, even though I've hounded him about replacing it. His shoulders challenge the seams of the jacket, and his pecs strain the buttons of the crisp white shirt. Any second, they're bound to pop off and blind people unfortunate enough to be in the danger zone. With one glance, anyone would know the man has a job in fitness, and he clearly loves showing off his physique. If he wasn't my performance coach and one of my best friends since kindergarten, I'd think he was an absolute douche for it.

"Looking like what?" I question, lifting my own champagne glass and knocking back its contents. I drag the back of my hand across my mouth before continuing. "Looking like I'm about to lose my career and fail to get my dick wet all in one night?" Because that's what it's feeling like.

I've worked too hard to get to where I am, and I refuse to leave Formula 1 until I'm good and ready. Is Argonaut Racing the best team on the grid? That's a joke if ever I've heard one. But if I'm going to break free from the midfield and land myself a seat at a top-tier team, they're my best bet.

Every driver aspires to win a championship, and my chances of ever doing that hinge on my performance now. I came up through Argonaut's driver development program as a kid, and I've only ever driven for the team, so I'm loyal to them in most respects, but I can't stay there forever if I want to win. And yeah, it's optimistic for a driver who's never won a single F1 race to be looking toward the championship, but I'm a dumbass with dreams.

The problem is that those dreams feel more out of reach with each passing day. Unless NASA starts designing Argonaut's cars, I'm never going to win a championship with them. I'm certainly not going to do it while Zaid Yousef and Axel Bergmüller are battling it out at the top, no matter what car I'm driving. Honestly, I'd be thrilled to place third or fourth with my current team, but that seems about as likely as the sun exploding tomorrow.

For now, though, my priority is staying in Formula 1 until I can prove that I belong in the upper *upper* echelon of this elite sport. I just have to keep my head down and perform well enough to garner the attention of the best teams' bosses. Zaid should be retiring in the next couple of years, so surely Mascort is thinking about his replacement. Or maybe Specter Energy will decide they need a new number two driver to support Axel, and if so, I'll be their man. That won't get me the title I'm after, but it'll be a step closer to it.

But none of that will happen if I lose my sponsorships and Argonaut cuts my contract short, all thanks to Jani's parting gift. The team may not rely heavily on the money I bring in, but no one wants a driver who has nothing but their talent to contribute. It's shitty, for sure, and yet it's how our little world works.

After this season, I have another year left with them, and

if I don't live up to—or exceed—their expectations? Fuck, if I think about the possibilities for too long, I might crawl into the nearest hole and never climb out.

"You'll get laid again, Dev, I promise," Mark says. "But only if you stop moping like a little bitch."

There's no missing how he ignored the first part of my complaint. I'm not the only one who's worried about my future in F1.

"I'm not moping," I mumble. But he's right. I *am* moping. I've always been the smiley guy, not the scowling one. This isn't who I'm supposed to be. "I'm just stressed, all right? It's a big night."

It's a big week is more like it. Tonight, I have to prove that I'm an asset to the world of racing, not a liability. Tomorrow, I have to grin my way through my media duties for Argonaut and pretend I don't hate my teammate. Then I have to get a solid time during free practice on Friday, qualify higher than P10 on Saturday—there's no way I'm scoring points otherwise at a circuit like Monaco, where overtakes are nearly impossible—and drive like my life depends on it on Sunday.

In a way, I guess it does.

"You're gonna get through it." Mark sounds assured, but I know he has his doubts too. "And if you don't believe me," he says, nodding to the other side of the room, "go ask Oakley. You know he won't sugarcoat anything for you."

I turn in the direction Mark's nodding toward, spotting our friend by the doors to the ballroom, where he's shaking hands and slapping shoulders.

Thank fucking god. It feels like I've been waiting years for that dickhead to get here and save me from the boredom these stuffy sponsor events always inspire.

I've known Oakley since before I could walk. Our families

have been neighbors for longer than I've been alive, and he and I grew up together in the karting circuits. We're the founding members of the Awkward White Dads Club, two mixed kids—Black in Oakley's case; Indian in mine—with white fathers, who bonded over never quite fitting into the motorsport world thanks to the color of our skin. And also, because our dads are easily the most awkward people on the planet. Nerds, the both of them, but considering Oakley's job these days, he's not far behind on the nerd scale.

Needless to say, we've been friends forever.

And I almost ruined it all in a single moment last year when I kissed his sister.

I shake the memory from my head before it can replant itself and grow roots again. I know better than to dwell on it—I've done enough of that already and faced the consequences. Besides, I refuse to let it interfere with my friendship with Oakley; it was a onetime mistake, never to be repeated. I know better now.

Before I can make a move to head in Oakley's direction, my agent steps into my path, blocking me from going anywhere. Great.

Mark, the bastard, manages to sidestep the glowering man and grins at my misfortune, lifting his empty champagne glass in a sardonic toast. "Catch you later, buddy," he calls to me before striding away.

A few steps behind my agent stands an exasperated Chava, his hands held out to the side in a universal *I tried* gesture. No doubt my assistant did his best, but there's no stopping Howard Featherstone when he's on a mission to make my life a living hell.

"Howard!" I call out, donning my signature smile and feigning enthusiasm. I knew he'd be here tonight, but I was hoping to avoid him for at least a little while longer. "How the hell are ya?"

"I've been better, Dev," he says flatly, those cold gray eyes leveling on me. "But I think you know that."

I'm tempted to stick my fingers in my ears and mockingly repeat Howard's words back to him, but I have to remind myself that I'm a twenty-five-year-old man—the appropriate response at my big age is to tell him to go fuck himself.

Thankfully, I've had enough media training to keep me from behaving either way in public, so I school my expression into one of understanding and nod solemnly.

"I hear you," I agree. "We've had some tough times lately."

He eyes me suspiciously, probably well aware that I'm putting on a front. But he's not about to call me out on it in case it leads us off topic. "We have. And it's past time to fix things. We could have started sooner if you weren't avoiding my calls."

I chuckle and drag a hand through my hair in an act of false sheepishness, though I can't resist lifting my middle finger just a little as I drop my hand back to my side. I haven't wanted to talk to him because I knew what he'd say. *You need to fix this, Dev. Hire someone to clean up your image. Get a full PR team in place. Let them turn you into a robot. Let them drain the life from you.*

"Sorry about that," I reply, boldly dishonest. "The last few weeks have been crazy, you know? Hey, did you catch the race in Azerbaijan? I managed to make it to Q3 in—"

"Cut the shit."

I can't help but cringe a little at the force behind his words. Oh, I'm definitely in trouble.

"*No one* is happy with you right now," Howard plows on.

"Not your team, not the sponsors. Certainly not me. And everyone else? They're *laughing* at you."

"I mean, I'm used to being laughed at," I point out, shrugging. "I'm a funny guy."

Apparently, this isn't the time for jokes, because the next thing I know, I'm nose to nose with him, his age spots and close-to-bursting veins the only things I can see.

"You keep this up, and you're done," he snarls. "There won't even be a seat for you in NASCAR."

I don't appreciate him insulting the chaotic art of turning left that is NASCAR, and I certainly don't like the way he's in my face. "I suggest taking a step back, Howard," I murmur. "This isn't the place to make a scene." And I *really* don't want to have to fight a sixty-year-old man who thinks he's hiding his growing bald spot with that comb-over.

As if suddenly remembering where he is, Howard blinks away his anger and takes a stumbling step back, huffing as he straightens his tuxedo jacket. He glances around to see if his outburst drew any attention, but it seems the only person watching us is a grimacing Chava.

"Get it through your head," he says after he's recovered, careful to keep his voice low. "Your image is on the rocks, and I can't save you unless you let me try."

I blow out a breath. I'm not interested in the angle he's come up with, one he's presented to me many times before. "Look, if Axel can come back from getting caught on camera screaming the N-word multiple times while rapping along to a song, I think I'll be fine with my fake STD."

Howard shakes his head like he can't believe I'd be so stupid. "You should know better than anyone that people will forgive racism far faster than a sex scandal."

That gets me to snap my mouth shut. Because as much as I hate to admit it, he's right.

Taking advantage of my silence, he squeezes my shoulder, holding my gaze. "Let me fix this, Dev."

The worst part is that I know he can do it. He can hire people that will sweep this all under the rug and make me look like the perfect little prince of the paddock. It would be so simple.

But I've done that before—I've given up control of my image and let them make the world believe I have the personality of a cardboard cutout. I wasn't allowed to talk about anything remotely political or "controversial," even if the issue I wanted to address affected me or people I cared about directly. I wasn't allowed to share my opinions or honest thoughts; I had to be the poster boy everyone else could project on. And I hated it, but I played along because everyone said that was best for me.

Yeah, right.

Jani was supposed to be the compromise. Instead of a full team, she was hired to handle my sponsored social media posts and anything mandated by Argonaut, maybe delve shallowly into facets of my personality for my fans. But she took it a step too far by trying to butt into my personal life and post it online. And after she attempted to get me to overshare one too many times, I was done.

So yeah. I'm uninterested in handing my image over to people I don't remotely trust.

"I can fix it myself," I say, though my voice hardly sounds like my own. "Just give me some time."

"You don't have much time left before people are going to give up on you." He takes a breath and straightens his shoulders. "I'm going to get a glass of champagne. But when I come back, we'll make the rounds together and remind everyone why you're such a delight to have in the paddock and on their billboards. Understood?"

"Yes, sir." I barely resist the urge to salute him.

As if he can tell, Howard glares at me and then stalks off, leaving me to lock eyes with Chava.

"Well," my assistant huffs as he approaches. His skin is close to the same shade as my own light brown, but it doesn't hide the flush that's crept up his neck. He hates Howard as much as I do. "This is a fucking mess."

"You're telling me," I grumble, wishing I had a whole case of champagne to chug right now. "I've got to fix this."

"Any ideas how? Short of hiring a PR firm?"

I shake my head. "I don't know yet." Sighing, I rest my elbow on his shoulder, suddenly exhausted. "I've got too many problems to solve right now."

"Including how every woman here is looking at you like you're tainted," Chava says dryly as a trio of ladies in expensive gowns side-eye me while they saunter by, giving us a wide berth. "And me, too, by association. Damn it, Dev."

"It's not my fault," I groan, dropping my head back. "But I've got to get laid. At the least, I need to fix *that* problem tonight."

There's a very slim chance that I'll find someone here who doesn't believe I'm currently being treated for an STD and will come back to my apartment, but I have to try. All I have to do is find a woman willing to give me the time of day and explain the situation to her. Just laugh it off like a joke, because that's exactly what it is. A cruel, cruel joke.

It's simple. I face harder strategies each and every race day. This is nothing.

Straightening up, I pass my empty champagne glass off to

Chava and run my fingers through my hair to sweep it off my forehead. I'm a good-looking guy, and I'm charming as fuck, so this should be a breeze. I'm writing off the past six weeks as a fluke. I just haven't tried hard enough. Now, though? I'm in it to win it.

But all my plans go out the window the second Willow Williams walks into the room.

CHAPTER 3

WILLOW

It doesn't matter that I'm wearing an outfit that costs more than a month's rent; I feel wildly underdressed in this crowd.

I know I look amazing in this baby blue silk gown and four-inch heels—even if I am tempting fate *and* my ankles by wearing them—but I still feel out of place. If there's anywhere in the world that could make me feel like I don't belong, it's a swanky party in Monaco.

Monaco. Just thinking the name has me nearly shaking my head in disbelief. Because honestly, who expects to be offered a last-minute invitation to visit a place synonymous with wealth and fast cars? Certainly not me and my barely used passport.

After flying into Nice this afternoon, I was picked up at the airport by a driver Oakley sent to fetch me. I kept my face glued to the luxury car's window as we made our way down the coast and across the border to Monaco, admiring the beautiful blue waters, lush greenery, and stunning cliffs.

Even if my brother hadn't mentioned the race this week-end, I would have known by the sheer number of closed roads and million-dollar yachts crammed into the harbor alone. It was controlled chaos. Excitement for the weekend was practically palpable in the warm spring air.

I video called Grace and Chantal to show them the sights as we slowly drove past them, but I nearly lost my ability to speak when we pulled up to the hotel.

I'm not a stranger to luxury. My parents have done well for themselves, and Mom's taste for expensive things is well-known, but I'd never seen extravagance like this. The building had old-world charm in the columns and aged facade, with purple and yellow flowers climbing in perfect patterns up both and hanging over the portico. The lobby, with its sweeping ceilings and eighteenth-century art, might as well have been a backdrop straight off a movie set.

I nearly giggled when a porter wearing a maroon uniform and a little hat asked me in accented English if he could take my bags. It was perfect.

The suite Oakley reserved for me was just as incredible— beautiful views of the water, a soaker tub, and a bed big enough to fit ten people. Clearly, he went all out for this graduation-slash-birthday present. Either that, or his company has sweeter benefits than I realized.

But I still haven't gotten a chance to thank him, because my brother has been MIA all day. He texted to tell me he'd be busy up until the start of the party, but that he'd meet me in the hotel's ballroom for tonight's event.

I spent the last few hours getting ready. I soaked, buffed, and moisturized my body into submission before slipping into the gown Grace had encouraged me to buy, even though I nearly had a heart attack seeing the price tag. But it *is* stunning, and I felt like a million bucks . . . until now.

I've always been a tiny bit self-conscious about my looks,

and one glance around has me shrinking in on myself. Every person drifting by me is somehow more gorgeous than the last. And here I am—short as hell, baby-faced, and the CEO of the Itty-Bitty Titty Committee. It's a trifecta that often results in me being asked where my parents are when I'm out on my own.

I'm envious of women like Chantal, with her long legs and curves. Unlike her, I'm convinced I could be replaced by a square piece of cardboard with a picture of my face slapped on it, and no one would know the difference.

But each time I start to feel like that, I remind myself of the attributes I *do* like. I love the bronze glow of my skin no matter what the season. I love my curls, even though tonight I've straightened them to within an inch of their life. And yeah, most days I love that I can get away with not wearing a bra under almost anything.

With those reminders, I push my shoulders back and lift my head, thankful for the boost from my heels. Without it, I wouldn't be able to see a single thing in this well-dressed crowd.

I take a few seconds to scan the ballroom, from its high ceilings with intricate molding and gilded trim to the shining wood floors. There's a Formula 1 car sculpted out of ice—complete with a shot luge—positioned on one side of the room, and a fire-breathing act is taking place on the other. Clearly no expense was spared, but I shouldn't be surprised. This is a sport that's always been about money, money, money.

"Wills!"

I start at the sound of my brother's voice and turn in the direction it came from, spotting him waving at me from beside the sleek bar. Blowing out a small breath of relief, I weave my way over. Ever the life of the party, he's surrounded by a crowd of people, but he's quick to excuse himself and meet me halfway.

He spreads his arms wide and I lean into them, squeezing him tightly for a few seconds. Standing back, he grips my shoulders as he looks me over. "Did you get shorter?"

I wrinkle my nose and knock his hands away. The moment of sibling love is decidedly over. "Did you forget I'm the perfect height to destroy your kneecaps? Don't try me."

"Yeah, I guess I shouldn't, especially with those shoes." He grimaces at my stilettos. "Should you be wearing those? I swear, if you dislocate anything, I'm *not* popping it back in for you."

I roll my eyes, but his concern isn't exactly misplaced considering my joints don't always like to stay where they're supposed to. Long ago, I learned that heels, no matter how stunning, weren't the best shoes for me, though that never deterred my love for them. Sometimes you've got to live life on the edge. Oakley has fast cars—I have high heels.

Still, I spend at least an hour every day either in the gym or on a yoga mat, working on strength exercises to encourage my body to keep everything where it belongs. With the help of physical therapy and a couple of surgeries, I'm not too worried about major injuries these days. But I'll always remain cautious. It's why I had to sit back while Oakley got to run reckless and follow his dreams of being an athlete.

I try not to be bitter about it, try not to let myself wish I was the sibling without chronic pain and weak connective tissue, but sometimes I taste it in the back of my throat.

"Relax, I haven't popped anything out of place in a while." I wave off his comment. "But it's nice to know you wouldn't help if I did. You're awful."

"We both knew that already." He gently grasps my elbow and turns me in the direction of the bar. "Let's get drinks and go find Dev. He's gotta be around here somewhere."

I nearly face-plant when my heel catches on air. If it weren't for Oakley's grip on me, I would have gone down—and hard—all at the mention of a name.

"Dev?" I repeat, wincing at the way my voice pitches high. I clear my throat, then clarify. "Dev Anderson? He's here?"

If Oakley were actually paying attention to me instead of eyeing a pretty blonde passing by, there's no way he wouldn't have picked up on my panic.

It's been seven months since I've seen my brother's best friend, and the last time I did? Let's say things didn't exactly go the way I thought they would, and I'm still mortified.

"Yeah, of course he's here," Oakley says as we elbow our way up to the bar. "SecDark is a sponsor of his team."

"Right." I knew that. I just . . . forgot. And by *forgot*, I mean I genuinely had no idea. "But I—I thought you sponsored a different team." There's no way I'm *that* oblivious. I may not follow F1 as closely as I do other sports, but it's on my radar. And so are too many things related to Dev, the boy I had a massive crush on for most of my childhood.

Oakley grunts as he lifts a hand to signal the bartender over, which I take as confirmation. "We started out with Deschamp, but Argonaut won the owners over with their 'all-American, all the time' bullshit. So yeah, we switched last year. Though Argonaut has yet to place on the podium this season, so it stands to be seen whether it's a better partnership."

I nod, trying to take all of that information in, but my mind is set to anxiety mode. Of their own volition, my eyes dart around the massive space in search of Dev in the crowd.

I knew there was a small chance I might run into him at the race this weekend, and I prepared myself for that possibility, but this feels like an ambush.

Oakley is still rambling on about racing statistics, but I've mostly tuned him out. I've heard it all before anyway. The guy could talk about these things forever. Usually, I dutifully listen, since I'm an amazing sister . . . and also because I find that stuff interesting, as much as I hate to admit it to him.

This time, though, I only pretend to pay attention, vaguely murmuring when it seems appropriate. But when my eyes land on a familiar form in the crowd, I can't keep up the ruse anymore.

Dev's trademark grin—the one he's never afraid to let loose—lights up the room. I swear his face was made for smiling and smiling alone, and the dark scruff on his sharp jaw only accentuates how bright it is. I've seen videos on my "for you" pages that constantly gift him the title of *best smile in the paddock*, and I can't disagree. No one on that grid—past, present, and probably even future—has humor more infectious than Dev's. None of them even come close.

As kids, it was rare to see him without a full-out grin on his face, and it hasn't changed a bit. Worries seem to roll off his back. It's not that he doesn't take anything seriously—he wouldn't have made it this far in his career if he didn't—but Dev just has the uncanny ability to always see the bright side, no matter how dark things may seem.

Without his positivity, I don't think I would have made it through the roughest points of my teenage years, a time when I hated my body for holding me back. It's a lot to credit someone with, but Dev and his smile and his little words of encouragement made all the difference.

My heart races like it always does when I see him, but

tonight, it's accompanied by anxious nausea. He looks . . . good. *Really* good. Better than I remembered, even with a mind that always paints him in the best light.

From where I'm standing, I have the perfect view of his profile. His jet-black hair is shorter on the sides and longer on the top. The strands curl and brush his forehead in that tousled way that looks intentionally styled, though it's more likely caused by the way he constantly runs his fingers through it. And that tuxedo . . . No man should look that good in a penguin suit, but I know a lot of people—myself included—would rather see him and his broad shoulders out of it.

Although, from what I hear, women aren't lining up to have that privilege these days, and I shouldn't be thinking that way either. Not because the rumor going around the internet is that he's being treated for an STD, but because he's beyond off-limits to me. Our kiss is a secret I plan to take to the grave.

"Oh, there he is." Oakley's voice cuts through my borderline impure thoughts and brings my focus back to him. In my periphery, he's looking in the same direction I am. "Let's go say hi."

"Huh?" The surprised syllable tumbles from my lips.

"You weren't even listening to me, were you?" He passes me a glass of champagne that magically appeared—along with an old-fashioned he's already sipping—while I was ogling his best friend. "I spotted Dev. I wanna talk to him before my bosses descend on my ass."

Oakley grips my shoulder and nudges me into walking before I even know what's happening.

But if there's one thing I do know, it's that I'm absolutely not ready to see Dev Anderson again.

CHAPTER 4

DEV

I'm in trouble. Big fucking trouble.

It feels impossible to be in even *more* trouble than I was five minutes ago, but it's the truth. Because with Willow here, I'm utterly screwed.

Sadly, not literally.

I have to leave the party. That's my only option, because if she spots me before I can find my composure, I'm going to . . . Well, I don't know what I'll do, but it definitely won't be anything good or smart or helpful to the recovery of my image.

Despite knowing I need to turn and power walk the fuck out of here, I can't seem to drag my attention away from her.

Across the room, she glances around, her delicate shoulders tensing as she looks for a familiar face in the sea of guests. If I were a braver man—funny, since I drive a car around a track at two hundred miles per hour for a living—I'd go over and greet her, tell her how great it is to see her again, and offer to get her a drink. Only, in my current state, there's a strong chance that greeting might come out as *What in the fresh* fuck *are you doing here?*

Thankfully, I'm a coward, so I stay rooted to the spot, and my focus stays trained on her.

She's wearing a dress that sweeps the floor and is held up by straps so thin I could rip them off with the slightest tug. It drapes a little in the center, emphasizing the soft slope of her chest, and while she's not the most endowed in that department, it didn't stop my hands from liking what they felt when I had the privilege of touching her. I examine the rippling blue silk, following it down to the soft curve of her hips, envisioning what it would be like to bunch it up to her waist like I did the last time we—

Shit. Fucking *shit*. I can't think of her like that right now. Correction, I can't think of her like that *ever*. I know better. We all know better, because we saw what happened the last time one of Oakley's friends got involved with Willow. And it wasn't pretty.

I've almost convinced myself to turn away when, suddenly, her face lights up. A smile blooms across it, giving me the same adrenaline rush that climbing into my car before a race does. But instead of spurring me to move, it keeps me frozen as I take in the full force of her joy.

She has dimples in both cheeks, deep ones that reveal themselves when she's smiling or laughing—or trying *not* to smile or laugh. They pop when she folds her lips in or scrunches them to the side. Even when she frowns, there's a hint of that dip in at least one side of her face. If there's a moment where they're completely hidden, it means she's sleeping or bored out of her mind.

And man, do I hate that I know that.

A rock of dread drops deep in my stomach as I catch sight of the recipient of her smile. Oakley sweeps his sister into a hug, and finally—*finally*—I drag my gaze away, because I know better than to repeat mistakes.

And kissing Willow Williams was the biggest mistake of my life.

"Earth to Dev. Anybody home? Hello? Did you *die*?"

When I blink and turn back, Chava's face is inches from mine. Mark is standing beside him, having returned from his great escape and looking at me like he's tempted to call the team doctor.

"You good?" Mark asks, leaning in and squinting, probably checking my pupil dilation.

I swat him away as Chava cackles. The two of them are ganging up on me as usual. It's like they've forgotten who signs their paychecks.

"I'm fine," I mumble as I drag a hand through my hair, but I find myself glancing around again in search of Willow.

I'm lucky she never told her brother about our little . . . incident. For weeks after it happened, I was convinced Oakley was going to show up and assassinate me himself. Considering he nearly killed Jeremy for what he did to Willow, I don't think my fears were unjustified.

Jeremy absolutely deserved what he got, though, and his crimes were far greater than a stolen kiss in a hotel stairwell. I'm practically innocent in comparison. But the guilt still weighs heavy in my gut.

"We were talking about trying to get him laid tonight, and then he zoned out," Chava explains. "He's probably praying he'll be more than a one-pump chump after this long."

His comment cracks me, and I'm grinning before I can stop it. I can't resist a joke at my expense. "Come on, I've got at least two pumps in me."

"There he is," Chava coos, pinching my cheek. If this guy wasn't one of my closest friends and the only reason I show up where I'm supposed to on time, I would have fired him by now. "Are we gonna find you a girl or what?"

"That's the plan," I reply. I can only hope it'll help take my mind off Willow. "First, I need another—"

But I'm cut off when Howard once again appears by my side, this time with a glass of champagne extended to me. Based on his scowl, it's not a peace offering.

"What you're going to do is take this glass and follow me," he instructs. "You've wasted enough time, and you've got a hell of a lot of ground to make up."

Sure, I wanted another drink, but this is not how I wanted to go about getting it. "Can you give me like a half hour?" I ask, holding back my exasperation. I'm sick of this guy breathing down my neck and ruining the vibe. "There are some people I need to say hi to first, then I promise I'll chat up whoever you want me to."

Howard shoves the glass against my chest with enough force that a few drops of the pale liquid spill onto my shirt. "Fifteen minutes," he concedes, and it's enough to keep me from wanting to sock him in the jaw. "But I'll be watching."

Again, the urge to mock him is strong, because the man is a walking villain cliché. I know he's only trying to ensure I get the best deals—and getting all he can from his cut of those deals—but he should really work on his bedside manner.

When he shuffles off again, I down the (possibly poisoned) champagne and hand the empty glass off to a passing waiter before glancing between Mark and Chava. "Think I could get away with sneaking out the back exit?"

Mark snorts. "No chance. Besides, Oakley will be pissed if you run away before he makes it over here."

My whole body tenses, and my eyes snap to where I spotted

Willow and Oakley in the crowd, but they're gone. Instead, a familiar deep vanilla perfume surrounds me, and I know it's too late to run.

I don't immediately join in when the greetings start. There's cheerful shouting and backslapping and good-natured cursing, but I'm coming to terms with being mere steps from Willow for the first time in over half a year. Apparently, I have no idea how to behave around her anymore.

C'mon, man. Just play it cool. Act normal. Easy as pie.

When it's my turn to face Oakley, I force a smile and let him tug me into his arms, hoping he hasn't suddenly developed the ability to read minds.

"It's good to see you, asshole," he says in my ear, thumping me so hard on the back that I swear it knocks my heart out of rhythm. Shit, maybe he *does* know what I did.

But there's nothing but warmth in Oakley's eyes when he pulls back, gripping me by the shoulders. He's still my best friend, the guy I came up with through karting, practically attached at the hip all the way to Formula 3. If he hadn't decided that racing was no longer his dream, I'm sure he would still be with me these days.

In some ways, I'm glad he's not. I've seen friendships destroyed by competition, and most of the drivers I know aren't particularly close with one another, no more than professional acquaintances. We're coworkers, really. They aren't people I'd share my deepest, darkest secrets with. But Oakley? He's my guy.

Or, well, he *was* until I did the one thing I could never tell him about.

Chava knows my secret, though, and he shoots me a knowing glance when Oakley pulls back and shifts to my side, leaving me with an unobstructed view of Willow. Mark's just hugged her, and now it's my turn, but I'm having a hard time getting my feet to move.

I don't know how I manage it, but I'm stepping closer, opening my arms, and folding her into them, all while my brain is still buffering.

The top of her head barely comes to my shoulder, and she's so slight that I'm surprised again and again by how tight her hugs are. She's always been delicate in my mind, soft and gentle. But while she might *look* fragile, I've seen her killing it in the gym. If she was determined to, the girl could probably bench-press me. And she's always determined.

It isn't to say she's unbreakable. Her condition means she's got a few more limitations than the average person, but underestimating her would be a mistake. She's stronger than most people think.

I let the hug linger only long enough to inhale her sweet scent and remind myself that my feelings for her are purely platonic, which is why that kiss was inappropriate on so many levels.

I'm met with a tentative smile as she drops her arms from around my waist, but she's watching me with those dark eyes, telegraphing a clear message: *Don't make this weird.*

Well, she doesn't have to worry about *me* making it weird because it already is. But I won't give us away, even if that means ignoring her for the rest of the night.

Is that rude? Yeah, for sure, but a man's gotta do what he can to keep from being murdered by his best friend.

Speaking of the guy, Oakley roughly curls his arm around my neck and asks how the season's been so far, saving me from having to strike up a conversation with Willow. I have no doubt that he's been keeping up with my career, which means he knows about my eighth-place finish in Azerbaijan

and my DNF in Miami—the high- and lowlights so far—so I
drop my voice and say, "I gotta tell you what really happened
with Nathaniel in Italy last week." He'll appreciate the gossip
about my teammate, plus I can't pass up a chance to chat shit
about the guy. "Spoiler: there was nothing wrong with the car
when he crashed."

I turn my back to Willow as Oakley presses me for the full
story. It's a solid distraction, even though Willow's melodic
laughter floats in the air around us as she talks to Chava and
Mark. I do my best to ignore it and press on until Oakley's
practically crying from laughing so hard. I did the same when
I heard the truth—Nathaniel puked in his helmet thanks to
the stomach bug he promised the team he'd recovered from.
The surprise of it caused him to lose control for a split second,
leading him to hit the barriers.

Oakley's still wiping at his eyes when something over my
shoulder catches his attention and his smile drops.

"Shit, my bosses are beckoning," he says, lifting a hand to
wave at them. "Hopefully this won't take long." With that, he
turns to his sister. "You good here, Wills?"

My back is to her, but I'm far too aware of Willow's presence behind me. "Yeah, totally fine," she reassures. "Go on."

Oakley nods and slaps my shoulder. "Don't have too much
fun without me."

As he walks off, I have no choice but to turn back around
to face Chava and Mark *and* Willow. I'm almost tempted to
run off and find Howard, but that's a step too far, no matter
how much I'd like to avoid this interaction.

"So," I prompt, glancing between the three of them, wanting to wipe my suddenly slick palms on my tuxedo pants.
"What's the—"

"You know what? I need another drink," Chava interrupts, disregarding my attempt to join their conversation. "Mark, come with me. We'll bring drinks back for Willow and Dev so they don't have to fight through the crowd."

Mark frowns at his half-full drink, a step behind Chava's scheming. "I don't need—"

"Let's *go*." Despite the daggers I shoot him, Chava grabs Mark's bulging bicep and drags him in the direction of the bar.

As much as I want to excuse myself and go talk to literally anyone else, I can't run away from Willow. Partially because Oakley would yell at me for being mean to his sister, but mostly because the second I look down at her, I once again find myself frozen in place.

I never used to be like this around her. So stilted and tongue-tied and . . . *uncomfortable.* And it's not like this is the first time I've ever been stuck with her one-on-one. Far from it. When we were kids, it felt like she and I were together more than we weren't. I wouldn't have called us friends, but we were a constant presence in each other's lives.

We would hang out and chat while I waited for Oakley to get ready to go out. We'd sit in my kitchen when my mom made jalebi, scarfing down each fresh batch. We'd throw popcorn at each other when our families went to the movies together. Hell, she once sat with me for hours when I had a concussion and no one else was around to keep an eye on me. Things between us have never been awkward.

Until now.

She's looking anywhere but at me, both hands clutching her nearly full champagne glass so tight her knuckles have gone pale. Knowing that she feels as weird about this as I do makes me feel a little better, but I need to stop being such a scared little baby and fix this surreal situation.

I clear my throat, wishing I still had a drink in my hand, both to wet my desert-dry mouth and for the liquid courage. "So, Willow," I begin, internally cringing when my attempt at nonchalance sounds more like disgust. I scrap it, knowing it won't work. Not with her. "How are things?"

Her big brown eyes finally swing up to me, and the grip on her glass loosens slightly. "Things are good," she answers, her breathy tone stirring something in me that should *not* be stirring. "You?"

I really don't want to talk about myself, so I redirect the conversation. "You just graduated, right? Sorry for not sending a gift. It was the least I could have done."

"You've been busy," she says, waving off my apology. "And this trip to Monaco is my gift from Oakley. You can tack your name onto it and call it a day."

I relax some at her joke and the hint of a smile pulling at the corner of her full lips, pleased that while this interaction is definitely strange, we can still find some sense of normality.

I snicker. "I'll happily take credit for someone else's work."

She laughs, and I can tell she's just as glad that we've found our footing again.

"Call your boss and ask if you can take an extra week off," I go on. "Oakley and I can charter a yacht."

I'm playing around—though maybe not; the yacht does sound like fun—but I must have said something wrong, because the smile disappears from her face.

Shit. What did I do this time?

"No need to make any calls, seeing as I don't have a job," she says, her chin dropping a fraction. "I've applied for more than I can count, but I've heard nothing from most of them. I might have to look outside of sports marketing."

Great, I've made her feel bad about her unsuccessful job search. It's only been, what, a couple of weeks since she graduated? Not many people are lucky enough to get hired that quickly, anyway. At least I don't think so. Not like I've ever been part of the real working world.

I know I can be a dick, and it's usually on purpose, but not this time. "I'm sure you'll find something," I reassure her, wanting to kick myself. "Don't even worry about it."

"Mm, yeah. Right."

She tucks a strand of hair behind her ear, and I follow her fingertips, remembering how she did the same thing right before I—

"Enough about me," she says, interrupting my thoughts before I can be dragged back into the memory. "You've certainly been making headlines lately. Everything okay?"

It's my turn to grimace, hating that she's the latest person to press on the bruise of my reputation. I hate that she even knows about it in the first place. "Ah, yeah. Things could definitely be better."

We're on equal footing now that we've made each other feel like shit, but Willow has always tried to find the lightness in heavy situations, so it's no surprise that she grins and says, "So you're telling me IYK Quick Results *isn't* paying you millions of dollars to promote them? What a scam."

That drags a laugh out of me, loud and genuine. "Upsetting, right? I've given them so much publicity that they *should* be paying me. And honestly, it's a great product."

Her grin remains, but there's a glimmer of worry in her eyes. "You've used it before?"

Ah, shit. Now she thinks the STD rumor is true. Am I cursed not to say anything right tonight?

"I'm just saying in general," I rush to reply. I *do not* need the rumor to spread any further, just like a— Nope. Not gonna make the joke. "Quick and easy testing could never be a bad thing. The product is good to have on hand, especially in a place like this where people aren't as cautious as they should be." I hold an arm out, motioning to the crowd around us. It's full of new money and social climbers. "Better safe than that burning sensation when you pee."

She closes her eyes like she can't believe what I've just said, head shaking almost imperceptibly. "Oh . . . my god."

I shrug. It's true. Condoms only go so far, and not every use is perfect, so what's so wrong with being careful? I've always thought STD shaming was shitty anyway, but now that I'm a victim of it without even having one, those feelings are even stronger. Maybe they *would* be the perfect sponsor.

Willow takes a deep breath and pulls her shoulders back, her eyes settling on me again, this time with a knowing sparkle behind them. It's been a while since she got a true taste of my sense of humor, but she's handling it the way she always has—with resignation and a refusal to laugh, no matter how hard it is for her to hold back. She finds me funny. She just won't admit it.

"What's the story behind those posts anyway?" she asks once she composes herself. "Were you hacked?"

I blow out a breath and tug at my bow tie. "The gist of it is that my social media manager got sick of my shit, so she quit. And that was her parting gift."

"I'll be honest, I haven't seen everything. Just snippets that people I follow have shared." She smirks, and I try my best to ignore how much I like the sight. "You're kind of a celebrity, I guess."

"I am. Thanks for finally noticing." I pull out my phone

and navigate to my Instagram archive. "And *you're* in for a treat."

My calloused fingers brush against her pink-painted nails as I pass the device over. She slowly scrolls through, reading the multi-paragraph caption Jani took the time to type up, and I can't look away. Willow's expression goes from passive to grimacing in a split second. At least I get to see a glimpse of her dimples when it does.

"Wow, you really pissed this woman off," she says, her eyes full of a mix of pity and humor.

I take my phone back, letting our fingers brush again. "I'll admit it. I did antagonize Jani."

Willow scans my face, the hint of amusement in her expression instantly eclipsed by dread. "Dev, what did you do?"

I have a laundry list of minor misdeeds, but I'll go with the worst of them all. "I . . . canceled her flight from Australia after the grand prix and left her stranded."

"No."

I put my hands up, palms out. "In my defense, she'd been hounding me all day about making some video using that sexy baby filter—you know the one going around everywhere—and then she snuck up on me after a bad practice session, and . . . yeah. Canceled it then and there. And didn't tell her."

The back of Willow's hand connects with my chest. "You're such a dick!"

"Never said I wasn't."

She lets out an exasperated breath, but then she studies me silently, like she's searching for something. Finally, she tentatively asks, "You haven't posted anything else since this happened?"

I shake my head. "I have no interest in handling social

media myself. I've got a million other things to do." Like drive a fast car without crashing.

"You're wasting an incredibly valuable opportunity to recover your image," she says with a frown. She's clearly looking at this from a marketing perspective, which makes sense considering her degree. "This post obviously did a lot of damage. Why not get Argonaut's media team to handle things, at least for now? Or hire a full-service PR firm?"

I wince. "Because you can always tell the guys who hire firms. All their posts come off so bland. Zero personality, you know?" I don't need to get into my deeper reasons for it. "And I don't trust Argonaut not to make me look bad."

"Come on, that can't be true," she argues. "Their whole purpose is to help you."

I snort. "Yeah, I wouldn't be so sure about that. They're so far up my teammate's ass that I'm not even on their radar. All I got for this incident was a five-minute lecture from the team principal. That was it. Ever since my teammate and his father swooped in with a bunch of money, they just . . . ignore me."

Her lips part in surprise, and my gaze drops to them. They're plump and pillowy, the bottom one just a little fuller than the top, like she's perpetually pouting. It's sexy as hell.

And *that's* something I am *not* allowed to think.

"Seriously?" she asks.

"Seriously," I confirm, forcing my eyes back up to meet hers. "They're not looking out for me. They're biding their time until my contract is up since they're too cheap to buy me out."

"That's awful."

It really is, especially because I should be their number one driver. I came up through their driver academy. I'm the one consistently scoring points while my teammate is red-flagging every other race. I'm thirteenth in the Drivers' Championship and the only reason we're not dead last in the Constructors'. But if my stats aren't enough to earn their support, then I don't know what is. Considering there's so much time left on my contract, I'm stuck twiddling my thumbs for now. Eventually, I'll have the opportunity to move to another team.

Maybe. God, I fucking hope so.

But who's going to want me if I can't prove my worth?

Instead of telling her any of that, I shrug and play it off like I always do when something bothers me. "It is what it is."

But Willow's not about to shrug anything off. The cogs in her head are already turning. "It doesn't have to be like that," she says, passion behind the statement. She's holding back, though, because when she's really invested, her voice shakes a little. She hates it, claiming it makes her come across as too emotional, but I disagree. It shows how much she cares.

And that once again proves that I know this girl too well.

"You can get their attention, Dev," she pushes on, both hands back to clutching her champagne glass. This time, the movement is one of excitement, not nerves. "You need to put yourself out there in other spheres. Pull in new sponsors and fans who will drop cash on your team's merch. We both know money talks. If you show up to the table with a fat check, they can't ignore you."

I cross my arms, impressed—and a little intimidated—by Willow's ability to throw a game plan together in five seconds flat. How she doesn't have a job yet beats me. Clearly, she's bullheaded and solutions-oriented, the perfect kind of employee.

Honestly, if I could, I'd hire her to fix this for me.

She's still talking, eyes alight as she outlines a plan. But

I'm no longer listening, because an idea has struck me, one I should have thought of sooner.

I could hire Willow to fix my dumpster fire of a reputation.

It's brilliant. I mean, Oakley might not love the idea, but this would be a strictly professional arrangement. He has no reason to think anything less than appropriate would happen between Willow and me anyway. And we both know better than to let it. With her help, I could be on the road to becoming Argonaut's number one driver. Maybe even on the road to a better team.

Willow could get me there. She obviously knows her shit, and she's got the degree to back it up. And, more importantly, she actually wants to see me succeed. This girl cheered for Oakley and me from the tiny stands at our karting races, and she's still cheering for me now. What else could I possibly want out of a fixer?

She's still talking, but the words leave my mouth before I can stop them. "I think I know how to fix this. All of this."

She stops, scrunching her brow. "And how's that?"

I take a deep breath. It's now or never. "You, Willow. I need *you*."

CHAPTER 5

WILLOW

"You, Willow. I need *you*."

The place my brain goes when Dev says those words is nowhere near appropriate for our relationship or current venue. I can only hope he can't see the way I've flushed from head to toe or feel the heat radiating off me, because I'm practically the same temperature as the surface of the sun.

I've had such a hard time keeping it together since Chava and Mark abandoned us that I've resorted to rambling on about marketing and image recovery in an attempt to avoid awkward silence, but then he had the nerve to open his mouth and say he *needs* me.

I think I'm going to faint. Or puke. Maybe both? Oh god, I don't know.

He's scrutinizing me, his eyes wide and his face hopeful. All I can do in return is gape at him like a fish.

"Can you . . . repeat that?" I request, amazed that the words are coherent.

I expect him to rephrase and tone down the way he's looking at me, because he's gazing like my face holds all the answers to the universe. Obviously, it doesn't, so I'd *love* to know what exactly is going through his mind right now.

But Dev's expression doesn't dull. Not one bit. And the next thing I know, he's gripping my shoulders and standing even closer. His proximity sends the scent of his cologne and something uniquely him wafting around me.

"You're exactly what I need, Willow."

Fourteen-year-old me would have absolutely lost her mind and collapsed into a puddle of goo at that kind of confession from Dev. Twenty-one-year-old me, however, takes a step back and puts her hands up. I don't like where this is headed. We've already made our mistakes; we don't need to make more.

"I'm gonna need you to explain your thought process here," I say slowly. "Because you're not making sense."

That gets him to blink, and some of the reverence in his eyes clears away. Another second passes before he drops his hands from my shoulders and takes a step back too. "Oh, shit. Sorry," he blurts, glancing around, likely checking to see if anyone noticed the interaction. "Got a little caught up."

"Uh-huh." The heat of his touch lingers on my skin, but I do my best to pay it no mind. "So . . . explain, please?"

"Yeah. Right. Okay." He inhales deeply, his hands lifted, palms pressed together like he's ready to beg or pray. "Willow . . . I think you can fix me. I think you can fix my image. I'd like to hire you to do it."

Once again, I'm lost for words as my brain tries to compute what he's just said. He wants to . . . hire me? To fix his image?

"Is this a joke?" I blurt, leaning to one side to peer around him, waiting for a camera crew or some guy with a phone to pop out and say, *Gotcha!* "Did Oakley put you up to this?"

Dev's brows furrow, and he drops his hands to his sides. "What? No. I literally came up with the idea while you were talking." He wets his lips and stares at me like he's searching for the right words to say.

He better search hard, because I can't take many more of these vague statements about being needed.

"I want you to help me do all the things you said would fix this. You're perfect." Oh god, again with the compliments that make my heart tumble over itself. "You clearly know how to handle situations like this, and I'd be lucky to have you working with me. So, what do you say?"

Right now, I can't say a single thing. There's no way he's asking what I think he is. "But why me?" I finally manage. "Yes, I know what I'm doing. Kind of. But don't you want someone with more experience? Someone with a proven track record? Someone who's actually done this as a job?"

Dev shakes his head. "I've had that, and it didn't work for me. Plus, I . . ." He takes a breath, his eyes darting away from me for a second before coming back. The vulnerability in their depths surprises me. "I don't trust many people at the moment, all right? The idea of handing myself over to just anyone scares the shit out of me."

"And you trust *me*?" I scoff.

I feel a little bad when the corners of his mouth flick down, but he's got to get this through his head.

"Come on," I try to reason. "I've known you since we were kids. I know all the stuff you and my brother got up to. I could make what your old social media manager did look like child's play. We both know I have more blackmail material than almost anyone."

"And you'd never use it," he counters. "You're not that kind of person."

It's my turn to frown. "You don't know that."

"Uh, yeah, I do." He says it like he really knows who I am at more than a surface level. Maybe he thinks he does, simply because we've known each other for so long, but we haven't spent much time together over the past few years. And I've changed. "If you never told our parents about the stuff Oak and I did, then you'd never tell the whole world."

"Okay, but what if you pissed me off and I pulled a Jani?"

"Like I said, you're not that kind of person."

God, this man is impossible. I don't like being told who I am and what I'm capable of, but he's right. I don't think I'd have it in me to drag a person through the mud, no matter how badly they wronged me. If I didn't do it when I found my then-boyfriend in bed with another girl, Dev's crime would have to be especially heinous to even get me to consider a revenge plot.

Dev clasps his hands together again. "I'll pay you whatever you want," he pushes on. "Name a number; it's yours."

My stomach drops. This is starting to feel more like a bribe than a job offer.

"I know your parents and your brother can support you, so that probably isn't the biggest draw," he concedes, which just makes my frown deepen. "But this would be the best thing for both of us. All you'd have to do is follow me around the world for a couple of months, and then you can put it on your résumé. Think about how good that'll look. You'd not only get the experience, but you could brag about rehabbing my image. It's a win-win situation. And, hey, you don't have to work for me forever. Just until my reputation isn't in shambles anymore."

"I don't do personal social media managing," I tell him,

shaking my head. "All my internships were for brands and teams. I can't do—"

"You can," he says, his eyes boring into me. "I'm not blowing smoke up your ass when I say you're the best person to do this. You know me, you know the sport, and you know how to fix this mess. Think of me as a brand, just one that's a little more . . . human. This reinvention needs to come off as authentic as possible. Like it's me personally behind it, even though there's no way I can be."

Silently, I take him in, pulling my lower lip between my teeth. I don't want to even consider his offer, but I . . . think I am. The spark in his eyes and the confidence he has in my abilities—even though he can't know for sure that I'm capable of what he's asking for—are making it difficult to say no. No one else has had that faith in me. At least no one with hiring abilities.

"Wills, please," he begs, his voice softening.

That tone makes my knees go weak and my resolve all but hit the ground. Besides, everything he's saying makes perfect sense. It *would* look good on my résumé. Amazing, even. And I could be back to my life in New York in a few months, hopefully having accepted a permanent position. This could set me up for the success I'm looking for. And I'd be making money in the meantime, so I wouldn't have to move back to San Diego with my parents.

I'm determined to stand on my own feet, and this is the perfect opportunity to prove that I can.

"What do you say?" Dev presses. He's standing so close that he's all I can see. The rest of the party has fallen away. "We could even put a hard end date on it. How about Alisha's wedding?"

His sister is getting married in mid-August, and considering it's practically June now, this would only be a two-and-a-half-month commitment. Like a summer job. I've had plenty of those throughout my life, so what's another? This time, though, instead of scooping ice cream or waiting tables, I'd get to do what I love.

I down the rest of my champagne and let Dev take the glass from me. Instantly, he makes it disappear like a bad magic trick. Right now, the world around me feels like an illusion, but I'm about to agree to something all too real.

"Fine," I say before I can overthink it. "I'll do it."

The way Dev's face lights up has me blinking like I'm staring into the sun. "Oh, thank—"

"*But*," I cut in before I lose myself in his smile. "Only if Oakley is comfortable with it."

His joy dims a fraction, though it's still practically blinding. I can already feel myself smiling back. His energy is so infectious it makes it impossible not to.

"Deal," he says, his eyes flicking to something over my shoulder. "But don't tell Oakley until tomorrow, all right? I'd like to have a good time tonight without worrying about what he'll say."

I shouldn't be so hung up on my brother's opinion, but after what happened with Jeremy, I owe it to him to get his approval first. The breakup wasn't my fault, I know that, but I still feel guilty for having a hand in shaking up Oakley's friend group. Now, when it comes to anything involving his friends, including a job offer from one, I'm determined to run it by him first.

Dev seems to understand that too. He was part of the wreckage. He and Chava and Mark took my side in the breakup, while two of their other friends defended Jeremy. The aftermath was nothing short of carnage.

"Yeah, I can wait," I agree, just as an elbow lands on my shoulder, always my brother's armrest.

"Dev, your agent looks like he's about to shit a brick," Oakley announces, though thankfully, it doesn't seem that he's overheard our conversation. "Go do his bidding so we can all get out of here and hit an actual club."

Ducking out from under Oakley's arm, I shake my head. "You can count me out of clubbing," I say as Mark and Chava rejoin, holding the drinks they promised when they abandoned me with Dev. "I'm jet-lagged and want to be able to function tomorrow."

Chava offers me a fresh glass of champagne and then his upturned palm. "You can ditch us tonight, but only if you dance with me now. Yeah?"

I don't miss how the question is directed at Oakley, who nods in my periphery. They do this like they think I don't notice, but they've been cautious around me since the Jeremy disaster. If I didn't still feel so ashamed, I might call them all out on it. For now, though, I'll continue to let it slide.

Still, I'm hopeful Oakley will sign off on me working for Dev, because the more I think about it, the more I want to do this. I want this step up. And honestly? Traveling the world and following a thrilling sport for a few months doesn't sound half bad either. Besides, he has no reason not to want this for me. Things might be different if he knew about the little indiscretion between Dev and me last year, but we seem to be on the same page about keeping it a secret.

I take Chava's outstretched hand and glance back at Oakley and Dev. I have no idea which way Oakley's going to go on Dev's offer.

But come tomorrow, I guess I'll know my fate.

CHAPTER 6

DEV

After an hour of kissing ass with Howard by my side, I bail on hitting the clubs with Mark, Chava, and Oakley, pleading a headache. Mark sends me back to my apartment with two acetaminophen, an electrolyte drink, an ice pack, and a recommendation for a guided meditation program. It took a hell of a lot of convincing to get him to even go out, ever the dedicated trainer and mother hen, but now I'm alone, and I can properly think about what I've done.

Positive: I hired someone to fix my damaged image. Negative: that someone is my best friend's little sister.

Willow's not beholden to her brother, but Oakley would never let her walk into a situation where she could get hurt, physically or otherwise. And after some of the things she's been through, I wouldn't be surprised if he wholeheartedly disapproved of my idea.

If that happens, I'll rescind the offer. No arguments. It's the best thing I could do, because Willow will fight Oakley on it if he says no and she still thinks it's an option. I won't come between the siblings. That'll just result in more drama that none of us want.

I probably shouldn't have asked her in the first place, but I really do believe she can pull this revival off. Not only does she know what she's doing professionally, she knows *me*. She knows my boundaries. Plus, she knows the sport, thanks to being raised around it. And I don't have to explain shit about my backstory because she was there for almost all of it. It's the perfect solution.

I kick off my uncomfortable dress shoes in the entryway of my apartment, not bothering with the lights. I make my way to my bedroom, guided by the soft glow of the city outside my windows, determined not to dwell on this more than I already have. My best bet is to sleep on it and see where my head's at in the morning. I've never made the greatest decisions with a belly full of champagne.

In the morning, when my mind is clear, I'll think it through again. But this already feels more right than anything has in a long time.

Willow can fix me. I know she can.

I'm dreaming of that night again, the one last year that led to my worst decision. Maybe it's a nightmare. I still don't know.

I'm shit-faced and so is Willow. She's leaning against the wall next to me as Oakley pukes his guts out behind the door to our left. He's retching and groaning, swearing off alcohol for the rest of his life even though he'll be drinking again tomorrow.

Willow and I barely got him to the club's bathroom before he spewed, but we drew the line at going in with him. Instead, we're out here waiting for him to finish so we can drag him back to the hotel, where he can spend the rest of his birthday in bed. I could handle it myself, but Willow, the good sister she is, wants to make sure he's okay.

"Only because our mom would kill me if something happens to him," she takes care to remind me.

She can say that all she wants, but I know the truth. She'd never admit it, but she actually *cares* about her brother. It's crazy. Absolutely unhinged behavior. I'd never confess to the same about my sister (even though it's also the truth).

Alisha's somewhere out in the main part of the club with her fiancé and the rest of our friends, celebrating Oakley. By some stroke of luck, I got them all to come out to Texas for the festivities, since my race schedule dictated that I had to be in Austin for the week. But getting us together always results in the best kind of chaos, no matter where we are.

I lean back against the cool cinder block wall and close my eyes as the world spins. I may not be losing my dinner right now, but I matched Oakley shot for shot tonight. I can't bring myself to open my eyes again until Willow stammers, "No thanks. I'm—I'm actually here with my boyfriend."

It takes a moment to understand what's happening in front of me: Willow is pressed to the wall, shoulders tight and half-turned away from the frat douche who's hovering in her personal space. The guy spares me a glassy-eyed once-over like he's sizing me up, hesitating for a beat before turning his attention back to her.

Boyfriend. Willow mentioned a boyfriend. It hits me then that she's referring to me. It's a ploy to get this dickhead to leave her alone, because, as far as I know, she's not dating anyone—and if she is, they're certainly not here. It's bullshit that she can't say no or *I'm not interested* and expect this fucker to listen, all because guys like him don't hold the same respect for women as they do for other men.

Seems like this guy doesn't respect anybody, though, because the mention of a boyfriend doesn't faze him. Neither does my proximity, apparently. He leans closer and whispers something in her ear that makes her turn her head and cringe in disgust. And that's all I need to see.

I'm really not itching for a fight tonight. I need to have all my faculties in order to drive this upcoming weekend, but I can easily take this guy and his fucking popped collar if I have to.

I don't waste another second before clutching Willow by the elbow and pulling her behind me. I smile widely to cover my rage as I'm left face-to-face with Popped Collar. "I'm the boyfriend," I tell him, fire burning just below the surface of my skin. "And you need to back the fuck off my girl."

Willow's hands are on my waist, pushing against me, trying to move me out of the way so she can handle this herself. But Oakley would have my head if I didn't step in and protect her, and I'd rather face Willow's wrath than her brother's. Besides, I wouldn't have stood by and let Popped Collar practically assault anyone, let alone someone I care about. Fuck that.

The guy has the decency to take a step back. He's not exactly steady on his feet, but his hands are fisted at his sides. "Who the hell do you think you—" But then his jaw drops open and his eyes go wide. And there it is. The recognition that's about to bring this all to a close. "Oh shit! You're Dev Anderson!" he slurs, throwing his hands up in excitement. Asshole. But at least he's not throwing a punch. "Dude, for real, I'm sorry. I didn't know she was your—"

"It's fine," I grit out, even though it's not. But I know better than to make a scene. If I do, it'll end up in the media. And that means I have to get him out of here before I do something unwise, like bruise my hand as I break his nose. "Enjoy the rest of your night, man."

After a few more seconds of open-mouthed staring, he finally stumbles off. Willow hasn't stopped poking my back since I pulled her behind me, so with a deep breath, I turn around to face her.

I dive in before she has a chance to give me hell, because there's no way she won't. "Before you yell at me"—I hold up both hands—"I know it's not fine, and if I didn't have to be careful about getting caught doing stupid stuff, I would have beat that motherfucker's face in."

But instead of verbally handing my ass to me, Willow grins. "*Actually*," she says, deep dimples popping in her cheeks, "I was going to say thank you, but I guess that's good to know."

I blink. Once, again, two more times. I'm too wasted to process the answer. "You're . . . not mad?" There's no way she's not mad. She has to be mad. Doesn't she hate when other people fight her battles for her? Has the real Willow been abducted by aliens and replaced with this mysterious, understanding angel?

She giggles. "Nah, not mad."

It's only then that I realize how close we're standing. We're practically chest to chest. The scent of her perfume surrounds me. If I wasn't already drunk, it would be intoxicating.

"That guy wasn't gonna leave me alone, no matter what. And, like, honestly? What you did was kinda hot." A silent beat passes, and then she presses her hand against her mouth, like she's trying to shove the secret back in.

I've heard it, though. And so has my dick, apparently, because it's twitching behind my zipper, just like it did when I first saw her tonight.

She's wearing the world's tiniest dress, a curve-hugging thing that leaves just enough to the imagination to be legal. It's black and slinky and ties around her neck in a pretty little bow that's been begging all night to be tugged open. Oakley tried to make her go back to the hotel and change. He even looked at me for backup, but I kept my mouth shut and turned to the rest of our friends instead. How could I say anything when I was already envisioning what it would look like on my floor?

Willow's a beautiful girl, I can admit that. I can also admit that I've thought it for a long time. But neither of those details matter because she's off-limits. Always has been. And the only boundaries I push are in a race car.

Doesn't mean I'm not tempted, though.

"Oh, crap," she says between more uncontrolled giggles. "I'm sorry. I shouldn't have—I shouldn't have said that. I'm not trying to make things weird, I swear."

I shake my head, mostly to clear away the thoughts I shouldn't be having. "No, you're good. Happy to play the fake boyfriend anytime you need me to." I might even be happy to play a real one.

Still laughing, she tilts her head back so it rests against the wall, her corkscrew curls falling around her bare shoulders. Yeah, she's drunk, and so am I, because all I can think is how pretty she looks under these shitty fluorescent lights.

"God, I'm glad you never told me anything like that years ago," she murmurs, eyes swinging toward the ceiling.

My brow furrows at her throwaway comment. "Why?"

She shakes her head, still not looking in my direction, wanting to let it slide.

"Seriously, tell me," I press. "Did I do something wrong back then?"

It's only then that she lifts her head to lock eyes with me. Hers are so dark I can practically see myself reflected in them. But there's a sliver, a quarter of her right iris, that's melted caramel. It's golden and deep. Some might call it an imperfection, an abnormality, but it's just . . . Willow.

"You don't know?" she asks.

"Know what?"

And then she makes a confession that changes the course of the evening. Maybe even my life. "That I had a huge crush on you."

The world around me spins, and I can't completely blame it on the seven tequila shots I downed tonight. "You did?"

"Yeah, but that's, like, *so* far in the past," she brushes off, waving a hand and nearly smacking herself in the face. "Like a kid thing. It's nothing. I really thought you knew." She giggles again, so sweet and so innocent. "I was so embarrassingly obvious."

"I didn't know," I say, but I'm already analyzing every interaction she and I have ever had. What the hell did I miss? *How* did I miss it? And if I hadn't, would things be different now? "Why didn't you—why didn't you tell me?"

She scoffs, but her lopsided grin remains. "It was a stupid teenage crush. Not like you were ever interested. And then Jeremy asked me out, so . . ."

Jeremy. Fucking *Jeremy*. The human embodiment of a piece of shit. A cheater, a liar, and an all-around terrible person. It kills me that we considered him a friend for so long, all because we grew up together. The warning signs were always there, and yet we just . . . ignored them. Put blinders on. Told ourselves that the way he talked to girls, the jokes, and the borderline misogynistic comments were fine—that it didn't mean anything. He was a good guy. We all were.

Except none of us were, because we sheltered him from the consequences. We took him at his word when he swore the girls he dated and broke up with were psychotic bitches who expected too much of him. We defended him when he was accused of cheating. Clearly, the girl didn't understand the meaning of *casual*. We even laughed along when he told us outrageous stories of the things these obsessive stalkers would do to get his attention.

When he started dating Willow, everyone was fine with it, even Oakley. They were both in college in New York, Jeremy a senior and Willow a freshman. It was perfect, honestly. He could look out for her, be a familiar face in the chaos of a new city.

"We all know how that ended," Willow finishes with a shrug, her smile a little less bright.

Yeah, it ended with her calling her brother in tears and Oakley getting on a plane to New York. It ended with Jeremy in the hospital, threatening to press charges, and our group of friends split down the middle. Thankfully, the case never went anywhere, but none of us were the same afterward.

But now I'm left to wonder what would have happened if I'd have made a move before Jeremy did. How different could things have been if I'd been the one to ask her out instead of him?

"If I had known, I would have—" I cut myself short, not even sure what I would have done if she'd told me about her feelings.

Have I been fighting my attraction to her for a while? Hell yeah, I have, especially since I tagged along with Oakley to visit her at college a couple of years ago. But I always thought dating her would cross a line, one I never wanted to venture over. Oakley might have been okay with it, just like he had been with Jeremy in the beginning, but it still seemed . . . wrong. Like a betrayal to my best friend, no matter how much I wanted it. How much I wanted her.

"What would you have done, Dev?" Willow presses when I don't complete the thought. She's watching me intently, her red-painted lips parted ever so slightly.

I don't know. I don't fucking know what I would have done back then. But right now, I'm tempted to make up for lost time, consequences be damned.

I don't realize my hands are on her hips until she covers them with her own, soft and warm.

I'm convinced she's going to pull mine away, but then she runs her fingertips up my arms, slowly, gingerly, until her hands rest on my elbows. She squeezes, an invitation for me to pull her closer, and I don't think twice before starting to—until a door slams open beside us.

I jump back as Oakley stumbles out of the bathroom, still looking a little green around the gills. "Let's get out of here," he groans, his eyes landing on me, then Willow. I may have put a little distance between us, but not enough. Based on the way his eyes narrow, Oakley probably sees the guilt written on my face. "Wait . . . what the fuck are you two doing?"

"Nothing," Willow says quickly. While my sins are reflected in my expression, hers shine through in her voice. She steps forward to grab her brother's arm, keeping her head down. "Let's get out of here."

"No, stop." Oakley holds up a hand, his unfocused gaze dragging between us. Being drunk off his ass isn't going to prevent him from connecting the dots. "Don't fucking lie to me. What were you doing?"

Willow takes a step forward and tugs on his arm, trying

to convince him to start walking. "Seriously, it was nothing, Oak. We were just waiting for you."

But he doesn't budge. His expression darkens, and he rips his arm from Willow's grasp. With his attention focused solely on me, he pokes my chest with one finger. "Were you just kissing my sister?"

"What?" I splutter, the reaction not helping my plight. "*No.* Fuck no. Of course not." Was I about to, though? One thousand goddamn percent.

I don't dare look over at Willow. I only hope she doesn't take it the wrong way. She seems to get it, though, because she grabs Oakley's arm again and forces him to look at her.

"I'm literally wearing red lipstick," she points out, motioning dramatically to her perfect mouth. "If we were kissing, it would be all over Dev's face, dumbass."

"Yeah, I'd be in full clown mode right now, man," I add to the defense. "And no offense to Wills, but that's not my shade of red."

A step behind her brother, she rolls her eyes, but he deflates in response.

"Oh," he mumbles. His anger quickly fades, replaced by the blank, wasted stare I much prefer. "All right. Good. Yeah." He drags the back of his hand across his forehead before it falls limply to his side. "But don't ever fucking try."

▀▖▀▖▀▖▀▖▀▖

I wake in a cold sweat with my sheets tangled around my legs. Shoving them back, I wrench myself out of bed and grab my phone, heading straight into the kitchen before blindly fumbling in the cabinet for a glass. I fill it with water from the fridge with one hand while I use the other to pull up Mark's contact on my phone. Both of them shake.

"If you're calling to see if I got back safely," he says upon answering the call, "then yes, Mom, I did. You can go to bed now."

Ignoring him, I put the phone on speaker and drop it onto the counter. "Mark, I think I fucked up."

He groans. "I swear, if you hurt yourself doing something stupid, I'm going to be so pissed. I can't let you out of my sight for one—"

"It's not bodily damage."

"Okay . . ." He trails off. "Then what did you do?"

I drag my fingers through my hair, still rattled from the dream and Oakley's warning—a warning I ignored later that weekend. "I hired a new social media manager."

Mark's quiet for a beat before he finally asks, "How is that bad? You need one. Unless . . . oh shit, don't tell me you re-hired Jani."

"It's worse than that." I drop onto one of the barstools in front of the marble island. "I hired Willow."

The silence that stretches across the line this time practically crackles with tension. Mark's shock and horror are coming through loud and clear. "No, you fucking didn't."

I close my eyes, chin dipping to my chest. "Oh, but I *did*."

"Fire her," he demands. "Right now."

"I can't do that." I sigh. "I'm the one who offered her the job. I need her help."

"Then you *really* fucked up. Do you need me to remind you of what happened the last time you got too close to her?"

He definitely doesn't. I'll never forget how I found myself in the barriers on lap thirty-seven in Austin because I couldn't get Willow and our kiss out of my head. When I finally made it back to the pit lane after riding on the scooter of shame behind a chatty marshal, I told my team principal that I just made a stupid rookie mistake and locked up the rear wheels, but all it took was one firm look from Mark to spill my guts.

"You crashed in your home race, Dev," he scolds. "Your home race!"

"Yes, thank you. I'm well aware," I mumble, rubbing my eyes as if that will get the images of Willow's face and my ruined car out of my head. "And technically, Vegas is my—"

"*Shut up*," he cuts in. "This is a bad idea and you know it. She's a distraction. Not only that, but we both know Oakley will cut your balls clear off if you ever make a move on her. You remember how he threatened me when I had the nerve to say she looked nice?"

Oh yeah, Oakley was touchy in the immediate aftermath of Jeremygate. We could hardly even look at Willow without finding ourselves on the receiving end of his glare. With time, he eased up, but his warning last October was a reminder of the lengths he'd go to for his sister.

"Yeah, that's because he knows what a whore you are," I joke, trying to lighten a quickly soured mood.

Mark scoffs. "As if you're any better. Need I remind you of Monza two years ago?"

"That was a onetime thing," I point out. "How can you not expect me to end up in bed with five women after making it onto my first F1 podium?"

"You barely got third, and that's because four other drivers got penalties."

"A podium is a podium, baby. Gotta celebrate what you can."

"You're ignoring the point," Mark huffs. "Oakley is never going to let any of us even get near Willow after—"

"I know," I interrupt softly. I hold the glass to my forehead, hoping the cold will shock some sense into me.

"And can you blame him? Jeremy wrecked her." He lets out a long breath. "And she's the reason *you* wrecked."

"Oh, fuck *off*. That was a terrible joke. I'm throwing tomatoes at you in my head. Boo, hiss, get off the stage!"

"I'm not kidding around." Mark's tone makes that abundantly clear. "You cannot let this girl get to you again, Dev. If you're really going to do this, you have to keep it strictly professional—for your sake and the sake of your friendship with Oakley."

Guilt simmers in my chest. He's right. I need to keep my distance from Willow whether she ends up working for me or not.

But after seeing her tonight—after dreaming of the words she said to me that drunken night last year—it'll be easier said than done.

Because Willow already has a hold on me, and I have no idea how to shake her off.

CHAPTER 7

WILLOW

Thank goodness for jet lag. Otherwise, I wouldn't have slept at all last night.

Dev and his job offer are the first things on my mind when I wake, my stomach twisted in knots and my head hazy. Before the fog clears, I briefly wonder if yesterday was a hallucination. But the glittering Monaco harbor outside my balcony doors is proof otherwise. So is my dress from last night's event, thrown over the chair in the corner. The half a dozen texts from Oakley telling me he's on his way up to my room solidify it. I'm really here. And Dev really did hire me to fix his problematic image.

Groaning, I drag myself out of bed and shuffle to the door when Oakley's complicated signature knock resounds from the other side. It's a remnant from our days playing ruler of the castle in our tree house. Back then, you weren't allowed entry without the secret knock, but nowadays, we use it to announce our presence to each other.

Without bothering to check the peephole, I pull down on the handle and haul open the heavy door, careful not to throw my hip out to the side for leverage as I do. I learned the hard way to use my limited upper body strength instead. I'm not interested in dislocating a hip again or spending hours in a Monaco hospital to get it put back in place.

"What should we do today?" Oakley asks as he strides inside.

It's barely nine, but he's already showered and dressed. I, on the other hand, am still in pajamas—cute long-sleeved pink linen ones, sure, but pajamas, nonetheless—and my hair is a mess since I didn't bother to tie it up last night, let alone wrap it in a scarf.

"We could hit the casino, do some shopping, get shit-faced on a yacht," he suggests. "Your choice. The world's your oyster, kid."

I don't know about any of that, but I do need to talk to Dev about how he wants to get started. Because the more I think about it, the more I realize just how big a job this is going to be, and it's got me panicking a little. What if I can't pull this off? But he wouldn't be pushing so hard to hire me if he didn't believe I could, right? He's in my corner, even if I'm still unsure about it.

Today would be perfect to get a crash course in what he expects. Thursdays are media days, chock-full of interviews, photo shoots, and other content creation for a driver's team and sponsors before the race weekend. I could observe, and he could show me the ropes.

First, though . . . I have to have a conversation with my brother. Nothing is going to happen until I get his approval.

Oakley throws himself down on my bed, leaving his legs hanging over the edge and his feet on the floor, and stares at me as he waits for an answer. I really wish I'd had time for a cup of coffee before launching into all of this, but here we go, I guess.

Perching on the chair I tossed my dress onto last night, I tuck my hands between my knees, needing the grounding pressure to keep from freaking out. "I'm up for whatever," I say, my voice as light and breezy as I can make it. "But . . . can I talk to you about something first?"

Nonplussed, Oakley circles his hand in the air to get me to come out with it.

I draw in a deep breath and exhale slowly. "As it turns out, you were right about me being offered a job by the end of the party."

He jackknifes to sitting in a move far smoother than I could ever manage, no matter how much I work on my abs. "For real?"

I nod in response. When he grins and his dark eyes light up, my stomach twists further in on itself.

"Wills, that's amazing. I *knew* you'd pull it off. Who will you be working for?"

Ah, crap, moment of truth. "You have to promise not to get angry or try to tell me I can't do it, okay?" I threaten without much real force behind it. He'll do whatever he wants anyway.

Oakley snorts. "What, did you agree to be a professional girlfriend to one of the old-ass team principals?"

"Ew, *no*." I flick my tangled hair over my shoulder. "But thank you for thinking I'm pretty enough to be hired as one."

He throws a pillow at me, leaving me to scramble to catch it before it hits me in the face. "Seriously, what is it?" he demands. "Stop being so cagey. I hate this shit."

I clutch the pillow to my chest, as if it will protect me from what I'm sure will be swift and harsh disapproval. "Dev wants me to be his temporary social media manager," I confess in a rush of words. "Just long enough to recover his public image after the Jani mishap without involving a big PR firm."

Oakley stares at me, blinking, his expression unreadable.

Oh no. This is it. He's going to tell me I can't do it. And even if I argue, I know Dev won't go for it if my brother isn't on board.

But to my surprise, Oakley shoots me a confused look. "Why would I be angry about that?" He scoots a little closer to the edge of the bed. "That's a great opportunity to get your foot in the door. And think about how sick that will look on your résumé." He scans the room, wearing a contemplative frown. "I don't know why I didn't think of it, to be honest. It's literally perfect."

Excuse me while I pick my jaw up off the ground. "You're seriously okay with this?" Could it really be this easy to get his seal of approval? I expected histrionics and threats to send me back to New York on the next flight.

Maybe I wanted it too. Maybe I wanted to be talked out of this. It's my nerves trying to take over, I know that, but I almost hoped someone else might point out the negatives I haven't discovered yet. There's got to be something I'm missing.

Oakley shrugs. "Of course I am. I just wish I'd thought of it myself. I want the credit."

"And you don't mind if I work for one of your closest friends?" I push, still searching for that out.

"No, I don't." A beat passes where he just watches me. Then his eyes widen. "Look, I know I told you I don't want you involved with another one of my friends, but this is a professional arrangement. Not . . . personal."

He has a point, and maybe I've underestimated his ability

to differentiate between Dev and Jeremy. Plus, he doesn't know about the kiss.

But I still have my own worries, no matter how much I want the job.

"What if Dev fires me and leaves me stranded in Australia like he did with Jani?" I challenge. "What would you do?"

Oakley lifts a finger. "First of all, the Australian Grand Prix already happened, so that's not possible." He raises another. "And second of all, he knows better than to leave you stranded anywhere. But if you mess up and get fired, that's your own problem." He lowers the first finger again, leaving his middle one raised as he smiles. "So don't fuck it up."

I launch the pillow back at him, letting out a delighted cackle when it hits him square in the face. Guess he lost all his amazing reaction times once he left racing.

"I'm glad you're leaving," he grumbles as he tosses the pillow to the side. "Let Dev deal with your ass."

"You barely see me anyway. You're too busy in Chicago," I huff as I slowly stand from the chair. It feels like a thousand-pound weight has been lifted off my shoulders. If Oakley can't see any drawbacks, maybe I really am making the right decision. "And this will only be for a couple of months. Just until Alisha's wedding."

Oakley gets a wistful look in his eyes when I mention Dev's older sister, just like he has for years, but he blinks it away quickly and waves me off. "Whatever. Go get dressed so we can leave. I want to get day drunk and gamble away my millions."

I snort but move over to my suitcase to grab an outfit for the day. "I think you're overestimating the number of zeros in your bank account."

"You don't know my life." He purses his lips and studies

me. "Hey, does this mean you need to check in with Dev? When do you officially start?"

"I don't know," I confess, pawing through sundresses and cardigans and ignoring the uptick in my heart rate. "I wanted to get your approval before moving forward with details."

Oakley mumbles something I can't make out. "Fine, call and let him know that the big, bad brother doesn't care what you two do. Just don't make things worse for him. He's already got it bad enough."

I roll my eyes as I pick out a dress with tiny pink flowers printed across it and a pair of white sneakers. My joints won't survive walking around this city without arch support, cute as my strappy sandals are. "You call him," I shoot back. "I don't even have his number, and you're the one he'd probably rather hear from anyway."

The first part is a lie. I definitely have Dev's number, unless he's changed it in the past seven months. And as for him preferring to hear from Oakley—well, it's not *exactly* a lie. I'm just too nervous to talk to him. Surely that doesn't bode well for our working relationship, but hopefully we'll fall back into our old camaraderie after a few days.

At least, I hope. Oh god, I don't know how I'm going to make it through this if I can't even bring myself to talk to the guy.

Oakley grunts but pulls his phone out of his pocket and taps the screen a few times before setting it on the bed beside him.

Dev's voice is hoarse when he answers, and I can't help but wonder what he did after the party last night. "What's up?"

"Hey, you at the circuit?" Oakley's question is directed at him, but he's looking at me, gauging my reaction.

There's vague rustling in the background, like sheets. I'm struck with the mental image of Dev naked in bed, brown skin against crisp white sheets, the necessities barely covered.

It's sudden and unbidden, but I like the idea of it more than I should. "Nah, haven't left my place yet," he says. "Why?"

"Come get your newest employee on your way over."

There's a long, crackling pause before he asks, "You serious?"

"Hi, Dev," I squeak.

"Willow. Hi." He clears his throat, and his voice loses some of that scratchy quality. "Oak, you're okay with this?"

"Yeah," my brother says. "I'm just pissed I didn't think of it first."

"Okay. Wow. All right. I guess I'll be there in a bit to pick you up, Wills."

Before I can panic about being alone with Dev, Oakley adds, "We can all go over together. I want the full backstage tour too."

"You already know what it's like," I point out, but I'm grateful that he'll be a buffer—and a reminder of why I can't let myself think the way I have been about Dev. "You've been to plenty of races. And you were literally a driver."

"Not in F1," he counters. "And Dev's always been too busy to show me around, the dick."

Dev lets out an exasperated breath. "Fine, we'll all go."

"One big, happy family," Oakley quips.

Yeah. That's certainly one way of putting it . . .

"Well, Willow," Dev says as I stare at the phone beside my brother's leg. "Welcome to Argonaut Racing. Hope you like red, white, and blue."

▗▚▚▚▚▖

Dev wasn't kidding about the color scheme. It looks like the American flag threw up all over him and ninety-nine percent of the people here.

This is Argonaut Racing's "All American, all the time" tagline come to life. Every person we've spoken to in the team's hospitality suite since we arrived five minutes ago has an American accent, and the team uniform of navy shorts paired with a red-and-white-striped polo screams patriotism. Or creepy nationalism.

A sneaky search on my phone while we're waiting for our coffee order tells me that Argonaut prides itself on hiring only US-based employees, from the factories all the way to the drivers. The team's owner and chairman, Buck Decker, is a Texas oil-money billionaire who took over two years ago and implemented the *all American* rule—along with putting his son, Nathaniel, in the second race seat alongside Dev. Before that, the team was a little more international, but they've always been an American constructor.

I slip my phone back into my purse as Oakley hands me a steaming vanilla-heavy latte, my preferred coffee order. At least I won't have to worry about getting a solid caffeine fix while on the road with Dev. Honestly, this hospitality motorhome looks like the lobby of a luxury hotel rather than a structure that's put up and taken down weekend after weekend in locations around the world.

A sleek rectangular bar takes up the center of the space, with high-top tables dotted around it, and there are TVs mounted on the walls every few feet. There are mini vending machines stocked with bottles from the beverage company that sponsors the team, grab-and-go snack stations, and what looks like a photo booth. There are even hanging plants to give the space a little greenery.

The uniforms are the only eyesore. Even Dev, who looks good in everything, comes off a little foolish, like a kid forced to wear an outfit his mom picked out for a Fourth of July parade. Not that *his* mom would ever do that; Neha Aunty would never stand for such tackiness.

And yet, even though he looks silly, Dev pulls it off better than anyone else here. The sleeves of the polo stretch tight around his thick biceps, and the buttons at the collar are undone just enough to show off a peek of his skin underneath. If the shorts were any shorter, they'd be borderline obscene, but as it stands, they show off solid thighs and, for an instant, what I swear is the swirl of black ink peeking out from the hem. But then he moves, and it's gone.

I don't mean for our eyes to meet when I look back up, but when they do, he watches me for a second too long. Like maybe he could hear me mentally thirsting over him and he's trying to figure out how to tell me to stop. But when I look closer, all I see is awe, as if he can't believe I'm here. That this is actually happening. I feel the same.

Finally glancing away, he nods in the direction of a back hallway. "Follow me."

I breathe a sigh of relief when he turns and navigates through the crowd like he owns the place. He greets people as we pass by, truly in his element. It's far more attractive than it should be.

"Before we do anything, we need to meet with the absolute light of my life," Dev says over his shoulder. "Patsy Beedle, Argonaut's head of communications."

Oakley and I trail behind him, and Chava falls into step with us as we head toward the offices at the rear of the motorhome. He's also wearing the hideous uniform, which doesn't bode well for me. It's beginning to look like everyone associated with the team and its drivers has to wear it.

"I hear you've joined Team Dev." Chava shoots me a crooked grin. "I'll help you get set up with everything you need, including hotel and travel bookings while we're on the road."

I shoot him a grateful smile, glad I have another ally here. "Thank you," I exhale. "This is all pretty . . . sudden. I wasn't exactly expecting a job offer last night."

"We weren't expecting it either," someone else cuts in.

I glance over my shoulder and glimpse Mark coming up behind us. Even though he's wearing a smile, it's not the authentic one I've seen him flash thousands of times. I've never had a problem with him, but he's never cared for me all that much. And I don't blame him. If I hadn't gotten involved with Jeremy, Mark wouldn't have been forced to choose sides, and he wouldn't have lost a handful of friends in the process.

I return his smile, hoping mine comes off a little more genuine. As Dev's performance coach, Mark is always with him, and if I have to maintain Dev's social media, that means I'm going to be constantly underfoot as well. There will be no avoiding each other, so for both our sakes and Dev's, I hope we can be civil.

Ahead of me, Dev comes to an abrupt stop. I peer around him to see what the roadblock is and catch sight of a petite middle-aged redhead wearing Argonaut's team uniform, though hers is modified with a navy pencil skirt and a star-printed accent scarf. Her smile says she'd offer up a slice of homemade apple pie in a heartbeat, but her eyes say it might just be laced with arsenic.

"There you are," Dev says to her, bright and beaming. He wastes no time looping an arm around her narrow shoulders and turning to Oakley and me. "This is Patsy. She follows me around to make sure I don't say anything slanderous to the press and get the team into trouble."

The woman heaves a beleaguered breath. "That is not my

job, Mr. Anderson." Her long vowels and honeyed drawl tell me she's from somewhere in the Deep South. She could insult my entire bloodline and make it sound sweet.

Dev shrugs. "It's close enough, right?"

Patsy opens her mouth like she wants to protest but closes it again and nods. "Honestly, yes," she admits, shaking her head before looking up at him and frowning. "What are you doing here so early? I usually have to send someone to drag you in on Thursdays."

"That's not true at all," Dev says to Oakley and me, wearing a shit-eating grin. *Yeah, right.* "I'm nothing if not punctual." He clears his throat to dislodge the lie. "*Anyway.* Patsy, I'd like to introduce you to my new social media manager, Willow Williams."

I stick my hand out. She wraps her own around it and squeezes firmly, but there's a confused crease to her brow.

"Nice to meet you," she says before dropping my hand and looking back at Dev. "It's just her?"

"Just her," he confirms, the note in his voice daring her to challenge him on it.

I've known the woman for less than a minute, but I already know she'll do exactly that. "Dev, we've talked about this. You need to hire a whole—"

"I know what I need, Patsy, and it's for you to take a beautiful vacation with your husband in the Tuscan countryside," he cuts in smoothly, smiling wide as if he's offering to send her on that holiday out of the goodness of his heart, not because he wants her to stop nagging him. "I promise, Willow is the best of the best. She'll have everything fixed like *that*." He snaps his fingers.

There's no way Patsy's buying what he's selling, but she has the courtesy to turn back to me. "Well, Ms. Williams, I'm

pleased to have you on board with us. You and I will be working closely to make sure this troublemaker doesn't have any
more . . . slipups."

"I'm looking forward to it," I tell her earnestly. Women are
in the minority around here—in most of motorsport, really—
so it will be nice to work alongside another driven female who
clearly doesn't put up with Dev's crap.

"Have one of these boys give you my contact info, and
don't be afraid to reach out." She turns back to Dev and ducks
out from under his arm. "I need you back here in an hour to
autograph driver cards and to do some filming. Now go ter-
rorize someone else."

She shoos us back, forcing us to clear a path as she saunters off. Am I a little intimidated by her? Absolutely. But I'm
equally awed and excited to work with her.

"And that was the woman of my dreams," Dev says wistfully as he watches her go. "I'm only slightly less scared of her
than I am of my mother."

Oakley snorts. "I'm sure Neha Aunty would love to hear
that." He glances around, no doubt antsy to get out of here to
see the cars. "Can we head to the garage now?"

Dev holds an arm out, motioning for Oakley to lead the
way. "Be my guest."

In a heartbeat, my brother is hustling through the throngs
of people. Mark joins him, but a light touch on my arm has
me hanging back. I peek over my shoulder in time to see Dev
pull his hand away.

To distract myself from how much I wish he'd left it there,
I take a gulp of my latte and end up scalding my mouth. God,
I need to get a *grip*.

"You good so far?" he asks, searching my face. When I
nod, he goes on. "Patsy's terrifying, but she really will help

you out. Lillie and Ransom are the team's social media admins, and Konrad is our main photographer, so if you ever need content from the team to post, they'll get it to you."

I nod again as I dig in my bag and pull out a small notebook and my favorite pink pen. I could type this information into the notes on my phone, but I remember details better when I write them out by hand. Plus, I'm less likely to lose them in the technological mess that is my phone.

Latte tucked into the crook of my arm, I jot down the names and titles. When I'm done, I look back up at Dev. He's smiling, but it's not the usual wide grin. This one is smaller, more personal. It's the same one he gave me last night. Like maybe he's impressed by me. I have to force myself not to read into it.

"You don't have to work this weekend," he goes on. "Get the lay of the land first, then on your way home on Monday, you can stop by headquarters in Dallas. I'm technically your boss, but you're also an employee of Argonaut, so you'll need to get all the legal stuff taken care of there. I'll make sure Chava gets the employment contract sent over tonight so you can review it."

I'd forgotten Chava was still with us until he salutes in my periphery. "Give me your clothing sizes, too, so we can get you a few sets of this beautiful uniform."

I can't hold back the grimace that takes over my face, and both guys laugh in response. Glad they're happy that I'll soon have the misfortune of donning the Argonaut uniform right along with them.

"The wardrobe's not great, but the benefits are top tier," Chava says, nodding to my latte, which is admittedly one of the best I've ever had. "Just wait until lunch. Practically a Michelin-starred spread at every meal."

"Maybe *you* get to eat that," Dev grumbles. "Mark will kick my ass if I try to eat anything other than chicken breast and grilled vegetables."

Chava rolls his eyes. "At least you got the chef to use your mom's secret spice blend."

That little taste of home must help, but I know it's got to be a challenge for Dev to have his diet dictated to him. He has to be careful not to gain weight or lose muscle mass, because every saved kilogram in the car matters when it comes to performance. He may not be running down a field or throwing a ball, but he's still an elite athlete.

The food issue was part of the reason Oakley left the world of racing. Part of the "normal" experience he craved involved not having to monitor every calorie that went into his mouth. He was miserable, I know that now, but back then I was jealous that he even had the opportunity to chase his dream. Sometimes I think I still am.

I push the thought from my head, because I'm chasing my dream right now. A modified version of it, sure, but I'm standing in the motorhome of a Formula 1 team, talking about contracts and perks of the job. I'm taking the next steps to get my career off the ground. And I'm doing it alongside people I've known for nearly my whole life.

I have Dev to thank for that. I stare up at him, taking in the easy way he jokes with Chava. He's got one hand in the pocket of his shorts, his shoulders are relaxed, and confidence rolls off him in waves. My heart stutters at the sight, but I'm sure it's just the caffeine hitting my veins.

"This is really happening," I murmur, mostly to myself.

But Dev must overhear, because he turns back and watches me as Chava shifts away, tapping at his phone.

"Yeah," Dev says quietly. "This is really happening."

I'd like to think I know what's going through his mind, because the same thing is going through mine: We're doing this. We're going to help each other. We're going to make the best of two shitty situations so we can come out of it on top of our respective games.

And we're going to have to be so, so careful not to make another mistake.

 **CHAPTER 8**

DEV

In a twist of fate, I don't qualify tenth like I was hoping for. Or ninth. Or even eighth. Today, I'm seventh on the grid.

Maybe Willow is my good luck charm, because I never imagined I'd make it this close to the front, especially in an Argonaut car. I'm certainly leagues clear of Nathaniel, who slotted himself into thirteenth. It's not terrible, considering he and I are usually somewhere in the back of the midfield, but his father is surely steaming that I'm rows ahead today.

Whatever. Buck can be as mad as he wants. I'm not here to coddle Nathaniel's ego. I'm here to score points for the team and work on getting out of this red, white, and blue hell.

Good luck charm or not, I haven't seen much of Willow since Thursday. I had a quick breakfast with her and Oakley this morning, and I've caught glimpses of them in the pit as the chaos of race day began. She snapped a few photos of me and then the car—though only in the moments right before I climbed in, taking the advice I gave her during our tour on Thursday to heart.

"Couple of things to remember when you're taking pictures in here," I told her as we moved through the garage. Oakley was busy talking to one of my mechanics on the other side of the space and out of earshot. "One, don't post any pictures where a computer screen is visible. Two, never photograph the car when the tires are off or if any sort of internal component is exposed. And three, try not to take too many photos of the back of the car in general. We don't need any of our competitors seeing that up close."

"No ass shots," she said, nodding thoughtfully as she scrawled in the little notebook she'd pulled out of her purse. "Got it."

"Willow Williams!" I gasped and nearly stumbled as I turned to her, genuinely delighted by the show of raunchy humor. So much for the innocent girl act. "When did you get so dirty?"

I was pressing my luck. I should have laughed it off and toned it down instead of entertaining more of that attitude. But that little quip had me craving more.

She held her hand up and circled her pen in the air. The bridge of her nose went a little pink, but otherwise, she held her own, even though she refused to look at me. "Let's just acknowledge the joke and move on."

"You've already spent too much time around me," I teased, ignoring the way my stomach twisted. "I'm rubbing off on you. I wonder what you'll be like by the summer break."

That got her to look at me. Her dark eyes sparkled, even though the rest of her face was devoid of humor. "I'm choosing to ignore that you said *rubbing off.*"

"*Willow.*"

She finally laughed, light and lyrical, and turned away to inspect one of the bays of tools and spare parts. "I'm not a child, Dev. I can hang with the big boys."

And that's my problem. She has truly grown up, and I can no longer rely on my go-to defenses in order to keep my attraction to her from multiplying.

I knew I was in trouble the second I saw her at the SecDark event on Wednesday night, but that unease has only increased tenfold since then. Especially after being near her, albeit briefly, every day since. How the fuck am I going to get through the next few months without throwing caution to the wind and doing something Howard would describe as "ill-advised"?

But I can't think about her right now. Not when I'm standing on the grid, ready to climb into my car for the formation lap. The second I'm in my seat, my mind has to be clear, my attention focused solely on the road in front of me. Any trouble I've made for myself can wait.

Because this is Monaco, baby. And I'm about to put on a show.

⌁⌁⌁⌁⌁

Okay, make that a *shit show*.

The challenging part of qualifying so high is keeping the position. I've been fighting for my fucking life since the race started fifty-three laps ago, and with twenty-five to go, there's still a strong chance I might not finish.

The car's reliability is starting to degrade, and the brakes are growing less responsive with each turn. I nearly lost my front wing after an Omega Siluro came around the hairpin curve and clipped me six laps ago, and my rear tires aren't feeling great. The only saving grace is that my pit stop was under three seconds and perfectly timed. That alone kept me from being put so far back that I couldn't easily make up the places I'd lost by stopping.

As long as I can hold tight and see this through, I'll finish P7. Sure, it's not the podium, and yeah, maybe it's optimistic to think the Deschamp car that's absolutely eating up my dirty air won't pass me, but I think I can pull this off.

"Keep pushing," Branny instructs over the radio. "Gap to Kivinen is two point six."

That's not something I hear often. The only time I'm close to Otto Kivinen or the Mascort cars in general is when I'm being shown blue flags to get out of their way. Otto and Zaid are always quite literally miles ahead of me, but this is a nice surprise. I doubt I have any chance of passing Otto, but my race engineer seems more optimistic.

It must mean Otto is having issues, and Branny confirms it for me. Mascort's number two driver is struggling. It could be a gift for me, but it could also be a trap if I push too hard and can't get these tires to last until the end.

"At this pace, you'll be ahead of Kivinen in three laps. Repeat, three laps."

Fuck, okay, all right. Otto won't give up the place easily, though, even if he's struggling, which means we'll have to battle for sixth. And if it comes down to it, can I manage on fuel and tire degradation? It's a careful balance, keeping the car from failing me while simultaneously pushing it to its limit.

Before I've had much time to consider it, Kivinen's rear wing is in my sights. I make to cut left, but he predicts my move and blocks. It's to be expected for a man who's been in Formula 1 for ten years; he's seen every play in the book.

But I'm not green, either, and I've learned a thing or two in my handful of seasons.

So I dummy him.

I move left, right, then left again before flicking slightly to the right once more. But as he defends to the right, I pull left. By the time he catches on, he doesn't have time to block me. We're already wheel to wheel. I close him off in the next turn, and what do you know. I'm ahead of Otto fucking Kivinen.

"Nice work," Branny praises. "Keep the pace."

I won't be able to make it any higher than this, but driving across the finish line in sixth feels like a win. Minus my mechanical DNF in Miami, I've finished in the points for every race. By comparison, Nathaniel's only done it twice in six grands prix—seven after today. According to Branny, he finished P15 here, losing two places from the start. If that's not an argument for who should be the number one driver on our team, I don't know what is.

Of course, if the press ever asks, Argonaut doesn't rank its drivers. It doesn't prioritize one over the other. That would be scandalous, because we believe in the ever-so-American value of *equality*. Except they absolutely do rank us, and Nathaniel is always the top boy, thanks to Daddy's billions.

But that can't continue if I'm consistently outperforming him.

I make my way to parc fermé and shut off the car as my side of the garage rejoices over the radio. Soon enough, I join them. I'm embraced by dozens of arms and slapped on the back by what feels like a million hands. It's not even a podium finish, but for Argonaut, this is fucking fantastic.

Except, they're not the ones I want to celebrate with first.

I thank all the team members who made this happen while scanning the people in the cordoned-off section of the garage where friends, family, and VIP guests watch the race.

I can't deny it—I'm looking for Willow. But Oakley's face is the first I see.

"Solid drive, man," he says when I make my way over, grinning wide and pulling me to him. "Almost made me miss this shit."

"We're all better with you sitting it out," I taunt as he joyfully pounds on my back. That earns me a loud laugh and another *thump* before he releases me.

I push my sweaty hair off my forehead, still searching for Willow. I get what I want when a small hand catches my wrist, and then I'm looking down at her beaming face.

"That was amazing!" she shouts over the sounds of the crowd outside cheering for the people on the podium.

I laugh as she jumps around in the limited space she has. She's still the shortest one in the area, even on tiptoes. I'm not the biggest guy either—being any taller or broader would have hindered my racing—but the way Willow is looking at me right now makes me feel seven feet tall.

I'm tugging her to me without a second thought. I wrap my arms around her shoulders as she squeals and complains about how gross I am, but she hugs me back fiercely. For a moment, I forget where we are and who's watching when I dip my head and brush my cheek against her hair. Like an addict, I inhale, needing a hit of her vanilla sweetness. Until now, I didn't realize just how much I'd been craving it.

It's ridiculous that I've been reduced to . . . *this*. Sniffing a girl's goddamn hair because that scent drags me back to a time when I had my hands all over her.

I pull back and cup her face in my hands, forcing her to look me in the eye. "You still want to do this? You want this craziness for a while?"

"More than anything." The brightness reflected back at me nearly makes me lean in so I can see it up close.

I'm grinning wider than I already was—a fucking feat in itself—and shoot her a wink before letting go and turning to the line of people vying for my attention, ready for another round of hugs and shoulder pats. Because if I'd have stared at her any longer, I'd have done something I shouldn't even be thinking about, especially with her brother standing right beside us.

But soon enough, Oakley will be gone, and the only thing holding me back from doing anything *ill-advised* will be myself. And I've never been known for my self-control.

CHAPTER 9

WILLOW

I'm still high on the adrenaline rush of the grand prix as I climb into bed that night.

The spectacle of Formula 1 is in a class all its own. The passion is unmissable, from the drivers to the fans. Getting swept up in it felt like the ultimate privilege. Even the post-race party, once again hosted by SecDark, was alight with the crackling energy of the day, and it was nowhere close to fading by the time I bailed. I would have stayed longer if I didn't have an early flight out of Nice tomorrow, and if my legs didn't ache from standing so much today. But at least I got a taste of the elite world before saying my goodbyes.

I'm hooked, no doubt about it, and now I can't wait for more.

It still blows my mind that I get to enjoy this, up close and personal, for the next few weeks. The work will be undoubtedly hard and the schedule will be grueling, but I'm ready for the challenge. So much so that I'm a little upset that I have to go back to the States tomorrow and miss out on the Spanish Grand Prix. The silver lining to this sad storm cloud, though, is that I'm flying straight to Texas to visit the Argonaut Racing headquarters, so I get to see where the magic begins.

Unable to shut my brain off after the whirlwind of a day I've had, I toss and turn. It's not only because of the excitement coursing through me from watching the race from the VIP area, though. *Maybe* it's a certain memory that keeps playing over and over and over again in my mind—the one when Dev pulled me to him for the sweatiest, hottest (temperature-wise), tightest hug after the race.

And the way he cupped my face like it was the most natural move? Like he didn't care who was watching? Like I was the only one in the entire garage? Yeah. That's definitely part of my problem right now.

It was innocent enough; Oakley didn't even bat an eye. But it felt like so much more. It felt like the moment in the stairwell a few nights after I made the most embarrassing drunken confession of my life—that I had a crush on Dev all through my childhood and teenage years.

If I'm being honest, I *still* have a crush on him, one that has always lingered in the corners of my heart. It's been locked away for some time now, but it's still there. It stayed imprisoned when I was with Jeremy, when I fell in love with a boy I thought would treat me well, but it worked its way back into the light once my heart was shattered.

Oakley was there for me in the aftermath, helping me pick up the broken pieces of myself after being cheated on and gaslighted. But Dev was there too. Not as often as my brother and definitely not to the same degree—he wasn't the one who put Jeremy in the hospital with a broken nose and a few cracked ribs. But in little ways, he made a huge difference.

He would text me just to check in and send photos from wherever he was in the world that week. He would email recipes he found when scrolling online, knowing that baking helps calm me when I'm stressed. He even sent me a custom dartboard with Jeremy's face on it. It was silly and an absolute waste of time and money, but it made me laugh, especially as I threw darts straight at "Jeremy's" eyes.

Now that we'll be working together, it's time to shove that crush back into the corner. Maybe even add a padlock for good measure. There can be no distractions. Nothing that might sully my professional reputation. This is my chance to prove myself.

Speaking of work, Chava has already sent me the log-in information for Dev's social media accounts, and since I can't sleep, I might as well use this time to scroll through his content. I *may* already be familiar with it, though. At least, I am with everything he posted up until Oakley's birthday last year, when I either unfollowed or muted him on every platform out of pure shame. That's why I didn't see the IYK Quick Results scandal in real time, but I'm kind of glad I missed it.

I haul my laptop over from the bedside table and plop it on my stomach, squinting against the harsh blue light as it turns on. After pulling up a new browser window, I start with Instagram. I type in Dev's email and password one-handed and hesitate before I click *log in*. I hold my breath as I wait for the page to load and let it out in a groan when red notification dots appear next to nearly every icon.

His Instagram grid, however, is empty. He must have taken everything down after Jani's infamous post. That alone will save me hours. It means I won't have to wade through thousands of likely wild or horrific comments. His DMs, on the other hand, are probably a circus.

Before tackling them, I navigate to his archive. Jani's

parting gift is there, like it was the night Dev showed me. So are hundreds of old posts. Since they're not published, there's no reason for me to scroll through them, and yet I find myself perusing one after another, pausing longer than I should on images of him grinning at the camera. His laughter is so infectious that a still photo has me fighting a giggle and a flutter in my chest.

There's no way around it—Dev is hotter than hell, and the pictures of him shirtless in his driver room with sweat glistening on his aggressively defined abs aren't helping me get a handle on this crush. I *should* be looking at his account through a professional lens. I *should* be considering how to incorporate elements of his old feed into something new and deciding on a creative direction for future posts. And I *should* be taking notes about how to make that all come together.

Instead, I'm fantasizing about running my fingers through the loose curls of his hair and pressing my lips to his stubbled jaw, then trailing lower and lower and—

I snap my laptop shut, plunging the room into darkness.

It's the shock to the system I need. From here on out, those thoughts are banned. Forbidden. Verboten. I don't need the complications of a crush, and I won't let it interfere with what Dev hired me to do.

Besides, we agreed to move on after the incident last year. And we're managing it fine so far.

As long as I stay away from tequila shots or anything else that has the potential to make me loose-lipped, it'll be fine.

I have absolutely nothing to worry about.

⬛⬛⬛⬛⬛

Chantal is waiting for me when I step into our apartment on Wednesday afternoon, quick to help with my suitcases.

Plural. I had to buy a second one after leaving Argonaut's headquarters with my new team swag.

"You better have brought a gift for me," she warns, shooting me a lopsided smile over her shoulder as she drags both bags into my bedroom.

I hike my overstuffed purse higher on my shoulder, shuffling behind her. "I made a special trip to a Starbucks in Monaco to pick up a mug, as requested."

She makes a little sound of happiness, then plops onto my bed and watches me expectantly. I drop my purse beside the luggage and collapse on the floor, achy and exhausted after sleeping in hotel rooms for a week and so many flights. I'm desperate to sleep in my own bed for at least a couple of nights. Soon enough, it'll be exclusively planes and hotel rooms for a while. Even the summer break won't bring much of a reprieve since I'll have to fly out to California for Alisha's wedding. It's going to be a lot for my body to handle.

"*So*," Chantal prompts, pulling me out of my thoughts.

She looms over me as she lies on her stomach with her elbows planted on the mattress and her chin resting in her hands. "Tell me everything. Actually, wait." She rolls onto her side to pull her phone out of the pocket of her shorts. "Let me get Grace on FaceTime first. She'll kill me if she doesn't hear this too."

"It's three a.m. in Hong Kong," I remind her, unzipping my first suitcase. If I don't unpack and sort through my stuff now, it won't get done, and I'll be scrambling to get things washed and repacked when it's time to join Dev on the road.

"She said she didn't care." Chantal waves it off, the familiar ringtone already echoing through my room. "You know our girl's a night owl anyway."

That she is. When I'm not wildly jet-lagged like I was this

weekend, I'm a morning person. On more than one occasion, Grace and I have crossed paths at five a.m. when I'm getting up to head to the gym, and she's about to go to bed. On those days, we sit together in the kitchen with steaming mugs— strong coffee for me and Sleepytime tea for Grace. My heart tugs a little at the thought. I won't see her or Chantal for the next couple of months.

Grace answers as if it's not the middle of the night, demanding that Chantal turn the camera so she can see me.

"Spill it, bitch," she commands, holding the phone close to her face. Her dark eyes are bright with the need for gossip. "And don't forget a single detail."

Having been given the order, I launch into a rundown of the last few hectic days, trying to keep it brief, even with the girls' interjections. My dirty laundry has been sorted into color-specific piles by the time I've caught them up, and Grace's excitement is practically oozing through the phone.

"You are literally the luckiest girl on the planet," she says, bouncing so violently her image shakes on the screen. "I would *kill* to go to those races, and you just get to waltz right in."

"Yeah, because I'm *working*," I emphasize, reaching for the suitcase full of Argonaut gear. "And I'm going to have to wear this"—I pull out a red-and-white-striped polo embroidered with the names of the various sponsors, brandishing it for Chantal and the camera—"every day I'm there."

Both girls grimace, Chantal going so far as to gag. "Okay, that is . . . not cute."

"Those colors have no business together unless they're on a flag or a Popsicle," Grace agrees. "But whatever. You'll make it work. And Dev is going to think you're hot as shit no matter what."

I shoot a weak glare at the screen, but I do kind of hope Dev likes what he sees. Of course, nothing is going to happen between us. Still, there's no harm in wanting him to think I'm attractive . . . right? "We're not going there," I say instead.

Chantal turns the phone so she and Grace can share a pointed look before shifting it back to me.

"Guess you shouldn't have told us all about your drunken confession and the kiss last year if you didn't want us shipping you together," Grace says breezily. "Because from where I'm sitting, you two are kind of the perfect pair."

"Stop it," I scold, tossing the polo into the suitcase again. I would agree, except there are too many obstacles standing in the way of Dev and me. My brother, for one. And really, I don't even know if Dev would *want* to be more than friends. Let's not forget the newest roadblock either: Dev officially becoming my boss. "I plan to keep things professional."

"Uh-huh," Chantal murmurs, clearly not believing a word coming out of my mouth. "Gracie, babe, how long do you give it before they're fucking?"

"Three weeks, tops," she answers without hesitation.

Heat rushes up my neck as I flash them twin middle fingers. The move earns a surround sound cackle in response. Ducking my head, I snatch various shirts, skirts, and pants from the bag and toss them into a pile of patriotism I hope won't run in the wash.

"Did you tell your brother what happened with Dev last year?" Grace asks. "Is that why you're so hell-bent on keeping this platonic? Did he warn you off the guy?"

My head snaps up again. "I absolutely did *not* tell him. And I never will, because there's nothing to tell. It was a one-time mistake, and I've moved on from it." Mostly. Kind of. Okay, not really at all, but whatever.

Chantal sucks in air through her teeth. "Girl, please. You're about to travel the world with a guy you've been obsessed with forever. Do you really think this is going to stay professional?"

I heave a breath, nervously sweeping my curls over one shoulder. "It has to. I won't ruin my career—one that hasn't even started yet, by the way—by hooking up with a man who is technically my boss. I'm not that irresponsible."

"I'd be irresponsible a hundred times over for a man as hot as Dev," Grace titters, fanning herself. "He knows you have a crush on him; you might as well go for it, see if he feels the same way."

"I *used to* have a crush on him," I correct, my face going even hotter at the lie. "Past tense. Not anymore."

"Yeah, right," Chantal dismisses. "You're still into that boy. Can't blame you either. He's a dream."

"Fine, let's say that I *am* into him." I throw my hands up. It doesn't matter how adamantly I deny it; they'll see straight through me. "Let's say that I still have a big, silly crush. It's not like I can *do* anything about it. Plus . . ." I blow out a breath and drop my chin. "Remember the Jeremy situation?"

The girls go quiet at that. *This* they understand. I can't and won't jeopardize more of my brother's friendships. Not once did he question me when I told him what happened with Jeremy. He just jumped to defend me the second I needed him to. I'll never be able to thank him enough for his loyalty and his faith in me. I can't throw that back in his face by hooking up with another one of his friends, no matter how deep my feelings are or how long I've had them. I won't run the risk of making another mess.

"All right," Chantal concedes. "Maybe not your best

option as far as boyfriends go. But I don't see anything wrong with a secret hookup."

"Chantal."

"Come on, it's perfect! You'll be traveling together and staying in the same hotels. It would be so easy to slip into each other's rooms and—"

"Not happening."

She tosses her braids over her shoulder and scrutinizes me. "Maybe it should. Maybe a few orgasms you didn't give yourself will make you a little less snippy."

I suck in a sharp breath, but before I can tell her to mind her business—and that I can't even remember the last time I gave myself one—Grace sighs dreamily.

"Summer is for falling in love, Willow," she says, drawing my attention to the phone again. "Why not open yourself up to it?"

"Not with him." I have to shut this down before they get any other wild ideas. "Listen to me: Nothing is going to happen. It can't."

Chantal turns the phone to face her again. I don't need to see Grace to know she's mirroring Chantal's eye roll.

"You guys don't know what you're talking about," I grumble.

Grace's laugh carries through my bedroom like she's right here with us. "You can say that all you want, honey. But no one knows you better than us."

▰▰▰▰▰

Feeling much more rested after a few days at home, I stream the Spanish Grand Prix preshow on my laptop while I sift through my clothes and consider what I'll actually need for the months away. For race weekends, I'll be stuck wearing the hideous uniform, but most weekdays, I should be able to wear whatever I want. Still, it's proving to be a challenge to narrow it down.

Other than one in Montreal, all the upcoming races are in Europe, so at least I won't have to worry about dramatic climate differences from one place to the next. But first, according to Chava, Dev wants me to join him in San Diego for the break before the Canadian Grand Prix in two weeks.

I don't really want to go home. I saw my parents when they came to New York for my graduation, and I'm not particularly interested in sleeping in my childhood bedroom, but in Chava's words, this trip isn't optional. So I guess I'm heading back to California.

"You good?" Chantal asks from where she's propped up against my doorframe. "You've been staring at that pile of flag knockoffs for a while."

I turn down the volume on the commentators predicting the outcome of the race and blow out a breath. "I'm trying to figure out what to pack," I admit. "I want to make sure I have what I need for all of the countries we're hitting."

"Rack up those passport stamps, baby." She sighs wistfully. "I'm so jealous. I have to stay here and work in an *office*. Ew."

"You should be jealous," I tease. "But maybe—oh, crap, my passport."

Chantal laughs as I scramble to my feet and snatch the purse I took to Monaco off the dresser. When I get my hands on the blue booklet, my shoulders sag in relief. I won't be going anywhere without it.

"You sure you want to do this?" she asks me as I carefully set my passport on my dresser so it'll be in plain sight at all times. "It's an amazing opportunity, don't get me wrong. But it does seem kind of . . . chaotic."

"It *is* chaotic," I agree, returning to my spot on the floor. Once I'm settled, I flip my little notebook open to my packing checklist. "But yeah, I'm sure. I want this."

A concerning smirk breaks out on her face. "You mean you want to ride Dev's—"

"Don't say it!" I screech, tossing my pen at her.

She dodges with ease, rocking back on her heels. "We both know you want to," she coos, stepping farther into my bedroom and nudging my toiletry bag closer to me with her pink-painted toes. "But fine, I'll drop it. For now."

"Gee, thanks," I grumble, grabbing the box sitting to my left. "So kind of you."

Chantal squats beside me, ignoring my sarcasm. "That the Big Box O' Pills?"

Holding up the glitter-labeled shoebox, I give it a shake. All of the bottles of anti-inflammatories, joint supplements, and in-case-of-emergency pain pills rattle around. I used to be embarrassed to travel with an arsenal of drugs, as well as several rolls of joint-strapping tape, but I've come to accept that if I want to stay comfortable and mobile, this Big Box O' Pills, as we affectionately call it, is a fact of life. Why be ashamed of something I can't change about myself?

"Locked and loaded," I tell her, shoving it into my carry-on suitcase. There's no way I'm letting that precious cargo out of my sight.

"Do these hotels all have gyms?"

I hold up my elastic workout bands before dropping them into my carry-on as well. "Pretty sure, but I'll be prepared no matter what."

"Keep those joints strong. And be careful, okay?"

"Don't know how careful you expect me to be if you also want me out there riding dick," I shoot back.

Chantal squawks in surprise at my comment, falling back on her ample backside. I roll my eyes and fight a smile as she clutches at her stomach and cackles.

"God, I love this side of you," she finally gasps. "You were so sweet when we met, and now you're a monster!"

Snickering, I slap her arm with the back of my hand. "That was *your* doing."

And I won't admit it to her, but Dev's influenced me recently too. It's hard not to let these things loose when I'm faced with his crude humor. Besides, I want him to know I'm not some passive, blushing little girl anymore. Maybe I was when I was with Jeremy, and even for a while afterward while my heart healed, but I'm about to walk into a brand-new stage of life. I don't want that reputation following me.

"I corrupted you." Chantal wipes away an invisible tear before throwing her arms around me and rocking me in her embrace as she fake cries. "My baby's all grown up. God, I'm gonna miss you so stinkin' much."

"I'm leaving in a couple days, not right this second," I complain, but I let her continue to tilt us from side to side. "You could at least make me want to miss you."

"Evil little thing," she babbles, clutching my head to her chest. "My sweet, pocket-size demon."

"You're the worst," I mumble as the opening strain of the Formula 1 theme song plays in the background. It's a reminder of where I'll be for the next few months—swept up in the world of racing, miles outside my usual comfort zone and far from my friends.

So I let Chantal hold me like a doll as the faces of the drivers flash across the screen. My breath catches when Dev appears, staring into the camera with an undeniable smolder. It doesn't matter that all of the other men have also looked directly into the camera. They didn't make me feel like this. Like they were staring straight at me.

But Dev is. And I'm suddenly no longer confident in my abilities to keep things platonic.

CHAPTER 10

DEV

I've been counting down the days until Willow's arrival.

Technically, she wasn't supposed to join me until next week in Canada, but I had Chava book her a flight out to San Diego first. She and I need to get started on fixing my image as soon as possible. We don't have much time, and after last weekend, I need some kind of win.

If my sixth-place finish in Monaco wasn't enough to prove that she's my good luck charm, then the utter bloodbath at the Spanish Grand Prix certainly is. There's no other way of describing it, considering I got my shit rocked from multiple sides five seconds into lap one and had to retire from the race because the damage to my car was too severe to carry on.

Three other drivers got caught up in the mayhem as well. The fucking FIA called the whole thing a "racing incident," even though Lorenzo Castellucci's obvious recklessness caused the crash. He should have been slapped with penalties and fines and firm warnings, because that guy is going to get someone killed one day.

"Are you sure you're not concussed?" Chava's voice comes

over the speakers in my car. Or really, my mom's car that I stole for the day. "You hate picking people up from the airport. And I'm your assistant. Isn't this in my job description?"

"I'm fine. Enjoy the day off with your family, dipshit," I tell him as I merge into the lane for the on-ramp to the arrivals terminal. "And if you make tres leches today, you better save me some."

Before he became my assistant, Chava was in culinary school. He dropped out after realizing he only liked cooking for fun and not for a career, and came to work for me instead. It was only meant to be a temporary position, something to save him from his parents' disappointment, but four years later and the guy's still with me. The restaurant world's loss is certainly my gain.

Chava sighs. "You know Mark is going to kill you if you—"

I'm saved from having to acknowledge the threat to my life and my diet when Chava's mom shouts, "*¡Salvador, ven acá!*" in the background.

"Sounds like Mama wants you," I say, grinning to myself. "And bring me cake! I deserve it after almost being murdered by Castellucci."

Chava hangs up after grumbling something highly offensive in Spanish that brightens my day with its filthy creativity. I wasn't kidding about deserving a treat after last weekend, and I have no doubt he'll be at my parents' house later bearing a plastic container full of cake and a blessing from his mother. I'm going to need both if I plan to survive the rest of the season.

Every time I get into the car, I take a risk. There's always a chance that I won't walk away unscathed. Advances in safety technology have saved my life countless times, but drivers like Lorenzo put that tech to the test every time those five red lights go out.

I'm lucky that he usually qualifies higher than I do. He's almost always near the Mascort and Specter Energy cars at the front, but his last flying lap in Q3 of qualifying on Saturday was cut short by a red flag. It left him down in tenth while I squeaked into twelfth, putting us a little too close for comfort for the race start. I should have predicted he'd try to muscle his way to the front. During his attempt, he clipped another car, causing them both to spin and take out everyone in their vicinity—me included.

Why Scuderia D'Ambrosi keeps him around is a mystery, considering all he does is ruin their championship chances over and over again. They're a legendary team, synonymous with F1 and elite racing, and supported by a fan base that runs generations deep. Despite his terrorism on track, Lorenzo is their poster boy. He's the Italian stallion, the pride of the paddock, and son of a former four-time world champion. He's amazing when he's not crashing, I'll give him that, but he's careless—still too young and cocky to have developed any kind of fear.

At twenty-five, I'm still relatively young, even by racing standards, but the twenty-one-year-old makes me feel like an old man shaking his fist and shouting at the clouds when I complain about him.

The blare of a horn distracts me from thoughts of Castellucci as I pull up in front of the airport terminal. It doesn't matter that I literally drive for a living; driving in the real world is a fucking nightmare. At least on track I only have to worry about nineteen other idiots, not thousands.

I park at the curb and put the flashers on, then turn up the volume of my playlist to drown out the sounds swirling around me as I settle in to wait. According to the flight tracker, Willow's plane landed twenty minutes ago, so she should be walking out at any second, if she hasn't already.

I scan the crowd milling around as the title track of a late-'90s Bollywood movie plays. The man singing waxes poetic about a woman's smile and something happening to his heart at the sight of it. It's sappy as hell and nothing I'll ever admit listening to on a regular basis, but damn if it doesn't throw me back into memories of lying on the living room floor, playing with toy cars while Mom watched her movies and spoke loudly into the phone to family back in India.

I'll also never admit that the Hindi lyrics make more sense when Willow breezes through the doors, a surprised smile lighting up her face when she spots me stepping out of the car.

Like in the lyrics of the song, there's definitely *something happening* to me too—it's just a little less chaste.

"Hi," she breathlessly greets as I join her on the sidewalk. She's dwarfed by a suitcase on each side. Her curls are a little windswept, and her pale green sundress flutters as she swipes her palms across her hips. "Sorry, I—I wasn't expecting you. Chava said he'd be here."

I grab the handles of her suitcases to keep from wrapping my hands around her waist. Every time I see her, my reaction gets stronger, which does *not* bode well for my promise to keep things strictly professional.

"Chava had errands to run." I drag the bags to the back of the black SUV. "You get me as your chauffeur today. Go ahead and get in."

She clutches her purse to her stomach as she heads to the passenger side, giving me a chance to get my shit together before I'm in an enclosed space with her. When I told Chava that I could handle picking Willow up from the airport—all right, when I *insisted* I'd do it—I was focused on getting a head start on my social media resuscitation. I didn't think her smile would send my heart into overdrive, or that I'd be fighting with my dick all because of the way her little dress skims her thighs.

And yet here I am, adjusting myself in my jeans after hefting her bags into the trunk, nerves and guilt eating at my stomach. God, I could really use that tres leches right now. Or a punch to the gut.

Once the suitcases are tucked away, I join her in the car. Heat surges to my face when notes of the embarrassing love song float between us, leaving me to desperately grab at the volume knob and turn it all the way down. I'm not sure which is worse though—Udit Narayan's crooning or the tense silence that's replaced it.

"Good to go?" I ask, choosing to ignore the lingering awkwardness.

Willow nods as she clicks her seat belt into place. "Thanks for picking me up. You really didn't have to."

"It's no problem." I turn off the hazard lights, tap the navigation back on, and shift the car into drive. Checking my mirrors, I ease the oversized SUV into the flow of cars attempting to leave. "Gave me something to do other than brood about how shitty my weekend was."

"Yeah, I watched the race. That was a tough break."

I snort. "That's one way of putting it. But I'm glad you're back. I've decided you're my good luck charm."

When she groans, I finally glance over and survey her quickly. "Don't put that on me! That's so much pressure."

"Too late. So you better live up to the hype," I rib her. "I'm planning to make it onto the podium next Sunday."

"Okay, *that's* a reach." She snickers as the voice coming

from the GPS tells me to make a left at the busy intersection ahead. "If I'm your good luck charm, what will you do when I'm gone?"

Focused on merging into the left-turn lane and driving defensively so that one of these dumbasses doesn't crash into me—I've had enough of that lately—I ask, "Who says I'll ever let you go?" The words snap off my tongue before I consider all the ways they could be taken.

Willow scoffs, thankfully interpreting my question as a joke, her laugh ricocheting through the car. "What, are you going to make me your hostage?"

I pitch my voice low and sinister, playing along, even though I'm not sure for once whether I was kidding. "Tell your family to pay a ransom of one million dollars, and I'll consider letting you leave."

She's grinning when I dare to look over, her dimples deep and her eyes nearly closed. "That's not going to help your image. Keeping a poor, innocent girl captive? Not a good look."

I hit the gas and make the left just as the stoplight above us turns yellow. "I don't think you're that innocent."

Instantly, the air shifts. Fuck, I should have kept my thoughts to myself. Mom calls my inability to do so a curse, and right now, I'm inclined to believe her.

Willow draws in a breath. "Okay, I . . . I think we need to address the elephant in the room."

"I told you to never bring up the size of my nose," I whine, going for distraction so we can avoid the conversation she's intent on having. I can't do this right now. Or ever. I'm just going to get myself into more trouble. "You *know* I'm self-conscious, Willow."

That shocks a snort of air out of her, and I grin in victory, even though she's quick to quiet herself.

"Dev, I'm serious," she says, though her grin and the laughter in her tone say otherwise. "And I thought you knew better than to buy into Eurocentric beauty standards. Shame on you."

That comment has me laughing before I can think better of it, still so surprised when she banters with me. She was like this when we were kids, keeping up with Oakley and me like it was natural. But the older she got, the more it faded. Like a shell was closing around her instead of opening up. She got . . . quiet. Reserved. Like her lightness had been stripped away. By the time I left to race in Europe full time at eighteen, she and I barely spoke anymore.

And it went on that way for years. It wasn't until after the Jeremy fiasco that I made a concerted effort to reach out, to make sure the glowing girl I'd grown up with hadn't let that light be fully extinguished. It started as a favor to Oakley, checking in on her and reporting back. But eventually, it developed into a need to know more for my own sake.

It was casual, though. We didn't have deep conversations or exchange more than a few texts every couple of weeks. But she was opening up again, even if it was only an inch at a time. It was why I was so surprised when she confessed that she'd had a crush on me. It was bold. Not something the closed-off Willow would have done, with the aid of alcohol or not. It was a glimpse of the old Willow. The fearless girl I'd known for so long. The one who could give as good as she got.

The one who has me feeling things I shouldn't.

"Okay," I force out. "Let's talk about it."

We finally get caught at a red light, so I take the opportunity to look at her full-on. If this is what she wants, then I'll let her guide the conversation. I'm not about to talk myself into a hole that I can't dig myself out of. I'm already on the edge of one anyway.

She scrapes her teeth across her bottom lip and watches the traffic through the windshield. "What happened over Oakley's birthday weekend last year . . ." she says, fingers twisting in her lap. "I don't—I don't regret it, okay? I won't sit here and try to tell you I was lying about my feelings or that I hated what happened. But I think we both know it was a mistake."

Keeping my mouth shut, I nod. She's right. It *was* a mistake. And it was a mistake to let the whole thing slide, as she requested I do that night, even though I didn't want to. I still don't want to, but it's not my call to make.

"It feels like it's hanging over our heads," she goes on, the words rushed. Her attention is still trained out the window as a flush touches the tops of her cheekbones. "I just want to move on and be friends—no weirdness, no flirting. We can do that, right? Put everything in the past and keep this cool?"

If it's what she wants, I'll do my best to make it happen, no matter how difficult it'll be. "We can," I answer, easing down on the accelerator when the light turns green. "I'm sorry if I've made you feel uncomfortable."

"You haven't," she blurts, finally turning to me. She has one leg tucked up under her, and her sundress is inching higher.

It's taking every ounce of willpower I have to rip my gaze away from her warm brown skin and keep it on the road.

"We're good, I swear," she continues. "And I'm glad to be working together."

I cling to the chance to change the subject before I yank the car over to the shoulder and push my hands under her skirt. "That's why I dragged you out here with me for the week. I wanted to get started on this as soon as possible."

Back on familiar ground, she brightens. "Then let's do it. I've been thinking about how to frame your return to the world of social media. You need a fresh start. Slate brushed clean, the past washed away, you know?" She glances out the window at the passing palm trees before looking back at me. "You feel like surfing today?"

I shoot her an amused look. "Is that actually a question?" I will never pass up an opportunity to be in the water. My love of surfing is second only to racing.

"Okay, good, because I have an idea," she pushes on, clearly ready to convince me even if I wasn't on board. "For our first post, I want to get some pictures of you coming out of the water. Think *The Birth of Venus*. But, like, *Dev Reborn*. A brand-new you."

"You saying you want me naked, Willow?" I tease as I turn in to our parents' neighborhood. "All you had to do was ask."

"Dev." She slumps back in her seat. "What did I *just* say?"

I groan. The innuendos are like second nature, especially with her. "No flirting. Yeah, got it. But come on, you set yourself up for that one."

"Okay, true," she concedes. "But that's it, all right?"

Is this censorship she's pushing for my benefit or for hers? To know she doesn't regret what happened between us is the kind of information I don't need, because it's certainly not helping me get past the lingering tightness in my chest and the voice in my head telling me to say, *Fuck it*, and flirt to my heart's content.

I finally pull in to our families' shared driveway and throw the SUV into park behind my father's midlife crisis mobile—

a Mascort 241 sports car. The same one I nearly got sued by Argonaut over when I posted a picture of me posing with it on my socials. I sure do love my team and their fragile ego.

"Let me grab my stuff," I tell her as we both get out of the car. "I'll meet you back here in twenty, and I'll take you to my favorite spot."

Without another word, I haul her bags out of the back and roll them up to her front door. I'm turning toward my house when her hand lands on my arm, dragging my attention back down.

"We're going to fix this," she softly reassures. "I promise."

Does she mean the tension between us or my fucked-up public perception? Unsure, all I can do is nod. For once in my life, words fail me.

That's one more thing I can credit Willow with. Not only is she my good luck charm, but she's the only person I know who can leave me speechless.

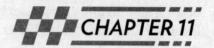

CHAPTER 11

WILLOW

Dev's golden skin shimmers in the sunlight like the rays were made specifically to beam down on him.

I'm mortified by how much I've been staring at him. And by staring, I mean gawking. Practically freaking drooling. I'm reaching throw-myself-into-the-ocean-and-never-come-out levels of embarrassment over it, but at least I can blame my job for all the attention I've directed his way for the past two hours.

"How about a couple of shots with your wet suit around your hips?" I request over the sound of the waves. God, I hope I've gotten enough sun today to disguise my undeniable blush.

Dev shakes his head, dark hair and water flying everywhere. "What did I tell you about trying to get me naked, Willow?" he calls back, but he's already pulling his arms free of the black neoprene as he wades closer to the shore.

I ignore the quip and lift my camera again, snapping shot after shot of him emerging from the waves, each one revealing a little more skin. I'm not the best photographer, but I took a couple of classes in college, so I know my way around a DSLR. Today, my goal is to capture images that are true to Dev.

People should know the real him—but only as much as he's willing to show. There's no point in invading his privacy; it won't benefit him more than it'll harm him, and that'll just put us back at square one.

"This good?" he asks once the wet suit is shoved down to his hips. The deep V of them is so defined that it's like an arrow pointing to hidden treasure. Treasure that isn't hidden all that well in the tight material. "Or do you want me in my birthday suit?"

"This is fine!" I shout, keeping the camera in front of my face to hide anything my expression may give away. "Could you turn around? Just look out into the water."

He does as he's asked, but the sight of his back does nothing to calm my hormones. The guy is just . . . ripped. Head to toe. I can't even begin to count all his abs. And I feel like a creep for ogling him like this.

I've seen him shirtless hundreds of times, but I can't deny the past few years have been incredibly kind to him. Maybe Chantal was right after all. Maybe there isn't any harm in a secret hookup, because who in their right mind could resist a man that fine?

I shake away the thought as quickly as it appears because there's *a lot* wrong with it. I've already made it clear to Dev that nothing can happen, but a couple of his comments in the car hinted that I'm not the only one with more-than-friendly feelings. It both boosts my ego and sets off warning bells in my head. But this is going to be a lot harder to resist if the attraction is mutual.

"Okay, I've got what I need!" I let the camera rest against my chest and wave him over to the edge of the water. "Want to see them?"

When he's beside me, I scroll through the snaps on the camera's small screen, snickering while he belly laughs at some of the less flattering action shots. It feels natural to be shoulder to shoulder, and I can only hope this ease between us continues for the rest of the time we're working together.

"They're great," Dev concludes, dropping down onto the sand next to his abandoned surfboard, arms stretched out behind him as he leans back. "Post whatever you want. I trust you to make me look my best."

"Daring words." I smooth my dress behind my thighs before sitting next to him and admiring the waves. I may have been apprehensive about coming home, but I can't deny that I've missed the beach, even as a self-proclaimed city girl these days. "I'll write up something about fresh starts and getting through tough times to go along with the pictures. From there, we'll start posting stuff from race weekends and brand deals, but we'll keep doing these more down-to-earth shoots too."

I glance over at him, unsure of how he'll react to my next question. "Would you be comfortable showcasing your sister's wedding? It doesn't have to be anything about her or the event. Just pictures of you and the setting. Something to show off how close you are to your family. Your sponsors would eat that up."

Dev lets his head loll back and grins. "Admit it, you want shots of me slathered in haldi so you can use them as blackmail."

"Don't put ideas in my head," I warn. "I can make that happen."

"I think I like it when you threaten me." His grin widens a fraction more. "And that wasn't flirting. Just a fact."

Shaking my head, I fight to keep from grinning along with him. The butterflies that once took up residence in my stomach make a triumphant return. "I can't with you."

"You better manage, because you're stuck with me for a while."

I can certainly think of worse ways to spend my time.

"Come on." He springs up and extends a hand, the top half of his wet suit still swinging down by his hips. "Your turn to get in the water."

"Yeah, no." I brace myself, sinking my fingers into the warm sand. "I'm good here on land."

"I'll let you paddle around on my board," he cajoles. "Remember how you used to beg Oak to let you?"

Oh, I remember. No matter what my brother was doing, I wanted to do it, too, from soccer to karting to learning how to surf. Except, unlike Oakley, who could do it all without a worry, I'd usually end up hurt. Even low-level physical challenges were a risk to my health. As I got older, I drew in on myself, tried fewer new things, telling myself I was content to stay in my own bubble. Content to just stay safe.

But Dev has never treated me like a glass figurine. While Oakley banned me from joining them out of worry, Dev almost always convinced him to let me try. Of course, I knew my own limits, but witnessing the way he'd go to bat for me melted my heart time and again.

"The water's too cold," I decline once more, even if I do appreciate the offer—that he remembered a small but important detail about me. "And I didn't bring a wet suit."

He points at me, staring hard. "I'm getting you in that water. Mark my words."

"Uh-huh, sure." I reach into my cross-body bag to check the time on my phone, but I forget my task when I spot my brother's name multiple times on the screen.

OAKLEY: Hope you haven't fucked up the new job!!!!
(jk I know you haven't, Chava would have ratted on
you already if you had)

OAKLEY: But he did say you guys are back home for
the week, tell Mom and Dad hi for me

OAKLEY: And tell Mom to stop sending me all those
recipes, I swear that woman thinks I only survive on
takeout

OAKLEY: Don't you dare tell her that I do

OAKLEY: Things going okay with Dev though? You
good?

Seeing his texts after exchanging undeniably flirty banter with Dev almost makes me feel like I've been caught doing something bad. Not to mention I've spent hours drooling over the guy, something I never would have gotten away with had Oakley been here. My chest may be tightening with anxiety now, but my brother's messages are a much-needed reminder of why I need to keep my feelings locked down.

WILLOW: All good, haven't gotten fired yet!! I should
have some stuff for Dev to post soon, keep an eye out
for it

I clear my throat after I send the text, trying to recenter myself as I look back up at Dev. "We should probably head home," I tell him, slipping my phone back into my bag. "I want to get started on editing these photos so we can get that first post up."

There's a beat of hesitation, like he's sensed something has changed for me, before he nods and turns his hand over again, offering to help me up. This time I take it, and the sensation of his palm meeting mine sends heat shooting up my arm. He's careful with how he pulls me up, closing his other hand around my elbow to keep from yanking too hard on my wrist. It's a move I taught him a long time ago, and one that's necessary in order to make sure the delicate joint doesn't slide out of place.

It's things like that, the details he's remembered for all these years, that weaken the resolve I've put in place to keep our relationship platonic. Honestly, if this is what I'm acting like after three hours with him, what will I be like after three days, let alone three *weeks*?

I thank him quickly and slip my arm from his grasp so I can lift my camera again. "Mind if I get a couple more shots of you walking away?" I need a minute to get a hold of myself again. "Kind of as an 'I'm coming back, you better watch out' message."

Dev smirks but picks up his board and walks away from me, calling over his shoulder, "I know you hate to see me go, but you love to watch me walk away!"

We're back in Dev's mom's SUV a little later. He's changed into shorts and a T-shirt, the kind of outfit I'm most used to seeing him in. Dev in a tux is a wonder, and Dev in a race suit is impressive, but Dev dressed down? That's my favorite version.

"Can we make a stop on the way home?" I ask once we're pulling back onto the road.

"Sure." He's relaxed in his seat, hands resting at the bottom of the steering wheel like driving a three-ton road car barely requires his attention. It's hotter than I'd prefer to admit. "Where?"

"Stella Margaux's," I answer, dipping my chin in embarrassment. But I'm desperate for a little treat to inhale while I'm editing photos for the rest of the evening.

He glances my way, his brow furrowed. "The macaron place?"

"That's the one."

"Huh," he murmurs, looking back at the road. "I didn't know you liked those."

"Probably a little too much," I confess. "Their location in New York closed for renovations, so I haven't had them in a while. I tried to make them myself but that, um, that didn't go so well."

"Isn't baking a stress reliever for you?"

"Never said I was good at it."

He frowns thoughtfully for a second, then nods, his lips lifting into a small smile, like he's picturing me burning desserts.

It's a quiet five minutes before we pull up in front of the lilac-painted building. The name is scrawled in beautiful cursive script emblazoned across the plate-glass windows. Everything about Stella Margaux's is a whimsical, pastel dream, from its display cases decorated to look like the macarons are floating on clouds to the Michelangelesque paintings on the ceilings.

According to several human-interest stories, the murals in each store are painted by marginalized artists from the local community, and a portion of the stores' sales goes to supporting arts education in public schools. In addition to making the best macarons in the world, Stella Margaux herself is a gem of a woman, the exact kind of person I want to be.

Too bad my baking skills will never live up to hers.

"What are your favorite flavors?" Dev asks as he ushers me inside, holding the door open.

"I love their summer peach and vanilla," I answer as the sweet sugar scent hits me square in the face. This is my happy place. "They also do an amazing lavender and honey, but all their classic flavors are fantastic too. I'll get you a pistachio to try. You'll love it."

But before I can make my way to the counter to order, Dev is gently shouldering me out of the way and smiling at the woman in a puffed-sleeve pink dress behind the counter. She blinks rapidly at the sight of him, a hand fluttering to smooth down her already perfect hair. I can't even blame her for reacting like that.

"Yeah, hi," he greets, skimming the display case before bringing his focus to her. "Can I get ten of every flavor?"

"Dev," I blurt, blinking at him in horror. "That's, like, two hundred macarons." I'm not saying I have the entire menu—seasonal flavors included—memorized . . . but I have the entire menu memorized, and that's *a lot* of macarons.

"Any particular boxes you'd like?" the woman behind the counter says without hesitation. She waves her hand delicately, motioning to the display of beautiful boxes in front of us.

Dev's smile widens, and I swear she swoons. "Surprise me."

"*Dev,*" I say again, this time grabbing his elbow. "What are you doing?"

He shrugs, pulling his wallet out and slipping a black credit card from one of the slots. "Business expense. You're on the clock. Besides, I want to see what the hype is about. I've seen these stores all over the world, but I've never gone in."

"We can't eat all of these!"

"We'll share with your family," he says with a shrug. "And if Mark asks what I ate this week, we lie. You've got my back, right?"

"Of course I do," I reply. I always have. Still, I scoff. "You're out of your mind for doing this."

"Hey, you said you liked them, right? Why wouldn't I do something that makes you happy?" He drags a hand through his hair, his focus trained on me. "You're doing me a huge favor, so this is nothing in comparison."

How am I supposed to respond to that? Another woman at the register is already tallying up our total, so I press my lips together and watch as he hands his card over and makes upbeat small talk with the employees. All the while, my stomach twists and turns, battling the fresh influx of butterflies.

I'm handed bags upon bags several minutes later, from pale pink to buttercup yellow, filled with boxes of my favorite dessert. I'll admit, I once ate fifteen in a sitting—a record that had me riding a massive sugar high for hours—but this is beyond excessive. Dev once again holds the door open as we exit, and then he helps me gently load all the bags onto the back seat of the SUV.

"I should take a picture of this haul and send it to Mark," I threaten weakly, but my brain is too busy repeating, *He bought two hundred macarons because you said you liked them.*

Laughing, Dev opens the passenger-side door for me, but not before he sneaks a box out of one of the bags. "I dare you. He'll yell at you, too, for bringing me here."

"Okay, fine. Your secret's safe with me," I concede as I climb up into the SUV. Mortifyingly, the breeze lifts the hem of my flimsy dress before I can make it into the seat, and my face flames at the idea that I might have just flashed Dev. I'm wearing a bikini bottom, thankfully, in case I had to go into the water, but the knowledge does little to settle my embarrassment.

His expression is just as light as it was before, giving nothing away as he holds up a sunset-orange and white box and raises a brow. "You wanna eat these with me? Or are you going to be a tattletale? Because snitches don't get macarons."

I offer my pinkie. "I promise, no snitching."

Our gazes meet the second his pinkie hooks around mine. The contact sends sparks arcing between us, stealing my breath away. It feels dangerous. Like a warning shot I should heed. Except the shot thrills me instead of scaring me off. It makes me want to slink closer, makes me want to push the limits. It makes me want to buck my promise to always be careful—with my body and my heart—and do something undeniably careless.

But then Dev drops my finger and the wave of wild desire ebbs again, bringing me back to my senses. I know better. And from the guarded gleam in his onyx eyes, so does he.

"Let's go eat our haul," he says, his voice carrying a hint of tension. Like he's holding back the words he really wants to set free.

I nod and let him shut my door, taking a second to breathe.

Get your shit together, the little voice in the back of my head scolds. Too bad it's drowned out by the memory of Chantal's knowing laugh.

CHAPTER 12

DEV

If it were possible to die from blue balls, I'd be deceased by now.

Between the dry spell that's lasted what feels like a fucking lifetime and Willow's big brown eyes all over me, saying things her lips refuse to, I'm pretty sure my dick is going to verbally scream for help at any second.

Sure, I could do something about it. Most people around here—honestly, most of my fellow Americans—don't know who I am, so it's unlikely the rumor that haunts me will be an issue. I could hit up a bar, pick up a random chick, and take her home. But knowing my luck, it would blow up in my face, and I'd end up with a new scandal on my hands. Something else to piss off Argonaut and finally end my career.

And, I'll admit it, I've got enough money and clout to get the number for a service that would send a gorgeous woman right to my door, but paying for sex doesn't do it for me. More power to the sex workers who enjoy their jobs, but I don't think I'll ever be one of the guys who employ their services, even though I know several people in the paddock who do.

Which leaves me with the option I've been relying on for weeks and the inspiration I've been using since that night in Austin: my hand wrapped around my dick and Willow on my mind. And I've got new material to add after today—the wind blowing her dress up around her hips, exposing the daisy-printed bikini bottoms that barely covered her perfect peach of an ass.

I was a gentleman at the time and pretended not to notice. But now? My mind is racing with nothing but filth as she steps into her house and turns to close the door, flashing me a small smile as she does.

I head for my house and move straight upstairs to my bedroom and the en suite bathroom. My parents are in Malibu for the day looking at Alisha's wedding venue, thankfully. Because one afternoon with Willow, and I'm sporting the biggest fucking hard-on known to man. Bless the macaron bags I managed to hide it with on the way inside. If not for their divine presence, this probably would have scared Willow away forever.

I'm out of my clothes and in the shower in the blink of an eye, head pressed against the cool tiles and hand gripping my cock as the water rains down. Her smile materializes in my mind first. Plump lips, pink tongue darting out to wet them, dimples flashing in her cheeks. From there, it's her slender neck, the swell of her breasts covered by the thin cotton of her sundress, the breeze catching the fabric and lifting it to her waist. Faded, pale stretch marks map her hips and ass, tempting me to trace each one, to dip between her thighs and elicit soft gasps from her. To feel her pussy gripping me. To bring her so high she cries out my name and shatters under my touch.

I'm coming in record time, eyes squeezed shut and braced

on one forearm. It would be embarrassing as hell if I had company. But fuck it. This is just what Willow and scandal-imposed celibacy does to me. I'm like a goddamn teenager all over again.

When I'm finished in the shower, I wrap a towel around my waist and grab another to dry my hair. A muscle in my shoulder twinges as I lift my arm. Shit. It's been a while since I've been tossed around by waves like that, and I'm undoubtedly going to be sore tomorrow. Considering I gave Mark the week off, I don't have anyone to fix me if I mess anything up too badly, so I pull on a pair of swim trunks and head out to the hot tub in the backyard—my makeshift physical therapist.

The sun has nearly set by the time I step out onto the deck, the twinkling lights Dad installed switching on automatically above my head as the sky darkens. The hot tub sits two steps down on the lower portion of the deck, where it can barely be seen from the house, and the tall fence to the left divides our yard from the Williamses'. The small opening Oakley and I cut out in the back corner is still there, never boarded over, even though neither of us could fit through it anymore. Only Herman, his family's Saint Bernard, uses it these days, and even he's pushing it size-wise.

After flipping the cover off the hot tub, I ease one foot into the water and then the other, sinking down until I'm fully submerged in one of the lounge seats. I drop my head back and groan as my muscles ease little by little. A press of a button has the jets firing up and hammering between my shoulders, but I'm distracted from the relief when the flickering of a light catches my attention.

From my vantage point, I can see the second floor of the Williamses' house, and the light is coming from Willow's bedroom window. The blinds are open, and there she is, an orange box in one hand and a macaron in the other. She stops and takes a bite, tilting her head back in pleasure as she chews, black curls tumbling down her back. Like someone has called for her, she glances over her shoulder, and her lips move. Then she's heading over to the window.

My breath hitches as I wait for her to catch me watching, but her eyes stay trained on the door as she pulls the cord for the blinds, closing off the glimpse I had of her life.

As I'm beginning to realize, even being with her for hours on end doesn't feel like enough anymore. How I went months without seeing her after the bad decision we made—okay, fine, the bad decision *I* made—I'll never know. But now that she's back in my life . . . Yeah, I'm fucked.

Completely and utterly fucked.

So I do the only thing I can. I close my eyes and lose myself in the memory of that night—the one when everything changed—once again.

It's Saturday night in Austin—*that night*—and I need to go the fuck to sleep.

Mark has already worked on my shoulders and neck so I won't be stiff when I get into the car tomorrow. Chava has been over our travel plans for Mexico next week. Jani has succeeded in pissing me off beyond belief with her little videos. And thirty minutes ago, after hours of playing video games with me, Oakley left my hotel room so I could get some rest.

But sleep eludes me. All because I can't stop thinking about Willow.

She's been on my mind since Wednesday night when we were all shit-faced at the club for Oakley's birthday. Her in that tiny dress, curls loose and tousled, the kind of sexy that had my eyes lingering for way too long. She's usually girl-next-door cute, but with that much skin on display and the heated haze in her eyes . . . Fuck, she was nothing short of a fantasy.

I can still feel the warmth of her skin, of her soft hips under my palms, of her hands over mine. I can hear her murmuring, "*What would you have done, Dev?*"

That's the thing. I still don't know what I would have done if I'd noticed her crush on me sooner. I haven't stopped agonizing over it since she asked, pushing myself to analyze every encounter she and I have had over the years and contemplate whether there was a chance when I could have made a move.

But if her feelings for me were so obvious, how could I have missed them? How could I have overlooked her for so long when I could have had everything I'm aching for? Was I *that* oblivious?

The answer is a bathroom door slamming open and being furiously accused of kissing his sister. Oakley. *Oakley* is the reason I missed every clue and hint and damn neon sign Willow tossed out there. Time after time, he was there to intercept them. He kept the blinders over my eyes and forcibly encouraged me to push Willow firmly into the she's-family category. He made sure I viewed her as an annoying tagalong and nothing more.

But Willow is *not* family. She's not my little sister. She's never been annoying or underfoot. Not to me. Never to me.

Yet I've always kept my distance. Arm's length. Eyes averted. Convincing myself that she's an extension of Oakley when she's been her own person all along. And it's taken me until this very week to realize that.

Burying my face in a pillow, I barely hold back a scream

of irritation. The universe has got to be playing a joke. The gods that hold my fate in their hands are enjoying fucking with me. Otherwise, I wouldn't feel like I got hit by a Mack truck of bullshit emotion all because a girl confessed that she likes me. Or used to. But based on how she responded to me, I'm willing to bet it's still a thing.

I'm not cocky enough to think I can have any woman in the world, but I race fast cars and make millions and have the looks and smile that drop panties. I'm loved by moms and daughters alike, a cheeky bastard with a penchant for flirty quips and dirty one-liners in interviews. I'm a goddamn *delight*, and women like to tell me as much. Usually without words.

So no, I'm not unused to confessions of crushes and batted eyelashes. I know how to handle a love declaration in a moment of passion and the tears that come when I say I don't feel the same way. I know how to avoid entanglements that end in drama. I know how to get myself out of trouble.

Except Willow makes me want to dive headfirst toward it. She's got me contemplating whether I should get out of bed and go find her. Because if I do, maybe there's a chance I can sleep tonight. I'd hate her for messing with my race weekend rituals if I wasn't so enamored of her—and if I wasn't stuck reminiscing about loaded words and an almost less-than-innocent touch.

Fuck, I've got to get it together.

What's messing with me the most is how we just . . . let it drop. Once Oakley told me never to make a move on his sister, I didn't bring it up with her again. Not the next day at breakfast, where we were both hungover as shit. Not Friday, when she stopped by the pit before heading out for a day in Austin with her friends. Not today, when she congratulated me for qualifying P12 and sat near enough at dinner that I could have pulled her for a private conversation without garnering any suspicion from her brother.

We're both pretending like nothing happened, like those damning words never left her beautiful mouth. But I can't pretend anymore, and I have to—

A light knock on the door drags me out of my half-baked plans to stalk down to her room and tell her how fucked up she's got me. Blowing out a breath, I roll out of bed and pull on a T-shirt and sweatpants. I'm not about to answer the door in boxers, even though it's probably someone who's seen me in far less than that over the years. I think I've been naked in front of Mark more times than any woman I've ever slept with.

But it's not Mark or Chava or Oakley on the other side of my door. It's not even Jani or Patsy come to torture me.

It's the current bane of my existence.

"Hey," I greet Willow, blinking in surprise. Shit, did I conjure her? Could she feel me thinking from floors above? Am I about to find out I'm actually a wizard? "What are you doing up here?"

Her eyes don't quite meet mine when she looks up from the carpet. They dart from my face to over my shoulder and back again. "I was looking for Oak," she explains, twisting her fingers in front of her stomach. "I locked myself out of our room when I went to the vending machine. I thought he might be up here with you and I could get the key from him."

I shake my head, mostly to clear away my earlier thoughts. I didn't conjure her, but it sure as shit looks like fate's out here conspiring again. The question is whether it's for or against me. "He left about a half hour ago." The guy's probably down at the hotel bar chatting up three different women right now. "If you want, I can go down to the front desk with you and get another key card made."

With the soft redness flooding the high points of her cheeks, I almost expect her to decline and rush away. But instead, she nods and lets out a relieved breath. "You wouldn't mind?"

I don't at all, especially since destiny brought her to my doorstep. Might as well take advantage of it.

"Not one bit," I answer as I pat the pockets of my sweatpants to make sure I have my own key. "The room's in my name anyway, so it'll be easier that way."

"Thank you," she says, shifting back to let me out after I slip on my sneakers. "It was so silly, I literally left the key sitting on the dresser."

"Happens to the best of us," I reassure, holding out an arm, motioning for her to lead the way to the elevators.

"Actually, is it okay if we take the steps?"

I smirk. "You still don't like elevators?"

As I fall in beside her, she lifts her chin indignantly, daring me to tease her. Which I absolutely will. "I avoid them if I can."

"You got stuck *once*, Wills." I can't stop myself from laughing. "And it was for all of five minutes."

"Once was more than enough," she huffs, shooting me a glare. "Now all my stress dreams involve getting stuck in an elevator that drops out of nowhere. My knees would prefer the elevator, but my anxiety doesn't."

"Okay, okay, I get you. Stairs it is."

I haul open the fire door to the stairwell and hold it so she can go first. I'm up on the ninth floor, so this won't be a quick trip, but I suppose that works in my favor. Now I have time to gear up to what I want to say, actually say it, and deal with the aftermath.

Willow grasps the handrail on the left, taking each step like she's afraid of missing one. She's wearing sensible sneakers with her white sundress, but I can't fault her caution. Little mistakes for her can result in big consequences. I know the feeling.

When we reach the landing on the eighth floor, I finally clear my throat, hoping it will help settle how hard my heart is beating against my rib cage. I'm not nervous, so I don't know what its problem is. No, not nervous at all . . .

"Willow, about the other night," I prompt. "I—"

"We don't need to talk about it," she cuts in, her eyes firmly locked on the steps as we round the landing and start on the next flight.

Good thing we have seven more floors to go. Clearly, this isn't going to be an easy conversation. "No, I think we do."

She blows out a breath, keeping her head dipped and her eyes down. "Can't we just leave it alone? I said some things I shouldn't have and put you in an awkward position. I'm sorry, okay? Let's just forget it and move on."

I blink, taken aback by her apology. "You have nothing to be sorry for."

"Of course I do. I made things weird between us."

"No, you didn't." I wet my lips, giving myself the opportunity to formulate my response and calculate how I want to approach this. "But you did make me realize a few things."

That gets her to look up. Wide, skittish, but cautiously hopeful eyes meet mine. And then she trips.

Racing has given me the gift of near-superhuman reflexes, honed over thousands of hours of drills, so I barely think about what I'm doing when I throw an arm out to catch her. I loop it around her waist and haul her back against my chest, nearly sweeping her feet off the ground. On contact, she clutches my arm, the breath leaving her lungs, pressing back against me like I'm her only lifeline.

I like the feeling more than I care to admit.

"Oh my god," she exhales, slowly regaining her wits and her balance before she peels her trembling fingers from my forearm. "Thank you for keeping me from breaking every bone in my body. That was close."

There's no way I'd let her get hurt. Never have, never will. Especially now that I'm coming to terms with what she's brought to life in me.

My heart is thundering in my chest. I'm sure she feels it. "You good?"

She nods, which should be a cue for me to let her go, but I can't bring myself to pull away.

Her body's warm and soft against mine, and her sweet perfume floods my senses. I'm struck by the thought that I could have held her like this ages ago if I hadn't been so fucking oblivious.

"I'm okay," she says, almost a whisper. "You can let go now."

"I don't think I want to."

That's my confession. It's on par with hers from the other night, but she laughs breathlessly in response, like it's a joke, and drops her head back against my chest.

"I can stand on my own," she promises, her deep dimples flashing as she grins. "You don't have to worry about me tripping again. I'll be more careful."

"That's not what I meant, Willow."

She freezes, then lifts her head slowly. Her smile has been

completely wiped away. If the deer-in-the-headlights look in her eyes is anything to go on, she's not going to ask me to clarify.

But that's fine. She's going to get it anyway, because I can't hold it back, even if this isn't the most romantic place for a confession. It'll be memorable, at least.

"What you said to me at the club," I murmur, loosening my grip so I can shift her to my side. I don't want to miss even a flicker of an expression. "I haven't stopped thinking about it. Thinking about you."

"Dev, don't," she warns, slipping out of my grasp and backing against the handrail. She grasps it on either side of her hips, bracing herself. "You don't have to do this." Her throat moves as she swallows hard, and her words are a little stronger when she speaks again. "You don't have to pacify me. I'm fine. I'm over it."

"Pacify you?" I repeat, nearly scoffing in disbelief. "Is that what you think I'm doing?"

"Obviously." She sidesteps down one of the stairs, still clutching the rail, and I follow without hesitation. "You make people feel better when they mess up. It's just what you do. Who you are."

The statement throws me off-kilter and halts my movements. Sure, I like to keep the peace and keep my life as chaos-free as possible, but that doesn't mean I'm constantly placating the people around me. Right?

But shit, is that what she thinks? *Is* that what I do? Is it what I'm doing right now?

The answer is a resounding *fuck no*. I'm not doing any of this to make her feel better about her confession. I'm doing it because I'm so hung up on this girl that I can't sleep. And I'm so focused on her that I barely care that I have a race tomorrow, one that I'm going to be woefully unprepared for. Her admission the other night opened floodgates that were being held back by a rusty lock, and now I'm stuck dealing with the onslaught. I'm selfish enough to want her in the disaster zone with me.

"That's not what I'm doing."

She takes another step down, making it to the next landing, and I follow. All the while, she keeps her back against the concrete wall, but her chin is lifted in defiance.

"And you didn't mess up," I say. "All you did was tell me how you felt."

She scoffs. "Yeah, and I was drunk when I said it."

With one more step, I'm in front of her. Toe to toe. Crowding her. "But does that mean it wasn't true?"

To her credit, she meets my gaze and holds. Her lips turn down as she searches my face, though I'm not sure what she's looking for. "Why do you care?" she finally asks.

"Because I can't get you out of my head." My hands find the dip of her waist as she inhales sharply, and I drive my point home. "Because I can't stop thinking about what might have happened if Oakley didn't interrupt." I splay my fingers across her back, pressing gently, nudging her to me. "What I wanted to happen."

"What you—" She cuts short, her lips parting and closing as she blinks, like she can't believe what I'm saying. With a huff, she tucks a curl behind her ear, ignoring it when it springs forward again. "Are you fucking with me right now?"

The blurted curse coming from her mouth has me tempted to laugh, but the open vulnerability on her face has any inclination dying in my throat. She truly doesn't believe me. Even with my hands on her body. Even after I told her I can't stop thinking about her, she thinks it's a practical joke.

"I'm not messing with you," I say, my voice low, like I'm talking to a scared animal ready to bolt. "Maybe this seems like it's coming out of nowhere. And maybe it is, I don't know. But, Willow, what you said, it made me see that . . ." Suddenly, the words dry up in my mouth, and nerves choke me. But words aren't doing shit in this situation, anyway, so maybe it's time to shift to a new drive mode. "You know what? Fuck it."

And I finally do the one thing I haven't stopped craving for days. I sink my fingers into the silken hair that spills over her shoulders, tug her head back, and turn her face up to mine. Her lips are parted, and her eyes are wide, like she's waiting for the other shoe to drop. But she doesn't try to pull away as I slide my other hand around her waist again.

We're so close that I could count each fleck of gold in the caramel sliver of her iris. I'm almost tempted. But there's something I want more.

"Dev," she murmurs, chest heaving against mine. But it's not a warning. It's an invitation.

The world goes hazy around the edges when our lips finally meet. I wish I could say that it didn't, that everything about this feels wrong, that I want to pull back and wipe away this mistake of a kiss before it goes any further.

But I can't. I can't do anything except tug her closer and let her soft heat melt into me. I can only fist her curls in my hand and slide my tongue across the seam of her lips. I can only squeeze my eyes shut and lose myself in her.

She lets me in easily, kissing me back, letting me take what I want and say everything my words can't express. But she must know exactly what I'm trying to tell her, because she presses her palms against my chest, then moves them upward to clutch at my shoulders, keeping me close, giving me more. I'll gladly take it all.

My veins ignite. Fire rushes through me. And Willow fans the flames with her sweet sounds of pleasure, her stuttered breaths, and her quiet moans. It's better than anything I could have ever dreamed of.

She gasps in surprise against my mouth when I tighten my arm around her and lift her off her feet. It prompts her to throw her legs around my waist and slide her fingers into my hair and grip hard, not letting me go. And I never want her to. She can keep me for as long as she wants.

With her back supported by the wall, I'm free to let my hands drift to her thighs, to the hem of her dress, and I roughly push it up to her waist. The heat of her core presses against my abdomen, daring me to slip my fingers to the edge of her cotton panties, to dip under the elastic by her hip.

I could do it. I *want* to. It would be so simple, and I'm fucking desperate to feel just a little more of her. The softness of her thighs is already tempting enough, and the way she tilts her hips against me is nothing short of pure provocation.

There's no way she can't feel how much I want her too. But this needs to stop before it goes any further. I need to know for certain if we're on the same page.

"Fuck, Willow," I mumble, drawing back enough to suck in a breath. I press my forehead to hers, feeling like I'm being dragged out of a dream. "Do you get what I'm trying to say?"

She's panting like she's run a mile, her eyes unfocused as they linger on my lips, but she nods.

I can't stop my hands from skimming over her hips, still under her dress. "You're not the only one who feels something, all right? I'm sorry it took me this long to realize it."

Just as she opens her mouth to respond, a door slams shut from somewhere floors below us, and it's enough to make her startle, shocking her out of the spell she's under. She blinks rapidly half a dozen times, then her horrified gaze settles on me.

She's quick to snatch her hands back, to plant them on my chest again, but instead of beckoning me closer, she's pushing me away.

As much as I don't want to, I grasp her waist and take a step back, settling her on her feet once more.

"You know—you know what?" she stammers. Her fingers flit across her lower body as she smooths out her dress again. "I can go down to the front desk on my own."

It takes me a few seconds to register her words. That's . . . it? Is she really going to ignore what just happened? "We still need to talk about—"

She puts up a hand and closes her eyes. She takes a deep breath in and holds it for a beat before looking at me once more. "This shouldn't have happened," she declares. The words are a knife driving into my gut. "And it won't happen again. It can't. We both know why."

The knife twists, because I know she's right. "Look, we should—"

"Don't, Dev," she interrupts, her voice firm. "Just don't. Let's forget about it."

The problem is, I can't. I don't think I ever will. And now that I know what she tastes like—sugar and the sweetest sin—I'll never be able to get her off my mind.

▚▚▚▚▚

Water splashing against my face has me spluttering and sitting up. My heart is still racing as the memory cuts out and

I'm dragged back to reality. Ramrod straight now, I scan the yard, looking for the culprit, and when I spy Chava standing on the deck, I groan and slump back down. At least I'm not about to be murdered.

"Man, how long have you been in this water?" he asks as he looks me over, concern written across his face. "You're redder than Mark when we leave him in the sun for more than five minutes."

Our poor pale friend tends to turn the color of strawberry jam when the sun finds him. I've never had the misfortune— god bless melanin—but sitting in practically boiling water apparently has the same visual effect.

"Fell asleep." I mumble the lie, running my hands over my face. "Thanks for rescuing me before I drowned."

"That would be one way to get out of your contract," he chirps. He then holds up a plastic container. "I brought cake."

"I knew I kept you around for a reason."

I haul myself up onto the edge of the hot tub, keeping my feet in the water as Chava toes off his shoes and does the same across from me, the container resting beside him.

"What did you get up to all day?" he asks, slowly kicking his legs. "I saw your board out front. You hit the water?"

I nod and drag a hand through my hair, still reorienting myself in the present as the night air brings my body temperature back down. "Yeah, Willow wanted to get some shots of me surfing, so we spent a couple hours out there."

"Oh, *Willow* wanted to spend time together, did she?"

I dip a hand into the water and splash him, leaving him cursing as he swipes it off his face. "It was purely professional, you dick."

"Uh-huh, sure," he says when he recovers. "When are you going to admit you're into her?"

I glance at the Williamses' house and back again. There's practically no chance anyone is going to overhear our conversation, but I still drop my voice. "When I'm sure Oakley won't murder me."

"Ah, so when hell freezes over." Chava nods sagely. "But honestly, man? I say go for it and deal with the consequences later."

"That's because you're a shit-stirrer with a death wish."

He snorts. "You do dangerous stuff every day." But then he levels me with a look that has my head spinning all over again. "What's one more risk?"

CHAPTER 13

WILLOW

I wake to Herman breathing loudly in my face.

With a groan, I sink my hands into the Saint Bernard's fur and push hard against his chest. Of course, he doesn't budge. He weighs more than I do, and my strength is no match for the love he has for me.

"Herman." I crack one eye open. "Buddy, you've gotta move. I love you, I do, but could you give me a little space?"

He huffs, hot and loud, but acquiesces and flops down beside me. I pat his big head and smooth down his ears before rolling to the edge of my bed. I sit there for a bit to make sure I won't get dizzy, then push myself up to my feet, grateful when my vision doesn't swim with black dots. According to the clock, it's a little after seven, though to be honest, I've been in so many time zones lately that time in general doesn't feel real.

My laptop sits open on my bedside table, next to an array of stuffed animals and below a poster of the K-pop group I was obsessed with in high school. The screen is dark, but one tap on the macaron-crumb-covered keyboard would bring up

Photoshop and the Word document I brain dumped a bunch of captions for Dev's future posts into. I thought they were pretty damn good at three a.m. Let's see if that remains true in the light of day.

That review can wait until I'm with Dev, and I'm hoping to put that off for . . . as long as I can manage. I came a little too close to making bad decisions yesterday, and I need some distance in order to steel myself against his charm. Sometimes I'm not sure he realizes how flirty he is, no matter who he's talking to. But other times I think he knows exactly what he's doing and the effect it has. Especially on me.

But I've spent years burying this crush. When I drunkenly confessed my feelings, I didn't expect anything to come of it; hell, I tried to brush the whole thing off. *He's* the one who made the first move. He's the one who pushed me against the wall and shoved my dress up and let me feel parts of him I never thought I would.

But I didn't say no. I didn't put a stop to it until he pulled away. Even then, I didn't want it to end, but fear kicked in, and I bolted down seven flights of stairs like an Olympic sprinter.

Some days I wish I hadn't run. I wish I had stayed with my back against the wall and my legs wrapped around Dev's waist. Who knows what would have come of it, but at least we wouldn't be stuck in this strange holding pattern of lingering attraction we can't act on. I'd give anything to go back to the way it was before I ruined it all.

It's too late now, though. That's for sure.

I groan as I lower myself onto the yoga mat under my window, needing to stretch and do a few strength exercises before I start my day. My lower back is achy from yesterday's flight, and it'll only get worse with all the travel ahead. I refuse to complain, though. I want this job, this place with Dev and his team, and I'll do everything I can to keep the pain from slowing me down.

Herman watches me from his place on the bed, only lifting his head when my phone buzzes on the nightstand. He looks from it to me like he's telling me to get my ass up and grab it.

"You could bring it to me," I suggest, but all he does is grunt and put his head back down.

I haul myself up and pad over to grab the phone, my heart giving a funny *thump* when a text lights up the screen.

DEV: My mom wants you to come over for breakfast

So much for avoiding him.

※※※※※

The scent of masala chai embraces me as I step through the Andersons' unlocked door—I can't remember the last time I knocked—and kick off my shoes, calling out for Dev.

"Willow!" His mother is the one who replies, her lilting voice guiding me toward the living room. "Come here! I want to show you embarrassing photos of Dev."

"*Ma*," Dev complains as I make my way in. He's sitting on the floor in front of the coffee table, where his mom has a collection of photos spread out. "She knew me as a kid. She's witnessed all of my embarrassing moments."

"Not all of them." She waves me over, smiling widely at me with the grin her son inherited.

Her skin is a few shades darker than his, and her black bob is streaked with gray, but the resemblance is strong. There's no doubt Dev's good looks come from her. "I need your help. I'm getting photos together for the wedding slideshow."

"How embarrassing are we talking?" I ask, settling on the floor next to Dev and scanning the photos in front of me. I do my best to ignore his eyes on me. "I could use some blackmail material."

Dev glowers as Neha laughs and hands me one of baby Dev splashing in the bath, a rubber ducky sitting on top of his head. "How's that?" she asks.

I'm already pulling out my phone so I can snap a picture of it. "Better than I could have asked for."

Dev throws his hands up but seems to know better than to interfere.

I spend the next twenty minutes helping his mother pick out photos of Dev and Alisha as kids before she claps her hands and ushers me off into the kitchen. A glass of chai, a plate of khaman dhokla with several chutneys on the side, *and* an omelet are set in front of me soon after. She watches me like a hawk as I eat every bite.

"So," she prompts once I'm stuffed to bursting. "You're working for Dev, yes?"

I scrutinize him from across the table. He's swiping his finger through the last bit of coriander chutney on his plate. When he puts it in his mouth, I have to look away. My mind has no business going to dangerous places a sight like that would instantly take me while his mom is staring me down.

"That's right," I answer, holding my warm chai glass to my chest. "He thinks I can revive his social media accounts, and I'm crazy enough to try."

She hums contentedly, head bobbing. "Good for you. He needs a lot of help to fix his terrible reputation." At that, she shoots her son a disapproving glare, but it disappears once she looks at me again. "Besides, I always thought you two made a good pair."

If I'd been in the middle of sipping my tea when she uttered those words, I have no doubt I'd be choking on it right now. Dev isn't so lucky, though. He coughs and thumps his chest with a fist, then turns to his mother and says something sharply in Gujarati that I can only dream of understanding. Despite his tone, she tosses her head back and laughs in reply. Dev's narrowed eyes tell me that wasn't the reaction he was going for.

He pushes back from the table, a muscle in his jaw twitching. "Willow, wanna show me what you've done so far?"

He's clearly eager to get away from his mom and this conversation. And . . . is he *blushing*?

I nod after a beat of hesitation, setting my glass back down. "Everything's on my laptop. I didn't think to bring it."

"It's fine," he says, already at the doorway. "I'll just go over to yours. Come on."

Well, I guess that's that. Flashing a smile at his mom, I stand and thank her for breakfast.

"See you later, Willow," she says warmly, catching and squeezing my hand before I can walk away. "Come back for dinner. I'm sure Dev would *love* that."

I let out an uneasy laugh as I squeeze her hand in return, then head out to find Dev. He's standing by the front door, tapping his thumb against the side of his phone impatiently. When he spots me, he hauls the door open. I slip my feet back into my shoes quickly, and then he's ushering me out. I'm tempted to ask what's up with him, but the way he avoids my gaze has me holding back.

"I'm leaving for Dallas tomorrow," he announces as we cross our shared driveway. "I need to get some time on the simulator at headquarters."

My stomach drops. He insisted that I fly all the way home,

and now he's abandoning me? "Oh. I thought we'd be here until we headed to Canada."

"You can say you're gonna miss me, Willow. It's okay."

I almost scowl, but then I catch sight of his grin, so I elbow him in the ribs instead. "Shut up." But I guess this means he's over the little fit that talking to his mom sent him into. "I just thought you wanted to do more content creation together. Kind of seems like a wasted trip."

"Sorry." He doesn't sound sorry at all. "I didn't know the team wanted me back there until last night." His easy tone turns bitter in an instant. "Guess they're worried about how I'm going to perform, even though Nathaniel's the one who crashed out the last two times we were there, not me."

I observe him, taking in the tension around his eyes. "I'm getting the sense that you two aren't besties."

Dev snorts as we step up to my front door. "You could say that."

When he doesn't elaborate, I cross the threshold into my house and wave to my dad in his home office off the foyer. The lanky man is hunched over in his ergonomic chair with four computer screens in front of him. Before Oakley started racing, Dad was a software engineer, and now that he's no longer managing my brother's career, he's gone back to his roots. Mom is a top cardiothoracic surgeon, so there's really no reason for him to work, but I think he does it just to keep himself occupied. I know he misses Oakley's racing days.

Dad returns our greeting with an enthusiastic wave of his own but is quickly distracted by something on one of his screens. I smile to myself as he turns away, then I head upstairs with Dev following close behind me.

"So, we'll meet up in Montreal?" I ask him when we reach the top landing. I'm disappointed that we'll be apart for nearly a week, but at least we have this time together. For business, of course.

"If that's okay," he answers.

I nod and push into my bedroom. "Yeah, it's fine. I have enough content for daily posts and stories until we're together again. But if you wouldn't mind snapping a few pictures while you're gone, I'd be grateful."

"Anything for you."

It takes a second, but then the words and their potential meaning hit me square in the chest. As I turn to him, Dev seems to have the same realization about what he's said, because he quickly follows it up with, "I mean anything you need for the job."

After his slipup yesterday and whatever he said to his mother this morning, I don't quite buy it. But I force myself to, because the alternative is having another discussion about why we need to keep things appropriate.

"Thanks," I say, flashing him a tight smile. I shuffle over to grab my laptop from my bedside table, then bring it to my desk and open it. "Give me a second to pull everything up."

Dev grunts his assent, and I swipe through the photos, bringing up the ones I want to show him. I edited everything into black-and-white, except for the last photo I'll include in the carousel. It's Dev with his surfboard under his arm. He's walking away, but he's turned enough that his trademark grin is on full display. It's a little crooked, and he's squinting against the sun, but he looks . . . happy. It's the Dev I've known my whole life.

The Dev I want the whole world to know.

"Oh my god. You still have this?" he asks from behind me with a laugh.

I freeze, still examining the photo, because who knows

what he's found. This room is full of relics from my child-hood. When I turn, he's holding up the small plush elephant I've had on my bedside table for more years than I can count. Ellie has been in residence in this space for so long that I barely remember she's here anymore. But suddenly, I'm very much aware of her again.

All because she was a gift from Dev a long time ago.

He won her for me at the county fair. Our parents had tasked Oakley and him with watching me that day, and when I laid eyes on the display of stuffed elephants at one of the game stalls, I couldn't be dragged away. While Oakley threat-ened to get Mom when I wouldn't comply, Dev shrugged and said he'd win one for me if I wanted it so badly. And so, he did.

Even at twelve years old, he had better hand-eye coordina-tion than most adults, and less than five minutes later, the woman running the stall handed over the toy. Dev held the elephant for a moment, savoring his win, then he handed it over to me. If I had to pinpoint when I fell in love with him, that might be it.

Gasping, I surge up from my chair and then rush toward him. "Put her down!"

Dev holds Ellie above my head and gazes up at her. "I can't believe you kept this thing."

"Of course I kept her." I scowl, reaching for the toy, but he keeps her just out of reach. "Ellie's too cute to get rid of."

"*Ellie?*" he repeats, still laughing. "Ellie the elephant?"

"I was *nine*, Dev. Children aren't exactly known for giving things the most creative names. Now give her *back*."

I jump for her, pressed up against him in order to give my-self a better chance, but Dev whips an arm around my waist and sweeps me off my feet, then unceremoniously drops me on my bed. It's not pretty, but he's gentle enough that it doesn't hurt anything other than my ego.

Still, it leaves me spluttering in offense. "Oh, you asshole!" But holy shit, that move has set something ablaze inside me.

He stares fondly at Ellie, paying me no mind. "You really have been obsessed with me forever."

I can't believe he's throwing that in my face right now. I'm pretty sure my jaw is hanging open. Never have I wished more that I hadn't let the tequila loosen my lips that night. Maybe we *do* need to have another conversation about this, because I'll die of embarrassment before we can even begin to fix his reputation if he keeps this up.

I'm about to scold him, but then Dev says, "Good thing it's mutual."

Somehow, that's worse than anything else he could have finished with.

I'm still lost for words, splayed across my bed, when he lovingly sets Ellie down and strides over to my desk like he hasn't just said something to wreck my whole world.

A minute ago, he was trying to course correct, trying to keep me from reading into his words, and now he's . . . uttering things like *that*. One old stuffed animal, and everything has shifted.

"You wanna show me these pictures now?" he asks, far more casual than I could dream of being.

Another beat passes before I can peel myself off the duvet. If that's all it takes for Dev to throw me off my axis, I'm in for a world of trouble.

"Sure." My voice trembles, and I clear my throat to keep it at bay.

I scramble up and make my way over to him. He moves aside, and I slip into my chair. I slowly page through the photos, holding my breath when he braces one hand on the edge of the desk and leans closer. His cologne and the lingering spices from the breakfast his mother cooked swirl around me. It both comforts me and has my heart hammering against my ribs, and when his chest brushes my shoulder, I swear I'm about to combust.

Finally, he nods in approval and shifts back some, though not enough for me to feel like I'm not still surrounded by him. I hold up a finger to signal that I have more to show him, and pull up the Word document with the caption I wrote for the post.

In my periphery, he scans the text. Honestly, it's more of a twenty-two-hundred-character essay than a caption, one that outlines why he disappeared—how he made a mistake and hurt someone who then wronged him in return—what's been going on in his life (making sure to sing the praises of Argonaut), and wrapping it up with a few optimistic lines about starting fresh and reintroducing himself to the world. I like to think it comes across as organic and heartfelt, but not too mushy. Like it could have come from Dev himself.

He drops his hands from my desk when he's finished and backs away, prompting me to swivel in my chair. Anxiety surges through my veins at the idea that he might not like the words I chose. I don't mind starting over, and his feedback will make a second draft stronger, but—

"This is perfect."

The fear floods away, leaving me to exhale a surprised laugh. "Really?"

"Yes, really," he affirms, dropping to the edge of my bed. His legs are spread wide as he puts his elbows on his strong thighs and leans forward, his focus never straying from me. There's no smile on his face. No humor. He's serious about how good this is. "I love it. I should have gotten you on this sooner."

I suppress my delight, but it warms me from the inside out anyway. "English degree coming in clutch," I joke. It doesn't crack him, though, so I clear my throat again. "You ready to get this out?"

He nods. "Let's do it."

With a few clicks and highlights and last-second edits, everything is copied, pasted, and uploaded to the pertinent places. All I have to do now is click *post*.

"Here," I blurt, picking up my laptop and shoving it at Dev. "You do the honors. It's your reputation."

But he pushes it back to me. "You're the one who did all the work. You do it."

I slide the computer back into my lap, frowning at him. "Are you sure?"

"Like I said before—I trust you."

Okay. Fine. My heart may still be stutter-stepping, but here we go. Shockingly, my hand doesn't shake as I navigate the cursor over the icon and peer up at him one last time. When our eyes meet, some of the lingering worry disappears.

He wants this. I want this. And we're dedicated to fixing this. Together.

I click.

CHAPTER 14

DEV

Fantastic news: only *some* people think I have an STD now.

Willow has been hard at work over the past week, posting daily to every social media platform I possess—and ones I didn't know existed before she came into the picture—to bring me back into the public eye. And if the curated comments she's texted me every day we've been apart are anything to go on, it's going pretty well.

Today, we've finally been reunited. We're sitting in the Argonaut motorhome set up at the Montreal circuit and chatting over breakfast. I have to leave for a track walk, a meet and greet, and a strategy meeting soon, but I'm savoring this time. It's a typical packed Thursday, made even busier by the dinner I'm set to attend tonight for one of our sponsors. Sadly, I haven't figured a way out of it just yet.

"What are the people saying today?" I ask Willow as I pick at the scrambled eggs Mark set in front of me.

She keeps her head down as she scrolls through her phone, a hint of a pleased smirk tugging up the corners of her glossy lips. "That your smile is the eighth wonder of the world."

"Solid."

I shouldn't have missed her as much as I did, but the week apart felt more like a month. And, admittedly, like a little part of me was missing the whole time. She's only been back in my life for a matter of weeks, and yet she's managed to brush the edges of my every thought. By the time we go our separate ways at the end of the summer, I'm worried she'll have taken over completely.

It's part of the reason I left San Diego early. Sure, I needed time on the sim and to talk with the crew at the factory in Dallas, but it wasn't as pressing as I led Willow to believe. I could have stayed in our hometown for at least a few more days, but I had to get out of there, especially after my mother literally laughed in my face when I told her nothing would ever happen between Willow and me. Then I compounded my fuckups when I spotted the stuffed animal I won for Willow when we were kids.

The idea that she'd kept the toy—*Ellie*—beside her bed for so long, a visual confirmation of her having been into me for years, made something snap in my mind. And when she pressed herself against me to get the plush elephant back . . . Fuck, it's a miracle all I did was toss her on the bed and blurt something about how her obsession wasn't one-sided, because all I wanted was to haul her in and kiss her until she was begging for more.

I tried to play it off and get back to the matter at hand—the work she was doing for me—but I'd already breached our agreement. Willow, thankfully, let it slide. Probably because she didn't want to get into it. What could she have said after that anyway? I knew the rules, and I flat-out ignored them. Scolding me for breaking them wouldn't have changed anything.

We're back to the easy laughs today, like everything last week has been forgotten. It helps that we have a buffer again. Chava sits across from us, scrolling through my social pages as well and reading out his favorite comments as he stumbles upon them.

Even Mark is taking part. He takes Chava's phone and snickers before he reads aloud, "'Chlamydia or not, I'd still ride him like those waves.'" His eyes slide to me. "Seems like your prospects are looking up, man. We might finally get you laid again."

I do my best not to glance in Willow's direction as I force out a laugh. "My chances might be better once people stop mentioning me and STDs in the same sentence."

"We'll get you there," Willow promises, and I finally dare to look over at her. She's perfectly composed, like Mark's comment hasn't ruffled her in the same way it's ruffled me. "To quote one of the comments I read earlier, you'll be drowning in pussy again soon."

Orange juice sprays from Chava's mouth, coating the table in front of him. Wincing, I use my napkin to wipe a few stray droplets off my arm.

"Jesus *Christ*, Willow." Chava's blasphemy is a cross between a cough and a laugh. "I didn't realize you even knew that word."

She shrugs, grinning back at him. The twinkle in her dark eyes has my uniform shorts feeling tighter. "I know a lot of words."

I bet she does. And fuck if fantasies of her legs wrapped around my waist and her lips at my ear while she whispers them don't assault me right there in front of everyone.

I stand abruptly, sidestepping from my chair to hide my

hopefully-not-obvious semi. "Lost track of time," I announce when confused expressions greet me. "Gotta pay Patsy a visit. See if she finally put me in the drivers' press conference. Maybe today's the day she'll give me the okay to tell reporters that Nathaniel's a cun—" I cut myself short, remembering where I am and who could be listening. "A sweet, darling, beautiful boy whom I respect *very* much."

"Uh-huh," Chava utters as Mark snorts.

Willow's frowning as she looks from me to Mark to Chava and back again. It's probably better that she doesn't fully understand the hatred I have for my teammate anyway. I don't need that inadvertently bleeding into the things she posts.

Besides, for her, I like to stick to being-positive Dev. Fixer Dev. Always-looking-on-the-bright-side Dev. She doesn't need to see the undercurrent of darkness and discontent that runs through me. I don't want to slip the rose-tinted glasses from her pretty eyes yet.

But if Argonaut continues to screw me over, she and the rest of the world may see more than they bargained for soon enough.

༄༄༄༄

Whoever said the world of Formula 1 is nonstop thrills and entertainment was a bald-faced liar.

"If I fall asleep, make sure I don't drop my champagne," I mumble to Mark, barely resisting the urge to slump against the small table we're posted up at. Some sponsor events can be a good time, but this one is a snoozefest. Who would have thought Swiss watchmakers were so *boring*?

Mark is my plus-one tonight. If I can't get both of them in, he and Chava take turns accompanying me. Though I might try to work Willow into that rotation soon. Is it a desperate move to get more time with her? Damn straight. Do I care? Not in the slightest.

Mark shoots me an amused glance. "As long as you flash that thing on your wrist as you do, I don't think anyone will mind the mess."

He's probably right. I shake out my wrist so the cuff of my shirt shifts up to show off the glinting timepiece. I gotta admit, the perks of this life are great sometimes. I'll probably never have to pay for a watch again.

Unfortunately, one of the shittier parts of it is making their way straight toward me.

"Incoming," Mark says from the corner of his mouth. "Don't do anything stupid."

My eyes lock on Buck and Nathaniel Decker, and I force a grin. It's sharper than it should be. "I would *never.*"

Mark heaves a sigh and straightens, pushing his shoulders back. He's taller than most of the men in this room, so it's really not necessary, but I'm grateful for my makeshift bodyguard. Not that *I* need protecting. No, more like I need someone to hold me back if Buck hits me with one of his famous microaggressions.

"Buck," I greet with fake warmth when he and his son approach. "So good to see you."

Argonaut's owner, clad in cowboy boots and a Stetson, flashes me a smile that doesn't come close to touching his cold eyes. He hates my guts, but he didn't immediately cut me from the team after my scandal, which means his need for me outweighs his hatred. Unfortunately, I don't know how much longer it'll last, and my contract stipulates he can buy me out whenever he wants, so I'll continue to try my best to stay in his relatively good graces.

"Dev," he returns, tipping his head so his hat briefly hides his eyes. "Glad you didn't skip this one."

I skipped *one* sponsor party last year when I was so sick with the flu that I couldn't get out of bed, and this guy is still holding it over my head. Every time I see him—which isn't often, thank god, since he's too busy running his evil empire to make it to many races—he gives me another reason to hate him back.

"Wouldn't miss it for the world." I turn my attention to Nathaniel, who looks bored out of his mind. I can't blame him. "How you doing, Nate?"

Only certain people are allowed to call him by his nickname, and I am not one of them . . . which is why I make a point to use it as often as I can.

He juts his strong chin out. "I'm good." His Texas drawl is only slightly lighter than his father's. "Excited about the weekend."

I bet he is. The team will do anything to keep him happy, so I can only imagine what hell they're going to rain down on me to make that happen. "Should be a good race if the weather holds out."

Nathaniel's eyes light up like he has more to say, but his father cuts him off.

"I'll see you in the paddock in the morning," Buck says. It's a dismissal, a promise, and a threat all wrapped into one. "Make sure you socialize tonight. I want everyone to see that you actually showed up. Honestly, I'm surprised you even made it here on time. Your kind of people aren't usually known for their punctuality."

I nod, biting back something along the lines of *fuck all the way off*. "Yes, sir."

He spares a glance at Mark but otherwise doesn't acknowledge my trainer, then clasps his hands behind his back and strolls off with Nathaniel reluctantly trailing behind him. For once, I feel bad for my teammate. With a father like Buck, no wonder he turned out the way he did.

When they've wandered into the crowd, I turn back to Mark and let my smile drop. "If that man keeps me until my contract is up, I'll be shocked."

"As if he'd waste the money to buy you out." Mark scoffs, but doubt flickers across his face. "The team would be at the bottom of the standings without you scoring points. He needs you."

Only until he can find someone he thinks is better, though. But outside of the top three teams, there are very few drivers better than me. No, fuck that. In the remaining fourteen, there aren't *any* better than me. If only I had a better car and the support of a team to help me prove it.

"We'll see for how long," I mumble, just as my phone buzzes in my pocket.

When I pull it out, I'm greeted by a notification. **Dev Anderson has uploaded a new photo.**

I follow my main accounts from the fake ones I set up after the Jani disaster, mainly so I could keep track of what people were saying about me after I disappeared from the public eye. Spoiler: it wasn't anything good. I stopped checking them after two horrible days.

Looks like Willow is on the job, though it's a little late to be posting. She's probably in her hotel room a few doors down from mine, already in her pajamas and lying in bed. That was her plan, at least, when I talked to her earlier. I like the image more than I should.

"Why are you smiling like a dumbass?"

I blink myself out of the fantasy, eyes swinging to Mark. "Excuse me?"

"You're a fuckin' goof on a good day, but this"—he waves a hand in front of my face—"is different."

I lock my phone and slip it back into my pocket without checking to see what Willow posted. I share just about everything with the man standing next to me, but I want to keep this to myself for a little longer. I don't need more of his judgment. "It's nothing important."

But Mark knows me too well. "Is it Willow?"

I pull in a deep breath and confess. "She posted something. I was checking the notification."

Knowing him, he doesn't buy it. He just witnessed my far-too-jubilant reaction to a notification that shouldn't have gotten more than a cursory glance.

"Right," he says slowly. "I saw how you were looking at her earlier."

I freeze under his hard stare and clench my jaw tight to keep from incriminating myself further.

"You know nothing can happen," he warns, dropping his voice as he goes into lecture mode. Might as well stand back and let him get it all out. "Stop entertaining the idea that it might." He lifts a hand to motion to the party around us. "Pick any woman here. Get this out of your system. You're only fawning over her because you're thinking with your deprived dick. I promise you, the second you get off, you'll forget about her."

He can believe that all he wants, but not a single woman has caught my eye tonight. If that's not proof that he's wrong, then I don't know what is.

I force a lopsided grin to my face, determined to navigate

the conversation away from the topic of Willow. "You think my reputation's recovered enough to make that happen?" I ask, trying to infuse the words with humor, even though all I feel is cold sweat dripping down my spine.

"The only reason it hasn't yet is because you've been too in your head." Apparently, Mark is done playing nice. "And now you're using it as an excuse because you want someone you can't have."

The truth is a punch to the gut. "You don't know what you're talking about," I snap.

"Yeah, I do." He gives me a once-over, not bothering to hide his discontent. "If the almost guaranteed prospect of ruining our friendship with Oakley isn't enough to convince you to stay away from Willow, then think about what it will do to her. Think about what being linked to you like that will do to her career. If you get involved and the public finds out, no one will hire her after you're done with her. They'll think she goes around fucking athletes to get ahead. You really want that for her?"

Ice spreads through my veins, freezing me to the spot and making it impossible to respond. Of course I don't want that. She deserves nothing short of the best. That's part of the reason I offered her a job in the first place—to make sure she was set up for future success. The last thing I want is to destroy it all.

"Don't do it, Dev," Mark murmurs. "Don't ruin this for all of us."

※※※※※

I go to bed alone.

If tonight is any indication, my reputation with women is improving. Unlike the last few months, a handful were brave enough to approach me, and I didn't hesitate to let the charm fly. But when I finally snuck away for another drink and to check on the notification I'd received, my desire to sleep with anyone else hit the negatives.

Willow had posted a photo from the meet and greet. In it, I had my head tilted back in laughter as a group of Desi girls held up a Photoshopped banner of me as the shirt-billowing hero of a Bollywood movie, with the rest of the drivers as my background dancers. I got a massive kick out of it and posed for several pictures with the girls. I didn't realize Willow was capturing the moment too.

The text under the post read *If racing doesn't work out . . .* which is word for word the joke I cracked then. But with the roar of the crowd and the distance between us, judging by this photo, there's no way Willow could have heard.

Had Jani been responsible for the post, she would have written something cheesy, something I would never dream of saying. But Willow understands my humor and what fits my brand.

She knows *me*.

I left the party soon after, done flirting with women I had no interest in. Mark shot me a disappointed look when I said my goodbyes, but I didn't care. Why waste my energy on something I don't really want?

But even if I shut down that idea, his warning lingers in my head.

I don't want to ruin Willow's career before it gets off the ground. The world is cruel to women in a way I'll never fully understand, but if she got involved with me, it would follow her for the rest of her life. I can't jeopardize that, no matter how much I want her.

Oakley's opinion alone isn't enough to stop me, but the

risk to Willow's career combined with the other consequences—
like probably dealing the death blow to our remaining friend
group—is.

Maybe. Fuck, is it?

It's not like I plan to break Willow's heart if we got involved, but I'm not a fortune teller. I can't read the stars or
predict the future. But if I had to choose between hurting her
and never racing again, I'd walk away from F1 in a heartbeat.

Cringing, I press a pillow over my face in hopes that it will
suffocate the idea out of me, but I'm still breathing, and all I
can see is Willow's coy smile from this morning. My not-so-
innocent girl.

I've known I was in trouble since Oakley's birthday last
year, but now? I'm deeper in it than I ever thought I'd be.

■✗■✗■✗■

The result of my restless night is a terrible practice session. It
carries over into Saturday, too, and I end up coming in thirteenth in qualifying. That alone isn't unheard of, but Nathaniel slotted himself into twelfth by two-thousandths of a
second, and that fucking stings. Buck is happy, and the entire
garage has released a sigh of relief. But me? I'm trying not to
be a sore loser before the race even starts.

In my driver room, Mark is pushing me through reaction-
time drills while Chava and Willow sit on the small couch,
each working on keeping my life running smoothly.

"Reid has space on his jet if you want to fly private tomorrow," Chava says as soon as I smack the last illuminated light
on the panel. "He says we're all welcome to join, and he's going home this week, so he'll be flying to Dallas anyway."

Reid Coleman is the third American driver on the grid. If
Scuderia D'Ambrosi hadn't snatched him up from F2 first,

I'm sure Argonaut would have wanted him. He's the quintessential all-American boy—golden blond hair, blue eyes, and ivory skin, though lately he's been sporting the kind of tan that hints to a winter spent somewhere warm. He's nothing like my brown ass. Some days I'm pretty sure Argonaut only brought me on because they wanted diversity points, but that's a conspiracy I'll never speak aloud.

Reid and I shared an apartment in Monaco shortly after we were signed to our teams. We were nothing more than boys barely out of our teens who found themselves living the dream of driving at the most elite level of motorsport. I can without a doubt credit him for keeping me sane that first year. Without him, I might have let my nerves get the best of me.

We've drifted a little since. It's the nature of being on different teams, and just a part of growing up, I suppose, but we still look out for each other.

Adjusting my race suit where it hangs around my waist, I nod. "I'm in. I'd rather not fly with the team again." Especially if they find a way to fuck me over today. As always, I'm trying to look on the bright side, but Argonaut makes it harder with every day that passes.

Willow clears her throat. "When you say we're all welcome," she begins, brows raised, "does that include me?"

Chava loops an arm around her neck and pulls her into his side. He lifts his free hand to ruffle her hair like he used to when we were kids, but before he makes contact, he pulls back. He's definitely made the right choice—I don't think she'd appreciate it if he frizzed her curls.

An unexpected jolt of jealousy lances through my chest at the sight of them pressed against each other. The vague chokehold he has her in is nothing but older brother shenanigans, and her hand is high on his chest only to keep him from squeezing her tighter. But regardless, it has my adrenaline spiking at a time when I should be keeping calm.

"Duh, it includes you," Chava says, grinning down at her, oblivious to my rising temperature. "You're one of us now."

Every instinct inside me is screaming to rip him away from her. To tell him to keep his fucking hands to himself. But before they can take over, Mark tosses me a warning look, his blue eyes piercing. So instead, I draw in a deep breath to steady myself and lower my heart rate. I can't risk the stress before getting into the car. Driving angry won't get me anywhere except in the barriers.

I do my best to ignore Chava and Willow's conversation as I motion for Mark to grab the torture device we use for neck training, but her giggles as Chava regales her with the perks of flying private float through the air and hit me one after another, like physical blows.

Mark nearly snaps my neck when he pulls the bands tight because I'm not properly braced. Thankfully, I manage to slip out of the head straps before he can truly do any damage. He fusses over me, hands brushing my head and shoulders to check for injury, but I duck away and turn to the couch.

"You guys mind heading down to the garage?" I ask, hoping they can't hear the tension in my voice. "I need Mark to work on my lower back, and I don't need you two seeing me in just my fireproofs. A boy needs his privacy."

With nods and noises of affirmation, they collect their things and move toward the door, though not before Chava tosses me a questioning look.

When they're gone, Mark gives me a disapproving frown. "You're distracted."

I pick up the training device again and put it back on. "I'm good. I promise. There was just too much going on." I motion to the cord. "You gonna torture me or not? I know you love to watch me suffer, baby."

He ignores my teasing, and the rejection burns. "You're letting her get to you."

"Shut the fuck up." It snaps off my tongue before I can stop it, but I'm sick of his little reprimands. I take a deep breath and close my eyes to center myself before reopening them. Mark is on my side. He's only looking out for me. "I'm sorry, man. I shouldn't have said that."

With a nod, he accepts my apology. "It's fine. I get it." He pauses, meeting my eyes. "But you gotta let her go."

I don't know which way to take his words. Let her go as in fire her? Or abandon the feelings I've developed? Either way, I don't know if I can do it.

"Let's get back to this." I offer the cord to him again. "I've got a teammate who needs his ass kicked."

◆◆◆◆◆◆

I'm back to feeling like myself once I'm down in my side of the garage.

The roar of engines and scent of motor oil have a way of bringing my blood pressure back to normal levels. The thread of adrenaline coursing through me now is thanks to the impending race and nothing else. I bounce on the balls of my feet as I have a last-minute strategy chat with Branny and Sturgill, our team principal. Sturgill isn't a bad guy, but he's Buck's lackey. And while the priority should be scoring points for the team, no matter which driver gets them, Sturgill has never made it a secret that *his* priority is keeping Buck happy.

That said, he's gone to bat for me before, and I've got to respect him for it. It's just a shame he can't do it more often.

Once we've wrapped up, I head over to where Chava's helping Willow adjust her headset.

Her expression is so bright that I almost have to look away. She's like pure sunshine, illuminating anything and everything around her, drawing me in like a moth to a flame.

"I've never looked better," she proclaims to Chava, framing her face with her hands and showing off the bright red headset. She's painted her nails to match, her ring fingers accented with glitter.

She's the only person in here who can pull off Argonaut's uniform. Her tight navy skirt hugs her hips, and she's got her striped polo casually tucked in at the front. She's tied her curls back with a star-printed ribbon, somehow sporty and gut-wrenchingly sexy at the same time.

One glance at her and I already know I'm in big fucking trouble. But I'm not interested in keeping myself out of it.

How can I let her go like Mark insists when she looks like an angel and has such a brilliant mind?

She spots me as I approach, her dimples deepening. "Good luck today."

"Don't need it," I tease, mirroring her grin. "I've got you."

That drags a groan out of her, and she drops her head back. "I told you not to put that on me!"

"Gonna get on the podium today, just because you're here."

"You're the worst." She sighs, then motions for me to move out of her way. "I'm going to find Konrad. He got some shots yesterday I want for your feed."

Thinking about her post from the other night, I step to the side, letting her pass. Everything she's done so far has been perfect, giving fans the glimpses into my life they're begging for, though never enough to make me feel uncomfortable.

She's been careful to keep the balance between personal and professional. Yesterday she even suggested a series of posts that focus on my relationships with the team members I work closely with—a gratitude tour of sorts, to show my appreciation for what each one of them does for me. In comparison, Jani shared more shots of me shirtless in the gym than anything else. It was as if her go-to strategy was to make me look like a self-absorbed prick.

After Willow strolls off, I turn to Chava, rolling my eyes at his knowing expression. Between his leering grins and Mark's disapproving comments, it's like having a devil on one shoulder and an angel on the other. I just don't know who's who.

"Don't say anything," I warn him.

"I wasn't going to."

"But you were thinking it."

A wicked grin splits his face. "Guilty as charged."

I sigh and reach around him to grab my helmet from the shelf. "I don't have time for this."

Chava clasps his hands behind his back and rocks back on his heels, ever the menace. "*Good luck today*," he mocks in a shitty imitation of Willow's voice.

"I'm going to kill you."

"Take a number, cabrón."

Once I'm in the car, the bullshit floods away.

The engine rumbles behind me. My helmet narrows my vision so the asphalt and the cars in front of me are all I see—including Nathaniel ahead on the right. The sight of him fills me with determination. Goal number one today: get around him as soon as possible. Though that'll only be possible if the

Omega Siluro in the grid spot ahead of mine gets out of my way.

Which, of course, doesn't happen.

He's slow off the line, leaving me to cut right, but Nathaniel makes a solid getaway, forcing me to slot in behind him. I stay close through lap one and keep my cool despite his dirty air slowing me at every turn, but the slipstream in the straights is worth it. By the time DRS kicks in, I have no doubt that I can pass him.

I give it another few laps, getting a little more heat in my tires until the car feels comfortable under me. I'm in my sweet spot, ready to push, knowing I can climb higher.

There's only one problem—my teammate won't get out of the fucking way.

He's defending like his life depends on it, which will be misery on his tires, especially this early on. His race engineer is probably telling him to take it easy, to preserve the two-stop strategy for new tires, but this guy is itching to ruin that.

"I need to pass him," I tell Branny over the radio, ignoring his calls to ease off Nathaniel's back wing. "My pace is at least a half second faster."

There's a beat of crackling silence before Branny announces, "Negative, you do not have permission to race."

I'm blindsided by the call. As it stands, we're both outside the points, and in order to change that, either I have to pass my teammate, or a handful of people in front of us need to run into considerable trouble. So why won't they let me do what's best for our standing in the Constructors' Championship?

Actually, that's a stupid question. I already know why.

"Then make it team orders," I demand. "Tell him to let me pass."

"Negative," Branny says immediately. Not even a second of thought goes into the answer. "Maintain and defend."

That's absolute *bullshit*. Even the commentators have got to see that my pace is better than Nathaniel's. If he let me through, I'd easily be seconds ahead of him. And there's a chance I could catch up to the McMorris in tenth.

But no, I'm stuck defending for my sack-of-shit teammate who only knows how to check his mirrors when I'm behind him.

I fume for sixty more laps, mentally cursing Nathaniel and Buck and every person who enables them, until I cross the finish line.

If I hadn't made up my mind before, I have now.

I've got to get out of here.

CHAPTER 15

WILLOW

"Looks like I'm not your lucky charm after all."

In a secluded corner of the Argonaut garage, Dev runs a towel over his sweaty hair. He pushes the loose curls back from his face and ruffles them, letting them fall at random. Even after a grueling race spent defending hard for his teammate, he looks practically perfect.

But the Dev standing in front of me now is a man I barely recognize. This one has slumped shoulders and a grim set to his mouth. He's unhappy, that much is clear, and he's hidden away in this corner so that no one else catches a glimpse of him like this.

He didn't want me to witness it, either, but I knew the half smile he wore when he shuffled into the pit lane was fake, so I followed him back here after Chava silently handed him a water bottle and a towel, clearly knowing better than me not to bother Dev in a moment like this.

Dev tried to protest when he noticed me trailing behind him, but he shut his mouth after my lucky charm comment. He still hasn't spoken, so I'm left watching him and racking my brain for a way to lighten the mood.

I heard the team radio, heard his race engineer tell him he wasn't allowed to pass his teammate. It resulted in a twelfth-place finish, eleventh for Nathaniel. Neither of them scored points. No wonder he's defeated and exhausted. All of that for nothing.

I may be new to the scene, but the tension between Dev's side of the garage and Nathaniel's is impossible to miss. It's obvious who the priority is, which no doubt has a little something to do with the team's owner. I don't know exactly why Dev hates Nathaniel so much, but eventually, I'll pry the full story out of him. For now, seeing firsthand how the team treats Dev explains a lot.

From the beginning of my venture as his social media manager, my goal has been to get the attention of the higher-ups at Argonaut, to make them see his value to the team. But maybe I'm looking at this all wrong. Maybe I need to organize a new game plan because, from what I've seen so far, this group will never have his best interests at heart as long as Buck Decker is in charge.

"When you're finished with interviews and debriefing," I say, "come find me at the hotel, yeah?"

There's a long pause before he gruffly answers, "Yeah."

Pushing my luck and the boundaries we've established, I press up onto my tiptoes and brush away a curl that's flopped onto his forehead. I don't miss the surprise in his eyes as I do so, but I choose not to acknowledge it.

"There," I proclaim, smiling up at him, my heart beating a little faster. "Now you're camera ready."

✴✴✴✴✴

It's after eleven when there's a knock at my door.

I unfold myself from the bed and pad over, placing my

fingertips on the smooth surface so I can check the peephole. I can't see the face of the man standing out in the hotel hallway. His arm is extended to brace against the doorframe, and his chin is tucked against his chest, but there's no mistaking it's Dev.

He slowly lifts his head when I haul open the door. He's showered and changed, but his expression is just as bleak as when I left him in the garage after the race. To my surprise, he's wearing a navy T-shirt with the Argonaut logo and a pair of jeans. After today, you'd think he'd choose something without the team's branding on it, but I'm guessing—just like the order he was given in the race—he didn't have a choice.

"Hey," he says, his voice low and rough.

"Hey." I step back from the door and extend an arm to welcome him inside. "Come in."

He watches me for a beat before he drops his hand from the doorframe and shuffles in. He kicks his shoes off just inside the threshold, then continues the trek to the armchair in the corner. With a sigh, he crashes into it and drops his head back against the cushion. His knees are spread wide, elbows hanging over the armrests. The pose is open but exhausted, and I can't help but imagine myself crawling between his legs, hands on his thighs . . .

Good god, girl. Get it together.

I stand in the small entryway for a second longer to compose myself before I turn and move to the bed. Perched on the corner closest to him, I tuck my hands under my legs and take him in.

"You okay?" I finally ask, even though the answer is obvious.

He closes his eyes, his lashes brushing his cheeks for a few seconds. Then he opens them again and fixes his attention on me. "I'll be fine."

In other words, he's very much *not* okay. Not that he'd ever let those words leave his lips. Not the perpetually content Dev.

"Do you want to talk about it?" I press.

"Not really."

I nod, letting the silence hang between us. When I asked him to find me, it's because I wanted to brainstorm a new strategy for getting teams other than Argonaut to notice him, but this clearly isn't the time to bring that up. He's in bad shape, waging an invisible battle that I'm not privy to. I don't know if I'll ever be.

Even though this isn't the right moment to talk strategy or push him to open up, I don't want him to go back to his own room and sulk alone. Sure, he could seek out Chava or Mark, but I doubt he will. I'm lucky he even showed up here with his guard dropped. I want to make sure he stays.

I heave myself off the bed, startling him, I think. But his eyes lose some of their distance as he tracks me.

"Let's watch a movie," I declare, holding his gaze for a beat before marching over to grab the TV remote from the bedside table.

I'm already logged in to my Netflix account—I watched an episode of a favorite sitcom while on FaceTime with Chantal earlier. So, when I press the power button and the screen comes to life, my profile and an array of rom-coms the algorithm thinks I'd like are revealed. I won't be going for any of those tonight, though.

"Are you still into horror?" I ask, sneaking a glance at him.

His frown isn't as severe as it was previously, but he furrows his brow at my question. "You remember that?"

I scoff, paging down to the next row of suggestions. "You mean do I remember getting the crap scared out of me every time you and Oakley had one of your horror movie marathons? Uh, yeah, I remember."

That drags a laugh out of him. It's scratchy, almost like he's forgotten how to make the sound. "I still like it, but I won't make you watch my favorite slasher flick."

I bite back a smile. At least he seems willing to stick around. If the only thing I accomplish is getting his mind off what happened today, helping him remember that there's more to life than racing and the politics that go along with it, then I'll consider it a roaring success. He's usually the one doling out the sunshine, bringing lightness to the lives of those in his orbit. And he deserves the same. It's his turn to be taken care of.

"Fine with me." I drop to the bed again, making sure to stick close to one side so there's ample space in case he wants to join me. "What do you want to watch?"

Straightening slowly, he searches me as I wait for his answer. "I have something in mind," he finally says. "But you have to promise never to tell anyone. Especially not Chava. He'll never let me live it down."

I rub my hands together like a supervillain and grin. "Ooh, something even Chava doesn't know? Do tell."

Exhaling another laugh, he shakes his head and glances away, like he can't look me in the eye as he admits it. "When I have a truly bad day . . . I put on a Bollywood movie."

I blink at him, waiting for the twist. When he doesn't go on, I scrunch my brow. "Okay? You're acting as if I don't know that you wanted to be a playback singer when you were eleven."

His attention snaps back to me. Wide-eyed, he points a threatening finger. "You better take that to the grave."

"Cross my heart and hope to die," I swear, trying not to

laugh. "But seriously, I'm not shocked that's your bad day go-to. Who doesn't want over-the-top drama and dance breaks when they're not feeling great?"

"It's a little more . . . specific than that." He takes a deep breath, lets it out in a rush, then confesses, "I usually put on *Kal Ho Naa Ho*."

I'm no connoisseur of Indian cinema, but I watched *a lot* of Bollywood when I was a kid, thanks to Neha Aunty. I'm pretty sure she's loaned every one of the DVDs in her collection to my mom in the decades they've been neighbors. And one movie has always stuck out more than others, because it's the one that had me crying for hours after it ended.

"I'm sorry," I say slowly, trying to battle my disbelief. "*Kal Ho Naa Ho* is your *comfort* movie? Are you serious?"

Dev weakly throws a hand up, once again avoiding my gaze. "I mean . . . yeah. It's about being proud of who you are—your background, where you come from—and living life to the fullest, even though you could die at any moment. If that doesn't explain my life . . ." He trails off and shrugs.

Okay, I see it. Though I never expected an answer like that. "I get it. But that movie made me sob the one and only time I watched it, so I'm nixing it for tonight. Give me another option."

Pressing his lips to one side, he scans the room, then brings his focus back to me, a small spark of hope alight in his eyes. "*Devdas*?"

I nearly choke. "You're out of your damn mind."

"*Dil Se..*?"

"It's like you *want* to be sad!"

He laughs again, but this time it's the warm sound I'm used to. "Fine, fine," he concedes. "How about *Om Shanti Om*?"

"Oh, I see." I nod sagely, putting together the puzzle pieces of his cinematic choices. "The theme here isn't depression—it's Shah Rukh Khan."

And there it is, the grin that makes my heart skip a silly little beat, even though it knows better. "You caught me. Can't go wrong with King Khan."

"I can get behind *Om Shanti Om*." I pick up the remote again and type the title into the search box. When I'm hovering over the image depicting a popular scene from the movie, I push my luck and pat the empty side of the king-size bed, a direct invitation. "Come over here. I don't want you craning your neck to see the screen. Mark will kill me if you pull a muscle."

The comment is casual, but we both know this is pushing the limits of our friendship, even with an ocean of space and a mountain of pillows between us. Sure that he'd say no and drag the chair over instead, I swallow back my surprise when he pushes himself up and walks over to the bed. He climbs carefully onto the mattress, one knee, then the other, and grabs one of the many pillows, setting it between us and dropping an elbow to it like it's an armrest as he props himself up against the headboard.

Over the last few days, I've lost track of how many times we've hugged or high-fived or sat shoulder to shoulder in meetings, so I shouldn't be sweating at the idea of him lounging nearly two feet away from me. But this feels intimate. We're alone, and we're literally in bed together, even if we're nowhere close to touching. The room is dimly lit by the table lamp, and the soft hum of the AC is the only sound, so the ambiance isn't helping the cause either.

Once he's settled in, I burrow down on my side of the bed. I'm going to pretend like this is nothing but normal, even if it's far from it.

"Ready?" I ask, lifting the remote. But before I can press play, I drop my arm again and sit upright. "Wait, hold on."

I toss the remote at him and hustle over to my snack stash on the dresser.

"I went on a snack run earlier," I explain, holding up two bags of chips. "You can't go to Canada without getting all-dressed and ketchup chips. Pick your poison."

He taps a finger against his lips, eyeing one bag, then the other. "Split 'em half-and-half?"

"I like the way you think."

I hand him the ketchup flavor first and make my way back around the bed to my side. Dev presses play on the movie as I open my bag and sigh contentedly at the first salty bite. I've eaten a few by the time the opening credits are over, and it takes me a second to realize that I can't understand a word of the dialogue.

"Dev, I need subtitles," I remind him, glancing over at where he's made himself comfortable, chips and the remote resting on his stomach.

"Oh shit. Yeah, of course." He scrambles to turn them on, flashing me a crooked, apologetic smile. "Forgot not all of us were forced to go to Hindi school."

"You may not have liked it, but I'm jealous you speak three languages," I grumble, shoving my hand down in the chip bag again.

"Five, actually," he says offhandedly, focus fixed on the TV as Shah Rukh Khan swans into the frame. "I learned French and Italian after moving to Europe. Made it easier to communicate in the paddock. Kind of sucks that everyone is just expected to speak perfect English."

I peer over at him, missing the translation on the screen. If I thought I couldn't be more impressed by Dev Anderson, here he is proving me wrong . . . and making more butterflies skitter through my stomach.

"I kind of hate you," I tease. "Stop being good at so many things. Save a few impressive feats for the rest of us."

Dev laughs. The sound is familiar and natural, and it comes so easily now that I have to wonder if the man who walked in here is the same one lying next to me. "You're good at a lot of things, too, you know," he says, meeting my eyes across the chasm of bedding that separates us. "Don't ever sell yourself short, Willow."

▚▚▚▚▚

At intermission—gotta love Bollywood—I get up to stretch while Dev grabs drinks from the vending machine down the hall.

We've shaken off the earlier awkwardness and fallen back into our old ways. I pelted him with gummy bears when he belted out "Ajab Si" like I was the one he was confessing his feelings for. We booed the screen together every time Mukesh appeared. Dev even promised to have every costume Deepika Padukone wore re-created for me after I gushed about them at least half a dozen times, probably just to shut me up.

We're in our own little world, where nothing outside this hotel room or unrelated to this silly movie masterpiece matters. I hope it's a reprieve for him, a chance to reset and shed all the crap this week brought him, because tomorrow is a new day, and I don't want those worries following him into it. I can't get rid of them completely, but I *can* make things a little lighter, even if it's just by watching a movie and eating junk food that he probably shouldn't be consuming.

The lock clicks, and Dev steps back inside. But instead of kicking off his shoes and coming back to the bed, he sets the waters and my key card on the small side table and drags a hand through his hair.

"I just realized what time it is," he says, his chin tucked and his expression a little less relaxed than it was before.

I move to the entryway and stop a couple of feet from where he's holding the door open with his foot.

"I should probably get to bed," he adds. "We have to head out pretty early tomorrow."

"Oh." I don't mean to sound disappointed, but the word slips out that way. Shaking my head, I force my tone lighter. "Yeah, you're right. And I still need to pack, so . . ."

"We'll finish the movie another time." With the reassuring smile he gives me, I know it's a promise. "You sure you want to come to Dallas for the week before we head to Austria? If you want to go back to New York, Chava can change your ticket."

I shake my head. We need to be in Europe in a week for the next race, and if Dev plans to spend the time in between at headquarters, then so do I. Having time apart won't be conducive to content creation, and since we'll be at the factory, I'll have the opportunity to talk to Argonaut employees there. It's the perfect chance to work on Dev's gratitude tour, which will still be good no matter what strategy we shift to.

"Still okay," I reassure him. "I guess I'll see you in the morning?"

He nods, holding the door open with his hand now, slowly backing away. "Car to the airport leaves at nine."

"Sounds good."

There's a beat of silence, like neither of us knows how to end the conversation. I don't really want him to go. Does he feel the same?

"Right," he finally says, taking a decisive step back.

I move to grab the door so I can see him out and hang on to these last seconds together. We'll meet up again in the morning, sure, but I want more of this before it fades away.

Dev is half-turned from me when his head snaps back around, his eyes suddenly bright. "One last thing."

I grip the door a little tighter. The butterflies are back in full force. "Yeah?"

"Whose abs are better—mine or SRK's in 'Dard-e-Disco'?"

The unexpected question shocks a laugh out of me. I can't even pretend to not find it funny.

"Stop fishing for compliments," I scold him. Because Dev's abs *are* better. And that's saying something.

His grin practically takes over his whole face. "Good night, Willow," he says.

"Good night, Dev."

He slips his hands into the pockets of his jeans and strolls off, shoulders back and chin lifted.

This is the Dev I know—confident and content. The dejection that followed him earlier has evaporated.

As I'm closing the door, motion farther down the hallway catches my attention. It's Mark, slinking back into his own room, though not before shooting the man coming toward him a sharp look. Dev doesn't acknowledge him, but it has me frowning.

Because I have a sinking suspicion that's why Dev had to leave.

 **CHAPTER 16**

DEV

Reid Coleman has charmed my girl.

Technically, Willow is not my girl. And okay, yeah, Reid charmed *everyone* on the plane with his adventure stories and his southern drawl. But the point still stands. Boy's on my shit list until the hearts disappear from Willow's eyes.

The oppressive Texas heat isn't helping the burn of jealousy as Chava, Mark, Willow, and I make our way across the tarmac to the awaiting SUV. Mark hangs back next to me as Chava and Willow walk ahead, recounting Reid's skydiving tale and acting like obsessive fangirls.

"You forgive me yet?"

I spare a glance over at Mark, hitching my duffel bag higher on my shoulder. "Nothing to forgive."

"We both know that's not true."

"We can pretend it is."

He exhales and keeps his voice low. "I'm just trying to keep you focused."

"I'm not distracted," I answer, but it doesn't lighten Mark's frown.

He worries about me; it's his job, but it's also because he's a good friend. Usually, it doesn't bother me, because ninety-nine percent of the time, he's right and I need to be guided back onto the correct path. But his warnings against Willow and the way he all but dragged me away from her last night aren't endearing me toward him.

"Look, it was a rough day. She just wanted to cheer me up," I explain, though when the implications of those words hit me, I elaborate before he can jump to conclusions. "All we did was watch a movie. And honestly? It helped. She . . ." I trail off, struggling to come up with a way to make him understand the lightness that Willow brings into my life. The way she chases away the storm clouds hanging over my head with her pure sunshine. "She fixed me."

Mark narrows his eyes in warning. "That's a lot of credit to give one person."

Maybe it is. Or maybe it's not enough. Because she dragged me out of the dark place I could have gone last night, and her presence now is what's keeping me from dwelling on how stuck I feel with Argonaut. We're about to step into the lion's den of my team's headquarters, but knowing she'll be there too? I feel no fear.

Bathed in the sound of her laughter, I keep my eyes on her bouncing curls. "She deserves it."

▰▰▰▰▰

The week in Dallas passes in a blur of meetings, extra-long gym sessions, and hours spent in the simulator. By the time we're on the plane to Austria, I'm certain I could drive the circuit with my eyes closed. I'm ready to fight again.

Whether Argonaut allows me to do that remains to be seen.

"Okay, time for your weekly update," Willow announces once the plane hits ten thousand feet and we're allowed to take out our electronics.

She hauls her laptop up from the bag by her feet and flips it open. When the screen kicks on, a slideshow appears. The girl's prepared.

We haven't spent much time together outside of meals lately. We've been too busy with our own responsibilities for much more than passing greetings and quickly snapped photos. Sitting next to each other in first class on a commercial flight feels like a stolen moment. But Mark's warning to keep my distance from her pops into my head as she clears her throat and prepares to start her presentation.

Willow deserves to apply these skills on a larger scale, to work for a team that will value her dedication and talent. I don't want to ruin that for her. So instead of leaning in like I want to, I nod and allow her to turn the screen in my direction.

"Followers are up an average of nine percent on all platforms," she begins. The first slide shows charts of follower and engagement growth.

Once I've looked over it, she flips to the next. This one is full of brand logos for companies that I'd be more than happy to work with.

"Howard has lined up two new brand deals for you. I have a full deck for each one if you want to review them later. We'll make sure they're a good fit."

"How insufferable was my agent when you talked to him?" I ask dryly.

She shoots me a knowing look. "Unbelievably."

"Sounds about right." I point to the computer screen, motioning for her to continue.

"Okay, you're absolutely welcome to shoot this idea down if you think it's too soon," she prefaces, "but the hosts of this podcast would like to interview you. I listened to almost every episode they've done so far, and these women really know their stuff. They're hilarious, too, and they've really taken off on the charts."

I lift a brow in surprise. She did all of that before she knew whether I'd even be interested? "You listened to every episode?"

"Nearly," she corrects. "Did my due diligence. And I listened to a few other F1-centric shows to see if they'd be a better fit, but I think this one's the best."

"God, I am so impressed by you."

The words slip off my tongue before I can stop them, but even as a flush creeps up her neck, I don't take them back. She deserves this praise and more.

"Thank you," she mumbles, keeping her eyes trained on the laptop as she flips to the next slide. "Anyway, I'll have Chava schedule everything. Then there's . . ."

As she continues, I try to focus on the screen and not her pretty blushing face. Every time she makes a suggestion, I agree. She knows best. That's obvious. I'm just along for the ride.

"Okay, let me coordinate with everyone and get it all on the calendar," she says, beaming, once she's touched on the final slide.

I have to resist the urge to trace the curve of her smile, because that is *not* something a boss should ever do. But the temptation is real, and the longer I spend with her, the harder it's going to get.

Maybe Mark was right. Maybe I should let her go. For my sanity and for her reputation.

Except that clarity disappears in a puff of smoke when she squeezes my hand, her excitement palpable. It's a brief touch, fully innocent. Just an expression of how happy she is to be working on all of this. I doubt she even thought twice about it.

With joy still lingering on her face, she puts her laptop away and pulls out her little notebook, then curls up in her oversized seat. She scribbles on the page, lower lip caught between her teeth as she concentrates. I know then that I'm fully hooked. I'm not letting her go anywhere unless it's by my side.

At least not until the summer's over and our time together is done. Fuck knows how I'll ever let her walk away again.

Sunday brings blue skies and sunshine as bright as my mood. I'm once again feeling like nothing out there can stop me. It's a welcome reprieve from the weight that's been pushing down on my shoulders.

Practice on Friday went off without a hitch, and I qualified eleventh yesterday. Adding to my buoyant mood, Nathaniel qualified seventeenth, so it's unlikely team orders will affect my race. Can't tell me to stay behind him if I'm already leagues ahead.

I avoid him as all the drivers gather at the back of a modified flatbed semitruck, which we'll be riding on for the drivers' parade. I greet Thomas Maxwell-Brown with a grin and a shot to the shoulder, teasing him about the douchey yacht pictures he posted last week. The guy's posher than a British royal . . . which he actually might be, if his bloodline was traced back far enough.

I've just climbed up on the truck when Zaid Yousef lifts his chin, motioning me to the free spot by the railing next to him—and away from the reporters. I freeze for a second before forcing my feet to move.

It's ridiculous, but I still get starstruck when I see Zaid. He's literally just a guy, and one I've been racing against for years, but he's been a god in my eyes since I was a kid. With seven championship titles under his belt and a near-infinite number of records broken, he's easily the greatest of all time. And as a fellow brown guy—the Middle Eastern kind of brown compared to my South Asian brown—he showed me that it was possible for people who looked like us to reach the highest level of motorsport.

"You good?" he asks me after we slap hands. His English accent is a little more working-class than Thomas's.

"Can't complain," I answer, trying to play it cool. I'm definitely failing.

"How's your mum?"

That's another thing about Zaid—he remembers the smallest details. He had a conversation with my mother *once* and still asks about her. "She's good. Still can't get her to stop working, even though she doesn't need to anymore."

Zaid flashes me a warm, knowing smile. "Mine's the same. She'd rather die than let someone else run our family's shop."

We chat as the truck starts to make its way around the circuit for the fans to see, but I'm bumped aside by a cameraman when the interviewers come over to ask Zaid about his chances at an eighth championship title.

There's an open spot next to Reid, so I step into it instead. "Thanks again for the flight to Dallas," I greet him. "How was your time back home?"

"It was a nice break." He rests his elbow on my shoulder

as he waves to the crowd. "Even if my grandmother spent the week nagging that I don't come home enough."

I laugh and wave as well, taking in the crowd's excitement. "Tell Dottie I miss her apple pie."

"Will do." He snorts. "Speaking of Texas and apple pie, you got plans for the Fourth of July?"

"Not past whatever Argonaut's doing." I'm not going home for it, considering it's in two days and the next grand prix at Silverstone is just a few days after that. "I'm heading straight to London in the morning in order to prepare myself for that shit show. You?"

"So you're going to be at the dinner?" he asks. "I'm still deciding whether I'm brave enough to show my face there, but I definitely don't want to do it alone."

"Oh, you mean the tacky party Argonaut's throwing?" I want to roll my eyes just thinking about it. It's going to be an England-bashing party . . . in the middle of London. "Yeah, they'll have my ass if I'm not there. Please come suffer with me."

Reid shakes his head, still watching the crowd. "No, I mean the dinner with Buck beforehand. It's a small thing, right? He said it'll be just key players, but I don't know if I want to be stuck with that guy for longer than I have to be."

My stomach sinks, and I frown, studying his profile. "What are you talking about?"

Reid stops waving and looks over at me, brow furrowing. The cameras are catching all of this, but at least they can't hear what we're saying. "You don't know about it?"

"No. I don't."

I'm not surprised that Buck is hosting something extra, but I *am* shocked that this is the first I'm hearing about it—and that he invited a rival driver.

My stomach is down in my knees at this point. It's obvious that Buck wants me out, but I doubt Reid would replace me. I can't imagine him leaving D'Ambrosi. He's happy at the Scuderia, and he's been fighting for third place on the podium all year. He wouldn't give that up to drive for a midfield team that hasn't had a win in ages.

But if Buck offered him enough money to make the switch worth his while, then I'm fucked. Because Reid is the all-American driver that all-American Argonaut has always wanted.

I have to fight to keep a smile on my face, to keep the cameras from picking up on the turmoil coursing through me. I don't want Reid to catch on either. "You got an invite because of the technical agreement, right?" I jokingly suggest. "I'm sure D'Ambrosi thinks that since you make our engines, you belong at all of our parties too."

"Right," Reid says, but it does nothing to comfort me. "I'm sure that's it."

▰▰▰▰▰

My gut churns as I pull into my grid spot, but the nausea is mixed with a burning anger now.

The engine rumbles as I flex my fingers around the steering wheel. I kept my head down and avoided everyone but my engineers after climbing off the drivers' parade truck, not wanting to lose the building fire in my chest. It's flaming bright now.

My heart slows as the red lights come on one by one, and it jolts as they all go out. I'm clean off the line and immediately pass two cars. By the time we hit the first corner, I'm in ninth. I keep the advantage on the inside, falling in behind a McMorris and sticking tight to its rear wing. The gap expands a little as the laps go on, but I'll be able to pass soon enough if I push a little more.

Branny is a mosquito buzzing in my ear. I tune out everything except the important stuff, giving clipped responses when necessary. We usually keep a good rapport going, but not today. Not after discovering the plot to kick me aside happening right under my nose.

By lap twenty-three I'm in front of the McMorris and the car is solid under me. My tires are holding out well, the balance is as good as it will ever get, and I'm eking out every bit of power available.

I'm driving to prove something. Whether it's to Argonaut or another team, I'm determined to exhibit what I'm capable of, why I belong here. There's a reason I was rookie of the year when I debuted. There's a reason sponsors flocked to me right out of the gate. There's a reason I beat out hundreds of other drivers on my way to F1. I'm here because I fought for it. And I'm going to keep fighting.

I push on, determined to close the distance to the car in front of me. I'm about to ask Branny what the gap time is when he crackles over the radio instead.

"There's something wrong with the car," he says. "We need to retire it. Slow down and box. Repeat, slow down and box."

I'm stunned into silence. The car feels as perfect as an Argonaut is capable of. "What's the problem?" I demand. "I don't feel anything wrong."

"There is an issue," Branny repeats, though he doesn't give any details. Maybe he doesn't want our competitors to know, but I'm driving the fucking thing. He could at least give me a hint so I could help judge the situation.

"Tell me," I grit out.

But again, I'm left in the dark.

"We can't risk it," he says. "Box, box."

I don't care that the whole world can hear me swear over the radio. I don't care that I nearly break the pit lane speed limit as I haul the car in. I don't care that my helmet lands with a sickening crack on the concrete inside the garage as engineers and mechanics rush around.

Steaming from head to toe, I grind my teeth to keep from saying something I'll regret to someone who doesn't deserve it. With my chin tucked to my chest, I dodge bodies determined to stop me to discuss. But I can't do it right now. I can't. I can't listen to the excuses.

Except Sturgill, the team principal, stands between me and the hallway that leads out of the garage, giving me no choice but to pass by him. I prepare to shoulder around him, to avoid his eye and all the bullshit he's going to spew at me, but the second I step beside him, his hand darts out, and he grabs my bicep.

I'm about to snarl at him to let me go, but I go rigid at the guarded look in his eye. The caution. The dark worry. So I let him drag me toward him. Once we're closer, he puts his mouth by my ear, not daring to be overheard.

His breath is hot on my skin, but my blood runs cold when he speaks. "There was nothing wrong with the car," he murmurs. "The order came from Buck."

CHAPTER 17

WILLOW

The second Dev storms into the garage, I'm moving toward him.

I rip off my headset and toss it down on the first available surface, homing in on him without a second thought. Not even the stiff ache in my hips from sitting in hard chairs and hours spent standing can hold me back.

Mark tries, though.

He grasps my upper arm, causing me to stumble to a stop. I pull my shoulders back, snapping my head up and shooting him a frown. We're both lucky he didn't pull hard enough to do damage.

Before I can open my mouth to reprimand him, he's shaking his head.

"Leave him alone." The words are low but firm, and there's little room for argument.

"I think I'll take my chances."

I'm equally firm, holding his gaze until he slowly loosens his grip. Reluctantly, he searches my face, and his fingertips graze the back of my arm as they finally fall away.

I ignore the way he calls my name in warning as I stride off again, heading to where Dev disappeared out the back of the garage. I'm not fast enough to catch up to him, but I think I know where he's going.

The door to Dev's driver room is closed when I reach it. I knock, though I don't wait for an answer before slipping inside and shutting it behind me.

Dev is on the other side of the small room, head down, fingers buried in his hair, pacing. The set to his shoulders is tense under his fireproof shirt, like he's barely holding back the urge to drop his hands and hit something. His unzipped race suit flutters around his hips when he turns at the sound of the door closing, and my heart breaks at the pain on his face.

I stay where I am. If he asks me to leave, I will, no questions. Until that happens, though, I'm sticking around. He shouldn't have to deal with this alone.

No one likes to drop out of a race early, but based on his reaction, this isn't *just* a DNF. Something else is at play.

"I have to leave this team," he declares, voice cracking on the last word. He finally drops his hands and balls them into fists at his sides, leaving his hair a mess. The heat of his anger has turned cold. "I can't stay here while they sabotage me over and over again. I'm wasting my whole fucking career."

I keep quiet. He needs to get this out before it eats him alive. Dev is always a positive force. Always a yes-man. But for once, he's allowing his true frustration to show.

"There was nothing wrong with the car," he goes on, speaking in a rush. "Sturgill said the order to retire came straight from Buck. He set me up. Asshole screwed me over so I'll stop embarrassing his son—and so I look less appealing to any team who might be interested in me." He grunts in disgust and shakes his head, his damp hair falling across his forehead. "I have to get out of here. Before they ditch me first."

It doesn't make sense that they'd do this to him. Dev is an amazing driver. He consistently scores points, keeping the team from being completely annihilated in the Constructors' Championship, so why would they want to ruin his chances of success? It's like cutting off their nose to spite their face.

"Don't you still have a year left on your contract?" I ask. "Don't they have to honor it?"

Dev snorts and shakes his head, returning to stalking back and forth across the floor. "That contract doesn't mean shit. I've seen guys get paid out and then never drive again. I don't want that to be me. It can't be. I won't let it."

He's growing agitated again, like a tiger pacing in a too-small cage. Argonaut is holding him back, and this is the first time I've ever seen him lose his shit over it. But I'm sure it's not the first time it's ever happened.

I never got to bring up the topic of changing the direction of his image revamp, but if he's going to leave Argonaut, he's going to need all the help he can get to find another team and stay in F1.

"If they're going to fuck me over, maybe I should do the same to them," Dev rambles on, stopping again in the center of the room. He's staring at me, but it's like he's looking right through me. "Crash in every practice and qualifying and race so they have to spend a ton of money to fix the car. We'd be constantly penalized because of all the modifications. It would be a disaster for everyone, not just me."

To snap like this, to consider sabotaging everything he's worked for, is extreme. But he's angry and reacting, and I can't blame him for it.

Wishing I could do more to soothe him, I softly say, "You're not going to do that, Dev."

He blinks in rapid succession like he's realizing for the first time I'm here. And then his shoulders slump and his eyes slide shut as he composes himself. When they open again, I'm no longer speaking to the caged predator. My Dev is back, even if he's missing that glowing lightness.

"Willow," he exhales, fingers uncurling from fists. "I'm sorry. I shouldn't have said any of that. I didn't mean it. I'm just . . ." He trails off, dragging a hand through his hair again before shaking his head with a sad, short laugh. "Fuck, I don't know what to do anymore."

I sink my teeth into my lower lip, wishing I could offer a solution past what we've already set into motion.

"Until teams stop seeing me as a liability," Dev goes on, defeat seeping into his voice, "no one's going to want me."

Pain sparks in my chest at his admission. It feels like a literal impossibility that none of the teams would want Dev. Maybe his reputation isn't spectacular right now—though it's improving by the day—but his racing speaks for itself. He's fought tooth and nail for every point he's scored with Argonaut. It doesn't take an engineer or a physicist to know the machinery he's working with isn't anywhere close to being on par with Mascort or Specter Energy, but his qualifying times are rarely more than a second off the leader's pace. And nine times out of ten, he outqualifies his nepo-baby teammate. His dedication is obvious, and a person would have to be completely ignorant to miss his hunger for more. He has everything it takes to be a champion, except for a team that can—or even wants to—make him one.

And yeah, he's talking about his racing career here, but I

wish I could tell him how much his friends, his family, and his fans love him and want him. How much *I* want him.

"We're fixing it," I declare. I'm itching to move closer and grip him by the shoulders to drive my point home. But I don't. It's best to keep my distance when emotions are running this high. "Things are already starting to look better. Does Howard know you want out?"

Dev nods and slowly draws in a breath, like he's tamping down his feelings so he can focus on logic. "I've told him to put feelers out, but he hasn't come back with any solid leads. He keeps telling me to stick it out here, to give it my all so my chances are better when my contract is almost up. But how can I expect my chances to improve when Argonaut won't even let me race?"

His composure cracks again, his expression twisting with anger and grief. Argonaut holds his dreams in their hands and can crush them at will. Hell, they're already squeezing—and hard.

I can't resist anymore. I take a few quick steps toward him, only halting when we're toe to toe and my palms are splayed on his chest. His heart is raging, battering his ribs. I'm pushing the limits right now, but he needs to know that he'll get through this. And that I'm on his side.

"Hey," I urge, scanning his face, noting that the resentment in his expression fades just a little. "It's going to be okay. We'll get you through this, and you're going to sign with a team that actually values you. It might not be tomorrow, or next month, or by the end of this season, but you're going to get what you want." I swallow past the emotion welling up. "Okay? I know it. And I'll do whatever I can to make sure of it."

I slide my hands around to his back and up to his shoulder

blades, then shuffle in to hug him tight, my cheek pressed to his chest. He's stiff in my arms, his own still down by his sides, and for a moment, I panic, worrying that I've done the wrong thing. I'm testing the boundaries of our friendship, of our professional relationship, but how am I supposed to leave him without comfort when it's clear he needs it?

I'm just loosening my hold, ready to surrender and pull away, when he gently wraps his arms around my shoulders. He drops his forehead to the top of my head, suddenly enveloping me in his hold. I've hugged Dev countless times, from quick one-armed squeezes to tackled embraces, but there's something so different about the way he's holding me now—like if he lets go, he'll break.

Holding him just as fiercely, I shut my eyes and breathe him in. I don't care that he's sweaty and smells faintly of gasoline. I only want to press myself closer and stay there forever. We fit perfectly, as if I was always meant to be wrapped up with him.

He exhales heavily against my hair and mumbles, "I'm sorry," but he doesn't lift his head. "I know this isn't what you signed up for. You're supposed to be posting silly pictures of me, not talking me off the ledge."

"I don't care," I reply, my voice muffled by his shirt. "You're allowed to be upset. Because this is incredibly shitty."

His chest vibrates under my cheek as he chuckles. "Hearing you curse is still so thrilling."

"Shut up." I squeeze him tighter for one more second before convincing myself to finally let him go. I'm afraid if I don't do it now, I never will.

He's wearing an exhausted half smile when I pull back enough to look up at him, and I let my hands linger on his pecs, soaking in his warmth. Then, with a slow breath, I make myself drop them.

"Thank you for letting me vent," he says. "And for talking me out of wrecking a multimillion-dollar car."

I snicker and shake my head, but I'm fighting a grin and the largest kaleidoscope of butterflies my stomach has ever battled. "I can't believe you let me see you being anything less than perfect."

"It happens sometimes."

His voice is warm, but the intensity in his eyes fills me with heat. I have to glance away. Otherwise, I'll be tempted to make another mistake.

"You want to finish *Om Shanti Om* tonight?" he asks, blessedly turning away so he can grab a towel from the shelf. He scrubs it over his face, wiping away that look in his eye. "I could use a laugh. And I could stand to get lost in someone else's drama for a while."

I absolutely want to spend the evening with him, but I'm quickly reminded of how our last movie night ended. "Is Mark going to come chase you away again?" I ask dryly.

He snorts and tosses the towel to the side, confirming what I suspected before. Mark was the reason Dev left my room so suddenly last week.

"We'll have to see," he says, snagging a bottle of water off the table and cracking the lid. "He may not even let me out after curfew."

I bite the inside of my cheek to distract myself from the little pang of hurt. Moving over to the small couch, I sit and draw my knees to my chest.

"I know Mark doesn't like me very much," I say. I've always kept that thought to myself. But if Dev's shown me anything today, it's that our hurts are better let out than kept in. "I get why, though."

"What?" he says, searching my face in disbelief. "That's not true."

I shake my head, averting my eyes. "You don't have to pretend. It's clear he doesn't like having me around. I probably remind him of everything with Jeremy—of how I ruined your friendship with him and the other guys."

"You didn't ruin anything." His voice is gritty and sure. "You know that, right?"

"Yeah, of course." I wave a hand, brushing away his question and my blatant lie. "It's just—"

"No, seriously." He sets the bottle of water on the table and stalks forward until he's standing in front of me. "None of that was your fault. Jeremy was an absolute piece of shit. That's why we cut him off. And the guys who sided with him? Also pieces of shit. We grew up together, sure, but that doesn't mean we were supposed to stay friends forever. I'm not interested in wasting time on people who think treating anyone the way Jeremy treated you is okay."

His words hit me like a wave of relief, one I didn't realize I needed. But none of that explains why Mark can't stand being around me.

"Then why does Mark hate me?" I blurt.

The second the words leave my mouth, I wish I could pull them back in. I'm a people pleaser down to my core. I've always cared more than I should about whether people like me. That habit has waned a bit over the last few years, which can certainly be attributed to Chantal's and Grace's influence. Their don't-give-a-fuck attitudes have rubbed off on me, but the need to please those around me and to be liked by my peers is so ingrained I'm not sure it'll ever fully dissipate. And it's why my unsuccessful job search stings so much—no one has liked me enough to hire me.

It's also why Dev's comment about being unwanted struck me so hard. Because I know what it's like to not be wanted. From jobs to Jeremy to being the fragile-jointed younger sister who couldn't do anything without getting hurt. I know what it's like to be shoved to the side and what it's like to feel pushed out.

Dev's expression softens as he crouches in front of me, hands resting on the outsides of my ankles. "Mark doesn't hate you," he murmurs. "I promise."

I swallow hard, wishing I didn't care so much. "But he doesn't want me around. And he doesn't want me around *you*."

The way the corners of Dev's lips pull up in a knowing smile has my heart beating harder and a frown tugging on my own mouth.

"I think you know exactly what that's about."

I stop breathing and watch him. He tenderly brushes his thumbs across the skin of my ankles just above my socks, and the way his brown eyes have melted has my insides doing the same.

"I don't know what you mean," I lie, though my voice breaks, betraying my words.

Of course, Dev still humors me. "He's afraid I'll throw the agreement you and I have out the window. He thinks I'll make a move on you."

"That's not going to happen," I say, going for resolute, but it comes out as more of a whisper. "He has nothing to worry about."

"He thinks he does. And I'm not sure he's wrong."

My heart has found its way into my throat. "Dev . . ."

I'm not sure whether the universe is trying to help me or

conspire against me, but a knock on the door has me jumping, my ankles jerking out of his grasp.

"The engineers are ready to talk," a deep voice calls from the other side. "Can you be down in five?"

Dev scowls, and the lines of his throat work as he swallows. "Yeah," he calls back, sounding a little pained. "I'll be there." A beat passes before his dark eyes swing back to me, some of their previous openness gone. "Guess I have to go face the Judases."

I'm torn over how to respond. I could jump back into our previous topic, clear it all up now. But I'm afraid of what I'll let slip if the conversation goes back. I'm afraid I might tell him that Mark's fears are well-founded.

So I weakly joke, "Remember, no destruction of property."

And there it is, that all-consuming grin he's known for. All bright white teeth and a hint of his usual mischievousness in his eyes. "I promise nothing."

He rocks back on his heels and plants his hands on his knees before he pushes himself up, once again towering over me. I glance away, knowing I need to get back to the garage and all the stuff I left behind. But before I can move, Dev presses his fingertips beneath my chin and tilts my head up.

"Thank you," he says, his eyes holding mine. "Seriously. I needed this. I needed you."

My throat is so tight I'm rendered speechless. He makes these comments so lightly, tossing them out like he utters them all the time, but every one hits me with the impact of a sucker punch. Doesn't he understand that he can't talk like that? He can't make me feel like I'm firmly ensconced in the center of his world when I'm supposed to stay on the periphery.

"I'll always be here for you," I finally say. Because I'm no better. I may have gone too far, but I won't lie to him about this. And it seems as though he's decided the same.

He cups my cheek for a split second before his touch falls away, his smile so sweet and so personal that it only reinforces his statement.

We both know what we want. What we need. The only question is whether we're reckless enough to go after it.

CHAPTER 18

DEV

Nothing says *I love America* more than a party in London.

Location aside, every detail of the club screams it. A moment ago, I was almost smacked in the face by an eagle piñata, and I'm pretty sure George Washington is doing Jell-O shots at the bar. The chants of *USA! USA!* are bound to start at any second.

Beside me, Chava's salivating over the model-slash-waitress passing by wearing nothing more than a red-and-white-striped bikini bottom and glittery star-shaped pasties. I won't deny that I glanced, but only to confirm that I wasn't hallucinating. Buck's Fourth of July parties have always been tacky and wild, but damn, this is a whole new level.

"I think I might be overdressed," Willow says on my other side, touching the short hem of her dress. It's red and silky with thin straps crisscrossing over her back. The second she walked out of the hotel wearing it, I wanted to tug on one of those strings and drag her back to my room.

It's been two days since Buck ended my race prematurely because of his overinflated ego—and two days since I told

Willow in so many words that I was ready to dissolve our agreement to keep things professional. She understood what I meant, yet she hasn't brought it up, and I haven't pushed.

But I don't know how long I can keep acting like I'm not fully obsessed with this girl.

"You're perfect," I tell her, throwing out any hope of keeping my fixation under wraps. Might as well speak my mind now. Dropping my voice, I add, "Not that I'd mind seeing you in those pasties."

"*Dev*," she warns in a horrified gasp, her eyes swinging up to me. And while her expression is one of shock, the underlying spark in her gaze heats my blood.

"Not sorry." It's flippant and true, and I'm done being subtle. With one hand cupping her elbow, I put my other on Chava's shoulder to guide them both. "Come on, they've got a taco bar."

Chava makes a dreamy sound, finally tearing his focus away from the waitress. "Nothing more American than Mexican food."

"And it's probably the best we'll get in this country. Let's go."

Chava pulls away as we move toward the serving line, grabbing a plate and eagerly awaiting his turn. I move a little slower, my hand still on Willow's elbow. If she questions my need to touch her, I'll say it's because I don't want her to trip in her giant platform heels, though she's managed just fine so far. If she's had any joint issues or been in pain since we've been traveling, she hasn't mentioned it. Either she's doing better these days or she's keeping it from me.

"You feeling okay?" I ask her over the din of conversations and an AC/DC song blasting in the background.

She nods and leans into me a little, making my heart

stutter. I'm not sure she realizes she's doing it, like it's natural for her body to seek out mine. It gives me hope that I sure as shit shouldn't be feeling.

"Just a little tired," she admits, smiling softly, seemingly recovered from my pasties comment. "I don't know how you travel like this and still manage to race. My head's spinning."

As I consider my response, I shift so I can face her before I speak, but her body moves with me. She's not just leaning into me like I thought. No, she's redistributed most of her weight to her right side, which means I'm supporting her far more than I realized. She has her left hip popped out to the side slightly, as if she's trying to take the pressure off it. She's clearly in pain—and probably a lot of it.

"Let me take you back to the hotel," I tell her, giving her a once-over, searching for any other clues that give away her discomfort. "You don't need to be here if you're hurting."

She frowns up at me, straightening a little. "I said I was tired, not hurting."

"Wills." I level her with a stare. "You're obviously uncomfortable. We can leave right now. I'll call Mark on our way so he can be ready to work on your—"

"I'm fine," she interrupts and pulls her elbow out of my grasp so she's standing on her own in those ridiculous shoes. "I took an anti-inflammatory before we left, so it should be kicking in soon. But if I need to leave, I can do it on my own."

The hell she can. I'm not about to let her wander back up a steep flight of steps and out onto the London streets to fend for herself. She's staying where I can see her at all times so I know she's okay.

I'm about to tell her as much, but she doesn't give me a chance to argue. "You need to put in as much face time as possible tonight." She looks out into the crowd, her attention snagging on something behind me. Probably Buck and his Texas posse. "I still can't believe he didn't invite you to that dinner."

My protectiveness scales back a little at the reminder. On the plane yesterday, I told her about Reid's comment. She and I sat side by side and caught up, since I'd passed out the second I made it back to my hotel room after my meeting with the engineers the night before. It was a blessing, really, that I'd accidentally bailed on her. If I'd shared the information then, there's no way she would have slept peacefully that night. Pissed doesn't even begin to describe how angry she was when I finally spilled the details.

If she didn't get why I have to leave Argonaut before, she does now. And she wholeheartedly agrees. I have to find a team to take me on, because my time here is ticking away. If I'm not careful, I'll be left without a race seat next season.

It's not necessarily a death sentence. Plenty of drivers have disappeared for a year or two, even three, and made a successful comeback. But I don't want to take that risk. I don't want to step back and find myself forgotten. I haven't made a big enough impact on the sport to remain in the collective consciousness for long. I need to make a splash.

I need to win.

"It is what it is." I pick up a plate and hand it to her. "I'll look for Reid in a bit and see what information I can get out of him."

"You think he actually went to the dinner?"

I shrug and reach for the tongs at the first taco station. "No clue. But Buck is a hard man to say no to, even if you're not interested in what he's selling."

Willow lowers her voice as I place food on her plate, her attention fixed firmly on my face. "And you think he wants Reid to take your spot?"

"Not like he's going to take Nathaniel's."

She falls silent at that, her red lips pulling down in a frown. She doesn't even protest when I pile five tacos on her plate. I don't expect her to eat them all, and she doesn't, but she surprises me by eating three and a half once we find a table, though she broods the whole time.

I don't interrupt her, and Chava peeled off to eat with a group of mechanics, so I soak in silence until she finally pushes her plate away and turns to me.

"It's time to kick things into overdrive," she declares, her eyes lit with a determined intensity.

I smirk, but my pulse picks up a little. She's sexy when she's scheming. "I think I know a little bit about that."

She angles her body toward me, her posture straight like she's no longer in pain. The drugs have likely kicked in, and being off her feet surely doesn't hurt. Not to mention the distraction of having a problem to solve.

"It's time to get out there and socialize," she instructs. "Talk to Buck and everyone he's with. Talk to anyone who looks remotely important, even if you don't recognize them. *Especially* if you don't recognize them. You're done sitting in the shadows and keeping your head down. The scandal's over; we've made a ton of progress on your reputation. It's time to go on the charm offensive and get people back in your corner."

My smirk morphs into a grin. I love watching the way her mind works. She's a phenom, a genius at what she does. And goddamn if I'm not getting a little hard right now because of how passionate she is about this plan. About me.

"This is just the first step," she warns. "Get ready to *really* put yourself back out there, including doing the drivers' press conferences again."

Argonaut hasn't sent me to one since Jani's post went viral, even though teammates are supposed to trade off. They've been coming up with various excuses as to why I can't attend, like that I'm recovering from an ear infection, or that I've lost my voice after a meet and greet. I wouldn't be surprised if they told the press that a giant whale came out of the ocean and swallowed me whole—but don't worry, I'll be fit to race this weekend.

I haven't complained. Willingly setting myself up for invasive questions after Jani's big fuck-you? No thanks. I field plenty of those in the media pen after races already, though I can usually count on Patsy to quickly guide me away before things go too far south.

But if Willow gets her way, I'm going to have to face it head-on.

"Time to tell the world that Dev Anderson is back," she finishes, nodding slowly, resolutely.

"No, not that I'm back," I correct her, brushing my fingers over her temple as I tuck her hair behind her ear, unable to resist touching the source of her brilliance. Maybe a little will rub off on me. "I want them to know I never left."

Her eyes are alight, and her grin radiant. I don't think I've ever wanted to kiss her more.

"That's right," she says. "You never left."

▚▚▚▚▚

Willow meant what she said about kicking things into overdrive.

My social media engagement is up a wild amount. I'm in

talks for a new brand deal with a major fitness technology company. And a few mainstream media outlets have even contacted Howard about doing interviews. I'm not sure what kind of black magic Willow has been performing behind the scenes in the last couple of days, but it's working. My name is very much back in people's mouths—and none of the talk is negative.

Today, though, it's on me to play my part. I'm waiting in the wings at Silverstone for the drivers' press conference to start. In a few minutes, I'll share a couch with Zaid Yousef, Thomas Maxwell-Brown, Axel Bergmüller, and Reid Coleman. Zaid and Axel are in the midst of a heated battle for first place in the championship, so the questions lobbed today will likely be directed at the two of them. But damn if I'm not just as interested as the rest of the world to see the bitter rivals sitting side by side.

When Reid shows up, we do the hand-slap, back-pat thing, and he dutifully nods to the woman standing next to me. I swear, Argonaut's head of comms only smiles when her favorite Texas boy is around.

"Hello, Ms. Patsy." Reid's drawl is always a little more pronounced when he's speaking to a fellow southerner. "Doin' all right?"

Patsy beams up at him and pats his arm. "Doin' just fine, sweetheart. You taking care of yourself?"

"Yes, ma'am," he answers. "Best I can."

After a minute or two of idle chitchat between them, we're given the okay to enter the press conference room. By then, my stomach is twisted in knots. Based on this interaction alone, it's obvious that Patsy would rather have golden boy Reid to look after instead of me. I've gotta catch him alone after this to see whether he went to that dinner with Buck, since I didn't see him at the party afterward. If my time at Argonaut is already up, I need to know.

Reid and I are the first ones on the couch, waiting for the drivers who can get away with being late to join us. Thomas is the next to stroll in. He greets the reporters in attendance warmly before he joins us onstage and says hello in the most hilariously stereotypical British way. Once he's sitting on Reid's other side and they strike up a quiet conversation, I scan the small audience.

Patsy stands guard in the back, phone in hand to record the session so she can replay it later and nitpick my every word. But the person I'm looking for is next to Patsy, little pink notebook clutched against her chest and big brown eyes surveying the room.

Willow doesn't have her curls tied back in a ribbon like she usually does when she's dressed in full Argonaut regalia. No, today she's left them to tumble over her shoulders. All I want to do is twist one around my finger, preferably while she sits on my lap. I wouldn't even mind if it happened right here on this uncomfortable couch.

Every day it hits me a little harder, sinks in a little more— I'd do anything, anywhere, at any time with her as long as it meant I got to have her near me.

I'm distracted from my fantasies when another figure walks into the room. Zaid. He waves and quietly apologizes for his tardiness before stepping onto the stage. With a nod to the rest of us, he takes a seat next to Thomas. He's the only one on the couch not wearing a bold color or pattern. His T-shirt is the Mascort black and silver; the understated palette suits him.

For a second, I let myself imagine what it would be like to wear it, to race for a top-tier team, to actually be a contender for the championship. Hell, I'd even take being decked out in British racing green like Thomas and the McMorris team, currently fourth in the Constructors' Championship. Or if Scuderia D'Ambrosi would take me, I'd happily trade my red, white, and blue for just red. If Buck's offer is good enough to convince Reid to come over, maybe we can trade. It's aggressively wishful thinking.

When Axel walks in, I see the last of the top-tier colors—the navy and neon yellow of Specter Energy.

The man barely spares us all a glance as he moves to my side of the couch, motioning for me to scoot down with a tilt of his head. There's plenty of room at the other end, but he's not about to sit next to Zaid. With the ugly history between the two, the most time they're willing to spend together is when they're on the podium, trading off between the first and second steps.

They've been passing the Drivers' Championship back and forth over the last four years as well. Axel won last year after an incredibly close season. This season, Zaid is leading, but not by much. Their point totals are so close that it's anyone's guess who will be lifting the trophy this year. But, as always, I'm rooting for Zaid.

Reluctantly, I shift closer to Reid, who follows suit and moves toward Thomas. To his credit, Axel thanks me as he sits down, something he wouldn't have bothered to do when he was younger and somehow even more of a selfish asshole. Considering we came up through the Formulas together and we're the same age, I know him better than I care to admit. Reid and Thomas raced alongside us too. The four of us came into F1 in the same season as rookies, but while the rest of us were friendly with one another, Axel kept himself apart.

I can't fault him for it. There's no rule that says we have to be anything more than coworkers. He and I aren't friends. We never have been. And I doubt we ever will be, since his behavior off the track isn't exactly what I want to surround myself with. He can shout racial slurs in song lyrics far away from me.

Steven Watters, our interviewer, has been sitting patiently across from the couch, waiting for us to get settled. Now that we're all here, he turns to the cameras and the audience, introducing us and getting the show on the road.

As expected, most of the questions are directed toward Zaid and Axel on opposite ends, and every eye in the place hungrily bounces between the two. It's tense, considering they both DNF'd in the last race, thanks to a daring move from Axel gone wrong. They're lucky they walked away from it unscathed, but if their battle heats up any more, that might not be the case.

"Dev, coming over to you," Steven says several minutes in.

Heart rate accelerating a fraction, I pick up the microphone I haven't had to touch so far.

"We're all aware of your . . . *scandal* following the Australian Grand Prix. You deactivated your social media accounts after putting out a statement refuting the claims and went quiet for a while, but it seems you've made a return."

Good for him for not beating around the bush, though the stilted way he mentioned my *scandal* is almost laughable. If the guy wasn't so stuffy, I'd be facing a slightly more pointed question.

"I have, yeah." I relax into the couch and drape an arm across the back. "Life's boring when you don't have something to scroll through while sitting on the toilet."

The audience of reporters and team representatives titters and chuckles as Steven clears his throat, looking a little flustered by my response. "Right. Well. What prompted your return?" he asks, leading me back to the topic at hand.

With a glance at Willow and Patsy, I resolve to get back to the script. Patsy may scare the shit out of me most days, but I'm more concerned about disappointing Willow.

Once the crowd and the snickering drivers next to me settle, I clear my throat. "It was time," I say easily, though I'm careful to keep from sounding flippant. "I like sharing parts of my life with my fans and supporters. Social media has made that easy, and I've felt detached without it. Like I'm missing out on an important connection."

I take a breath and scan the crowd. "Look, I know the internet can be a lawless place. There are people waiting around every corner, determined to bully and tear others down. But there are some incredibly supportive people out there too. They're the ones who fuel me to keep pushing, to keep doing my best. I don't want to let them down, because I wouldn't be here chasing my dreams if it weren't for them in my corner. I want to fight for them. I want to give them my all."

That group also includes the girl across the room who's wearing a smile that lights up her entire face. How anyone could see it—see *her*—and not want to melt blows my mind. Just the sight makes me want to blurt out to the whole world that she's the reason I can sit on this couch without wanting to throw up from nerves. The topic of conversation isn't the most comfortable, but I'm doing it because she told me it's for the best.

And she's right. Without her encouragement, I'd still be hiding from the world.

"So yeah," I force myself to finish before I accidentally confess something I can't take back. "Prepare to be sick of me."

Another round of muffled laughter spreads around the room, but my attention lies firmly on Willow and the way she lifts a hand to her lips to cover her own laugh.

I don't look away from her as Steven moves on to Reid, and I only faintly register the question he asks about how Reid thinks D'Ambrosi will fare this weekend. Willow's staring right back at me, a question in her eyes, making it impossible to focus on anything else. I answer the look she's giving me with a wink. I barely notice the flashes in the crowd of photos being snapped, and I'm sure there will be a video clip of me online in no time.

But that's fine. Let them wonder who I'm trying to charm. All that matters is that she knows.

And that she understands that I'm not holding back anymore.

⬛⬛⬛⬛⬛

"Reid. Wait up."

He turns and steps aside in the hallway, waiting for me to catch up. We have fan signings to get to, but he waves off his own comms director so we can have a little privacy.

"I'm amazed Steven asked either of us a single question," he says once I'm leaning against the wall next to him. "They should have just called Zaid and Axel up today instead of making the rest of us sit through that rivalry bullshit."

"Agreed," I say, though I quickly lean in closer and drop my voice. Their rivalry isn't what I want to talk about. "Hey, I wanted to ask . . . did you go to Buck's dinner the other night?"

Reid shakes his head, leaving me simultaneously relieved and disappointed. "Nah, I had something else come up. Didn't go to the party either."

I blow out a breath. "Okay. Got it."

"Dev." He puts a hand on my shoulder and squeezes once. "I have no interest in going to Argonaut, no matter what Buck offers. I'm happy where I am, and"—he shifts his gaze to the hallway behind me and then over his shoulder—"between you and me, I'm about to sign a new deal with D'Ambrosi. I'm staying for three more years."

"No shit," I breathe out in shock. "That's amazing, man. Congrats."

He squeezes my shoulder again, leveling me with a hard stare. "You tell a soul, and I'll make what Jani did look like child's play."

"Your secret's safe with me."

We part ways a minute later, my head swimming. At least I don't have to worry about Reid taking my race seat. Buck will have to go back to the drawing board if he wants to find another American driver to partner Nathaniel, which will buy me a little time. It doesn't alleviate my fears, but it'll do for now.

I can take a breath, shallow as it might be.

And I take a deeper one when a soft hand lands on my arm.

"You ready to head out?" Willow asks, looking at me with a smile. "You were great up there."

I relax under her touch. This hint of contact is enough to soothe my frenzied thoughts for the time being. "Were my answers up to your standards?"

"They'll do," she teases, but she quickly sobers, her expression softening. "I'm really proud of you. This situation has sucked, but you're facing it now, and you're going to come out stronger because of it."

"*And* I'll be less of an asshole to the people who work for me," I joke. "Trust me. I never want this to happen again."

"You're not an asshole," she says, perfectly serious, making something in my chest twist. "You're human. We have our good days and bad. We put up with as much as we can until we can't take any more, and sometimes we react in less than perfect ways." She slides her hand down to mine and grasps my fingers. "But you're learning to do better and you're moving forward. That's why I'm proud of you."

Would she still be proud of me if I dipped my head and kissed her, right here, right now? Because that's all I want to do.

I want to taste the words on her lips. I know they'd be sweeter than honey, because everything about her is. That sweetness is sliding over me now, working its way into my veins, reinforcing the truth of what she's said. Making me want to live up to who she thinks I am.

"Thank you," I force myself to say. I want to tell her so much more. But this isn't the time or the place for a confession, even if shitty places—like back hallways in sketchy nightclubs and hotel stairwells—are where all our big moments have happened thus far. "You coming to the signing?"

I change the subject because if she says another kind thing to me, I might lose the last bit of control I'm hanging on to.

She nods. "I'll be out in the crowd taking some videos. Once we're through with the gratitude tour for the team, I want to focus on the fans. I might try to do some mini interviews with a few of them today." She shrugs, but she's undoubtedly in her element. "Who knows. We could end up with something great."

Just knowing she'll be there, watching and helping, is

enough to make the rest of the tension leave my shoulders. With her faith in me, I can face anything.

"Whatever you want to do," I say, "I support it."

She's beaming up at me now, and I swear my heart doesn't know what to do at the sight of it.

I'm down so fucking bad.

CHAPTER 19

WILLOW

With a week between races and no desire to fly back to North America, only to have to turn around and fly to Hungary a few days later, I'm back in Monaco—with Dev.

If we're going to push on with our plans to show other teams why they'd be lucky to snatch him up, we kind of need to be together. *Together* in the physical sense. Well, not *that* kind of physical, but physical as in being in the same place. Yeah. That.

The saving grace is that he's put me up in a hotel instead of insisting that I stay with him at his apartment. I have no doubt he was tempted to offer, but he was smart enough not to try.

In the last several days, the tension between us has been stretched taut, and it's threatening to snap. I've tried to keep my distance while still doing my job, no matter how difficult that's becoming. And *difficult* feels like an understatement at this point.

This past weekend at Silverstone, he started and finished eighth. Nathaniel, on the other hand, was forced to start from the pit lane because of a gearbox replacement, which meant the team had nothing to hold over Dev's head in order to make Nathaniel look better. Still, Dev used the slight from the week before as inner fuel to push as hard as he could, and seeing him do so made me want to work even more diligently. I'm determined to help get him out of Argonaut and to a team that actually deserves his talent.

But that means spending more time with him, and *that* means fanning the flames of my crush more fervently. I didn't think it could get any more intense, especially after the Fourth of July party and the way Dev winked at me at the press conference. And yet my heart swelled when he pointed me out to his fans for being the one behind some of their favorite videos of him, or when he smuggled a vanilla latte in for me before the full team meeting on Saturday because I'd been running late and hadn't had a chance to grab one.

I've been careful to keep my feelings firmly in the *crush* category, avoiding any other labels. Nothing like falling in love, even if that might be a more apt term for what I'm feeling. I can't let it be that serious.

Thankfully, he's given me some time to breathe and get a handle on my emotions, since he insisted I take a few days off over the break. And even better, it has coincided perfectly with the last-minute trip Grace planned after she called me on Friday night to ask where in the world I'd be next week— perks of having the summer off and no concerns about money.

So now the oxygen is being squeezed from my lungs as one of my best friends hugs me. Or maybe she's trying to kill me. I'm not quite sure.

"I missed you so much," Grace coos, somehow clutching me even tighter. "I've been so *bored*. I absolutely needed to go somewhere fun."

"You've been in Hong Kong," I point out once I manage to suck in a slight breath. "Objectively one of the coolest places on the planet."

She waves a hand, brushing off my comment and also giving me a much-needed reprieve from her embrace. "Yeah, yeah. It's a cool hometown, but still a hometown. But this place—" She sweeps the same arm to motion to the hotel we're standing in front of. "*This* is what I'm talking about. This is the vacation I needed."

"Don't get too excited," I warn her as we turn for the lobby. Behind us, an employee of the hotel is loading her luggage onto a cart. She's staying a week, but that didn't stop her from packing six bags. "I'm not exactly a high-rolling gambler, and I definitely don't have the budget to spend more than five seconds on a yacht."

That said, my paychecks from Dev and Argonaut have been eye-wateringly large. They'll be enough to keep me living comfortably in New York for the next year, even if I don't find another job after leaving this one.

The reminder that Dev and I will part ways at the end of August, just a month from now, makes my stomach lurch. The past several weeks have been some of the best and most exciting of my life. I'm going to miss the action and the thrilling pace of the sport—and I'm going to miss Dev.

Even knowing I won't see him again until the end of this week sends a wave of disappointment washing over me. Grace's presence takes the edge off the sting, but still, I just . . . miss him.

"So, have you fucked him yet?"

I blink in surprise and dart a look at Grace. One of her black brows is raised, and the smirk on her lips says she's got me all figured out.

"*Excuse* me?" I splutter.

She uses one perfectly manicured nail to circle my face. "That look. You were thinking about Dev."

"Was not," I say entirely too quickly to be believable.

"You *sooo* were." She pokes her finger into my forehead, grinning as I bat her hand away. "I know that look. You were thinking about a boy, and the only boy you're interested in is Dev. Thus, my question: Have you fucked him yet?"

I shush her, whipping my head around to make sure no one overheard her. "Keep your voice down," I hiss, grabbing her arm to drag her into the lobby with me.

"What?" she protests, taking one step for every two of mine. "It's a legit question. I need to know if I won that bet with Chantal."

I barely resist the urge to groan. "You're awful. And neither of you is winning."

"Are you saying you *don't* want to fuck him?"

This time, a few sets of eyes swing our way, and I quickly pull her into an alcove by the elevators for some semblance of privacy. "What I do or don't want doesn't matter," I say. My tone is firm, but my heart is thudding away and threatening to make my voice shake. "We're working together, and we don't need that kind of complication, or the backlash, no matter how we feel about each other."

She tilts her head, studying me. "So, the attraction is mutual then?"

Dev's voice echoes in my head, telling me how much he'd like to see me in pasties like that waitress was wearing. I nearly choked at the time, but it also sent heat shooting through me, making me seriously consider whether we'd be missed if I dragged him off to the nearest dark corner.

When I don't immediately reply, Grace goes on, twirling

a piece of her inky hair between her fingers. "I only ask because there's this clip of him going around right now. He's winking at someone in the crowd, and all the girlies are going wild over it. You wouldn't happen to know anything about that, would you?"

The question is deceptively innocent, but I know her game, and I won't be declaring that the wink was directed at me. "Not a thing."

"Huh. Shocking."

I roll my eyes, not wanting to play this game right now—or ever. "Come on," I grumble, grabbing her arm again to get her to the elevator. "Let's get you away from the general public."

She giggles but follows me willingly, a bounce in her step. "I better be a bridesmaid when you and Dev get married!"

▧▧▧▧▧

A few days later, I don't think there's a single street in Monaco I haven't seen.

Grace may not be from here, but she's the ultimate tour guide, and I have to respect the spreadsheet she made to make sure we didn't miss anything. We've checked off nearly all of it, but there are still a few spots we've yet to hit.

She's explaining our itinerary for the day as I swipe on some mascara, kneeling on the bathroom counter so that I'm tall enough to see myself in the mirror. This hotel suite was *not* made for those of us who stopped growing in fifth grade.

"After that we could hit up—" Grace cuts herself short, frowning in the direction of the bedroom. "I think your phone is ringing."

I glance down at the counter, looking for my phone among the makeup scattered over the surface. I could have sworn I brought it in here, but it's nowhere to be seen. Scrambling onto my feet, I right myself quickly and slip by Grace, who's hovering in the doorway of the bathroom. Hustling over to the bed, I discover that my phone is indeed lit up and buzzing.

"It's probably just Oakley," I tell her as I grab the device. We spent most of yesterday sending each other ridiculous F1 memes, which has been our primary method of communication lately. You can say a surprising amount about how you're feeling with a single photo of Thomas Maxwell-Brown's hilariously expressive face.

But surprisingly, it's not Oakley calling.

My heart surges into my throat when Dev's name flashes at me. I hesitate for a split second before dragging my finger across the screen, answering with an embarrassingly breathy "Hey."

"Hey," he replies. "I'm sorry to interrupt your morning, but I need you."

Again, I'm thrown by Dev's phrasing, and I lose the ability to speak for a beat. Thankfully, he continues, saving me from having to fight to find words.

"I know I said I could handle it myself, but I might need some help with this podcast," he explains, and I blow out a quiet breath. "When I do interviews, Patsy's usually hovering a foot away, making sure I don't say anything I shouldn't. And we both know I'm an idiot with no filter, so it might be a good idea to have someone close by to tell me when to shut up. Which means . . . would you mind being my Patsy today?" He pauses for a second, the words fast when he speaks again. "I mean, unless you already have plans. I know you have today off, so—"

"I'll happily be your Patsy," I interrupt with a laugh. "But just as a heads-up, one of my friends is in town, and—"

"Oh, shit, I'm sorry. Forget I even asked, Wills. Go have fun."

"No, no, it's fine," I reassure, eyeing Grace, who's watching me with a curious brow raised. "I just wanted to ask if it would be okay if she came with me."

"Of course. The more people to keep me from putting my foot in my mouth, the merrier."

I snicker, trying to fight a grin so that Grace doesn't start hounding me about Dev again. It's no use, of course. I can't help smiling. The second I hang up, I can expect a litany of lascivious comments to fly.

"Great, we'll see you soon," I say.

I've barely hit the button to end the call before Grace is throwing herself on the bed beside me.

"Am I about to meet Dev?" she demands, a sparkle in her dark eyes that I absolutely do not like.

I push up from the mattress and busy myself by packing my purse for the day. "If you embarrass me in front of him, I will never forgive you," I threaten. "Promise you'll be on your best behavior?"

Her smile is nothing short of Cheshire. "Oh, *absolutely*."

Thirty minutes later, I'm standing outside Dev's apartment door, my sweaty hand poised to knock, with Grace at my side. Before my fist can hit the solid wood surface—and before Grace can nag me again to hurry up—it swings open with a rush of air. And then there he is, hitting me with the full force of his smile.

"I'm so fucking glad you're here," Dev says, grateful eyes locking on me.

I think my response is intelligible, but my brain is short-circuiting at the sight of him.

Grace bumps me out of the way and stretches her hand out to him. "I'm Grace." She's practically buzzing. "It's nice to *finally* meet you."

I swear Dev's smile changes just a fraction as he focuses on Grace. It doesn't fade or shrink, and it doesn't come anywhere close to disappearing, but it's . . . different. It's the one meant for his friends and his colleagues and his family. It's different from the one when he's focused on me.

I'm too busy dwelling on what that means to focus on their conversation until we're inside the apartment and Grace announces, "Willow's been lost without you these last few days."

I whip my head around to her, horrified. I'm trying to splutter a denial out when she follows up the statement with, "Seriously, girl's a workaholic. She doesn't know how to relax."

The clarification pacifies me a little, but it doesn't stop my cheeks from flaming. "Yeah," I laugh, the sound choked. "I've been working on a few things. I couldn't help it."

"See? Doesn't know how to take a break to save her life," Grace goes on. She's quickly distracted by the race simulator set up in the corner of the living room. "Ooh, I *have* to try that."

As she scurries over and climbs into the low seat, I turn to Dev, offering an apologetic grimace. "I'm sorry for her. She has no filter."

Dev chuckles, slipping his hands into the pockets of his jeans. "Don't apologize." He's looking my way, but his focus is fixed on something over my shoulder. "I appreciate her honesty."

I can read between the lines on that. He and I certainly aren't being honest with each other these days. We're still dancing around the elephant in the room, watching it grow by the minute. Before long, we're either going to have to own up to how we feel or let it crush us under its giant feet.

"Plus, I don't want you burning out." He finally looks at me, a hint of worry in his eyes. "I feel bad about calling you on your day off."

I shake my head, but I do appreciate his concern. "It's fine. I'm happy to be here."

That's the truth. A few days apart has left me missing him more than I thought possible. I've tried to push thoughts of him aside and enjoy my time with Grace, but it's been difficult. So much of my life revolves around him right now. It's kind of hard *not* to think about him when my camera roll is filled with photos of him, when this city is full of Formula 1–related media and merchandise, and when all I want is to curl up in bed beside him again and giggle over a cheesy Bollywood movie.

Taking a quick breath to center myself, I nod toward where his laptop is sitting on the coffee table in front of the couch. "You ready to do this?"

The cheeky grin is back, the one that's just for me. "You ready to make sure I don't say anything that'll make my reputation worse?"

"Let's see what we can do."

By the time the interview is finished two hours later, Grace has crashed on the racing simulator about sixty times, and

I've nearly cried off all my makeup from laughing at Dev's out-of-pocket—but never offensive, cruel, or incriminating—answers. Dev, of course, has managed to charm the hell out of yet another group of people.

His quick banter and quips with the Australian hosts made the hours feel like minutes, keeping me so entertained that I almost forgot I was there to prevent him from saying anything he shouldn't. Turns out, he didn't need me at all. The man has had enough media training and has done enough interviews to know what he should and shouldn't do. I was essentially a spectator. Not that I minded; it only proved that my crush isn't misplaced. Dev is more than worthy of any and all adoration.

"Well, that wasn't as much of a shit show as I thought it would be," he announces after closing his laptop. With his arms raised in a stretch, he drops back against the couch cushions.

It's a challenge to keep myself from inspecting the expanse of skin revealed between the top of his jeans and the hem of his black T-shirt or the lines of his biceps straining against the sleeves. God, he's gorgeous. And, thankfully, seemingly unaware of my attention.

Unfortunately, Grace notices me noticing Dev, and her wicked expression tells me we're absolutely going to have a conversation about this once we're out of here.

"You did so well," I say to him, ignoring Grace as I tuck my notebook and phone back into my purse. I snapped a few pictures of him that I've already posted, and I've made notes of some of his responses so I can pull clips from the podcast once it's live. "They'll probably have to edit out my cackles in the background. But that just proves people are going to love it."

Dev grins back at me, eyes following my every move as I stand and smooth my sundress around my hips. "As long as I made you laugh," he says, slowly dropping his arms back down. "That's all that matters."

Grace makes a faint choking sound from across the room, but I refuse to look in her direction.

Dev either doesn't notice or is choosing to ignore her too. Though judging from the way he's staring up at me like I'm the only other person in the room, I'm putting my money on the former.

It's thrilling and unnerving and has me quickly gathering my things and inventing a fake lunch reservation that Grace and I are in danger of being late to. If I don't make my escape now, I'm bound to do something silly like crawl into his lap, wrap my arms around his neck, and gush about how great he is. His ego doesn't need that, and I certainly don't need to encourage the butterflies flitting through my stomach, so I grab Grace by the elbow and wave goodbye before tugging her out of Dev's apartment.

We make it into the elevator before she steps in front of me, hands on her hips. "Girl," she says. And then again, more emphatically: "*Girl.*"

I slump against the steel wall behind me. I'm going to need the support for this conversation. "Yes?"

"You know he didn't need help, right?" She regards me with a hard stare. "He just wanted to see you. And make you laugh."

She's right, but I'll never live it down if I admit it. "I'm sure that's not true."

"Willow." Any traces of humor are gone from her voice. "The way that man looked at you when he opened the door? I've never seen anyone light up like that."

Again, she's right. There's no point trying to deny it. But saying it out loud means it's no longer just a fantasy or a simple delusion. Grace has noticed, which means I'm not making it up—and *that* means my ability to keep from acting on my feelings for Dev is practically gone.

"That's just how he is," I argue weakly. "Literally, he's known for having the world's best smile."

"I'm not talking about his smile. I'm talking about his entire reaction to you. Just the way he—" She shakes her head, then levels me with a no-nonsense look. "I get that you want to keep things professional. And I get that we as women have to tolerate being slapped with ugly names and labels when we get involved with men in positions of power. And I even understand that you don't want to jeopardize your brother's friendships. But, Willow, if you let that man slip away . . . then you're a coward."

As if to punctuate her words, the elevator shudders to a stop on the ground floor. My world feels like it's been rocked by an earthquake.

"Go get what you want," Grace finishes. "And don't let yourself regret it."

CHAPTER 20

DEV

It's raining.

No, not just raining, it's absolutely pissing down, and right now, the Hungarian circuit resembles a shallow lake. If things clear up, it's possible we can race, but for now, all we can do is sit and wait for the rain to end.

"Go fish."

"Fuck!"

From my quiet corner, I snicker, chin tucked to my chest, trying not to draw attention to myself while the bored pit crew plays children's card games in the middle of the garage. I chose to sit this round out, but that doesn't mean I wasn't dominating the Uno game that came before this.

Nathaniel has disappeared to places unknown, avoiding everyone as always and not making any friends. Good thing he doesn't have to; as long as his daddy's in charge, his seat is safe.

Unlike mine.

I no longer care about fighting for my place with Argonaut, but I'll work hard to stay on good terms with the vast majority of people here. So many of them have actually helped me—my mechanics and engineers, the entire support staff, even Konrad, who's currently shoving his camera in my face. They all deserve my best, and I'm not about to let them down.

Speaking of people I don't want to let down, Willow moves in from the back of the garage with Patsy by her side. For once, Patsy is actually smiling, and she's got a hand on Willow's shoulder as if commending her. Whatever it is, it's well deserved.

The podcast episode Willow arranged for me was released three days ago, and from the snippets I've heard and the comments I've seen online, the response has been mind-blowing. It's as if people actually *like* me again. Not that they should have stopped in the first place, but she's brought me back from the brink, and I'm once again sitting pretty in the court of public opinion. It's a miracle.

No, that's wrong. It's not a miracle. It's not an otherworldly phenomenon. It's Willow and her brilliant brain.

The praise she's getting now is only a drop in the bucket of the veneration she's owed. But I want to be the one to give it to her. If she'll let me.

And that's the problem. I don't know if she will.

"What's with your face?" Konrad asks me, sounding vaguely disgusted as he pops out from behind the camera. "Why do you look like you might puke?"

All right, cool, so my *lovesick* ass looks literally *sick* at the idea that Willow may not reciprocate my feelings. That's good to know.

Konrad moves off when I don't give him an answer, hopefully assuming that I look like this because I'm apprehensive about the race. Honestly, the rain doesn't faze me, and I take a massive risk every time I climb into the car anyway. So, racing on a wet track, while objectively more dangerous than a dry one, doesn't make me anywhere near as nervous as watching Willow walk toward me does.

The scent of pure, sweet vanilla hits me as she slides over and stands close, surveying the rest of the garage and the pit lane outside the door. There's a soft crease between her brows, and her deep brown eyes are a little wider than usual as they swing to me.

"Do you think they're going to cancel the race?" she asks.

It takes me a second to register her words. I'm too distracted by the mere sight of her and the way my heart thumps erratically in my chest.

Even the horrible Argonaut uniform can't hide how stunning she is, but my sunshine girl never notices the stares that follow her—and plenty do. I've seen several of the mechanics watch her breeze by, although a pointed glare from me usually encourages them to get back to work.

Everyone knows she's off-limits, which probably means there are rumors about why. As long as they aren't the reputation-destroying kind, I can live with them. I just hope she can too.

At her question, I spare a glance over at the engineers, who are watching the weather radar on their screens. I'm no meteorologist, but it seems like the front is moving on from the circuit. "Doesn't look like it."

Right on cue, Sturgill strides across the garage and starts barking orders as he returns to his station. A second later, a message from race control flashes on one of the engineer's screens. He reads it out loud, proclaiming the delay will end in fifteen minutes.

It's time for me to get to it.

Before I can tell Willow as much, her hand is on my shoulder, squeezing softly. "Be careful out there, all right?"

There's worry in her eyes, but it's nearly overshadowed by a sheen of hopefulness, of reverence. She understands and respects the risk I'm taking, and she's concerned for my safety, yet her expression is full of pure faith in my abilities. She believes I'll go out there and come back to her in one piece, because I'm excellent at what I do.

"I'm always careful," I tease, but I quickly sober and put a hand over hers to drive my words home. "I promise I will be. Besides, you're my good luck charm."

She shakes her head and kisses her teeth, pulling her hand back, though not before pinching the side of mine in retribution for the comment. "Haven't brought you very much luck so far, but okay," she says, sighing in resignation. "Go get 'em, tiger."

This is going to be chaos.

After one formation lap and five seconds of sitting in my grid box, that's obvious. There's no way there won't be carnage. Two cars spun out on the way to the grid. One of them crashed, ending his race before it could begin. The other recovered, though a move like that would rock the confidence of even the most self-assured driver. He won't be willing to take risks and will probably be at the back of the pack by the end of lap one.

Me? I have seven cars to fight my way past and zero plans to hold back. If there's a single bright spot that comes from being with a team that barely develops their car from year to year, it's that I know its limits. I know what I can and can't get away with on a track this slick. And if there's one thing this hunk of carbon fiber does well, it's race in the rain.

I tighten my grip on the steering wheel, watching the red lights above me come on one by one before going dark.

I hit the gas, surging out of my box, and keep right down the straight as the cars ahead weave in and out. An Omega Siluro slows in front of me, forcing me left into the gap that miraculously appears when I need it.

That's when disaster strikes.

Not for me, though, because today clearly is my day.

The massacre I predicted is playing out, but it's worse than I thought. In a split second, a Mascort takes out a McMorris, then a Specter Energy car collects a D'Ambrosi on its way to the runoff area. I manage to maneuver around and through, avoiding and swerving, and then . . .

No. What the fuck? What the actual *fuck*?

I'm in second.

It's only Zaid ahead of me, the spray from the back of his car distant enough that it's not impeding my visibility. Of the top six, it looks like he was the lone driver to escape the mayhem. I can't see much in my mirrors as I round the next turn, but I can certainly see the scuffle for position and the debris that continues to fly. Shit, when I make it back around the circuit, I'll have to dodge all of it to avoid ruining my tires.

"Could be a safety car soon," Branny warns over the radio. Then, less than five seconds later, he declares, "Safety car deployed. Watch your speed. And you're in P2. Very nice job getting through that."

Never one for overenthusiastic praise, that man, but I'll take what I can get.

"Can you give me an update on the cars behind?" I need

to know who I'm going to have to fight in order to keep this position. Because now that I'm up here, I'm not giving it back.

He reads off the next five cars, but Reid, Otto, Thomas, Lorenzo, and Axel aren't on the list. Fucking hell. *All* of the top runners, save Zaid, were taken out. There's a possibility some of them might recover and rejoin, but this is my chance. If I just hold on, I have a shot at the podium. The safety car will make that tough, though. The reduced speed will bunch up the pack and give the racers behind me the opportunity to regroup and catch up. And if there's a red flag—

"And that's a red flag," Branny says. "Box now. Line up in the pit lane."

My stomach sinks a little. If it's a standing restart, I could fall into the midfield again and lose my chance at a podium. "Copy."

I do as I'm told, following Zaid into the pit lane and lining up behind him, watching as the teams' mechanics rush out with tire blankets.

"I'm going to get out of the car if that's all right."

Branny approves my request and tells me to stay close. We'll get a warning before the restart, but I need to shake off some of the adrenaline the race start and being in P2 has brought me.

One of the mechanics helps me out, and another brings over an umbrella as I take off my helmet and balaclava, even though I'm already soaked. From what I can tell, the rain has nearly stopped, and with as hot as it is today, even with that torrential downpour, the track is going to dry quickly.

And that means we have to get rid of these slow-ass wet-weather tires and switch to the faster slick tires ASAP.

I stop at the pit wall to check the weather screens and tell Branny and the race strategists what I'm thinking, then head into the garage, seeking one person. Mark tries to catch me as I come in, but I wave him off and make a beeline for the back corner. Some of the tension floods from my shoulders when I spot her, and I swear she looks just as relieved to see me.

It takes everything in me not to gather her in my arms, although I can't resist the urge to run a hand down her arm and pull her a little closer. I dip my head to her ear as if I'm trying to have a private conversation. There are cameras around, so if we're caught on film, it'll look perfectly innocent. Which it is . . . even if there's nothing particularly innocent about the way I feel standing this close to her.

I don't actually need to talk to her about anything. All I want is to be close, to bask in her presence and let her bring me back from the sharp edge of realism that I probably won't keep P2 for long. I need a reminder that I can do this, even if the odds are stacked against me. From her, all it takes is a glance and a smile, and a surge of confidence reemerges.

The look she gives me is one I've come to crave. One I'll miss far more than I could have imagined possible when our time together is up.

Big brown eyes meet mine, and there isn't a shadow of doubt behind them. She believes I can do this. That I can do anything. It fills me up. Convinces me that she's right, that I *can* do anything, including win this race, even if there's a seven-time world champion in front of me.

"Think you can give me a pep talk?" I request, though I don't really need one now.

Her laugh has my heart racing and a grin spreading across my face. I'd do anything to keep hearing that sound.

"Okay, let's see what I can do." She takes a deep breath, then launches into it. "I watched you and Oakley compete in this one karting race when you were fourteen. It was raining, and I was so upset that my dad dragged me along that weekend, because I was stuck wearing this ugly plastic poncho the whole time. The thing covered up my outfit—one that I'd picked out in the off chance that you'd notice me."

I blink at her confession and pull back a little so I can look her in the eye, but she grips my arm, keeping me where I am.

"Not that you ever did," she goes on, her tone full of humor. I'm dying to see it on her face, but she hasn't loosened her hold. "But that doesn't matter. What matters is that I forgot all about my ruined outfit and my terribly frizzy hair as soon as you shot off the line like there wasn't a drop of water on the ground. You had zero fear. Oakley, on the other hand, played it safe. He finished fourth. But you won."

Contrary to what Willow thinks, I was scared shitless the whole time, but I refused to let that stop me. I learned young that I could feel the fear and still drive hard.

"I know you're still that fearless fourteen-year-old," Willow continues, strong and certain. "So, go back out there and drive like it. Go win."

Finally, she drops her hand from my arm and lets me pull back. I study her open expression, the dimples peeking out from both cheeks even though her smile is small and a little bashful.

There's a wash of red on the high points of her sun-kissed face, but her eyes are alight. There isn't a touch of shame or embarrassment there. She's aware of the implications of that story, acknowledging the crush that never went away, and it's taking every ounce of strength I have not to kiss her and show her that crush is anything but unrequited now.

"Fuck, that might be the best pep talk I've ever gotten," I admit, my voice a little raspy from the effort of holding back.

She gives a mock curtsy, her dimples deepening as she grins. "Always happy to help."

I hope she means that, because I don't think I can live without it now. I don't think I can live without her.

"Restart in fifteen!" rings out from behind me, and I'm dragged back to reality, forced to leave the bubble of happiness. "Standing start!"

I exhale, knowing I need to get my head back in the game. But I'm more confident now than I have been in years.

"I better get back out there," I say, though I don't let go of her arm.

Willow nods, not pulling out of my grasp. "Guess you should."

"Not going to tell me to be careful this time?"

She wrinkles her nose, and goddamn if it doesn't make me want to press my lips to hers even more. "Nah. You know what you're doing."

"Yeah. I'd say I do."

There's a beat of quiet between us as I try to convince myself to leave, though it's not the least bit awkward or weird. Finally, I shoot her a wink and take a step back.

That's all it takes for me to be swept back up in the madness. But I'm freshly determined, and I've got my eyes set on the podium.

I make my way out to the pit lane but frown at the intermediate tires on the car. They're far better than the full wets, but they're not what I asked for.

"I said I wanted slicks," I call out when I reach the pit wall.

One of the strategists shakes his head, turning in his seat to face me. "Dev, that's not—"

"Give me the slick tires." I'm not asking anymore. I won't

let these people fuck up my chances. Not this time. "I know this track, and the sun's already out. If we're going to maintain our stop strategy and keep P2, you need to put me on slicks *now* instead of waiting."

"Mascort is sending Zaid out on inters," he argues. "The only ones daring to go with slicks right now are the ones who have nothing to lose and are willing to take that risk."

"Yeah, well, I'm willing to take it too."

He pauses, carefully assessing me. My jaw is set and my hands are planted on my hips. I'm not backing down from this. He can fight me, but deep down, he knows I'm right. They all do. It's about whether they're willing to take the risk with me.

"Fine, all right." The strategist sighs, leveling me with a hard stare. "But if you crash, the blame lies solely with you. Be careful what you ask for."

꒰꒰꒰꒰꒰

Sitting in the P2 grid box is absolutely surreal. It's almost hard to remember the last time I was this far up—what it was like to have nothing but a beautifully clear straight in front of me.

There's one thing I definitely remember, though. I may not have won an F1 championship yet, or even a race, but I'm an F3 and F2 champion in my own right. And champions never forget how it feels to win.

I was right about the track surface. The small, dark patches of wet tarmac shrink before my eyes as I wait for the remaining cars to finish the formation lap. But there's a very likely chance that I could catch one of those patches and spin out, especially on these tires.

Passing Zaid is going to be the challenge of my life, but he's starting on intermediate tires. They're not going to last long, and he'll undoubtedly pit early. The only question is, will I be far enough ahead to maintain P1 when he does?

The lights go out once again, and I'm off the line nearly faster than Zaid, but he has a better getaway and I have to yield the first corner. We're back on equal footing as we come out of it, battling for position as I fend off the cars behind. But down the next straight, I pass him—without the aid of DRS—all because of the tires.

I've just passed Zaid fucking Yousef, my idol and the man I could only dream of being like. He's a seven-time champion for a reason, though. Even with terrible tires, he still has more skill, more experience, and a better car, and he's immediately back on me.

But the track is too dry for inters, and he falls back just a little, trying to find clean air, when we hit the next corner. He'll have to pit soon, and he'll lose time because of the tire change. He'll probably come out behind several other cars, if not dead last. It'll take a hell of a lot to make up those places, and if I can push harder and expand the gap, I can win this.

Just as I expected, Zaid dives into the pit lane when we make it back around, and my next competitor is already several seconds behind, probably thanks to their unfortunate tire choice as well.

"Okay, Dev, you're leading the race," Branny says in my ear. His voice is a little higher than usual, like he can't believe it.

I can't even blame him. The last time I had no one in front of me, I was winning my last F2 championship. But to lead my first F1 grand prix? God, I hope they can't hear me laughing over the radio.

Still, I keep my head down and push. As the laps fly by, Zaid slowly works his way back up the field. I pit for new tires on lap thirty-seven, one lap after Reid—who was previously the closest man behind me—does. The stop is blazingly fast, and I come back out ahead of Reid again, though I'm stuck behind a McMorris that's yet to pit. Sure enough, two laps later, it heads for the pit lane, and I'm once again the race leader.

Fortunately, it's difficult to pass on this circuit. And because of that, I actually have a chance to win. I just need to expand the gap between Reid and me and defend like I never have before once Zaid undoubtedly makes his way back up.

I can do this. I can win.

Branny continues to give me updates on driver positions and my lap times, guiding me through it all. Everything is going perfectly—even if none of this was in Argonaut's plan. A win might not change much for them, but it absolutely does for me.

The future's looking brighter than ever.

The moments after I cross the finish line in first are a blur.

There's the chaos of congratulations over the radio while I navigate my way to parc fermé and come to a stop behind the first-place sign I thought I might never see again. There's the crush of my team as I join them by the barrier meant to keep them back. I'm fielding shouts and back slaps and hugs so aggressive that I'll probably have a cracked rib or two after this. I catch a glimpse of Willow's curls in the crowd, but I can't get to her, no matter how hard I try. And fuck me if I'm not doing everything I can.

Then there are officials leading me away to be weighed and guiding me to the postrace interview. I thank the team and my family, and I'm pretty sure I don't say any swear words, but I'll have to watch the playback later to actually know what happened. Then it's the cooldown room with Zaid and Reid. I shake their hands and take in their commendations, but I'd be hard-pressed to remember their exact words.

But on the podium, everything comes into sharp focus.

I did it. Five years in Formula 1, over one hundred race starts, and I'm finally here. The American national anthem plays, representing both Argonaut and me. I've never loved the song more.

Champagne rains down as Reid and Zaid point their bottles in my direction, and I spray them in return, laughing so hard I'm not sure if the moisture dripping down my face is champagne or tears. This is it. This is what I've worked for, and now that I've had a taste, I want more. But for now, I'll let this be enough.

We pose for pictures when the bottles are empty, then I'm being ushered off the podium and directed to get cleaned up before I'm needed for interviews. I can't wipe the grin from my face—not that I'd want to—as I make my way through corridors and back to the motorhome, cheering with everyone I come across on the way. I want Willow to be one of them, but I still haven't found her. She's the first person I'll seek out once things settle down. This win is hers too.

The adrenaline wanes as I make my way up the steps to my driver room. Mark trails after me, but after hugging him tight, I promise that he can work on me later. For now, I need a chance to sit and savor this alone.

I did it. I really fucking did it.

As he heads off, I open the door to my room—and promptly freeze.

The pictures catch my attention first. On the wall across

from me is a collage of photos. Some are of me, some of fans wearing my number, some of my family at my karting races when I was a kid. Then there are the letters and posters, all handwritten, all cheering me on, all showing the sheer force of the belief these people have in me. There's even a portrait of me, done in a modern style with flashy colors. My smile, of course, is the most prominent feature.

But it's Willow kneeling below all of it, still setting things up, that has my heart beating harder than I ever thought it could.

She turns with wide eyes and a soft gasp when the door opens. The photo in her hand slips to the ground as she climbs to her feet, using the massage table next to her for leverage, but then she twists her fingers nervously in front of her.

"I thought you'd be gone longer," she says, a slight waver in her voice and a hesitant smile. "It's not done yet, but I . . . wanted to surprise you."

My throat is tight, locking in the words I want to say. I'm dehydrated from the hot race, sure, but that's not what's rendered me speechless. This is all because of Willow.

"You did all of this for me?" I finally choke out, scanning the space, then settling my focus on her again. "What if I hadn't won?"

"I've had this planned for a while," she admits, still twisting her fingers, but her smile is growing. "This isn't a shrine to your win or anything. I just wanted you to see how loved you are by so many people. I wanted to remind you of why you should keep fighting for what you want."

I appreciate the sentiment, undoubtedly. But my reason to keep fighting is standing in front of me.

Maybe it's the lingering adrenaline. Maybe it's the recklessness that flows through my veins. Or maybe it's merely the sight of her. But whatever it is, it sends me striding toward her before I can think twice.

I stop when we're toe to toe. I'm so close she has to crane her neck to look up at me. Her gaze is uncertain but hopeful, like she's prepared for me to let her down gently but wishing for more. I'll give her whatever she wants.

"I love it," I tell her, though the *it* is nearly a *you*. "It's perfect."

She exhales, soft and a little unsteady. She opens her mouth like she wants to say something, but the words die on her tongue when I curl my hand around the back of her neck.

"You're perfect," I murmur.

I drop my gaze to her mouth, then flick it back up. When the look in her eyes goes from unsure to expectant, I don't waste any more time. I've squandered enough of it already.

I kiss her.

CHAPTER 21

WILLOW

Dev's lips on mine feels like a win of my own.

He did the hard work, yet I'm reaping the reward, even if it's not the prize I anticipated. But this is absolutely what I want. What I've wanted for a long, long time.

So I kiss him back.

His tongue brushes mine, and my body hums in response. He tastes sweet, like the electrolyte drink he downs after every race, a hint of cherry and something else I can't place. It's a reminder of the feat he's just pulled off, and a fresh wave of joy rolls over me.

He did it. He won. And he did it with an unreliable car and a team that doesn't support him the way they should. It's a victory he deserves to celebrate in any way he wants. And if it's me he wants . . .

His stubble scrapes against my skin, and I sink my fingers into his sweat-damp hair to pull him closer. A groan rumbles low in his throat as he hauls me to him, hands firm on my waist, possessive, his touch nearly searing. I grip him tighter, holding him to me, possessive in my own right, not wanting to give this up.

Only, this can't last. It was never meant to, as proven by the end date of our arrangement. And maybe this is part of that—a perk of the job. It, too, will end when we walk away from each other. More likely, it ends when one of us walks out that door.

I push those thoughts aside and focus on the here and now, like the way his mouth slants greedily over mine. I tilt my head in invitation and melt into him, shivering as his hands wander from my waist and brush under my breasts, to the slight fullness at the sides. Goose bumps follow his course up to my collarbones and neck. He finishes the journey by cradling my face so tenderly I can't help but let out a little sigh. It's both a plea for more and gratitude for his gentleness. He knows how to handle me, knows what I like. He even seems to know, as he slows his movements and eases up, that if this lasts any longer, I won't be able to resist taking this further.

His last kiss lingers, somehow sweeter than the rest, and he strokes my cheekbones with his thumbs as I slowly wake from the dream.

"I've been wanting to do that again since last year," he murmurs, his lips a whisper away from my own.

I release my hold on his hair and slide my hands to his chest, fingers curling into his race suit. I'm still lightheaded and kiss-drunk, so I ask the question without a second thought. "Then why didn't you?"

His mouth pulls up at the corner. "I'm pretty sure we both decided it was a bad idea."

I swallow hard, but I don't let him go, even if reality is pressing in again. "You're right. We did."

My stomach sinks an inch at a time. The end is already here. We're about to pull away from each other and once again agree this was a heat-of-the-moment thing. That it meant nothing, even if we both know that's not true.

Except Dev's hands don't leave my face, and the flash in his eyes tells me he's not going to lie about what's happening.

"If this is such a bad idea," he says, his voice tight, "then tell me why I want to kiss you again. Why I can't get you out of my head. Why, every time I see you anywhere near another man, I want to drag him away from you and make sure he never comes close to you again. Tell me, Willow. Tell me why I feel that way."

My throat constricts as he stares down at me. The burning passion in his gaze makes me want to push up onto my tiptoes and kiss him once more just to get him to close his eyes. He can't look at me like that, or we'll make choices that can't be taken back.

Instead, all I can do is whisper, "I don't know."

He releases his hold on my face and lets out a heavy breath, dropping his head back before righting it again. But he doesn't step away. He settles his hands on my waist, keeping me close. His message is clear. He's not about to let me walk away.

And I don't plan to go anywhere. I'm not ready to reach the end of this.

"Then tell me how *you* feel," he urges, a faint note of desperation in his tone. "Tell me I'm not the only one going crazy."

He must already know how I feel. But maybe we both need to hear it again to believe it. "It's not just you."

He presses his forehead to mine and shakes his head just a little, like he can't believe this is the situation we've found ourselves in, even though he's the one who made the move—the one who once again changed everything for us. "*Fuck*, Willow."

"I know," I whisper, tightening my grip on him.

His jaw works as he takes in several steady breaths, his fingers pressing into my back. The pressure keeps me grounded at a time when I could easily float away.

"I know this . . . this is a lot," he finally says. "But I don't want you to decide later that this was a mistake. It wasn't for me. And it wasn't the last time either."

I don't regret calling it a mistake. It was the right thing to do, the right way to play things back then, but I can't say the same now.

"This isn't a mistake." It's the truth, but it's not as simple as that. "But I don't know what any of it means."

We can let out all our long-held secrets, make all these confessions, but they don't matter if we can't figure out where and how things go from here.

Dev draws back enough to look in my eyes. "It means I don't want to pretend it's easy for me to stay away from you. I'm done acting like I don't want to be near you every second I can." He sweeps my hair over my shoulder, fingers lingering on my nape. "I like you, Willow. So much that sometimes I forget what's supposed to be keeping us apart."

He might, but I can't. My brother, this job, the risk of relationships and reputations ruined . . . There's so much at stake. And yet that doesn't stop me from saying, "I like you too. A lot."

His smile turns teasingly smug, but I can practically feel the excitement thrumming under his skin at my admission. "Yeah, I kind of knew that. I mean, you *did* already drunkenly confess your feelings for me."

I scoff to cover a laugh. "Shut up."

The humor he's brought to the moment makes some of my worries drift away. It's like we're ourselves once again. Dev and Willow, class clown and the girl trying not to laugh at all his jokes.

He twirls one of my curls around his finger, his grin back but his gaze still soft. "Nah, if I shut up, then I can't tell you how much I wish I hadn't let you walk away from me back then. I should have gone after you."

I shake my head. "I wouldn't have listened. I was too embarrassed."

"What about now?" He searches every inch of my face. "Still too embarrassed?"

"No. Not in the slightest."

He's leaning in again, and this time I'm ready for the kiss. So I close my eyes and tilt my head back, waiting for his lips to graze mine.

But a loud knock on the door has me rearing back. Dev doesn't let me go far, though. He reacts quicker than I can, looping an arm around my waist, keeping me to him. It's like he's not concerned that the person on the other side of the door could burst in and catch us like this.

Thankfully, he's right. Only a voice floats through, telling Dev that he's needed for interviews.

Over my head, he responds, and then he dips his chin again to look at me. "They love to interrupt us, don't they?"

Glancing away, I force a chuckle at his joking comment. I don't find the idea of getting caught very funny.

Dev cups my jaw, prompting me to look at him again. "Hey," he says softly, the humor gone. "We'll talk more about this later, all right?" He waits until I nod slightly before continuing. "I have to get back to the team, but this isn't me walking away from you. Clearly, there's something between us. And we have to figure out where it goes from here."

I nod, swallowing hard. "We do."

"We will." His lips find mine for a parting kiss that leaves me breathless. "Go back to the hotel," he murmurs, drawing back just far enough to say the words. "Get changed. We're going out tonight."

"I saw the race!" Chantal screams when she picks up my call. "I can't believe your boy won!"

I breathe out a laugh, imagining her jumping up and down in our apartment while I'm getting ready alone in another nondescript hotel room. I miss her even more now that I have something major to tell her.

"Yeah, it was a big surprise," I say, cradling the phone between my ear and my shoulder as I paw through my suitcase, searching for an outfit to wear tonight. "Hey, are you . . . are you busy right now? I can call back later."

"Pfft, as if I've got anything better to do." Something that sounds like a chip bag crinkles in the background. She must be settling in to get caught up on *Love Island*. Normally, I'd be right there with her. "Hit me. What's up?"

I've been dying to talk to her about what happened with Dev since the second he stepped out the door of his driver room, leaving me to press my fingers to my swollen lips and replay the memory. It was . . . amazing. Fantastic. I felt absolutely schoolgirl giddy, but what comes next makes me anxious. Undoubtedly, I need a second opinion. I'll probably force Grace to go through it all with me, too, once she answers my texts.

"I . . ." How the hell do I even start this conversation?

"Dev, he . . ." I take a shuddering breath. Fuck it, I just need to get it out there. "Dev and I kissed today," I blurt.

Her gasp is followed by shocked silence that lasts so long I worry the call got disconnected. But nope, she's still on the line when I pull the phone back to check. And I'm glad I do, because her shriek a second later might have burst my eardrum if I hadn't.

"I *knew* it would happen!"

I wait another beat before putting her on speakerphone, setting the device next to my suitcase and sitting cross-legged in front of it. "Yeah, you and Grace called it," I mumble, still in disbelief that it happened. "I probably should have listened to you guys in the first place."

It might have saved me some restless nights and days of pining if I hadn't insisted that Dev and I keep things strictly friendly. But honestly, I don't regret the path we've taken, because it means we've both had time to think about it. To let our feelings grow without the pressure of knowing that this was on the horizon. I like how we got here. I like how we've found our way to each other. It feels right, even if we have a lot of details to work through.

"I'll forgive you for this misstep," Chantal teases. "So, are you done acting like you two aren't in love with each other?"

My face flames, and I freeze with my hand on a pile of dresses. "I—I wouldn't go *that* far," I stammer. "But . . . I don't think we're just friends anymore."

Her voice is softer when she speaks again. "You haven't been for a while, babe."

She's not wrong. We've been dancing around our feelings for ages now. But am I ready to give in to the pull, the magnetism, that exists between us?

"I don't even know what I *want* from him," I confess to

her. "A onetime hookup to get this out of our systems? A friends-with-benefits situation? An actual relationship?"

Saying the options out loud makes everything feel a little too real. As anxiety rises in my chest, I barrel on. "Maybe a hookup is all this can be. Once my contract is finished, he'll still be traveling around the world while I'm back in New York, and there's a chance I won't see him again for months. How's a relationship supposed to work like that?"

"There are plenty of drivers who have partners and families," Chantal points out. "They seem to be doing just fine. Why would you and Dev be any different?"

I suddenly can't seem to think of any of those reasons, but I'm sure there are thousands just waiting to spring up and tear us down. Do I want to risk that? Can I take the leap of faith that would be necessary to even pursue something with him?

"No matter what we do, it won't be easy," I finally say. That's the only conclusion I can come to right now. Because the idea of being without him feels just as hard.

"Easy is overrated," she counters. "What matters is making yourselves happy."

And therein lies the problem—I don't know how to do that.

There's one thing I do know, though. "I'm scared, Chantal," I whisper.

Being with Dev in any form means opening myself up to another chance at heartbreak. I can't imagine he'd ever cheat like Jeremy did, but I also can't imagine being his forever first choice. Now that his reputation is repaired, he can have any woman he wants, so why would he settle for me?

I'm fragile and weak, practically held together with glue and stretched-out rubber bands. Some days I can barely keep up with the breakneck pace of following the team around the world, and it's nothing short of a miracle that I haven't fallen completely behind or gotten seriously hurt. Someone should slap a sticker on my forehead that reads *handle with care*.

Would he really be up for tolerating that? And for how long?

Then there's my brother. I've already torn Oakley's friend group apart once. I don't want to be the reason it happens again. If Dev and I broke up, no matter how amicably, there would always be a lingering awkwardness between us, and I have no doubt that it would carry over into his relationship with Oakley.

And even if we *didn't* break up, if it led to a wedding and kids and a happily ever after, their friendship would still change. Could I handle that? Could I be confident in my choice, knowing that Oakley would still be affected?

"I just don't think being together is a good idea," I tell Chantal, but the words taste bitter on my tongue.

There's a beat of disappointed silence before she says, "You can't really believe that."

I don't, but this is fear talking. Right now, there's only the burn of panic in my veins. It's activating my fight-or-flight response, and it's telling me to run.

But I don't *want* to listen to the fear. I don't *want* to let it deprive me of the happiness that being with Dev would undoubtedly bring me, even with the consequences, even if only for a short time.

It can keep singing its siren song in the back of my mind, but I refuse to let it lure me under. I won't drown in the current of emotions and let them wash me, broken and bloodied, onto the shore. I won't let it turn me into a shell of myself like I've been before. Or steal the fire I worked so hard to build and build and build until it blazed bright once again.

So that leaves me with two options. I can be selfish. I can

put myself first and dive into the unknown. Or I can defer to the greater good and let this all come to an end, keeping the status quo intact.

And that means I have to make a choice.

"I'm just afraid I'll have to give something up to be with him," I finish weakly.

She's quiet for a few seconds, considering my words. She understands where I'm coming from, even if I don't explain my thought processes. She knows all my hang-ups and self-doubts, and she's seen all the versions of me—from the wide-eyed innocent coming into college, to the brokenhearted girl after the Jeremy situation, all the way to the woman I am now, in part thanks to the way she and Grace helped build me back up.

"I understand that," she finally says. "And it *is* scary. But, Willow . . ." She takes a breath, her next words gentle but determined. "You could have *everything* with him. Please don't let the fear win."

CHAPTER 22

DEV

My phone has been ringing nonstop since the end of the race. So have Chava's and Mark's. I don't think I've ever heard from so many people in my life. Shit, I didn't realize I even *knew* this many people.

I'm tucked into the corner of my hotel room, video chatting with my mom, my dad, my sister, and a handful of friends who watched the race with them. It's a riot of cheers and toasts in a combination of English and Gujarati, and I can't make out half of what they're shouting.

"You did well, beta," Mom says for the millionth time, but I'll never get tired of it. Praise from her is like gold. "Bring that trophy home so I can see it for myself."

"If I had known you planned on winning, I would have been there!" Dad shouts, his arms wrapped around Mom's shoulders. "I'm so proud of you, kiddo."

"I *guess* you did okay," Alisha teases from the edge of the screen. "You better enjoy the attention now, though, because next month it's going to be all on me."

Her fiancé snorts, chucking her gently under the chin. "Ah, yeah, just you. Not like it's *our* wedding."

It's obvious from the way he looks at Alisha that he's madly in love. Is that how I look at Willow? If so, it's a fucking miracle no one has called me out on it already.

And it's a miracle that I held out until today to finally kiss her again. But seeing her in my room, setting up a display to remind me how loved I am . . . I couldn't stop myself. I had to make my obsession known.

But now she and I have a lot to talk about. The conversation has been coming our way for a while, but I undoubtedly sped it up with my actions today. And for me, there's no going back to how things used to be.

I want more. But it's up to her to decide what *more* is. The risks are far more serious for her than they are for me.

After promising to call again tomorrow, I disconnect the video call and turn my attention back to Chava, who's just setting his phone down as well.

"I talked to Oakley." The announcement suddenly fills my stomach with lead. "He said don't worry about calling him back. He just wanted to congratulate you."

Fuck. I've pushed Oakley to the back of my head, and this is *not* the reminder I needed after having my hands all over his little sister a few hours ago. As reasonable as he is, I don't think he'd appreciate that detail. Especially if he knew this wasn't even the first time.

But Willow is her own woman. She can make her own decisions. I just don't know whether they'll lead to more friendships destroyed. Guess all I can do is wait and find out.

"Let's get out of here," Mark says from across the room, slipping his phone into the pocket of his slacks. "I'm letting you off the leash tonight, Dev. You better make the most of it."

"Oh, I plan to," I reply, choking back the guilt that threatens to bubble up into my throat. I undo the top button of my shirt as if that will help, but it only draws a wolf whistle from Chava, who must take it as a sign that I'm ready to let loose rather than a nervous tic.

He loops an arm around my neck, putting me in a headlock. "Gonna finally get you laid tonight, mano. Everyone wants to suck a winner's dick."

The comment surprises a laugh out of me before I can stop it, but it eases my guilt as he drags me to the door. If he knew I had zero plans to go for any of them, he'd razz me to no end.

"We gotta grab Willow," I remind Mark and him as we step into the hall, nodding to a few other Argonaut guys who are headed out as well.

Tonight's going to be chaos—the good kind this time—for the team. It's a great fucking feeling knowing that I'm the reason everyone is happy, and I'm already desperate to keep it going. But that's only if Buck will let me get away with it again.

Chava leads the charge to Willow's room at the end of the hall and pounds on the door, crooning her name as Mark and I catch up. I open my mouth, ready to tell him to cut it out, but I'm rendered speechless as the door swings open.

If there were any lingering doubts in my head about getting into a relationship with Willow, they're gone now. Because everything I need is standing right in front of me.

"You ready to hit the town?" Chava asks as she steps across the threshold of her room. Somehow, unlike me, the man resists drinking in every inch of her.

She looks good in everything, but in tonight's little black

dress that dips low in the front and shoes that can only be described as fuck-me pumps? Keeping my hands off her is going to be an impossible task—though maybe that was her aim. By this point, she knows exactly what she does to me.

Her red-painted lips curve into a smile as she beams up at Chava. I'm only a little jealous that the sparkle in her eyes isn't for me.

Okay, fuck it. I'm a lot jealous. She should be looking at *me* like that.

"Where are we going?" she asks as she pulls the door closed behind her. "I'm up for whatever, but I wouldn't mind knowing the game plan."

Chava's reply barely registers as I watch her step farther into the hall, unable to look away. I've always been aware of Willow—how she moves through a space, how she speaks, how she reacts—but it's different now. The awareness is so much stronger, like there's a string tethered between us. Like it's tugging me to her.

It's not until her attention finally shifts to me that I realize I've been holding my breath, and a hit of warm vanilla floods my senses as I inhale. As Chava and Mark walk ahead of us to get to the elevator, the former still chatting away, she falls in next to me. And, *finally*, there it is—the smile I've been waiting for, that look of pure and open adoration, the one she gave me before I went out and won the race. It sets every cell in me on fire.

"Hey, champ," she quietly teases, long lashes batting as she regards me. "Excited for tonight?"

I nod, but I'm not interested in talking about myself. "You look amazing," I tell her, glad we're out of earshot of the others.

It's a weak compliment, but it'll have to do for now. I'll

save the poetry and the Hindi movie lines for when I have more time and the privacy to worship her in the way she deserves.

Her smile shifts into a smirk, her eyes flicking over me. There's a new heat in the dark depths when she meets my gaze again. "You don't look so bad either."

Fucking hell, I'm so gone for this girl.

"You doing okay?" I ask her. I need a distraction to keep myself from doing something unwise—like dragging her back to my room in front of all these people.

"Yeah," she says. The back of her hand brushes mine as we walk slowly toward the awaiting elevator. "I am."

I search her face in profile. We've had a little time to think about what happened earlier, and I need to be sure we're still on the same page. "Promise?"

"Promise."

The conversation we're dancing around will have to wait until we can sneak away. Whether that can happen tonight remains to be seen, but I'm desperate for it. I can't let what's hanging between us linger. I want to make moves. Make decisions.

Make choices that could change everything for us forever.

The club is loud and hot and decorated with more American flags than I'd ever expect to see in Hungary, but I've certainly had worse nights out. The champagne is flowing, the music is decent, and the people gathered to celebrate are having a good time. I can't even complain about how packed the place is, considering it's why Willow has been practically pressed up against me for the last hour.

At Chava's insistence, we're all out on the dance floor instead of in the VIP section like I'm sure Mark would have preferred. Willow's in the middle of our group, moving back and forth between me and Chava. The two of us are competing to see who can break out the worst dance moves to make her laugh the hardest.

I am *not* a bad dancer—my mother would disown me if I was—but I'll happily act a fool to make Willow smile. I've done it before, and I'll do it again. As far back as I can remember, I've played the clown so that I can watch her face light up. So I can watch those deep dimples appear like little craters in the moon. And what's more beautiful than the moon?

For now, it's my turn with her. With my arm wrapped around her waist, I dip her back dramatically, pulling the sweetest laugh from her lips. When I lower her a little more, she reaches out for me, her fingers clutching at my shirt. There's no way I'd ever drop her, but still, I don't pull her up right away. With a pounding heart, I savor the way she clings to me and the thrill that flashes across her face. She still has that daredevil streak, the one I watched fade into an ember as she got older. But it's flaring back to life now—her desire to push the limits and explore the things she thought were out of reach—and I'm more than happy to be her guide.

She squeals as I right her again, hands still pressed to my chest. They're all that separates her body from mine. It wouldn't take much to tug her closer, to dip my head and seek out her lips, to steal a kiss on this crowded dance floor. And if the spark in her eyes is anything to go off, she'd let me.

But before I can make the move, my phone buzzes in my pocket. Keeping one arm looped around Willow, I pull it out, preparing to send yet another congratulatory call to voicemail.

Except it's Howard's name flashing at me this time.

I hesitate, torn between wanting to continue dancing with

Willow and needing to know what my agent wants. He's never been one to waste time with flattery, so there's likely another motive behind this call.

I bend to shout, "Sorry, I've gotta take this!" in Willow's ear before motioning for Chava to come closer. When he does, I'm quick with my instructions. "Watch her, all right? I'll be right back."

He nods once. "Got you."

I'm reluctant to loosen my hold on Willow, and she watches me with disappointment in her eyes, like she's just as opposed to letting me go. But Chava's quick to sweep her into his arms, and the jealousy doesn't surge through me like I expected. I'm who she wants. And Chava wouldn't dare try to sway her feelings—unlike Mark, who's been shooting me unreadable glances all night. As I slip away from our group, I get another one of those looks from him.

I make my way through a crowd of Argonaut crew members, fielding toasts and more slaps on the back as I head to a quieter back hallway. The thudding bass reverberates through the walls, but the volume is dulled enough that my agent should be able to hear me.

"You calling to congratulate me, Howard?" I greet, phone pressed hard to one ear and my free hand cupped over the other, suddenly warm from all the champagne. "People are telling me I won a race today."

True to form, Howard doesn't react. "I'm calling because there are whispers that Otto Kivinen is leaving Mascort at the end of the season."

My agent's words slap me into soberness. Did I hear that correctly? Because there's no way he's just said what I think he has. "You're fucking with me."

Otto has been at Mascort for as long as I've been in

Formula 1. He's the peanut butter to Zaid's jelly, the perfect number two driver. Exactly the kind of person a team wants supporting their champion as he fights to win his eighth title. He's a consistent points scorer and one of the best defenders on the grid. He's exactly who I'd want as a teammate if I were a championship contender.

As far as I know, Otto's been in contract negotiations with Mascort for next season, but if these whispers are to be believed, they must not be going well. Zaid's been vocal about how much he respects Otto and how much he wants him on the team. And Mascort is nothing but supportive of the guy, so this must be something Otto's pushing for.

Not everyone wants to be the number two driver forever. I know the feeling.

"Like I said, whispers," Howard goes on. "Loud ones. And whispers that Mascort's on the hunt for his replacement. They're considering options now."

My heart pounds in my ears, my blood hot and rushing through my veins. Howard wouldn't be sharing this information unless it related to me. "Am I one of those options?"

"More than an option after today's performance," he reveals. "And I have it on good authority that Argonaut is willing to let you go for the right price."

Of course they will. Buck may have his billions, but he'd rather make money by getting rid of me than let me stay and lead his team to victory. It's obvious he was already looking for someone to replace me next year. This just means he won't have to buy me out to make that happen.

"You're lucky you've turned things around for yourself," Howard continues. "People are starting to see your true potential."

"It wasn't luck," I automatically reply. "It was Willow."

And she's the first person I want to tell about this news. I want to run to her now, sweep her into my arms and murmur against her lips that everything we've worked for is within reach.

Howard grunts. "Whatever it was, keep it up." He pauses, letting the news wash over me—letting me imagine what I could have. "Congratulations on your win today, Mr. Anderson. I'll be in touch when I hear more."

I'm moving before he hangs up, escaping the hall and maneuvering through the crowds again, determined to get back to Willow. In the blink of an eye, I'm in front of her. I think I bump Chava out of the way, earning myself a string of Spanish expletives from him in the process, but I don't care.

My hands find Willow's waist, and I dip my head low so she can hear me when I say, "I need to tell you something."

She pulls back to look up at me, worry flooding her eyes. "Is everything okay?"

"It's good news, I promise." I squeeze her waist, then snag one of her hands. "Come with me."

I guide her through the club and to the back hall I just emerged from. There are a couple of people milling around a few yards away from us, waiting in line for the bathroom, but they pay no attention when I back Willow against the wall.

She leans against it willingly, like she's grateful for the reprieve from dancing and the crush of bodies. Her posture may be relaxed, but her gaze is expectant and hopeful.

"So?" she prompts, squeezing my hand. "What's the news?"

I take a breath to center myself. Am I really about to say this? "I just got off the phone with Howard. He thinks I have a shot of going to Mascort next year."

There's a beat of silence as Willow processes the information. Her eyes widen when it registers, and she claps a hand to her mouth to cover a quiet scream before dropping it to my chest instead. "Dev, oh my god! That's amazing!"

I bring my hand up to cover hers, to keep it pressed to my heart. "Nothing's for sure." I try to temper her reaction as well as my own, but I can't stop the grin that splits my face. "I think it looks good for me, though."

"I'm so happy for you." She slips her fingers from mine and throws her arms around my neck. "You're going to get what you want. I know it."

Her hold on me forces me down to her level, so I wrap my own arms around her narrow waist and tug her close. Willow's embrace is fierce, as if she's pouring every ounce of love and strength and belief she possesses into me, like she knows I'll need it for the journey I'm about to go on. And I do. I need it more than anything. Because as excited as I am at the possibility that I'll soon have the race seat I've always wanted, the challenge of getting there is still daunting.

Willow knows that, yet she already thinks I'm more than capable of getting it.

Her grip on me loosens a little, and we shift so that we're eye to eye. As always, there's an undercurrent of energy between us, but it crackles now, threatening to ignite into something bigger. Brighter. An inferno that can no longer be ignored.

"This is familiar," she whispers.

It is. We've found ourselves in yet another club hallway, another place I can add to our list of unfortunate spots for unplanned confessions, but I wouldn't change it for the world.

"Don't tell me your brother's going to burst out of the bathroom," I tease.

Her gaze drops to my mouth, and her fingers curl around the back of my neck, making her intentions perfectly clear. "I don't want to think about him right now."

"Neither do I."

This time when we lean toward each other, there are no interruptions.

Her warm, soft mouth meets mine, and everything else in the world falls away. All the bullshit. All the drama. All the worry. It's gone, and all I know is her. My sunshine. My moon guiding me in the darkness. My Willow.

I hold her tight as I deepen the kiss, coaxing entry past her lips until our tongues are brushing. There's nothing tentative about it, no hesitation from her like there was earlier. That split second of waiting for her to kiss me back took years off my life, but this has returned them all to me. It's given me a whole new existence.

A low moan escapes the back of my throat when she rakes her nails against my scalp. My hands find the generous curve of her ass in return and haul her closer, my knee slipping between her thighs and hiking the already high hem of her dress even higher. The gasp she lets out tells me she can feel every inch of me straining behind my zipper, but she stays where she is.

"Dev," she says between kisses, fingers still tangled in my hair. "What are we doing?"

"Celebrating," I mumble against her mouth. "Isn't it obvious?"

Her laugh is breathy and sweet. I inhale it like the purest oxygen before diving in for another taste of her.

She lets me take it, body molded to mine, hips grinding against me, but she quickly backs off. And good thing she does, because after months without sex, there's a strong chance I'd come right here, right now, with the way she moves against me. Crazy thing is, I'd probably still thank her for it.

"We need to talk about this," she pants.

I flick my tongue across her lower lip, needing more. "I know."

"We should do that now."

"We should." I kiss her again.

"You have to stop kissing me."

"I don't want to."

She exhales in relief, sinking further into me. "Good. Neither do I."

The way our lips meet is nothing short of reckless this time. It's like lightning during a summer storm—hot and bright, threatening to burn us down. This is not the appropriate venue to let this carry on, but I don't want to stop.

"You feel so good," I whisper. I've finally found the strength to break away, but my mouth still hovers over hers. "Being so close to you for all these weeks but not being able to touch you the way I wanted? I've been losing my mind. I can't go back to the way things were."

Her lips are swollen, her curls swept over one shoulder, her eyes a little hazy but locked on mine. "I don't think I can either." The confession is breathy and soft, but the words are clear. She means it.

"But I don't want to jeopardize your career or your reputation." I force myself to go on, pulling away a little more at the same time. I peer down the hallway in either direction, but the few people who were lingering near the bathroom are gone. "I don't want to do anything you're not comfortable with."

She nods, her eyes clearing, and there's a glimmer of apprehension in them along with the clarity.

"We shouldn't rush into anything," she agrees, trailing her fingers down my neck to rest on my shoulders. "Even if it's just physical."

There's no rushing to be done. I've been grappling with my feelings for her for nearly a year now, and in the time we've spent together, she's become my rock. But Willow has always been in my corner. This isn't new. It's just constant now, and I'm afraid of ever being without her.

That right there tells me this is more than just physical. That I'm attracted to so much more than just her wide eyes and bright smile and the curves I want to trace every inch of.

I'm done fighting the pull I feel to her. Will there be consequences? There sure as shit will be. But I'm willing to handle them.

"I don't want it to be just physical," I tell her. There's no point in lying or keeping the truth from her. "I want all of you, Willow. I have for a long time. And I don't think I can settle for anything less than that."

The pulse point at her throat beats wildly as she studies my face, probably looking for any trace of deception. When she doesn't find it, her gaze locks on mine again, full of tentative acceptance. If she can't fathom that I want her—body, mind, and soul—then I'll have to try harder to prove it.

But it's up to her to tell me what she wants. She knows where I stand.

"Think about what you want," I urge. I cup her face with both hands, making sure she can't look away. Making sure she doesn't miss the weight of my words. "Take all the time you need. Don't rush it. And don't force it." I let my thumbs skim across her cheekbones, praying this won't be the last time I get to touch her like this. "But just know that I'll be here waiting, because I know exactly what I want—and it's you."

CHAPTER 23

WILLOW

My body aches like I've been hit by a truck when I roll out of bed the next morning.

I barely drank last night, so I can't blame this on a hangover, but I overdid it in other ways. I stood for too long, danced too hard, and wore impractical shoes without thinking of the consequences. Now I'm paying the price.

The torn labrum in my left hip—the one doctors have repaired three times already and refuse to fix again—catches within the joint as I take a tentative step toward the bathroom, and it threatens to give out on me. The pain is sharp and intense but blessedly fleeting, though when I try again, I know it will do the same thing.

I need to hydrate, pop an anti-inflammatory, and do some gentle stretching ASAP. I've been slacking on taking care of my body, and it's come to bite me in the ass.

Yet, if this is the consequence for last night, I'll take it without complaint.

I fight back a smile when the memory of kissing Dev in that dim hallway surfaces. Sure, it wasn't the most romantic setting, and yeah, it was once again a heat-of-the-moment thing. But *god*. If my hip didn't hurt so badly, I'd be kicking my feet like a giddy kid.

I promised Dev that I wouldn't rush into a decision about where we go from here, but if he knocked on my door right now, I'd probably throw myself at him. And *that* means I need to avoid him until I've had a chance to weigh the pros and cons and come to a conclusion about what I want. What I *really* want—and what to make of the repercussions that could come with it.

I text Grace and Chantal as I lie on my yoga mat, grimacing through the discomfort of the stretches and welcoming the distraction of my friends' nearly incoherent messages as I update them on the Dev situation. Twenty minutes later, my body doesn't feel much better, but my mind's a little clearer. Both my best friends wholeheartedly encouraged me to follow my heart. Knowing I have their support makes this easier, although I've never been worried about them and their opinions when it comes to Dev.

But on my way down to breakfast, I run straight into one of my concerns. Literally.

Mark steadies me, his strong hands gripping my shoulders. The collision is my fault—I was so distracted by forming my mental list of pros and cons that I didn't see him stepping out of his room until it was too late—but maybe this is fate intervening, forcing me to face my anxiety head-on.

"Are you okay?" he asks, his brow furrowed in genuine concern. Considering he's a foot and a half taller than me, it's warranted. He could have easily wiped me off the face of the earth.

"I'm fine," I say, though stopping so quickly has made my pain flare up again.

"You don't look fine."

Trust Mark to be blunt.

As I gingerly move away from him, I think about lying again, but today's pain is so acute, there's no way it isn't written all over my face. "My hip is giving me a little trouble," I explain. "No big deal, though. I promise."

He frowns and takes a few steps back, putting at least ten feet between us. Then he lifts his hand and motions me forward. "Walk toward me. Let me see how it's affecting your gait."

I blink in surprise. He's gone into full physical therapist mode in a heartbeat, watching me expectantly, waiting for me to comply with his orders. He's a professional, and he'll probably tattle to Dev if I try to brush off my pain again, so I do as I'm told and walk toward him. I can't mask the slight limp.

His frown deepens as I approach, then he grasps my elbow to support me when I reach him. "You need to stay off that for a bit," he instructs. "I can work on you. See if we can get that hip sitting a little better in the joint."

My jaw goes slack as I scrutinize him. "You'd do that for me?"

"Of course," he says with a scoff. "You really think I'm that much of an asshole?"

"No," I blurt. My face goes hot with embarrassment, but he's seen right through me. I didn't think he liked me enough to go out of his way to come to my aid. "I just—I didn't think—you're here for Dev, not anyone else."

He rolls his eyes as he tightens his grip on my elbow, taking on more of my weight as he turns me toward the elevators. "I'm here for the people I care about, and you're one of them." He gently nudges me into walking, watching each of my steps. "Come on. Let's get some breakfast, and then we'll see if we can get your pain level down."

I let him guide me, thankful to him for both the literal support and for being so open to helping me. "Thank you," I tell him quietly as he hits the button for the elevator.

He doesn't look at me as he says, "I've got you, Wills. You should know that."

I certainly do now.

Mark doesn't let me go even as the elevator descends. Surprisingly, the silence isn't the least bit awkward, but I do have to break it. "I don't want Dev to know about this."

I can feel Mark's eyes on me, though I continue to focus on the steel doors straight ahead. It has nothing to do with hiding who I spend my time with from Dev, but because I don't want him to know that I'm hurting. I don't want him to take on that worry.

Blessedly, I don't have to elaborate. Mark gets it. "I'll send him down to the gym after breakfast," he answers. "He needs to sweat out all that alcohol from last night anyway."

I snicker, finally peeking up at him. "You're cruel. I like it."

A hint of a smirk creeps up his face. "I have a feeling you won't like it for long."

▬▬▬▬▬

An hour later, I'm lying on the massage table that Mark keeps set up in his room so he can work on Dev at any time. I have to respect his preparedness, but right now, I kind of hate him for it.

"Holy *fuck*," I grit out.

This time, Mark's smirk makes me wonder if he's a sadist.

He's perched next to me on the edge of the table with my knee hooked over one of his shoulders and his hands wrapped around my thigh over my compression shorts. We're all up on each other, but there is nothing even *remotely* sexual about this. Honestly, he's lucky I haven't kicked him in the face yet.

"Breathe out," he says calmly.

Obediently, I force a puff of air out of my mouth as he gives my leg a controlled tug.

The relief is immediate, like the ball part of my hip isn't jammed into the socket any longer. The excruciating "massage" he gave me first has even encouraged the usually tight muscles surrounding the joint to relax. I'm in heaven.

My head is spinning up in the clouds when Mark asks, "So. You and Dev, huh?"

Panic assaults me, dragging me back down to earth, before I stutter, "I—I don't—"

"Stop." He moves his hands a little lower on my thigh so he can pull it at a different angle. "I already know."

I let out a heavier exhale as he yanks my leg again. This adjustment is almost better than the first. "Did he tell you?"

There's no avoiding Mark's questions; I'm truly at his mercy right now, so I might as well be honest.

He shakes his head. "He didn't have to. I saw you kissing last night."

My stomach plummets to the floor. Oh no. If he saw us, that means *anyone* could have. It means we've been careless and rash. We let our emotions lead us without considering the possible outcomes. Though Dev asked me to think things through, we've pretty much already thrown caution to the wind, and now I could be facing down a nightmare.

"Do you think anyone else saw?" I ask, dread creeping through me.

"No." His answer is firm. "But even if they did, every person there last night was from Argonaut, and we've all signed NDAs. Nothing is getting out."

The fear subsides a little, though not completely. If Dev and I keep acting like horny teenagers, there's no way this will stay under wraps, whatever *this* is or might turn into.

"Okay," I respond weakly. What else is there to say? He already knows my secret.

Mark continues to work on my hip in silence, offering me more relief than I've felt in months. It isn't until he asks me to turn over onto my stomach so he can work on my hamstring that our conversation resumes.

"You need to tell your brother before he finds out from someone else."

My cheek rests on my folded arms, so my words are muffled when I say, "There's nothing to tell him yet."

All Dev and I have done is sneak kisses here and there. My brother, the ladies' man he claims to be, wouldn't have leverage in the argument that a couple of kisses equates to something serious. I haven't agreed to date Dev. We're not in a relationship. And we haven't done anything more than divulge that we have feelings for each other. It could all be written off so easily.

And there's still a tiny chance I might do just that.

"What's going on with me and Dev . . ." I trail off, my heart cracking a little at the words on the tip of my tongue. "I don't even know if it's going to go anywhere. I don't know if it can."

Regardless of the Oakley issue, I have to think about my professional reputation. I don't want to be branded with misogynistic labels and face the rumors that I slept my way into a job. Juicy stories sell, and one like that could ruin my career before it's even started. As much as I want to, I can't single-handedly change how women are viewed and treated, and I can't follow my heart to a place that would lead to the destruction of what I've worked so hard for.

Yet there's a part of me that believes that Dev is worth the risk.

"It can go somewhere." Mark once again speaks in definitives. "And if you want it to, it will. That boy's head over heels for you, Willow."

"I know," I whisper, wishing I could be so confident in my possible future with Dev. "I feel the same way about him."

It's strange confessing this to one of my brother's best friends—one of Dev's best friends. Mark and I have never been close. We've always skirted around each other, and this is by far the most direct conversation we've ever had. There's no rule that says I have to share any of this, but it feels like the right choice to trust him.

"I'm going to be completely honest," Mark goes on, digging his thumbs into the muscle behind my knee. "I didn't like the idea of Dev hiring you—at all. You distracted him. Made him take his eye off the prize." His thumbs slide higher, though he's definitely taking it easy on me. His words are harsh enough. "Did you know he crashed in Austin last year because he was thinking about you?"

I inhale sharply, my head snapping up so I can gauge Mark's expression. "*No.* There's no way. He said he crashed because he locked up and—"

"It was because of you." Mark dips his chin and focuses on the work he's doing to my leg. "He told me himself."

I stare at him in disbelief for a few more seconds, then drop my forehead to my arms in shame. "Oh my god," I mumble. "You were right not to want me around." Maybe I'm still at risk of being a distraction. Of ruining everything for him. "Maybe I should cut this off. I was so worried about my own career that I didn't even think about his. I don't—I don't want to be the reason he loses focus, I can't—"

"You're not. Not anymore." Mark's touch disappears from my thigh, then he's pushing on my shoulder, signaling for me to flop onto my back. "Now, if you walk away, I'm afraid he'll fall to pieces."

I take Mark in, torn between believing his first impression and his current one. "Do you really think that?"

"Dev has been trying to hide his feelings about you because he knows I disapprove. Or, well, I used to. Yesterday showed me . . ." He takes a breath and rests his hand on my bent knee. "Willow, you make him want to be better. *Do* better. Before you came back into the picture, he was close to giving up. He'd never admit it, but he'd lost that spark. He could talk all he wanted about getting away from Argonaut and working toward being a champion, but he wasn't doing anything about it. You changed that."

I'm speechless. If those words had come from anyone else, I might not be convinced. I might think they were humoring me. But Mark isn't the type to lie or sugarcoat. If he says it, he means it. And he truly believes Dev is better off with me around.

So I might as well ask the question that all of this really comes down to. "Do you think I should give us a chance? Me and him?"

"I do."

He gives my knee the lightest squeeze. It's nearly imperceptible, but it pulls some of the crushing weight of this decision off my shoulders.

"Okay," I exhale. "As long as you approve. You're the one I was the most afraid of pissing off."

Mark laughs as he straightens my leg again and starts to work on the outside of my thigh. "More than Oakley? Damn, am I really that scary?"

I shoot him a dry look and tick off my reasoning on my fingers. "You are a giant. You always look angry. For years, I've been convinced you hate me. *And* you're currently digging into my IT band, meaning I am in *unimaginable* pain. So, uh, yeah. You are."

"My bad." With a sly glance, he presses harder.

I let out a little squeak, but the pressure gives me sudden relief. It's amazing and awful. "God, you're such a *dick*."

He shakes his head, fighting a grin and losing. "There she is. The menace I remember."

I laugh. "You're probably going to regret telling me to go after Dev. That means you're stuck with me too."

"How terrible," he deadpans.

Before this conversation, I might have believed he meant that. But as it turns out, Mark's not my enemy. If anything, he's the best wingman in the world.

I let him torture me for another ten minutes before I tap out and allow him to help me sit up slowly. But before I can hop down from the massage table, he clamps a hand down on my shoulder and looks me hard in the eyes.

"Talk to your brother," he insists. "After the Jeremy fiasco, I don't know how open he'll be. He knows Dev would never hurt you on purpose, but he might need time to work through his feelings about it all."

I take a deep breath and blow it out. "I'll talk to him," I promise. "But it's got to be face-to-face."

Mark nods and lifts his hand from my shoulder, offering to help me climb down from the table. Once I'm standing, I give his fingers a tight squeeze.

"Thank you, Mark," I say, glad to have this newfound camaraderie. "For both therapy sessions. You should charge me double."

That drags the loudest laugh from him I've ever heard. It's still relatively quiet in the grand scheme of things, but I'll take it.

"This one's on the house," he teases. "But next time, you're paying full price."

▰▰▰▰▰

That afternoon, I sit with Chava on the plane to Belgium, headed to the last race before F1's summer break—and the last race I'll be joining the team on the road for. The flight is less than two hours, but it's still too much time to be stuck sitting next to Dev.

On Tuesday and Wednesday, I wander around Spa and Francorchamps, snapping photos to post to both my own social media and Dev's.

On Thursday, I watch from the back of the crowd as Dev charms his way through interviews and meet and greets, then slip away before he can seek me out.

On Friday and Saturday, I hide behind Mark and Chava in the garage, doing my best to keep my interactions with Dev to a minimum. He constantly tries to catch my eye, but he seems to know better than to engage me.

Staying away from him has been torture, but I need the space so I can determine how I want us to move forward from here. My head goes fuzzy when he's too close, and all reasonable thoughts disappear when the familiar warmth of his cologne hits me. God forbid he brush my hand or sweep my curls over my shoulder; I'm an immediate goner. Nothing but a pile of goo on the floor.

I'd be disgusted with myself if I didn't know that my feelings were reciprocated. Honestly, I might be the slightly less obsessed party here—though not by much.

I want to be with him. That much I've already settled. But it's *how* and *when* we make that happen that I'm working on. It would probably be best if we held off until my contract with him and Argonaut is up at the end of August. I don't think we could go public until a few months after that, or at least until I landed a job on my own merit.

But that feels like an excruciatingly long timeline. Though if it's the safest way for us to be together, then maybe it's how things have to be. Still, it's going to be torturous to hold out.

I'm hoping my resolve will stick around as I take the stairs up to Dev's driver room. We have a couple of hours before the race, and I need to snap a few photos of him getting ready, since those always perform well. People really like seeing him in his tight fireproofs for some reason . . .

Chava and Mark disappeared while I was still sipping my latte, so they should be up there already. At least they can act as an intermediary. It's worked okay so far, especially after my chat with Mark. He wants me to be sure of my decision, so if he can help, he will. Even if it means keeping Dev and me apart for the time being.

But the boys are nowhere to be found when I step into Dev's room and shut the door behind me. He and I are completely alone—and he's half-naked.

"*Oh*," I hear myself say, cringing when I do. But that doesn't stop me from staring at him in those incredibly tight pants that leave nothing to the imagination. "Sorry, I can—"

"Good, you're here." He snags the fireproof shirt hanging up on the rail he's standing next to. "You want to get some photos? It looks like people are digging my helmet for this weekend."

I couldn't care less about his new helmet design and how much people like it when I'm staring at his rippling back muscles.

"Uh-huh." God, I need to snap out of it. I clear my throat as he finally tugs his shirt on. "Where are Chava and Mark?"

When Dev's head pops out of his shirt, his hair is sticking up in every direction. "Mark had to grab something and Chava had a call to make." He sweeps his hair back. "They should be here in a little while." He turns to inspect me, a brow raised in challenge. "You done avoiding me?"

I wasn't trying to be sly, but it warms me that he knows exactly what I was doing. "I have no idea what you're talking about," I say lightly, making sure he can see my smile.

He chuckles as he reaches for his race suit next. "I'd be offended if I hadn't told you to take time to figure things out."

"Yeah, you kinda brought this upon yourself."

"I can pretend you're not here if that makes you feel better."

I can't help but laugh. "That's okay. I think we can exist in the same space."

The glance he shoots me says that he doubts that, but he nods to the shelving unit across the room. "Go ahead and get some more shots of my helmet."

I'm grateful he's not about to convince me to have a chat about what decision I've come to. Not that he'd want to have such a deep conversation right before the race, but it's a relief regardless.

I make my way over to where his helmet and the backup sit, though a small pastel orange box on the shelf beside them steals my attention. I pick up the Stella Margaux's box and turn to him with a grin. "Are macarons your new prerace snack?"

He keeps his back to me as he steps into his race suit and pulls it up. "No, those are for you," he says.

I blink, confused. "For . . . me?"

"Yeah, I know how much you like them."

My mind whirls, trying to remember where the closest Stella Margaux's is—and it's not anywhere nearby. "I'm pretty sure the closest location you could have gotten these was Paris."

"Yeah." With his back still turned, he slips his arms into the sleeves of the suit. "Had them flown in this morning."

He says it so casually. Like it took nothing to pull that off, even though I know it was a lot more than that.

"What if you hadn't seen me today?" I ask, my throat getting tight. "What if I was still avoiding you?"

He shrugs, and I hear the sound of the suit zipper pulling up. "I would have had Chava bring them to you. I just thought you might need a treat."

There's a pinching tightness in my chest, one that only happens when he's around, my heart being squeezed by all the feelings I have for him. I was right to keep my distance over the last few days, because this man . . . this man makes me reckless. He makes me forget all my concerns.

Makes me forget that there's a world outside the two of us.

"Dev."

He finally turns to look at me.

My breathing goes shallow. The macaron box drops back to the shelf.

I'm in front of him before my mind can catch up to my body. My hands find his jaw, cupping it, my thumbs tracing the hollows of his cheeks. I pull his face down to mine, ignoring the surprise in his eyes.

And then I kiss the hell out of him.

Despite his shock, he responds almost instantly, looping his arms around my waist and lifting me. I wrap my legs around him, my skirt hiking up to my hips, and hold on for dear life. A shelf digs into my back as he pushes me against it, but I barely register any sensation other than the press of his lips against mine.

I tilt my head to deepen the kiss, wanting more of him. All of him. I've made up my mind.

The logistics can get fucked. We'll figure it out when we have to.

There's nothing controlled or gentle about this kiss. There's no more taking it slow. It's urgent and eager and hungry, an explosion of emotions that have been bottled up for days and weeks and months. Maybe even years. It's desperate. It's a plea for so much more.

It's exactly what I want.

"You done thinking about things?" he pants when we break apart to catch our breath. "Made up your mind?"

I nod, nearly knocking myself out on the shelf behind me, but I don't care. Dev's ready to hand his heart over to me, and I'm ready to take it from him.

"If you want this—if you want *me*," he says, "I'll fight for it. I'll fight for us."

"Yes," I gasp, sinking my fingers into his hair. "I want to make this work."

The bliss that floods his expression makes my heart thump against my rib cage. I slant my head to kiss him again, to seal this promise we've made. But before I can, the door swings open.

Rearing back, I actually hit my head this time, wincing when Mark and Chava come into view. The two stare at us for a beat before Chava swears in Spanish, then jams his hand into the pocket of his uniform shorts and pulls out his wallet.

"Seriously?" he grumbles, slapping a hundred euro note into Mark's outstretched palm. "I thought they'd at least wait until *after* the race."

I gape at them. They *bet* on Dev and me? "Are you guys for real?"

Dev watches them, obviously biting back a grin. "Not cool," he says, clearly thinking otherwise but trying his best to back me up.

I push against his chest until he sets me on the ground. Shoving down the hem of my pencil skirt, I glare at the boys at the door. "I can't believe you."

Mark puts his hands up in surrender, but the money he's holding doesn't help his case. "Hey, at least you got what you wanted, Wills. Can't be too mad."

I suck in a breath, ready to retort, but nothing comes to me. Because he's right. I *did* get what I wanted.

As if to remind me of that, Dev brushes his knuckles against my jaw, featherlight. Heat blooms up my neck, and I soften again as I look at him.

"Let me go win another race," he says quietly, the words meant just for me. "Then we can talk. Okay?"

I swallow hard, ignoring the kissy noises Chava makes in the background.

"Okay," I murmur. "I'll be waiting."

CHAPTER 24

WILLOW

Dev doesn't win again.

But a ninth-place finish in that tractor of a car is commendable, and I'm immensely proud of him all the same. Hopefully, it's more than enough to keep him on Mascort's radar.

He catches me in the garage after the race, his damp hair brushing my temple as he shifts close. "Sturgill's on my ass about this debrief. We'll have to talk at the hotel. Stay up for me, baby."

The command and the endearment ignited a blaze inside me. I've been on edge for hours, alternating between pacing my hotel room in my pajamas, frantically packing to head home tomorrow, and doing PT exercises in an attempt to burn off some of my nervous energy. Yet it's nearly midnight and—ignoring the fact that my body would never hold up for it—I'm wired enough to run a marathon.

When a knock on the door finally comes, I throw it open and find Dev with a hand braced against the doorframe. The crooked smile that pulls up one side of his mouth is so achingly familiar.

"Hey," he says. "Can I come in?"

The words have barely left his mouth before I step back and motion him in, my heart rate picking up when the door clicks shut behind him. Neither of us speaks for a beat, the quiet hum of the AC the only sound as we stare at each other. The entire day has been leading up to this, but now that it's here, I don't know how to proceed.

Thankfully, Dev does. He closes the distance between us, then he tucks a loose curl behind my ear, his hand lingering on my neck when he's done.

"I'm sorry it took me so long to get here," he says, gaze steady on me. "You still up for talking?"

There are other things I'm far more interested in right now. Even so, I nod and grab his hand, guiding him over to the bed. We sit so we're angled toward each other, our knees bumping. It's the tiniest bit of contact, but for the time being, it's enough.

"I meant it when I said I want to make this work," I begin, pulse thudding in my ears. "I don't know what that looks like for us. But I want there to be an *us*."

"I want the same." His fingers inch across the duvet, his pinkie finding mine and hooking around it. "We don't have to figure it all out right now. Or any of it. We just need to be honest with each other about how we're feeling. This won't work if we aren't."

"I'm being *very* honest with you right now," I point out. There's definitely a gaping hole of vulnerability in my chest.

He chuckles. "I know. But this won't be easy, and I need you to tell me if it starts to feel like too much to handle."

He's right. The only way we can make this work is if we're open with each other, because right now, there are more than a few barriers in the way of us having a public relationship. "I promise I will."

"We'll take it one day at a time, yeah?"

"Yeah," I breathe. It feels so damn good to be following my heart, in spite of the risk.

"Can 'one day at a time' include taking you on a date, though?" he asks. His voice is tentative, like he's worried I might say no. "I don't want to half-ass this, Willow. I want to date you—be with you. I'm in this, fully and truly."

I nod, pressing my fingers closer to his. "You can absolutely take me on a date. In fact, I insist on it."

At that, he blows out a relieved breath. "Thank fucking god. Don't know what I would have done if you'd said no." He grabs my hand, then lifts it to his lips and places a few rapid kisses to my knuckles. "That's where we'll start. I promise, this is going to be the best date of your life."

"It better be," I say, laughing with a lightness that only he brings out in me. "Good luck trying to impress me."

"Don't worry, I've already googled 'cool date ideas in San Diego' for inspiration." He tugs me to my feet, backing toward the door. "Next time we see each other, I'll have the magnum opus of dates planned."

My stomach drops at the *next time*. "You're leaving?"

He comes to a stop in the small entryway, his expression softening as he squeezes my hand. "It's been a long day," he says gently. "I'm sure you're exhausted."

"I'm not that tired." My reply is quick, no hesitation. I lace my fingers with his, gazing up at him as I steel myself to ask for what I want. There's no sense in backing down now. "Don't go, Dev."

His breaths are slow and measured as he quietly watches me. "You sure?" he finally asks, his voice a little gravelly.

"Absolutely."

"To be clear: Are you asking me to sleep over?"

I squeeze his hand a little tighter. "I am."

"All right," he agrees, glancing away for a second, then turning back and studying my face. "Yeah. Maybe we could watch another movie. How about *Dilwale Dulhania Le Jayenge*? It's a classic."

"You and your SRK obsession." I playfully roll my eyes but sober again quickly. "But no. I don't want to watch a movie."

Judging by the way the humor in his dark eyes is replaced with heat, he's starting to catch my drift. "Would you rather eat snacks and gossip about our crushes?" he offers, taking a step closer.

"I'm thinking something a little less wholesome."

He gives a soft but dramatic gasp. "Don't tell me you want to play spin the bottle."

"Maybe more seven minutes in heaven," I suggest. "Preferably longer than seven minutes, though."

He stills, all amusement gone now. "Careful, Willow," he warns.

He can caution me all he wants. I know how I want the night to go.

"I'm done being careful." It's time to shed this label of innocence that's been shoved upon me. Being the baby sister, the fragile one, the girl left brokenhearted, doesn't equate to being naive. I don't want anyone, least of all him, thinking it's true. "Do you understand what I mean?"

His Adam's apple bobs as he swallows hard. "I think I'm beginning to."

To prove my point, I run my hands up his solid chest, over his pecs. Then I journey downward over his abs, slowing but not stopping when I reach the waistband of his jeans. I'm not a virgin. If my ex deserves credit for anything, it's showing me the highs my body can reach.

But I have an inkling that Dev can get me higher than anyone else ever could.

When my fingers brush the button of his jeans, he seizes my wrists in his grasp. His expression is tense, and I'm briefly terrified I've done something wrong.

The worry disappears when he tugs me flush against him. He then drops his hands to my thighs and curls them around the backs, lifting me in one smooth motion. On instinct, I wrap my legs around his waist as he takes on my weight. It's reminiscent of the encounter we had in his driver room, but no one's going to interrupt us tonight. I won't allow it.

We're back across the room in no time. He lowers himself into the armchair in the corner and pulls me down to straddle his lap. My pajama shorts might as well be nonexistent they're so thin, and he's growing hard beneath me. There's no doubt we want the same thing.

He stares up at me, hands resting where my thighs meet my hips, his chest heaving with every breath. His voice is reverential as he says, "You're all I want. Are you really going to let me have you?"

I brush my lips across his and answer, "I'm already yours."

Our kiss turns scorching with my admission. He slides both hands to my ass and squeezes, hauling me closer. I roll my hips against his in response, and he drops his head back, breaking the connection long enough for him to groan, "*Fuck,* Willow."

His mouth finds mine again a moment later, consuming me. I grasp at the soft cotton of his Argonaut T-shirt as his teeth scrape my bottom lip. There's nothing gentle about it, and the roughness has me arching against him even more.

My hands fall to the bottom of his shirt and push it upward, over the contours of his abs. He quickly gets the hint, tugging it off over his head, then throwing it to the floor before grabbing me again. But I press my hands firm against his chest so he can't pull me toward to him. I need a second to take in the masterpiece beneath me.

I've seen Dev shirtless countless times, but this is different. This time I can admire and touch and do everything I've fantasized about at night under the covers for literal years.

"You're unreal," I exhale, running my fingers over the grooves, reveling in the way his muscles flex under my touch. "What did they do, make you in a lab?"

The sound he lets out is a cross between a laugh and a groan. "If they did, I would have asked them to make me a little taller."

I snicker and dip my head, finding his stubbled jaw with my lips as my hands continue their exploration. "I like you the way you are." He's practically a foot taller than me anyway; neither of us needs to strain our necks more than we already have to. "I wouldn't change anything."

"Feeling's mutual." He twists his fingers in the hem of my T-shirt, a question in his eyes when I shift back again. "Can I? I want to see you."

A shiver speeds down my spine. "Yes. Please."

He pulls it up and over my head and sends the fabric floating to the floor to join his, leaving me only in my bra. And just like I did, Dev takes his time to admire the view.

His breath hitches, and I swear the hardness in his jeans grows even more as he drinks me in.

Normally, I'd be conscious of all my flaws—like the faded stretch marks that map the tops of my breasts and the ones that trail down from my waist and dip past my shorts—but just like I've seen him half-undressed before, he's seen me like this too.

There's something freeing about having known him my whole life. He's seen me at every stage—a skinned-kneed five-year-old, pimple-faced at fourteen, stumbling drunk at twenty-one. He's seen me on the beach, getting knocked down by waves and brushing sand out of my hair. He's seen me ten seconds after rolling out of bed, bleary-eyed and wearing hand-me-down sweatpants.

I don't need to hide a single aspect of myself from him. He's already seen it all. And yet he's still here, looking at me like I'm the center of his universe.

"You're perfect," he breathes out, shaking his head a little like he can't quite believe it. He tilts his chin up to find my lips again, giving me the gentlest kiss to punctuate the compliment.

"Me?" I mumble, eyes barely open, too intoxicated by him. "You're the one who's perfect."

He doesn't acknowledge the words, like he doesn't even hear me. He just continues tracing up and down my spine, the warmth of his touch seeping into me. "Fucking flawless," he continues. "God, look at you. How did I get this lucky?"

He drags his lips down my neck and over my collarbone, then places soft kisses between my breasts, touching me like it's his absolute honor to do so. As he does, I work my way down to the waistband of his jeans, searching for the button. I want more of him.

"Not yet," he says. "I want to feel you first."

He pushes my fingers away from his zipper, then slides his hand between us, the heel of his palm brushing against my core through the thin fabric of my sleep shorts. I gasp at the electricity that shoots up and through my belly. But I lose my breath completely when he pushes my shorts and underwear to the side, his fingertips gliding over my sensitive skin.

"You're so wet," he murmurs as he slips a finger inside me.

The move drags a moan from my throat. When he adds a second and curls up to brush against a tender spot, my head falls back and I clutch his shoulders, trying to keep my hips from bucking.

"Don't hold back," he insists against my neck, letting his teeth drag over my skin. "Ride my fingers."

My eyes slide shut as I do what I'm told, rocking forward on his lap. His fingers move in rhythm with my motions, helping me along, and when he adds his thumb to the mix, swirling it around my clit, I swear I see stars. If I could form words, I'd tell him how fucking good it feels.

"Just like that. Good girl."

Even in the haze of pleasure, I can hear the rawness of his voice. When I manage to crack my eyes open, he's studying me, gaze dark and heavy. It's enough to make me grind down on him, and when I do, flames spark through me.

My breathing grows frantic, like there's not enough oxygen in the room. It's all been stolen, fed to the fire blazing at my center. Dev brings me even closer to the edge when he claims my mouth with his, stealing that last bit of air. And when his thumb moves just a little faster, I'm there, falling headfirst, with no desire to ever stop.

I turn away to gasp for breath, lowering my forehead to his shoulder and resting my hands limply on his chest. He eases his fingers out of me, and wetness trails down my thighs with them. If I wasn't soaked before, I absolutely am now, and even though I've just come, I'm still desperate for more of him.

From the corner of my eye, I watch as he brings his fingers to his mouth. A pleased sound rumbles from the back of his throat.

"You taste just as sweet as I imagined."

That's it. That's all it takes.

I lift my head, chest still heaving as I suck in air. "I need you to fuck me. Immediately."

"*Willow*," he admonishes, but his grin is wicked. "Such a greedy girl, aren't you?"

"Shut up," I groan as I press my lips to his, tasting myself on his tongue. "I want you inside me."

He inhales sharply, turning his head to break the kiss. "That really what you want?"

"Yes." I hold his face between my palms so he's forced to look at me. So he can see just how sure I am. "So badly."

He stares up at me with an adoration I want to bask in, but then a flash of disappointment overcomes it. "I don't have a condom," he explains. "I wasn't expecting this to happen."

I kiss him again, hands still cupping his jaw. "It's fine," I say when I force myself to break away again. "I'm on birth control, and I haven't been with anyone in . . . in a long time."

Suddenly, we're moving, his hands under my ass as he stands, bringing me up with him. "I think you already know I don't have any STDs."

I stifle my laugh, wrapping my arms around his neck to hold on as he strides across the room. "I don't know. Maybe we should grab one of those IYK Quick Results tests, just to be sure. I hear they're really accurate."

"You're awful," he says as he sets me on the bed and kneels on the edge.

I shoot him a smug grin. "You love me anyway."

"You're right. I do."

My heart stutters as his words wash over me. The comment was a flippant phrase that rolled off my tongue without thought. And I certainly didn't imagine that kind of reply.

"Dev . . ." I whisper, giving him the opportunity to take it back in case he didn't mean it.

I don't realize I'm inching away until he grabs me by my calves so I can't escape. He holds me there and hovers over me, knowing better than to pull me toward him.

"That's not how I expected it to come out," he admits on a soft, self-deprecating laugh. "But that's how I feel, Willow."

He cages me in with his arms, but I'm not trapped by him or by his words. I feel . . . safe. With him, I always have, even when we were young and he was encouraging me to be a little reckless. He made sure I never got hurt, and here he is, doing the same thing now. How could I not love him for that?

"You don't have to say it back," he continues, his nose brushing mine. "I don't expect you to. I know it's a big thing. But I need you to know."

I swallow past the lump forming in my throat and blink away the burn behind my eyes. "Okay," I choke out, but what I really want to tell him bubbles up behind it. "I do love you, though."

It's his turn to go still, his eyes searching my face the only motion. "Fuck," he exhales after a beat. "That felt even better than I thought it would."

A giggle escapes me, a surge of giddiness rushing through my veins. Dev loves me. And I love him. If I could go back and tell my thirteen-year-old self that we'd end up here, that girl wouldn't have believed it. Yet here we are.

"Does that mean you'll fuck me now?" I ask, both teasing and hopeful, and the laugh it drags out of him makes my heart skip a beat.

"Whatever you want, jaanu," he says before kissing away every bit of composure I have left. "I'll give it all to you."

I'm breathing hard when he reaches behind me to undo

the clasp of my bra. When he slips the straps down my arms and lets it fall to the floor, my nipples are already pebbled, aching to be touched.

He takes another moment to admire me. "Beautiful. You are so beautiful," he repeats. I don't think I'll ever get tired of hearing it.

He dips his head and takes a nipple into his mouth, rolling it with his tongue, drawing a shaky exhale out of me. When he pulls back to move to my other breast, he covers the first with his hand, saving me from the sting of the AC. It's so considerate I could cry.

Dev continues his exploration of my body, pressing kisses down my sternum to the softness of my belly. My stomach twists when he hooks his fingers into the waistband of both my shorts and my underwear and gives them a tug, a silent request for me to lift my hips so he can pull them off.

This is it. I know I can back out at any time and he would respect that decision. Not that I *want* to stop this, but . . . shit, this is really happening. Whether reality lives up to all my fantasies remains to be seen. Though, so far, I've been more than satisfied by this turn of events.

So I lift for him. And then, finally, every inch of me is bared.

Once more, he takes his time to admire, eyes sweeping over my body, a hard set to his jaw like he's holding himself back from devouring me. Based on how he lowers his head to resume kissing across my hip bones, he's about to do just that.

I stop him with a trembling hand when his lips are a hairsbreadth above my most sensitive spot, and he glances up at me in question.

"Another time," I insist, though the heat in his eyes almost makes me regret my choice. "I want you inside me."

"Greedy *and* impatient," he teases, kissing his way back up my body. "But fine. I'll take my time with you when we do this again."

Again. We haven't even gone all the way, and he's already got me thinking about how mind-blowing the next time will be. After how quickly he got me off with only his fingers, I can only imagine the kind of delicious damage his tongue can do.

"Take those off." I motion to his jeans. I want to see all of him too. If he thinks I'm impatient now, he's in for a surprise. "Hurry up."

"All right, all right," he concedes, laughing as he rises from the bed and finally undoes the top button of his jeans.

I observe, rapt, as he drags the zipper down, taking in his black boxer briefs and the bulge behind them when they come into view. But when he pushes the jeans down his thighs, I gasp.

"You have a *tattoo*." I prop myself up on my elbows to get a better look at his left thigh, where there's a mosaic of blooming flowers, a roaring tiger, and lines of script in various languages that I can't fully make out. "I *knew* it."

Dev snickers as he steps out of his jeans and once again kneels in front of me on the mattress. "Don't tell my mom."

His position gives me a better view of his ink . . . and more. "Your secret's safe with me," I promise, but my mouth is suddenly dry.

I want to lie back and look at him, but I want to touch him more. I sit up straighter and hook my fingers in the elastic waistband of his underwear. He leaves his arms hanging at his sides, letting me do what I want. I suck in a sharp breath when I pull down on the material and his cock springs free.

"Oh my god." I don't even realize I've murmured the words until he speaks.

"Don't worry, baby," he says, voice rough. "You can take it."

I'm not so sure, but I'm no quitter. Especially not when I've been waiting for so long. I curl my hand around him. My fingertips don't even come close to touching.

His sharp intake of breath barely registers. I'm too focused on the sight in front of me. "You gonna do something with that?" he asks, finally garnering my attention. "Or should I show you what I want to do with you?"

I swallow, searching for my voice. "The second one," I croak.

"We can make that happen."

He has me flat on my back in a flash, his hips slotted between my thighs, boxer briefs gone. There's nothing between us now. My legs part easily for him. They'd go much farther, but they shouldn't, unless I want to find myself in a Belgian emergency room to pop my hip back into place.

My stretch marks and surgery scars don't bother me much anymore, but I'm still sheepish about having to advocate for my comfort. I shouldn't be embarrassed, I know that. It's a condition I have no control over, and it's a fact of my life. Always will be. And yet, I'm flushing from head to toe, trying not to shrink in on myself as I lock eyes with Dev.

"Be gentle with me, yeah?" I whisper, cupping his neck as he braces himself on his forearms.

I don't have to ask him. He knows how to handle me. He has for my whole life. Still, I say the words for my own peace of mind.

"I know you can get your leg behind your head. Stop playing." He punctuates the joke with a soft kiss. Then he pulls back enough to murmur, "I promise I'll never hurt you."

This man could snap me in half, and I'd say thank you. But if I want this to happen again, we have to be careful.

Our lips catch and release, lazy and sweet, but our breaths are growing heavy, and my impatience takes over again.

As if he can sense it, Dev runs a hand down my body and dips two fingers into me, and a moan falls from my lips. "You ready?"

"Please," I choke out.

That's all the encouragement he needs. He flicks his thumb over my clit as he drags his fingers back out. My wetness glistens on them as he grips himself and aligns with my opening.

Oh god, this is it.

The head of his cock nudges against me, meeting a little resistance as he notches inside. I breathe through it at his murmured insistence in my ear, and soon, I'm lifting my hips for more. He sinks into me inch by inch, giving me time to adjust to the feel of him, to the way he stretches me, fills me. I expected pain or more discomfort. It's been so long since the last time I had sex, and there's no way around it: he's huge. But he does it with such ease and care that I'm convinced we were made for each other.

"Fuck, you're so tight," he groans against my neck. Lifting his head, he studies me. "This okay?"

I nod. The accompanying *yes* lodges in my throat, and all that escapes when my lips part is a breathy moan.

He rocks back and forth to stretch me a little more, his motions gentle but sure, and then he's seated fully inside me, his hips pressed against mine.

"Still okay?" he asks, barely above a whisper.

"God, yes." This time the words flow freely, as if he's broken through every wall within me. "Don't stop."

The demanding throb between my legs can only be satiated by his movements. I'm ready to lose myself to him.

I grip his shoulders as he moves, slowly at first, still shallow. But then he gives me more, little by little. His hips roll into me, driving in deeper, each thrust a little harder than the last. I arch my back and draw him into me, my body begging for more, because the friction is impossibly spectacular.

"Faster," I plead, instinct taking over.

He's more than willing to comply, and his careful control wavers.

It's not long before I'm desperately meeting him thrust for thrust. My peaked nipples brush his chest, and the combination of sensations has me pressing up into him, desperate to feel every inch of his skin against mine as the pressure builds and builds and builds. I'm hovering on the cliff, ready to fall. I just need that little extra push to go spiraling down.

I get it when he slips a hand between our bodies and presses down on my lower stomach, finding my clit with his thumb. I'm suddenly electrified, every inch alight, crashing over the edge with such force that it drags a groan out of him as well.

"That's it, baby," he pants, still moving as I clench around him. "Ride it out. I've got you."

And he does. It's why I let myself melt into him, let him steal my breath with another earth-shattering kiss. I want to float off and close my eyes, get lost in all of the sensations— but he's not done.

He moves slowly, allowing me a chance to recover before his pace quickens. A soft cry escapes my lips when he does, even more sensitive now. Pulling my legs up, I hook my ankles behind his back to take him at a different angle. The sensation isn't as sharp like this. It's more like an ache that grows and grows, and soon, I'm begging. For what, I'm not sure, but I'm whispering, *"Please, please, please,"* over and over again.

"Give me another one," he demands in my ear, stubble scratching my skin as he brushes his cheek against mine.

I shake my head, trembling. "I can't," I gasp out, squeezing my eyes shut tight.

He grasps my chin. "Look at me."

I force my eyes open, absorbing the intensity of his stare. He holds my gaze as he drives into me, no hesitance in his strokes, determined to take what he wants from me—determined to give me everything in return.

It's all enough to wring another orgasm out of me. My cries are lost when he dips his head to kiss me. Euphoria spirals through me, and my head spins. I'm so drunk on him that I barely notice when his hips stutter. But the praise and worship whispered and slurred into my ear soak deeply into my consciousness. Not all of it is in English, but I understand the sentiment perfectly.

He's deep, so deep inside me. I'm a woman possessed, every inch of my body on fire. There are no coherent thoughts in my mind. Nothing more than him. Nothing more than us.

I want this forever.

He buries his face in my neck when he explodes inside me, his mouth against my pounding pulse, his teeth grazing my skin. I stroke his shoulders, savoring the way he collapses against me—though he's careful not to crush me or hurt me. He gives me just enough of his weight so that I know he doesn't want to let me go.

He's not the only one. I'll hang on to him for dear life if I have to.

Because there's no going back now.

CHAPTER 25

DEV

I may not have won the race today, but having Willow in my arms feels better than winning ever could.

We've both cleaned up, but the sight of her slick thighs as she climbed out of bed did something to my brain. I almost went full caveman and threw her back onto the mattress so I could leave her with my mark all over again.

But I managed to resist. Barely.

Watching her face as she came . . . *fuck*, I've never seen a more stunning sight. The sound of her little gasps and breathy moans will be seared into my memory for the rest of my life. The day I forget them is the day I die. It's been five minutes, and all I want is to hear them again.

And again, and again, and again.

My love confession may have snapped off my tongue as an easy reply to her taunt, but it's true. This girl is *it* for me. I just wish I'd realized it sooner, because no matter how much time we're given together, it will never be enough.

I extend an arm to invite her to rest her head against my chest, and she accepts gratefully, pressing herself into my side and hooking her thigh over mine. I've dreamed of this so many nights, but now it's actually happening. Shit, maybe I *am* dreaming.

"Do you need to go back to your own room soon?" she murmurs against my pec, big brown eyes swinging up to look at me, telling me exactly what my answer should be. "You probably don't want to get caught sneaking out of here in the morning."

"I don't care." Anyone on this floor who sees me knows to keep their mouth shut. "I can stay as long as you want me to."

She snuggles closer, a contented sound escaping her lips. "Good. I don't want this night to end."

Neither do I. And I can only hope all of our nights from now on look exactly like this one.

I press a kiss to her forehead, then litter more across her curls until she giggles and pushes my face away. With a grin, I pull her in and pin her down to steal all the kisses I want, but the muffled buzz of my phone in the pocket of my jeans on the floor distracts me. I consider ignoring it, but it could be Howard, and I'm not about to miss the call that could shape the rest of my life.

"I'm not done with you," I declare, planting one more hard kiss on her lips before leaning over the edge of the bed.

Except when I yank my phone free, Howard's name isn't the one flashing on the screen. It's Oakley's.

Willow lifts a hand to my chest, a concerned crease between her brows. "Who is it?" she asks.

I don't want to wreck her peace, but I won't be dishonest. "Oakley."

As I anticipated, she stiffens beside me, though to her credit, she doesn't pull away. "Answer it," she instructs.

Without second-guessing it, I slide my finger across the screen and say, "Hey, man."

All I hear at first is the rush of air, like he's driving fast with the windows down and the call on speaker. "What time are you getting into town tomorrow?" Oakley shouts over the noise.

I frown, watching Willow. She can likely hear his side of the conversation in the quiet of the room.

"Are you in San Diego already?" I ask.

"Got in earlier," he answers. "Our moms have already fed me at least six meals. I had to get out for a drive before they made me eat another." He snorts. "Good thing I'm not the one racing these days. I wouldn't be able to fit in the car."

I force out a laugh. "Maybe I'll put off coming home for a few more days then. I can't risk it."

"Nah, fuck that. Get your ass back here ASAP. I'm bored without you, and Neha Aunty is starting to go a little wild with all this wedding stuff. I need reinforcements. Which brings me back to my original question: When will you be here?"

I glance at the clock on the bedside table. It's two a.m., which means it's five p.m. *yesterday* in California. I've been traveling the world for most of my life, and the time zones still get me wildly fucked up.

Today is technically the first day of the summer break. I promised Oakley and my family that I'd come home as soon as I could so that I'd have plenty of time with them, plus some time to relax before the whirlwind of Alisha's multiday wedding starts. I'm supposed to get on a California-bound plane at some point today—along with Willow and Mark and Chava—but I'd be hard-pressed to say when. I was a little too busy having sex with this guy's sister to bother looking up my itinerary last night.

I squeeze my eyes shut, then open them and focus on Willow's perfect face. "I don't know," I mumble. "Check with Chava. He's the one running my life."

"Already called him like three times. He didn't answer," Oakley counters. "Maybe Willow knows. She's usually an organized control freak about this kind of stuff. I'll call her now. Talk to you la—"

"No!" I blurt, just as Willow's eyes go wide. Shit, now I have to cover. "It's like two in the morning here, man. Stop calling people and waking them up. When I find out, I'll text you."

Oakley heaves a sigh that's almost lost in the wind. "Fine. Just don't leave me here alone for too long. I miss you, you dickhead."

Even though my stomach is roiling with guilt, his words make me smile a little. "Miss you too. See you soon enough."

I hang up and toss the phone back to the floor, groaning as I scrub my hands down my face.

When I open my eyes again, Willow has her chin tucked to her chest and her lower lip pulled between her teeth.

The phone call has officially burst the bubble we created for ourselves.

"How is this supposed to work, Dev?" she asks. Her voice is small. Scared. "How are we supposed to do this?"

I run a hand over her hair, wanting to soothe her, but I'm just as terrified. "How do you want to handle it?"

"I don't know," she murmurs. "I want to be with you. I *am* with you. But I'm afraid of telling Oakley." She takes a breath and lifts her chin, even if it wobbles a little. She's being as strong as she can right now. "Can we keep this between us for a little while? I want us to be sure about this—all on our own—before we tell anyone. No distractions. No doubts. No one trying to talk us out of anything."

I'm already sure, have been for entirely too long now, but she's right. There can't be a single doubt from either side when we take the plunge. The waves we make will be big, and loving each other might not be enough to keep them from drowning us.

"I think Chava and Mark might already know," I joke in an attempt to lighten the quickly darkened mood.

That drags a soft laugh out of her. "You might be onto something." She plays along, but she quickly grows serious again. "I don't think I can keep this from Grace and Chantal either. They'll figure me out in no time."

"So, seems like Oakley will be the only one out of the loop." I sigh. I don't like it, but I get it. If anyone's going to try to convince us not to be together, it's him, and we don't need that kind of influence this early on.

"Yeah." Willow wets her lips, the wheels turning in her head. "We can't hide it from him for too long, though. What if . . . what if we tell him right after Alisha's wedding? That's two weeks from now." She waits until I nod before continuing. "We can take that time to figure out how we want to handle going public. Plus, that's at the end of my contract with you and Argonaut."

She's right. But I don't want to think about what things will look like when her contract's up and she's not by my side at all times. Then again, when she's not my employee, what we're doing won't be so frowned upon.

"Okay," I agree, tugging her close to me again. "Looks like we're going to be sneaking around for a while. You up for it?"

She braces a palm on my chest as she hovers over me. Even in the low light of the bedside lamp, I can see the caramel sliver in her eye. Her perfect imperfection.

"If it means I get to be with you," she says, "then I'm up for anything."

I slide my fingers over her neck and bury them in the tendrils of hair at the back of her head. "Hey. I love you."

Relief flickers across her face. "So that wasn't an accidental, heat-of-the-moment thing?"

"Not in the slightest. You?"

"Nope. I meant it." She purses her lips, like she's considering telling me a secret. "I think I've been in love with you for most of my life." It's a vulnerable admission, but she eases the seriousness by teasing, "About time you caught up."

She can joke all she wants, but she's right. It took me too fucking long to see what was in front of me and run toward her.

But at least we've made it here. I just hope we can stay.

The first things I notice when I wake, before I've even opened my eyes, are the scent of sweet vanilla and the warmth of Willow's body seeping into mine.

I can tell she's awake, even though her back is to me and she's trying to keep her movements small and limited. She's always been a restless sleeper. I remember how she would end up out of her sleeping bag or halfway across the tent floor when our families went camping together. Clearly, nothing has changed over the years, though now I'm worried she does it because she's uncomfortable. I can't imagine staying in one spot for very long is easy on her body—especially after the multiple rounds I put her through last night.

"I know you're awake," I mumble against her bare shoulder.

She stills at my words and turns her head a little, though she doesn't look back at me. "I didn't mean to wake you," she whispers. "I'm sorry."

"Mm, don't apologize." I sweep her hair out of the way and kiss the nape of her neck, reveling in the shiver it sends through her. "I don't want to miss a moment with you."

She shifts a little more toward me, and this time, I can see her smile. "Do you go to sleep at night with all these lines planned?"

I grin against her skin in return. "Want to hear another?" When she nods, I whisper, "I'm convinced the gods dropped you right in my path."

"Ooh, good one," she says, showing me those dimples. "What Bollywood movie is that from?"

I laugh, my face already aching from the width of my smile and the pure fucking joy she inspires in me. "If you find out, let me know." I kiss her neck again, and this time I'm rewarded with a contented sigh from her. "But I mean it. I think this was always meant to happen."

"What, falling into bed together?" she jokes, rolling onto her back and squinting up at me sleepily.

"And everything that led up to it." I punctuate the theory with a kiss on the corner of her jaw. "How we needed help from each other. The time we've spent together because of it." My lips drift to her collarbone. "How close we've been able to grow without being questioned about it." I flick my tongue across the fluttering pulse point at the base of her throat. "It was all perfect. Like it was written in the stars."

"Written in the stars, huh?"

"Pure fate. Kismet. Red string and all that."

"And you believe in it?"

"Considering you're in my arms right now, I have to."

"Sap," she mumbles, threading her fingers through my hair. "Keep talking."

I could go on about her all morning, but Willow's phone chirps on the bedside table, interrupting my attempt to tell her how the Indian astrologers my mom claims she doesn't believe in but utilizes anyway couldn't deny how compatible we are.

Willow huffs as she pulls away from me to grab the phone.

"It's Chava," she says, her face falling just a little as she reads his text. "He wants to head to the airport in an hour."

Reality is calling, and it's time to face it. We have a lot to stare down.

"All right." I kiss the corner of her mouth, knowing this will be the last time I can do that until we're alone again. And I have no idea when that will be. "Let's head home, jaanu."

CHAPTER 26

WILLOW

"I'm so sore," I quietly whine to Dev as we step out into the sunshine. "How am I supposed to sit on a plane for . . ." My stomach lurches at the thought of traveling from Brussels to San Diego today. "Oh no. How long is this flight?"

"Long," he answers, grabbing the handle of my suitcase from me, our fingers brushing in the process.

I'll take all the contact I can get. Now that we've left the privacy of my hotel room, we have to act like there isn't anything—like a red string of fate—between us. We're separate entities instead of a united pair.

My chest aches a little at the idea. We agreed to keep this a secret, but in the light of day, sneaking around seems way more difficult than it did when we created this plan. All I want to do is lace our fingers together and declare to the world that we're an item.

At least . . . I think we are. We didn't exactly put a label on things.

Doesn't look like I'll be asking Dev about what he considers us, though, because Mark and Chava join us on our way to the awaiting SUV. They may have caught us making out and even bet on it happening, but we shouldn't involve them any more than they already are. They're Oakley's friends, after all, and who knows what one of them—okay, it would totally be Chava—might let slip.

They're not the only ones I have to be careful with. I have to remember that Dev is a celebrity, no matter how hard it is to wrap my mind around that fact. He's under constant scrutiny because of it, and by association, I have been too. My photo has already popped up in various publications. They're harmless, usually just shots of Dev and me walking side by side in the paddock, but my name is out there now. I've been identified as his social media manager, and for the time being, that should be my only title.

When we reach the SUV, I make accidental eye contact with Mark as he loads our bags into the trunk—and, yep, he *absolutely* knows what Dev and I were up to last night. My face goes hot when he winks at me, but at least he approves.

Chava, thankfully, seems none the wiser as I slip past him and scramble into the third row of the SUV. Dev soon joins me, his hand finding my thigh while the other guys linger outside on the sidewalk. It's a private enough moment, so I let it endure, even shifting so his fingers slip underneath the edge of my shorts.

"Before we're stuck with our families," he murmurs close to my ear, "let me take you on a date."

I glance at him from the corner of my eye, resisting the urge to turn and press my lips to his. "Is this going to be that best date ever you promised me?"

"Shit, I've got a lot to live up to, don't I?"

"You brought that upon yourself, bud."

"I suppose I did." He blows out a heavy breath, but there's

humor behind it, and the way his hand slides a little higher tells me he's not worried. "As soon as we land, I'm stealing you away. We'll tell everyone our flight got delayed."

I frown. "Chava and Mark are literally on the same flight. No one's going to believe that if they show up and we don't."

"They'll cover for us. I promise."

And that's when I notice Chava. His grinning face is pressed to the window, his hands cupped over his eyes so he can see in through the tinted glass, watching us like an exhibit at the zoo.

Clearly, there are no secrets here.

I sigh. "Fine. I guess that's the least they can do."

Sixteen hours later, I'm stiff, achy, and ready for bed, even though it's three in the afternoon here in California. I'm not fit for any kind of date right now. I'm not even fit to be seen by other humans.

Still, Dev herds me into another waiting SUV and nods goodbye to Mark and Chava before climbing in beside me. I try to wave to them in thanks, but I'm so exhausted my hand flops like a limp fish.

"I don't think I'm up for anything," I say wearily.

"You'll be up for this, I promise."

I'm not sure about that. But he hasn't let me down so far, and this is supposed to be the best date ever, so . . . I guess I'll play along.

But the longer we drive, the more confused I get. We're sticking close to the coast, heading into one of the fancier San Diego neighborhoods. Maybe we're going to a private access area of the beach. I wouldn't mind napping in the sun, but we could do that any day. Not exactly "best date" material.

So when we turn into the driveway of what's easily a ten-million-dollar home, I frown and shoot Dev a curious look. "Don't tell me you bought an entire house for this date."

He snorts and undoes his seat belt, then mine. "Just a rental. Don't worry. Not that I wouldn't buy a house just to impress you. I'd pick a more exciting city, though."

That pulls a laugh out of me. "I'll keep that in mind."

He gets out of the SUV first, then helps me down, his warm hands wrapping around mine briefly before his arm finds my waist. We make our way up the flagstone path to the wide front porch. It's decorated with wicker chairs and a swing, but it's the paper grocery bags that catch my eye.

"Did you order something?"

Dev's grin is crooked, his eyes sparkling. "You're really intent on ruining my surprise, aren't you?" He drops his arm from around me in favor of scooping up the bags, then he punches in a code on the door to unlock it. "Ladies first," he says, stepping off to the side.

Turning the knob, I obey, but only because I trust him enough not to lead me into a trap or into the awaiting machete of a murderer. Perks of knowing him my whole life, I guess.

Thankfully, there's no horrific surprise or serial killer on the other side of the threshold. Just a stunning open-concept floor plan with warm cherry oak floors, cozy neutral-colored furniture, and a chef's dream kitchen. But the view is the real selling point of this place.

A wall of floor-to-ceiling windows overlooks the ocean and the narrow, twisting stairway that leads down the rocky incline to the beach. There's a patio tucked into the side of the cliff, complete with more wicker furniture and a firepit. Best of all, it's hidden from anyone who might wander by on the narrow stretch of beach below.

I kick off my sneakers and pad toward the windows, taking in the view as Dev sets the bags on the kitchen island. "This is gorgeous," I exhale, staring out at the dark blue waves that lap onto the shore. "And peaceful."

His laugh carries across the space. "Exactly. We won't be getting much peace once we're home. I wanted one last escape before the wedding chaos begins."

I can only imagine the riot Alisha's wedding is going to be. I saw a few of her vision boards the last time I was home, and every aspect looked exciting, lavish, and expensive as hell. But as incredible as the three-day event is almost guaranteed to be, it's going to be an exhausting time for everyone involved.

"Come on. Let's check out the upstairs," Dev says, sidling up beside me and extending a hand. He's cradling a small white bag in his other arm, but I can't make out what's in it.

He leads me up the wide staircase, past all the lovely black-and-white nature photography lining the walls, to the second floor. The main bedroom practically hangs over the ocean, boasting even more stunning views. I'm immediately tempted to crash on the bed and let the dull roar of the waves lull me to sleep.

"Almost there."

He steps around the king-size mattress and tugs me toward another doorway, this one leading to an en suite bathroom done up in sleek marble. The focal point is the oversized claw-foot tub that sits by another expansive window.

"Ta-da," Dev announces. He lets go of my hand and turns on the bathtub's chrome tap. "Figured you could use a soak before we really start our date. Get undressed."

"Hey, buy a girl dinner first."

He laughs. "That's next. But first, you need a bath." He

sets the bag on the counter. It's lavender-scented Epsom salt. "Hopefully this will help your muscles. After last night and that flight, I know you're hurting."

My throat tightens, and I swear my heart skips a beat. No one has ever put so much thought into caring for me. No one has ever understood how I feel as innately as he does. "Thank you."

He shoots me a wink as he pours a generous amount of the Epsom salt into the steaming water. Immediately, the soothing scent of lavender fills the room.

"Come downstairs when you're done," he instructs, dropping a kiss on my forehead before moving to the door. "I have more surprises."

He steps out and then I'm alone, smiling goofily to myself as I blink away the tears that threaten to spill over my lashes. If my heart bursts from an overabundance of love, I know exactly who to blame.

I make quick work of getting out of my clothes and piling my curls on top of my head, then lower myself into the water, groaning as the heat slowly loosens all my knotted muscles. I stay submerged until my fingertips go wrinkly, and when I finally convince myself to get out, I find the world's fluffiest towel waiting for me.

Once I'm dry, I move into the bedroom. My suitcase stands next to the bed, but on the mattress is a container of my favorite vanilla-scented body butter and a brand-new sundress. It's white with the most delicate violets dotted across it, and it's from a brand that carries a significant price tag. Even if this doesn't turn out to be the best date of my life, it's definitely the most expensive one I've ever been on.

When I'm moisturized and dressed, I head back downstairs and find Dev coming out of the kitchen toting a tray of sandwiches, lemonade, and what I'm sure are Stella Margaux macarons. He nods to the open sliding door that leads to the patio.

"Come on, let's have a picnic."

I follow him out and settle in on the cushioned love seat. I turn my face up to the sun and let the sea breeze ruffle the frizzy ringlets that have escaped my bun. Everything about this moment is perfect.

Silently, he sets the tray down and hands me a glass of lemonade before sitting beside me. "How did you plan all of this so quickly?" I ask as the drink cools my palm.

With an arm draped over me, he presses a single finger to my shoulder. "One, I am *very* wealthy. I can pay to make just about anything happen. And two"—he presses another finger into my skin—"I know how to use the internet to order things."

I lift my glass to my lips to hide my smile. "Dick," I mumble into the drink.

"Oh, absolutely. But do you like it?"

Scanning the stunning surroundings, I sip my lemonade and pretend to consider my answer. "Hmm . . . I *guess* you did okay."

He grazes his lips across my jaw and nips at the corner in revenge. When I turn my cheek to press against his, I can feel his grin.

"Smart-ass," he murmurs. "I like you in that dress, by the way. I think I chose well."

"I won't ask how you knew my exact size."

"Then I won't admit that I pawed through your clothes while you were in the shower this morning."

I laugh and pull back a little, cupping his cheek and losing myself in the dark depths of his eyes. "I know I said it already, but thank you. This is . . . this is amazing. It's everything I could have wanted out of a date." Because all I really need is him.

His gaze flits over my face, his brows drawing together a fraction. "You don't ever have to thank me for stuff like this, Willow. This is how you deserve to be treated."

Tears once again prick at the backs of my eyes. I ward them off by pressing my lips to his. The kiss is chaste and closed, but it's achingly sweet.

Dev pulls back first, inspecting me for a second. With a soft chuckle, he dips his head and ruffles his hair like an embarrassed teenage boy who's just had his first kiss. For a man I'd enthusiastically describe as incredibly sexy, the move is adorable.

"All right, enough of that," he says, grabbing a plate of mini sandwiches off the tray. "Eat."

I take one gratefully and sit back, biting into the soft bread and cheese. "Are you happy to have a break from racing?" I ask when I finish chewing.

He nods as he grabs a sandwich as well. "As much as I love it, I love the downtime too. It's nice to not have to rush from one place to another for a few weeks."

I can appreciate that sentiment after following him all over Europe. But it hits me then that I won't be doing that anymore. I'm . . . done. I won't have to jump on red-eye flights or cram into the vans that take us to circuits. Malibu is our last stop on this whirlwind adventure, and at the end of Alisha's wedding weekend, my contract with Dev is up.

Grief punches me in the chest, nearly knocking the air from my lungs. I don't want this part to end, even though it'll allow us to bring our relationship out into the light. Helping to pull his reputation back from the brink has been an honor.

I've loved getting to know the people at Argonaut—minus Buck and Nathaniel, who never spoke a single word to me—and I loved thanking them via Dev's accounts for all the work they do. I've loved . . . all of it.

I never thought I'd enjoy a job like this, one full of travel and fast-paced events. For so long, I've envisioned myself working in a huge marketing department for a sports team, sitting at a desk, clicking a mouse all day. Something quiet and safe. To work closely with just one person originally felt like a step back. But now? I couldn't imagine spending my days in a cubicle and likely never meeting the athletes I was promoting. The days when I strived for just that feel like a lifetime ago. Like someone else's life.

"What will you do once I'm not working for you anymore?" I ask Dev, doing my best to keep my voice level, even though my heart is pounding up into my throat.

"I'm going to hire a PR firm like Howard originally asked me to." His answer comes so easily that it's clear this isn't the first time he's considered his options. "You got everything perfectly back on track for me, so all they have to do is maintain it. And once I'm at Mascort next season—"

"Don't jinx it!"

"Once I'm *hopefully* at Mascort," he amends, "they'll probably have a list of people for me to choose from that they've already vetted and approved. They're the real deal. Unlike Argonaut, who pretty much told me to figure it out all by myself." He rolls his eyes.

I have to tamp down the desire to blurt that I want to stay with him. That I want to keep doing what I'm doing, even if he really doesn't need my help anymore.

But I swallow back the words. It's not a viable option if we want to have a public relationship, and especially if I ever want to have any kind of career unshadowed by rumors of sleeping my way into a job.

"I'm crossing my fingers you get the Mascort contract," I say instead.

Dev blows out a breath, blessedly unaware of the turmoil raging inside me. "Me too. I know it won't happen overnight, but I can't take another season at Argonaut."

And Argonaut probably wouldn't take another season with him either.

"Can I ask you something?" I unnecessarily preface. He'll answer any question I come up with, but I've been curious about this for ages. "Is there a reason you hate Nathaniel so much? Other than the team always prioritizing him. And him being a dick."

Dev snickers and finishes off his sandwich. He wipes his hands on a napkin, then opens his mouth like he's about to answer, but then he closes it again and surveys the patio for a few long seconds.

"When Buck bought the team," he finally begins, "he threw this party so he could introduce himself to us. Everyone at Argonaut was excited to welcome him and Nathaniel. Probably because we were desperate for the cash influx. But the team needed new blood anyway.

"I won't lie, I was thrilled about the whole thing. More money meant that we might finally be competitive. Plus, Nathaniel had made a name for himself in F2 the year before, and since I wasn't the one getting pushed out by his arrival, I was happy to have him there." Dev gives a short, dry laugh. "I should have known better."

I take his hand in mine, a silent show of support. He curls his fingers around it, but he looks out at the waves when he speaks again.

"I introduced myself to him and Buck, and he just . . . ignored me," Dev says, shaking his head a little like he still can't believe it. "Straight up acted like I wasn't even there. Buck was the only one who spoke to me, but even that was brief. I caught Nathaniel alone later that night and asked if there was a problem. I don't remember exactly what he said, but he made it very clear that he had no interest in getting to know me as a friend, acquaintance, or even a teammate. Talked to me like I wasn't worthy of his attention."

Dev blows out a heavy breath, finally glancing back over at me. "It's why we rarely do any videos or events together. And when we do, we always have a buffer. I swear we haven't been alone in a room together since that night. Which is fine. I'm not interested in spending time with people who treat me like that."

I squeeze his hand, my stomach in knots. No one deserves to be treated that way, especially not Dev. He might as well be the human embodiment of sunshine.

"I'm sorry that happened," I say quietly, intent on lightening the mood again. "Okay, so he's obviously the driver you respect the least out there. Who do you respect the most?"

He sits a little straighter, and his expression brightens. "Zaid. Easily. He paved the way for guys like me. Showed me that little brown boys had a place in motorsports. Without him, I don't know if I would have stuck out the hard times."

"And now you're about to be his teammate. Amazing."

He side-eyes me. "Weren't you *just* telling me not to jinx it?"

"You'll be fine." I wave it off, grinning. "I'm so proud of you. You're going to have to get me paddock passes. I *have* to see you in that car. Hopefully I'll find a job that gives me vacation time right off the bat."

His smile wavers for a split second before it comes back at full force, but his eyes have dimmed a fraction. I don't love the reminder that I'll no longer be following him around the world, either, but he's the one who already has a plan in place for when it happens. Even still, maybe it hasn't really hit him that I'll be returning to my life in New York in just a couple of weeks.

Maybe it's time to broach that subject, as much as I dread the sadness that comes along with it.

"I guess we should talk about how to make long-distance work," I say, quickly following it up with, "if that's what we decide to do."

"It's not what I *want*," Dev answers, the words measured. "But if it's the only way we can be together, then that's how it'll have to be." He exhales a sardonic laugh, peering at me in profile. "Can I make a confession? It's been a really long time since I had a girlfriend."

My heart stutter-steps in my chest. Is he . . . Did he just put a label on this? I mean, I like it, but it feels . . . big. Bigger than professing our love for each other somehow.

I choose to ignore it. I'm not ready to discuss what we are right now. "Oh yeah?" I ask, my voice artificially light. "When was the last time?"

"I—" He cuts short, scrunching his brow in concentration. "Shit, freshman year of high school? Priya. Her mom *hated* me."

I gape at him. "Seriously?"

"Oh yeah, that woman thought I was the—"

"No, I mean you really haven't had a girlfriend since the start of *high school*?"

Over the last several years, I've tried my best not to keep up with him or read tabloid fodder about his love life. I didn't want to come across something I couldn't unsee. But he hasn't had a girlfriend since he was what? Fifteen? He's always come off as such a romantic—case in point, this date—so I assumed he had a string of monogamous relationships over the years. Guess I was wrong.

Dev shrugs. "This lifestyle makes it hard to have a partner. I really have to be invested in a relationship to want to make it work. That's not to say there haven't been women. I'll be honest, Willow. There have been . . . a lot." He seems only a little sheepish about admitting that.

"Huh," I muse, but it doesn't particularly bother me. He's a hot, rich, successful man who could charm the pants off just about anyone. And it sounds like he did. But I have no right to judge him for it. Besides, I'm the one he's rented out a whole house for, *just* so we could have a date. The women in his past aren't my concern. "No wonder that STD thing hit you so hard. It could have been true."

He barks out a surprised laugh. "Okay, *ouch*. I was always careful, thank you very much." He elbows me gently in the ribs and grins. "But yeah, it did hit a little close to home. The paddock might as well be a petri dish, so it's important to be safe."

A flash of a memory hits me—the two of us skin to skin last night—and suddenly I'm flushed from head to toe. Sure, a conversation about STDs does little to get me hot and bothered, but his scandal meant that he wasn't with anyone else over those months. Considering we laid the rumors to rest what feels like ages ago, he could have easily found someone to take to bed in the meantime—yet he still held out. For me.

He chose *me*.

"You okay?" I hear him ask. The note of concern in the question snaps me out of my daze. "Is it too warm out here? We can head back inside if you want to."

I shake my head, both to turn down the offer and to clear away the thoughts that have me wanting to throw caution to the wind and declare our relationship to the whole world right this instant.

"I'm fine right here." I inch as close to him as I can manage. "I was thinking about how I never want to leave, actually. Do we *have* to go back home?"

He chuckles and tucks me under his arm, resting his chin on the top of my head. "Unless you want my mom to hunt us down, we should probably drag ourselves over there in the next few hours. But until then . . ." His other hand finds my knee and traces upward under my sundress. "I have a couple of ideas for how we can spend our time here."

CHAPTER 27

DEV

I'm more afraid of facing a house full of aunties than I am of climbing into my car before a race.

Alisha's wedding will be in Malibu—a three-hour drive from San Diego—so I optimistically thought that would prevent our family from descending on us at home in the weeks leading up to the big day. Unfortunately, it seems like everyone has decided to join us here, and I can't escape.

Every time I try, I'm cornered and interrogated about where I'm going and what I'm doing with my life and when I plan to settle down. If I wasn't making so much money, they'd also be complaining about my nontraditional career choice—a.k.a. anything other than doctor or lawyer or engineer. Even so, they still lob underhanded comments about how Dad encouraged me to follow my racing dreams.

Thankfully, Mom comes to my defense whenever she hears those remarks. She's good at reminding them that I'm more successful than the majority of our family members. She also can't help but throw in a little humblebragging, either, about how at least one of her kids is following in her footsteps of being a doctor.

It's been a week of this. A week of being trailed by little cousins and accosted by uncles wanting grand prix tickets. A week of making wedding favors and pulling out my credit card to pay for last-minute additions. A week of being forced apart from Willow.

I knew the transition from spending most of our time together to having to keep our distance would be hard, but this has been fucking torture, especially knowing she's just next door.

Oakley, on the other hand, I've seen plenty of. He got roped into helping out with wedding stuff, too, while Willow lucked out and found herself being invited along on shopping trips with my mom and hanging out with Alisha to do whatever brides do before they get married.

As grateful as I am for the time with Oak, it's killing me not to blurt out, *Hey, man, I'm in love with your sister, and for some bizarre reason, she loves me back. Please don't break my ribs.*

Yeah. I'm suffering.

"I can't believe you roped me and Chava into dancing at the garba night," Oakley grumbles for the millionth time as we stuff trinkets into tote bags monogrammed with Alisha's and her fiancé's initials. We're sitting in my parents' living room, raising our voices over the sound of cackling aunties and shrieking kids. "How come you're not making Mark do it?"

"Because he's a little too"—I point at my palm—"for that."

"You and I are literally half-white," Oakley says, scoffing. "How do you know I didn't get my dad's horrible sense of rhythm and his love of Steely Dan?"

"You lose your mind every time a Panjabi MC song comes

on. Stop acting like you're not excited about this." I shove a box of horrendously expensive chocolate truffles into a bag. "Besides, do you *really* want to witness Mark trying to shoulder shimmy?"

Oakley grimaces, surely imagining our extremely long-limbed friend attempting it, just like I am. "All right, never mind. No one needs to see that."

No, they don't. To be honest, I don't want to be seen dancing either. The guest list is huge, and there's no way clips of me won't end up on the internet minutes after the rest of the guys on Alisha's side and I finish our performance.

Shit, with my luck, it'll probably be live streamed. Maybe I can beat them all to the punch and have Willow do it. If you can't beat 'em, join 'em, right?

Again, for what must be the millionth time today, my thoughts shift to her. Our date last week feels like a lifetime ago, and if I don't get her alone in the next twenty-four hours, I might combust. But the only way to do that is if I sneak out of here tonight—and sneaking out of a house full of nosy aunties? Forget it.

As Oakley continues to shove favors into bags and complain about it, I pull out my phone and send a text to Willow.

DEV: I'm coming over later. Leave the hall window unlocked.

Her response comes within seconds.

WILLOW: When exactly is later?

DEV: Just don't go to bed early.

All I get in return is a string of question marks, but I don't bother to reply. She'll see what I mean tonight.

"Who's got you smiling at your phone like that?"

My head snaps up. Oakley squints at me, top lip lifted in a hint of a sneer, but there's a curiosity behind it all. Shit.

Clearing my throat, I lock my phone and slip it back into my pocket. "Just the drivers' group chat. Thomas was saying stupid shit again."

Oakley grunts in response, though I can't tell if he believes my lie. Thankfully, we're interrupted when Alisha bursts through the front door, struggling under the weight of what looks like fifty garment bags.

"Any one of you fuckers want to help me?" she huffs, glaring at us, then at the other guys sitting around.

"Language," Mom snaps as she comes in the door behind Alisha, but her expectant gaze lands on me. "Well? Are you going to help or sit there like lumps?"

Oakley is the first to scramble up. He mumbles an apology to my mother and swoops in to help Alisha. I don't miss the sidelong glance he gives her, lingering just a moment too long. He used to be more obvious about it, back when he thought I wasn't paying attention. But I was.

He's had a thing for my sister forever, even if he'd never admit it, and I never pressed the issue. It wasn't like Alisha was ever going to look his way. Being five years older than us and (unfortunately) cooler than we could ever dream of being, she was so out of his league they were playing different sports. Guess that's why I just ignored it.

It gives me leverage when it comes to the Willow situation, though. He can't blame me for falling for his sister when he obviously fell for mine. And here he is, still looking at her like that a week before her wedding . . . Yeah, I'll use it for ammunition if I have to.

I just hope it won't come to that.

By midnight, the house is quiet. The aunties have been a rowdy bunch the past few nights, staying up until two and three in the morning, but maybe they've finally gotten it out of their systems. Better for me. At least Willow won't have to stay up half the night waiting.

After sneaking downstairs and through to the dark kitchen, I peek out the back door and across the yard. Lo and behold, Willow's bedroom light is still on. The rest of the Williams house is dark. Hopefully that means I won't have any run-ins tonight.

With one last glance over my shoulder, I head out into the backyard. I slip around to the side and stick close to our shared fence, then dart onto their property. I've done this so many times, it's like muscle memory. Except it's only ever been to sneak in to play video games with Oakley past our curfews. Never to sneak in to (fingers crossed) do something less than wholesome with his sister.

Once I've made it to the Williamses' without setting off the motion-activated floodlight, I reach for the wisteria-covered trellis that stops just under the window of the upstairs hallway—the window I told Willow to leave unlocked for me. Now I've just got to hope she did.

I start my climb, putting one hand over the other and hooking my sneakers into the holes of the lattice that I swear have gotten significantly smaller since the last time I did this. Then again, the last time I did this, I was probably fifteen. Fuck, I'm too old for this shit.

Still, I make it up to the window without breaking a sweat and hold my breath as I shove up the glass pane. It moves without a sound.

I may be a little less than graceful as I slip through the opening and essentially somersault onto the soft carpet, which, thankfully, dulls the volume of my impact. I'm in. And it looks like I'm in the clear since the lights are still out and no one is—

Oh, fuck. I'm not in the clear. I forgot all about one family member. The worst of them all.

I forgot about Herman.

The Saint Bernard is standing six feet away, head lowered, his eyes locked on me and his tail wagging slowly. I scramble to my feet and put my hands up so I can ward off the impending attack of slobber and kisses. The behemoth of a dog would never bite me, but when he gets excited, he gets *loud*.

"Herman," I whisper, slowly stepping closer to the wall as his tail picks up speed. "You're my boy." I inch along the carpet, Willow's closed door in sight. "Do me a solid and don't blow this for me, all right?"

The dog steps closer, the tail-wag morphing into a full-body wiggle.

"Herman," I warn, still slowly sidestepping. "*Herman.*"

The gods must be looking out for me tonight because I get my hand wrapped around Willow's doorknob just as Herman lurches for me, and I slip into her room a split second before his lolling tongue can find my leg. But I'm in and he's out, and all is right in the world.

"Dev? What are you doing?"

At the sound of Willow's surprised question, I turn and press my back to the door. She looks too fucking cute in her messy bun and linen pajamas, the blue fabric dotted with little lemons. The fruit choice and color palette remind me of the Amalfi coast, so I make a mental note to take her there the next time I have a break.

Like I told her before: I'm rich. The world's our oyster. And I'm taking her everywhere as soon as I can.

"What am I *doing*?" I repeat, keeping my voice low and hoping Herman can't hear me. If he gets any more excited, he may start barking. "I'm performing a grand romantic gesture by sneaking into your home at midnight and trying to avoid a make-out session that your dog is *very* insistent on having. I feel like that calls for a better greeting than 'What are you doing?'"

Willow rolls her eyes, but she's trying to tamp down a smile. "If you're here to have sex, you might as well turn around. That's absolutely *not* happening with my brother and parents across the hall."

"Not what I came here for." It's sort of what I came here for. "I really wanted to see you. And Ellie." I nod to the stuffed elephant still sitting on her bedside table. "I came to tuck you both in."

The corners of her mouth flick up a little more. "How considerate."

"I wouldn't climb up a trellis and risk being slobber-attacked by a dog for just anyone. Too dangerous."

"Says the race car driver."

I finally crack, grinning so wide it almost hurts. I'm just so glad to see her again, up close and personal. "Come here, Wills."

Despite her sarcastic comments, she doesn't waste a second throwing herself into my arms. I gather her body to mine and hold her close, inhaling her sweetness. With each breath, a little more of the stress of the last seven days washes away.

"I missed you," she mumbles, her face buried in my chest. "You've been next door this whole time, but it felt like miles."

"You know you could have come over, right?" I tease as I rub her back, grateful to feel every divot and groove of her spine. I want to memorize every inch of her. "You could have come up with an excuse to steal me away. I'm sure there was social media stuff to be done. I'm disappointed with your lack of creativity and effort."

She snorts into my shirt. "Yeah, right, and have all your aunties descend on me? I don't think so. Besides . . ." She drops her hands from my waist and pulls back as far as I'll let her. "I didn't want to interrupt your time with Oakley."

It's kind of her to give me that opportunity, but she's forgetting that I'll have to learn to balance my time with her and with her brother soon enough if we're going to make a relationship work. I hope this doesn't mean she's having any second thoughts.

"You still in this with me?" I ask, dipping my head to catch her eye. "No doubts?"

She regards me straight on, eyes nearly black in the low light. "No doubts," she says firmly. "I want to tell Oakley after the wedding. I don't want to risk ruining Alisha's day—well, *days*—if telling him goes wrong."

"Yeah, if he beats the shit out of me, I won't be able to dance," I joke.

Willow doesn't seem to find the humor in it. "I really hope it doesn't come to that." She worries her bottom lip between her teeth, glancing away. "And I don't think it will. He only did that to Jeremy because of how terrible he was to me."

"So don't be an asshole, and I'll be fine. Got it."

She blows out a breath, shoulders slumping. "Dev . . ."

"I'm sorry," I say quickly, cupping her face so she looks at me again. "You know I resort to terrible jokes when I'm nervous."

I'm desperate to change the subject now, to get away from anything that steals her light. I scan her room, homing in on the Desi clothes hanging up on the edge of her closet door. "Are those your outfits for the wedding?"

She brightens again, leaving me to exhale a small sigh of relief.

"Yeah, I still need to pack them up," she says. "You like the colors? Neha Aunty helped me pick them out."

I survey the chaniya cholis, lehengas, and saris, taking them in a little more closely, something nagging at the back of my mind. "Do you have them in order? Like, for all the events?"

"Yep." She points at each one as she goes down the line. "Pithi, mehndi, garba, wedding ceremony, and wedding reception." Yellow, pink, green, orange, and purple.

It clicks then. "I can't believe that woman."

"What?"

I release my hold on Willow and run a hand through my hair as I fight the heat creeping up my neck. "I hope you don't mind color coordinating with me, because those are the exact same as all my outfits—which my mom also picked out."

"Oh my *god*," Willow whispers fiercely. "*No.* She wouldn't do that."

"She would and she did."

"But she doesn't know about us!" she practically shouts. Her eyes immediately go wide, and she drops her voice again. "Wait, wait, wait. That morning when I had breakfast at your house, right after I started working for you—you said something to her in Gujarati, and she practically fell out of her seat laughing. Why?"

I should have known Willow wouldn't forget that, and now I have an embarrassing confession to make. "Because I . . . I told her that nothing was ever going to happen between you and me."

Willow blinks up at me for a beat, and then she doubles over in quiet giggles. "I can't *believe* you," she gasps, her body shaking. "Literally a minute later, you were telling me you're obsessed with me!"

I grudgingly pat her shoulder, grateful for the low light so she can't see how red my face probably is right now. "Yeah, all right. Maybe I did. But I—"

"Don't even try to deny it," she says, grin so wide and dimples so deep that when she looks up at me, I can't help but dazedly smile back, blinded by the pure joy emanating from her. "I guess she was right to laugh."

"Truly." I shake my head. Mothers are the world's best fortune tellers. "Come on, let's get you and Ellie to bed."

She finally straightens up. Taking my hand, she leads me over, and I hold up the sheets as she climbs in. I tuck her in as promised, arranging Ellie beside her before I sit on the edge.

"Sweet dreams, jaanu," I murmur, stroking a thumb over her cheek. She looks so peaceful that I don't dare ruin it by climbing in beside her, no matter how much I want to. "I'll see you from afar tomorrow."

# CHAPTER 28

DEV
_____

The big weekend has finally arrived, and I swear I've been scrubbing haldi stains off my face for half the day.

"This shit is a nightmare," I hiss, still pissed that I, the brother of the bride, had to be covered in that stupid yellow turmeric paste as part of the pithi ceremony. "There's no way Alisha would stand having this spread all over her. That girl threw fits as a kid when I got washable marker on her while we were drawing."

Chava spares me a disinterested glance from where he's lazing on my bed, scrolling through his phone while Mark and Oakley do the same thing beside him. They have their own bedrooms in this sprawling Malibu beach house my family rented, but, of course, they've posted up in here instead. I hate to say it, but I think we're attached like conjoined quadruplets at this point.

Downstairs, the thudding drumbeats grow louder, and excited shouts and laughter accompany the music. It's the first night of the wedding, and the men from both sides are here to celebrate while the women get their mehndi done at their own party next door. I don't know how Alisha found *three* high-end rental properties on the same street, but my bank statement says she pulled it off. They're so nice that I can't even be mad about it.

The house across the street, with its lush green yard, will be home to the garba tomorrow night and the wedding ceremony on Sunday, but this place and the one next door will be used for the rest of the events and ceremonies. Plus, we put our close family and friends up here. It's the perfect way to keep the celebration going twenty-four seven.

"I saw her," Chava says offhandedly, his attention still fixed on his phone. "She looks great. Glowing. And you look . . ."

"Jaundiced," Mark finishes for him.

I throw the yellow-tinted washcloth into the sink. "Fuck *off.*"

"You look fine," Oakley calls as I stalk out of the en suite bathroom. "Not like you have anyone to impress. It's just the men tonight."

I'm careful not to react to that, because I don't plan to just hang out here all night. No, I'll be heading next door the second I can slip away without being noticed.

This already feels like a taste of how life will go when Willow and I are forced to make our relationship long-distance. Endless texts, phone calls snuck in spare moments alone, sending silly pictures of the most mundane things. This morning, I stared at a photo of a stack of pancakes for several minutes, all while imagining I was sitting at the table next to Willow. It was the highest degree of pathetic.

I'm in love with her. I've known as much for a while, and I've already confessed it, but I didn't expect love to hurt like this. To ache. To burrow deep into my bones and physically *pull* me toward her. She's part of me, wrapped around every nerve and muscle and bone, and to be separated from her is like missing a piece of myself.

And she's just next door. How wretched will it feel when she's half a world away?

Fuck. Right now, I need to be the joyful brother of the bride, not the moping lovesick puppy who's just been kicked by reality. But *man*, this is miserable.

"Are you really that mad about a little turmeric?" Oakley asks, surveying me closely. "I've never seen you scowl this much. Didn't even know you could."

Doing my best to school my expression, I turn toward the mirror and adjust the collar of my navy button-down. I'll be back in Indian clothes tomorrow, coordinating with Willow again, though hopefully no one other than my scheming mother will notice.

"Just a little on edge," I admit when I can't conjure a relaxed expression. "I still haven't heard from Howard. My future's kind of up in the air, and it's silly season, so . . ." I shrug without finishing the thought.

Heaving a sigh, Oakley gets up from the bed and stands beside me, clapping my shoulder and making eye contact with me in the mirror. "You could just retire," he says, smirking. "Life's pretty good on this side."

That gets me to snicker. I shake my head. "I'll pass, thanks. I like my job."

"Shame." He uses the hand that was on my shoulder to slap me upside the head. "Stop moping. Let's go get shitfaced. You don't have to drive this weekend."

He's right about that, and I plan to take advantage of it—just not in the way he's suggesting. "All right, fine," I concede, managing a smile this time. "Wanna bet on how long it'll take for one of the uncles down there to ask me for paddock passes?"

Oakley snorts and guides me to the door. "I'm giving it no more than ten seconds."

If racing doesn't work out, I might have a future career as a spy.

After plying all the boys with drinks and leaving them singing completely unintelligible Bollywood karaoke, I've made my escape. It's a little after ten p.m.—still incredibly early when there are wedding festivities in full swing—but I can't take another second of waiting.

I texted Willow twenty minutes ago and told her to meet me here—the laundry room in the house where the ladies are partying tonight. It's the only place I could think of where we wouldn't be interrupted, because who's doing *laundry* at a party? And with wet mehndi on their hands? Never happening. Besides, all those sparkly outfits are dry-clean only.

The party is taking place in the backyard, meaning I could sneak into the house unseen. My stomach sinks a little when I step into the small room off the kitchen and realize Willow isn't here yet. She responded to my text with a kissy-face emoji, but now that I think about it, it wasn't exactly a re-sounding *Yes, I'll meet you*.

Well, shit. Maybe I blew it. I should have gotten confirma-tion. I could text her again or maybe even call or—

The door, which I left ajar, suddenly swings open, nearly smacking me in the nose.

"Oh, shit!" Willow gasps. She shuffles into the room under the weight of her embroidered chaniya choli, bumping the door shut with her hip. "Are you okay? Did I hurt you?"

I'm more surprised by the curse leaving Willow's pretty little mouth than I am by nearly getting taken out by the door. "I'm fine," I tell her, still blinking away my shock.

And once I do . . . Fucking hell, she's a vision in soft pink and gold. Willow decked out in clothes from my culture absolutely does it for me. It's the second time today the sight of her has almost knocked me on my ass. The first was at the pithi ceremony, when she wore that marigold-yellow outfit and truly embodied the warmest ray of light. It's proof of how well she fits into my life, how easily she adapts to and appreciates this part of my world. All of it fits her beautifully, and I don't just mean the clothes.

"Okay, good," she exhales before giggling. "I'm so happy to see you, but I can't stay for long."

Her cheeks are flushed, and she's holding her hands out in front of her awkwardly. Her positioning draws my attention to the swirls of intricate mehndi designs twisting all the way up to her elbows. From the look of things, she's been having a great time with my family.

"I promise, no one will notice," I tell her. "Things are about to get rowdy out there."

She blinks a few times, the glitter on her eyelids catching the light. "Seriously?"

"Seriously." I lean against the washing machine and smirk. "Pretty soon they're gonna be telling Alisha all about how to perform her wifely duties."

Willow stops blinking and gapes at me. "You don't mean . . ."

"Oh, I absolutely do mean. Did you see anyone carrying around an eggplant out there?"

She balks.

"I'll take that as a yes."

"I thought they were talking about cooking," she says weakly. "I really should learn Gujarati. No wonder they were all cackling. Curry isn't that funny."

I bite back a laugh at her wide-eyed innocence, curling my hands around her waist and pulling her to me. "Don't worry," I reassure. "I'll teach you one day. And I'll help you practice for your future wifely duties."

She comes to me willingly, though she doesn't dare touch me in return. "Oh yeah? When should we start on these future wife lessons?"

"No time like the present."

Willow squeals when I lift her off her feet and turn to place her on top of the washing machine. "Dev," she warns, hands lifted between us. "My mehndi is still drying."

I bend, finding her ankles and the hem of her long skirt. "Guess that means all you can do is sit there and look pretty while I wreck you."

"Dev!"

I watch her through my lashes and lift the fabric to her shins without shame. "Can I?"

"We shouldn't," she whispers, but her knees fall open.

"We shouldn't," I agree as I slowly push her skirt to her thighs. "But I want to. Do you?"

A tense beat passes as she observes my every move closely. Then she nods.

"I need to hear you say it, Willow."

"Yes," she exhales, slipping forward to the edge of the machine, skirt rising with the motion. "Yes, I want to."

"That's my girl. Now spread your legs for me, baby."

She does as she's told, and I slip my hands up to her hips and curl my fingers around the edge of her cotton panties. I drag the soaked material down her legs. I want nothing more than to worship her pussy, to taste her like I've been dreaming of.

"So wet already," I murmur. My cock is aching, but this is all about her. This is all I want.

"Just what you do to me," she pants, inching closer. "Touch me, please."

How could I resist such a sweet plea?

Dropping to my knees, I push her glittering skirt over her hips, revealing her to me. I palm her ass, pulling her closer as I lean in, tracing her slit slowly with my tongue. She tastes like everything that makes life worth living.

The moan that escapes her is the filthiest thing I've ever heard, like she's been on edge the whole time we've been apart, waiting for me to touch her. And now, judging from the way her hips buck forward, she's done being patient.

I close my lips over her clit and suck, earning another shuddered sound of pleasure. Her back arches, and her hands hover over my head. She wants to touch me, to grip my hair. She's barely resisting the urge, lest she smudge the paste staining her skin. I don't want it to budge. I want it to darken to the deepest brown so I can trace the lines and swirls and flowers for weeks to come. Her skin is already the most beautiful canvas; it deserves unmarred art.

But I have no problem corrupting the rest of her.

I glide the tips of my fingers over her folds as I greedily devour her, her skin slick and scorching, and I take what I want. I slip one finger into her first, relishing the way her walls flutter around me. Then I add a second, eliciting another heavenly sound. She practically chants my name, begging for more, grinding against my face like a woman possessed.

"Dev, please," she whines.

I glance up and take in the sight of her head thrown back and her hands lifted as if in prayer. I choose to believe she's praying to me.

"I'm . . . I'm . . ."

Pulling back slightly, I murmur, "Let go, baby." And then my tongue is back on her clit and my fingers are curling up, working inside her to bring her all the way to that peak.

She crests it with a loud moan. I keep my mouth pressed to her as she rides it out, still tasting her, slowing my movements until she goes limp against me. With soft kisses to her inner thighs, I slip my fingers out of her, pleased with the way they glisten under the fluorescent lights.

"I've wanted to do that for days," I say, sitting back on my heels and dragging the back of my hand across my mouth. I grin wickedly up at her. "Too bad you didn't let me when I snuck into your house."

She watches me with a look somewhere between smitten and annoyed. Like she's torn between telling me she loves me and kicking me in the face. "If you'd done that," she says, chest heaving and breaths still labored, "there's no way this would still be a secret."

She's right. My girl is loud and wild when she finally lets go, and I'd never want to hold her back.

Her eyes go wide then. "Oh god, you don't think anyone heard us, do you?"

I shake my head. "With the music that loud? I'd be amazed if anyone out there could hear themselves think."

She drops her shoulders and exhales, and I soothe her with a kiss to the inside of her knee. Then I rearrange her skirt, letting it fall back to her ankles, turning her back into the picture of decency—minus the missing panties and the glow in her cheeks.

"Soon we won't have to keep this such a secret," I promise. "Two more days."

"Two more days," she repeats breathlessly.

And they're going to be the longest days of my life.

CHAPTER 29

WILLOW

Dev smudged my mehndi.

It's not particularly noticeable, but I know why the lines on my fingertips aren't as sharp as they could be or why the flower on my wrist looks a bit more like an invasive weed. It's our little secret—just like our relationship will be for one more day.

I haven't seen him since last night. He's been busy with religious ceremonies and lunches with his grandparents all morning and afternoon, but I've been counting down the hours until the start of the garba. According to the clock on the bedside table, we're only an hour away. I'm so excited I could scream.

To distract myself, I called Grace and Chantal for pep talks and filled them in on all that's happened over the last several days. I've steamed both my lehenga and my mom's for tonight. I've washed, deep conditioned, and styled my hair. I've repainted my nails to match the emerald green of my outfit. I even went for a long walk on the beach like some sort of cliché. I'm just so ready to see Dev.

After helping my mom get ready in my parents' room, I make my way back down to the first floor where my bedroom is. The Andersons truly went all out for this wedding. This house—and the two others—is a testament to that. It'll probably take some time to adjust when I go back to New York because my entire apartment could fit into the living room here.

Not wanting to think about going back to the city, I push the thought away. I love New York and I always will, but I'm not ready to return to the life it represents. Giving up this whirlwind that I've grown so fond of over the past few months will be tough, and staying in one place rather than hopping on a plane to a new city nearly every week seems so . . . dull. Boring. Gray.

Following Dev around the world has brought color into my life. Color I didn't know was missing. I never thought I'd find my passion in the world of motor racing. It's always been part of my life, my brother's dream until he decided it wasn't, and something I thought wasn't for me due to a myriad of reasons. But it *is* for me, and I don't want to leave it. I certainly don't want to leave Dev.

The universe must know how desperate I am to stay with him, or at least to get my fill of him before we're officially parted, because there he is standing outside my bedroom door. He's leaning against the doorframe, phone in hand, wearing a green kurta that matches the color of my lehenga so perfectly it's like they were cut from the same cloth.

My feet are moving before I even know what I'm doing. As if he can sense me there, he looks up from his phone. And then he smiles.

Yeah. There's no way I could ever walk away from this man.

I'm beside him a second later, drinking him in from head to toe. "Wow, you look . . ."

He straightens up. I swear he even puffs out his chest a little.

"Handsome?" he supplies for me. "Dashing? Hot as fuck?"

"Wrong," I lie. "I was going to say like a leprechaun."

"That is rude for so many reasons that I don't have time to get into."

As much as I want to admire him and banter, I'm struck with nerves. He's here waiting for me out in the open where anyone with a bedroom down this hallway could see. Oakley, thankfully, is staying in the house next door with the rest of the guys, but any number of people could catch us.

"What are you doing here?" I ask, lowering my voice and glancing over my shoulder to make sure we're alone.

Dev's unconcerned. His signature grin is in place, and his body is relaxed. "I was sent to escort you and your parents across the street to the party."

"I'm pretty sure we could have found our way," I point out, but I relax a little. At least he has a valid reason to be here.

"Better safe than sorry. I've been told there are some crazy brown people in this neighborhood."

I scoff at his terrible joke and shake my head. Then, emboldened, I open my door and tug him in with me.

"You'll have to wait to be our escort," I tell him once we're inside. "As you can see, I'm not dressed."

He gives me a thorough once-over, taking in every inch, even though I'm wearing yet another simple pink sundress, something he's seen me in a thousand times before. And yet he looks at me like it's the first time, assessing every curve and inch of skin on display.

I flush under the attention and turn away. If I let myself bask in it, we won't be getting anywhere on time.

Grabbing the lehenga choli hanging up in the closet, I move to the bathroom. "I'll be right back."

But Dev catches my wrist. "No point being modest, baby. Pretty sure I've already seen you naked—a few times. And I can help you with the ties on your lehenga."

He's not wrong on either count, so . . . fuck it.

I shove the outfit at him and pull my sundress off over my head.

Even though he was the one who suggested I change in front of him, his jaw goes slack, and he's back to studying me as I stand before him in just my skimpy lace underwear. Last night, when I didn't think anyone would see what I had on underneath, I'd gone for basic cotton. I certainly wasn't going to make that mistake again today.

"I see you're not fond of bras," Dev murmurs as he drags his focus back up to my face.

I shrug, reveling in the way he's trying to resist staring at the peaks of my nipples. "No point, really. Not like I've got that much going on."

His voice is hoarse when he says, "Oh, you've got enough."

I grin as I nod to the choli. "Help me, yeah?"

It takes a beat or two before he gains enough wits to pull the blouse off the hanger and motion for me to lift my arms. I do as I'm told, and then he steps forward. As he pulls the top carefully over my head, I close my eyes and soak in the warmth of him.

"Your mehndi looks fantastic," he murmurs. He doesn't back away once my choli is in place. "Very dark. It means someone loves you a lot."

My eyes reopen. "You smudged it, you know."

He cocks a brow in challenge. "I seem to remember telling you to sit there and look pretty. You're the one who went wild."

"All because you made me," I whisper back.

"Careful, Willow." He brushes his nose against mine, his lips inches away from my own. "Keep this up and we won't be going anywhere tonight."

I'm tempted to take him up on that offer. I could have this blouse off in a heartbeat, drop my panties to the floor, and be on my back on the mattress in seconds. We could make it quick. We could—

I clear my throat and step back, but my heart pounds from the effort it takes to resist. "You have to go dance," I remind him, sounding entirely too breathless. "And I have to record it for the whole world to see."

Dev hesitates, his teeth sinking into his lower lip, but finally, he steps back. "Can't wait to make a fool of myself again on the internet," he says. Then he crouches and holds open the skirt for me to step into. "You gonna cheer me on, jaanu?"

"I have to stay quiet for the video." I grin, relieved by how easily we can set the tension aside and get back to our easy conversation. "But I'll be cheering you on in my head. You're going to do great."

He snorts as he lifts the skirt. He settles it around my waist and does the side tie like a professional—not too tight, not too loose. "Yeah, just gonna channel my inner Shah Rukh Khan." His eyes flick to mine, the corner of his mouth pulling up in one of those beautifully personal smiles. "I would dance on top of a train for you."

That declaration is nearly better than a love confession. I can already hear "Chaiyya Chaiyya" playing in my head. "I'd love to see that."

With both hands on my waist, he holds me in place and angles in to press a tender kiss to my cheek. "You better not change your mind once you see me dance tonight."

Nothing could change my mind about him. "I wouldn't dream of it."

I can easily say this is the most fun I've had in ages. Sure, traveling around the world and watching fast cars zoom around is great, but dancing and cheering and eating what has to be about ten thousand jalebis? It can't be topped.

Dev, Oakley, Chava, and a few male cousins from the bride's side are set to perform soon. Which is perfect, because my feet are already aching in my heels, and if I don't want to puke up all the sweets I've eaten so far, I need to sit down and rest. I'll kill two birds with one stone—gear up for the next round of dancing and film Dev making a fool out of himself. Win-win.

Just as I settle into my seat toward the edge of the low stage in the backyard, Dev appears. He should be off preparing for his grand entrance, but instead, he's crouching in front of me, holding out his phone.

"Hold on to this for me, please?" he asks, big brown eyes with those thick lashes I'm incredibly jealous of fixed on me. "I don't want it bouncing around in my pocket while I'm up there."

I nod and take it from him, our fingers brushing. The touch sends a zap of electricity up my arm, and I'm once again desperate to steal time alone with him. Desperate to get our secret out in the open.

"I've got it." I set it on my lap, the screen reflecting the red and gold lights strung up around us. "Good luck up there. Don't fall flat on your face."

He rolls his eyes as he straightens, hands on his hips like a Bollywood hero. "Never. I'm a professional."

"Uh-huh. Sure. Right."

With a wink, he strolls off to find the rest of the guys. I snap a few pictures of the crowd and the decor, having already gotten permission from both Dev and Alisha to post about the wedding. For the sake of safety, I won't put anything up until we all leave on Monday, even though my contract with Dev will technically be over by then. Doesn't matter, though. As long as he doesn't kick me out of his accounts, I want to keep helping.

My attention snaps back to the stage when the volume of the music pouring from the speakers increases. The lights dim until the stage is dark, and then the spotlight flares and the song's beat kicks in. It's not a song I recognize, but the Desi portion of the audience certainly does, and I make quick work of shifting from still photos to video.

My brother appears first, looking surprisingly dapper in his bright pink kurta. Chava is the next to swan into place, and one by one, four of Dev's cousins appear. Then there he is, Dev in all his glory, arms spread wide as he saunters to the center of the stage. In any other scenario, this entire routine would absolutely give me the ick, but it's a big, fat Indian wedding. This is exactly how it's supposed to go.

I trade off between watching Dev lip-synch and dance in real life and on my phone's screen, already imagining how I'll edit this. I swear he's singing straight to me, and even if I have no idea what the lyrics mean, it's still classic Bollywood—there's no way it isn't wildly romantic.

I nearly laugh when Oakley and Chava almost run into each other during a transition, but I'm distracted when Dev's phone buzzes in my lap. Holding my own phone steady, I glance down.

Howard's name is flashing across the screen.

My heart surges into my throat. I dart a look at my phone, still recording, then at Dev's again. *Shit.* Howard wouldn't call unless he had news, but Dev's only halfway through the routine. It's late, and it's the weekend, so if I let this go to voicemail, Howard may not answer when Dev calls back. That would leave Dev waiting in agony for who knows how long, especially with the wedding festivities tomorrow. He'll have little opportunity to take calls. Which means I have to make a choice. Right now.

Biting my lip, I tap the screen of my phone to stop recording. I dump it into my lap and scoop Dev's up instead. Then, after a deep breath, I answer.

"Hi, Howard, this is Willow," I greet, hoping he can hear me over the booming music.

The pause that follows lasts so long I pull the phone back to make sure the call is connected.

"Willow?" he questions after another second, his tone full of disdain.

I breathe a small sigh of relief that he's there, regardless of his attitude. We've spoken a handful of times before, but maybe he needs a reminder of who I am. "Yeah, I'm Dev's social media—"

"I know," he cuts me off. "Is there a reason Mr. Anderson isn't answering his own phone right now?"

"He's . . ." I trail off, watching Dev up on the stage, taking in his grin and his moves. "He's a little busy right now. Can I take a message?"

"No." Howard's tone leaves no room for argument. "I'll call back in the morning."

"Wait!" I shout so loudly that the people seated near me turn and stare. "Can I at least know if it's good news?"

He pauses for so long again that I wonder if he's hung up, but then he finally says, "It is."

Oh my god. This really is the phone call Dev wouldn't want to miss. "Okay," I breathe out. "Please, just . . . hold on one second, okay?" I shoot to my feet and wave to the boys onstage with my free hand, hoping to get the attention of at least one of them. "He's going to want to hear this as soon as he can."

"I don't have all night," Howard grumbles, but I barely hear him.

Somehow, Dev is the one who spots me, and the second he looks my way, I point to the phone and shout, "It's Howard!"

That's all it takes.

He's jumping off the stage a second later, landing like a true action hero, then he's sprinting toward me. Dev has the phone out of my hand before I can blink, skidding to a halt and lifting the device to his ear.

"Howard? What's going on?"

The music is still booming, and the other boys are finishing the routine, a little half-assed, but at least they're doing it. I keep my focus locked on Dev, though, watching his every shift in expression.

"Is it official?" he asks. He presses his lips together as he listens, his face unreadable. "All right. Yeah. Thank you, Howard. I appreciate you calling."

My heart pounds so hard it threatens to break free from my ribs. The anticipation makes it hard to breathe. "So?" I prompt. "What's going on? What's the news?"

Another beat passes. The music comes to a deafening crescendo. And then Dev smiles, wide and bright and beautiful.

"I'm going to Mascort."

CHAPTER 30

DEV

Following five grueling hours of negotiations over a video call last night, Howard sends the Mascort contract in the morning.

I sign it with both of my parents standing behind me. My mother showers me with kisses and blessings while my dad squeezes my shoulder, tears shimmering in his eyes. Alisha would be here, too, if she wasn't busy getting her makeup done. Somehow, she wasn't pissed at me for stealing just a sliver of her spotlight. Still, I'm determined to make sure she gets all the attention today.

The rest of the morning passes in a blur. Alisha hides away as the baraat begins. The music from the procession is loud enough to be heard from all the way down the street. And then it's finally time for the wedding day to begin.

I head out of the house to join the guests who have already settled in their seats and greet the ones from the groom's side that are trickling in. When the groom himself finally arrives, my mother greets him first, and after invoking a few traditions I'll never understand—like grabbing his nose—she escorts him to the elevated mandap.

The four-post dais is wrapped in red, white, and pink roses, and dozens more cascade down from the draped cream silk covering it. Before it are six ornate chairs—two facing the crowd and two on each side. They're perfectly placed around a spread of items on the red and gold rug. It's beautiful, just like every other aspect of this weekend.

I scan the growing crowd, which will be two hundred people strong when the ceremony starts, looking for one face in particular.

At the tap on my shoulder, I turn around.

Willow is wearing the deep orange sari I saw hanging up in her room the night I snuck in, and the color brings out the warm brown of her skin. She's standing next to her parents and Oakley, which means I can't say the things I desperately want to, and I certainly can't let it show on my face either. No matter how hard it might be, I can't give us away. Not yet.

I've been accused of being a romantic. A sap. But how could I be anything different? I grew up on Bollywood movies with men spinning around in fields of flowers, singing about how the girl they love is more beautiful than every daisy, rose, and tulip in the world. How the fuck am I not supposed to tell Willow that she's brighter than all the stars in the sky? How can I look at her and say, *You look nice*, when I want to scream from a snow-covered mountaintop that just the sound of her voice could raise me from my grave?

And yet I force myself to clear my throat and say, "You look nice."

Her happiness is blinding, like staring into the sun. I don't want to look away. I'd let her steal the sight from my eyes, the breath from my lungs. I'd let her do her worst and still be eternally grateful.

"You look all right," she jokes before sparing a glance over at her family and remembering our audience. "I can't wait to see Alisha."

I chuckle. "I think you'll love her grand entrance. Me and the boys get to carry her in like a princess." Then I force myself to greet Dr. and Mr. Williams. "Thanks for being here this weekend. I know it's been pretty overwhelming."

Dr. Williams beams at me. The same dimples that dot her daughter's cheeks appear in her own. "Neha told me to brace myself, but I never could have imagined all this. I've loved every second of it, though. Can't wait for your wedding next."

The last comment is said teasingly, but I'm already imagining myself under that mandap with Willow.

Slow your fucking roll, my guy.

From the corner of my eye, I see one of Alisha's bridesmaids leaning out the back door of the house, waving to get my attention.

"That's my cue," I say to the Williamses with a nod to Oakley. He's going to help with this part since he's practically family. "Almost time to escort the bride in. We'll see the rest of you later."

Dr. Williams gives me a quick hug before shooing us off. But before I turn to go, I lock eyes with Willow.

Tonight. We're finally telling Oakley.

My sister is officially a married woman. Which means that I've become the target of all the aunties' matchmaking attention.

"Beta, my friend Sonali has a granddaughter who is a trauma surgeon," one of the older women coos. "She would make a great wife. She could fix you back up after you crash!"

The women surrounding me cackle, bangles and jewels

tinkling as they clap their hands like it's the funniest thing they've ever heard.

The reception has been in full swing for half an hour, and already, I've faced more offers like that than I can count. It's going to be a long night if this keeps up.

I extract myself from the group of aunties as smoothly as I can and weave through the crowd of people mingling and eating and dancing, praying I don't get caught by another woman who wants to set me up. A few people greet me as I go, but thankfully, they let me step out of the giant marquee.

Out in the night air, I draw in a deep breath, relieved to have escaped the direct assault of noise after such a busy day. Thankfully, every detail went smoothly, from the vows to the cocktail hour, and finally, the newlyweds' grand entrance at the reception. But I need a break.

I've caught sight of Willow a few times, though every time I've tried to approach her, I've been intercepted by someone who wants to talk about my future and romantic prospects. I'll find her later. How much later, however, remains to be seen.

"Long day, huh?" comes from behind me.

I glance over my shoulder and find Reid sauntering my way.

I try to laugh, but the sound that escapes is more of a pained grunt. "And it's not anywhere near being over."

Reid snagged an invitation to the wedding thanks to my mother, who practically adopted the kid when he and I lived together in Monaco. Every time my parents came to visit, she insisted that it was her duty to make sure he was taken care of, especially once she found out that his mother had passed away years ago and his elderly grandmother was his only remaining family. After that, he was invited to every family vacation and gathering, though he always politely declined. This was one invite he couldn't turn down, though.

"Gotta admit," Reid says, coming to stand next to me as he looks up at the shimmering fairy lights draped over our heads like a canopy. "This is probably the best party I've ever been to. Y'all really know how to make a wedding fun."

"That we do," I agree, clinking my champagne glass against his.

He laughs and sips his drink, watching me thoughtfully. "I saw Willow in there taking pictures. She still running your social media?"

I nod but stop myself quickly. "Actually, today's the last day of her contract."

"No shit?" He blinks, brow raised. "I'm surprised you're letting her go. She's really pulled you back from the brink."

She most certainly did, and if I could, I'd insist she keep working for me. Working *with* me. But her reputation is too precious to destroy, and I want her to find the biggest successes in life.

"I was honestly prepared to bribe her so I could woo her away from you," Reid continues. "I need someone like her running my social media."

"I won't lie, your image is pretty . . . stuffy," I agree as diplomatically as I can.

He sighs, almost defeated. "I know. Some days I'm amazed people even remember my name. I'm outscoring Lorenzo in the points, but he overshadows me in every other way." He slides me a look from the corner of his eye. "Is Willow looking for a new contract, by chance?"

I'm struck by the question. We haven't really talked about what she's going to do next, but I assumed she'd return to

New York and get a job there. Then again, if Reid is offering what I think he is . . .

Fuck, could this be the solution to our long-distance problem?

"Possibly," I hedge, my brain already working through how we could make this happen. "Let me talk to her, and I'll let you know."

Reid's face lights up, activating his golden boy charm. "Tell her I'm all in," he insists. "If she wants the job, it's hers. Immediate start date. I'll call up my lawyer and D'Ambrosi tonight. We can get her the necessary contracts by the morning."

"You really don't waste time, do you?"

He chuckles, lifting his champagne glass in a mock toast. "I've seen what she's done for you, and I want that. Not the whole 'I'm a lovesick sap' thing, but the other stuff."

I wince. "You caught on to that?"

Reid's smile is faint but kind. "You look at her like she hung the moon, Dev. Kind of hard to miss."

That is exactly why Willow and I need to talk to Oakley very, very soon. There's no more hiding this.

"Let me talk to her about the offer," I tell him before downing the rest of my champagne.

He slaps me on the shoulder. "Be persuasive. I want her on my team. The *winning* team."

"Yeah, yeah. I'll do my best, asshole."

Reid's laugh follows me back into the crowd. My only goal is to find Willow. Now that I know there's a chance we can truly be together, to not end up separated in the way we expected, I'm desperate to talk to her about it. But will she go for it?

It's a big ask. She has a life to return to, and this was never supposed to be more than a temporary job. Her goal when we started working together was to land a position at a much bigger marketing firm, so would she be up for a little more of this? Especially if it's with someone she doesn't know well?

I finally spot her near the edge of the tent. She's cradling a fresh jalebi in her hands, and by the time I reach her, it's gone and she's got her fingers pressed to her mouth in an attempt to hide her puffed-out cheeks.

"Hey." Fuck, I sound rushed, like what I have on my mind is urgent. But in a way, I guess it is. "Can I talk to you? In the house?"

She swallows, her brows knitting together in concern. "Everything okay?"

I nod, already turning to guide her away. "Everything's great. Don't worry. Come on."

She doesn't question me. She just trails along as I weave back outside, glancing over my shoulder every few seconds to make sure she's following. Once we're away from the tent and on the grass, I slow and offer my arm to her so she doesn't have trouble if her heels sink into the soil. She accepts without hesitation, letting me lead her into the house.

When we're alone in the dim back hallway, she slides her hand down from the crook of my arm, her fingertips brushing my wrist, and presses her palm to mine. I spread my fingers reflexively, and when her fingers slot between mine, I curl my own up to keep her hand in place. It's a perfect fit.

I draw her to a stop between the door to the bathroom and the one to the home's impressive library a little farther down. I can't take another step until I get this off my chest.

"Dev, what's going on?" she asks softly, her eyes locked on mine.

Her face is so pure and full of love that my throat goes

tight for a second. "I . . ." I swallow, trying to dislodge the lump. "I have kind of a crazy question for you."

She tilts her head, red-painted lips turning up at the corners. "Okay, hit me with it."

I pull in a steadying breath, hoping the words don't come out rushed and jumbled. "If you could continue working in F1, would you want to?"

A crease appears between her brows, and confusion swims in her eyes. "That's what's so important?" When I nod, she nibbles on her bottom lip and averts her gaze a little, like she's deeply considering her answer. "Truthfully? I never thought I'd say this, but . . . *yeah*. I really love it. It feels . . . right."

Relief surges through me, and I swear my heart stutters. She wants to stick around. But I want more confirmation before I lay out Reid's offer. "And that's not just because you love me, right?"

"That has a little something to do with it," she says with a light laugh. "But it's a fascinating industry, so I'd love to see more of it."

When I don't immediately reply, her amusement fades away, leaving her searching my face and the crease between her brows reappearing. "What are you trying to say, Dev?"

This time, I draw my thumb across her brow, erasing the question there. "I was just talking to Reid and . . . he told me he needs someone who can make him stand out," I explain, trailing my hand down to cup her cheek. "He saw what you did for me and wants the same thing. I agreed that you're the perfect person for the job."

She drops her shoulders. "You're kidding me."

"Not in the slightest."

She's still scrutinizing me like she doesn't quite understand what's going on. "He really wants me to work for him?"

"He does. Told me he'd call D'Ambrosi *tonight* to make it happen."

The pulse in her neck is fluttering against my wrist, or maybe it's my own racing. Because if she decides that this won't work, I don't know what I'll do. I can't let her go now that I know what it feels like to hold and kiss and touch her. How it feels to love her. To be loved by her.

I need her with me. Always. As close as I can get her.

"Think on it," I tell her, shifting closer. I need the contact, especially if she decides that life in New York is what she wants. "You don't have to make a decision right—"

"I don't need to think," she blurts, covering my hand with hers to drive the words home. "I want to do it. At least for the rest of the season. I'm not ready to be done. And I'm . . ." She takes a shuddering breath. "I'm not ready to leave you."

I'm laughing before I can stop myself. Nothing about this is funny, but I'm so fucking relieved that my body can't do anything else. I can only let it out in the most natural way it knows how.

"We'd still have to be cautious," she follows up. She's grinning against my palm, which softens the weight of the words, but she's right. "I think it could work for us, though. And we wouldn't have to be apart."

We wouldn't. I wouldn't have to give up my sunshine. My guiding star. My heart and soul. "I want to kiss you so badly right now," I breathe out. I want to seal this agreement with our lips pressed together, with her body molded to mine.

Her grin turns teasing. "You'll smudge my lipstick."

"You can touch it up."

"Fine," she whispers as I lift my other hand to her face as well. "Kiss me, Dev."

"Don't have to ask me twice."

I dip my head and close my eyes. I don't need to see to find her kiss. We're magnets drawn to each other. It's all inevitable. It's how it was meant to be.

It's fate.

But my eyes fly back open when the bathroom door next to us bangs against the wall. We both jerk at the sound, though I don't pull away from her, my hands still cupping her jaw.

And then Oakley steps into the hall.

CHAPTER 31

WILLOW

Oakley knows.

I can tell by the look in his eyes. My lipstick may not be smudged, but there's still no denying it like we did nearly a year ago. We've been caught.

"What the fuck is this?"

It's only then that Dev's hands slip from my face. But, to my absolute surprise, he curls his fingers around mine at my side. We're doing this then. It's not how I envisioned us breaking the news, but we're caught. No sense in lying when Oakley knows exactly what he was looking at, despite the question.

God, I think I'm going to be sick.

"Well, Oak," Dev says after a long inhale. "I was about to kiss your sister."

I wince. My brother isn't going to take that answer well at all. The journey of emotions that cross his face, starting with disgust and morphing into surprise, then grim anger, confirms that suspicion.

"You fucking *asshole*," he hisses, stalking forward, though he's forced to stop when I step between the two of them and hold an arm out. "I should have *known* something was going on."

"Oakley, please," I blurt, but I already know he can't hear me over his own screaming thoughts. "Let's just—"

"And *this*." He waves a hand, motioning wildly between Dev and me. "This clearly isn't new."

From one glance, he's got us all figured out. He knows us both so well—*too* well—that our connection is obvious to him. I might have appreciated that under different circumstances, but right now, his words are like a dagger to my heart.

As I struggle to explain, Dev cuts in.

"You're right," he says easily. "It's not new. Not really."

All I can do is shoot him a pleading look over my shoulder as my brother gapes at him. Oakley probably expected denial and guilty glances, but Dev is facing this head-on, even if I want to cower.

"How long?" my brother finally grits out. "How long has this been going on?"

I open my mouth, ready to answer this time, but Dev squeezes my hand, as if to say he's got this.

"Well, Willow has had a thing for me for most of her life," he replies, keeping his voice low and even. "And I've been obsessed with her since your birthday weekend last year when she accidentally confessed her crush. But it *is* new in the sense that we've only just acted on our feelings in the last couple of weeks."

"Weeks," Oakley repeats, his focus finally drifting down to me, his eyes hardening. "Since you started working for him?"

My throat tightens, and tears burn the corners of my eyes. "No," I say, the word wavering as I shake my head. "No, not that long." It's the truth, but if Dev is going to be brave and tell the entire story, then I owe it to them both to do the same. "We kept it professional—*friendly*—for a while. But I didn't want to ignore what was between us any longer."

"*We* didn't want to ignore it," Dev corrects, squeezing my hand a little tighter, letting his strength flow into me. "We realized we wanted to be together."

Oakley's throat works as he swallows, his eyes still narrowed and bouncing from me to Dev and back again. I can't blame him for being shocked and upset, and my heart aches that it came out this way.

"So if I hadn't let you work for him," he rasps, focused on me again, wearing that look of crushing betrayal, "this wouldn't have happened."

I want to deny it, but he's right. Without Dev's idea and Oakley's approval, we wouldn't have grown closer. It was the perfect setup. And my brother had no idea what he was signing off on.

"Jesus Christ," he says when I don't answer, a maniacal note in his voice as he shakes his head. "I can't believe this. I can't believe you'd—that you'd *lie* to me like this." His eyes snap up to Dev. "*Either* of you."

My heart pounds, and then suddenly stops. It restarts with a hard, dramatic *thump* as I take in his accusation. He's mad about us . . . lying?

"This whole time, you kept it from me," he goes on. "There were so many chances for you to tell me, but instead, you lied. Do you understand how fucked up that is?"

I peek back at Dev, who's staring at Oakley like he's still trying to wrap his head around what he's saying.

"I'm . . . sorry?" Dev stammers, faltering for the first time since my brother stepped out of the bathroom.

Oakley rolls his eyes and scrubs a hand down his face. "It doesn't *matter* that you're together," he urges. "You're an adult and so is she. I don't run your fucking lives. But it matters that you lied to me."

Oh god. We've gotten this all wrong. We were so worried about whether Oakley would approve that we forgot to consider how he'd feel when he found out we were keeping it from him in the first place.

"We weren't sure how you would react," Dev says, his voice low and gentle again. "You literally told me to never try it with her. When the whole Jeremy thing happened—"

"Jeremy was a pathetic excuse for a man that we should have cut off years before we did," Oakley spits. "Don't use him to justify your bullshit. He had it coming for what he did to her."

"Okay," Dev concedes, lifting his free hand. "But you know you wouldn't have approved of anything happening between Willow and me. You can't just write that off."

Oakley works his jaw from side to side, his teeth grinding like he's holding back his anger until he can express it more clearly. "Fine," he admits. "I *don't* like the idea of you together. At all. I don't like the idea of another one of my friends dating my sister."

Behind me, I can feel Dev gearing up to defend what we've done, his chest swelling as he takes a breath. But before he can speak, Oakley pushes on.

"How I feel doesn't matter, though. Because that's *my* problem. Not yours. So stop tap-dancing around me like I'm an idiot who can't handle being uncomfortable, and just stop *lying*."

We really did get this wrong, and I don't know how we didn't see it before.

"I'm sorry," I whisper, reaching out with my free hand to touch his arm. Thankfully, he doesn't immediately shrug it off. "I didn't—"

"If you had just told me," he barrels through my apology, "I probably would have been surprised, yeah. And definitely not happy. But I would have gotten over it a lot faster than I'm going to get over this."

Oakley inspects us both. Some of the anger that's got him wound tight ebbs, but it's replaced by a hurt expression that makes me feel even sicker.

"Look," he says quietly, addressing Dev. "I'll always be protective of Willow. But I also want her to be happy. And you're supposedly my best friend. I want you to be happy too."

"Even if the two of us are happy because we're together?" Dev hedges, and I can only hope we're finally starting to make progress here.

"Are you serious about her?" Oakley demands in reply.

There's no hesitation when Dev answers. "I am."

My brother's eyes snap back to mine. "And you *actually* want to be with him?"

"Yeah," I say, my throat somehow even tighter. "I really do."

Oakley draws in a deep breath and nods sharply. With a quick step back, he holds both palms out. "Then fine. *Fine.* I just have to accept it. It's my thing to get over."

I almost collapse in relief. My knees go weak, and I have to slump against Dev to keep myself upright. It doesn't escape Oakley's notice, and the set to his jaw hardens.

"But if you hurt her," he warns Dev, "I'll break both of your hands so you never drive again."

Dev nods solemnly, clearly not doubting the threat. "Understood. No plans for that to happen, though."

"And you," he barks at me, eyes narrowed. "If you hurt him—"

"I won't," I interrupt before he can finish the threat. "I promise, I won't."

Oakley stares at us both for a few long seconds, leaving my stomach to churn with anxiety. But then he abruptly slaps Dev upside the head and socks me in the shoulder, though not hard enough to hurt me.

"Man, fuck you both," he groans.

And then he pulls us in for a hug.

"You're shitty people," he mumbles against the top of my head, clutching me to his chest while he has Dev in a head-lock. "I hope you're happy together, you absolute losers."

That surprises a laugh out of me, and the tears I've been holding back finally pour over. "We are."

"Good. Someone better be, because I sure as shit am not."

With one last squeeze, he shoves us away.

"I'm not over this," he says, pointing at Dev and then me. "But since we're here to celebrate love today, I'll suck it up. All right?"

"Got it," I squeak. "Thank you, Oak."

With that, he rolls his eyes and stalks off.

It's a few long seconds before I finally work up the nerve to turn to look at Dev, blinking in shock.

"Did that . . ." I trail off. "Did that really just happen?"

Dev wets his lips, fighting for his voice. "I think it did."

"He knows. He knows, and he didn't kill us."

"Uh-huh."

"We're no longer a secret."

"We're not," he agrees with a hint of disbelief. "No more hiding from him."

"No more hiding," I repeat, dabbing under my eyes to wipe away the slowing tears. My makeup is certainly ruined by now, but I don't even care. "I can't believe it."

Dev huffs out a laugh. "Yeah. Neither can I. But I'll take it."

He slings an arm around my shoulders and tugs me into him. I go willingly, sliding my arms around his waist as I lean against his solid chest. It feels like we've survived a battle.

"I don't want to go back out there," I mumble against the purple silk of his kurta. "Not after that. I need to take some time to just . . . breathe."

"We don't have to go back to the party," he says. "But there is somewhere else I want to take you."

He pulls back, lacing our fingers together once again as he leads me down the hall. We turn a corner, then another, before we come upon a sliding glass door that leads to a patio on the side of the house. Dev lets go of my hand to unlock and open it, then ushers me outside.

From here, I can hear the music playing inside the tent, but we're shielded from view of the backyard by a lattice wall of climbing roses. The flowers scent the air, petals fluttering in the soft evening breeze. I swear it's the most romantic place I've ever been. I even spin to take it all in, my sari twirling around my legs.

"I love this," I exhale, tilting my head back to take in the bright stars and the slim crescent of the moon.

When I look back down again, Dev is offering me his outstretched hand. "Come here," he says. "Dance with me."

The laughter that bubbles out of me is light. It pushes away the lingering tension from our encounter with Oakley. I still don't feel *good*, but the pain is easing.

"You know I can't dance," I remind him, though I kick off my heels and nudge them to the side in preparation. "Remember my parents' anniversary party?"

"I'll never forget Jeremy's howl when you stepped on his toes with your stilettos." He snickers, motioning me toward him with an arm extended. "Stand on my feet. I'll move for both of us."

"Dev, I don't want to hurt—" My protest dies when he sweeps an arm around my waist and lifts me briefly. A moment later, he settles my feet on top of his.

"Hold on to me."

So I do. And he sways with me in his arms, moving our feet in tiny steps.

"This can't be comfortable for you," I giggle, glancing down at my bare feet on top of his very expensive designer shoes.

"I'm always comfortable when you're in my arms."

"Charmer."

"You know it."

I have nothing else to say to that, so I rest my head on his chest and let him take over. Almost instantly, the song shifts into something slow and romantic. Like the universe just knows.

His heartbeat is slow and steady under my cheek, a reminder of the conditioned athlete he is.

When it ticks up a notch, I lift my head and eye him. "What's wrong?"

"You're going to think I'm crazy," he says. "But you make me nervous, Willow Williams."

"Me?" I have to scoff. "Why?"

"Because I'm so in love with you that it hurts."

My breath catches and my heart stutters at the open

honesty on his face. I nearly tear up again, because I know exactly what he's talking about. I know that deep soul ache. And I feel the same about him.

"Me too," I whisper back.

He cups the back of my head with one hand, guiding my cheek back to his chest, to the steady beat of his heart.

We stay like that for several more songs until the rhythm changes again and the roar of the crowd in the tent breaks through the magic.

"I was wondering," I say as I step off his feet and onto the smooth stone of the patio, my own heart racing. "Should we . . . should we put a label on this? I mean, you've already *technically* called me your girlfriend, but still . . ."

And there it is, that famous grin, the one that internet poets have written volumes about.

"Willow," he says, mock-scandalized, eyes wide. "Are you asking me to be your *boyfriend*?"

Refusing to smile back, I pinch my lips tight. But there's no hiding how I feel. Not from him. "Maybe."

"Then I wholeheartedly accept."

He drops his lips to mine. And finally, Dev smudges my lipstick.

 **CHAPTER 32**

DEV

My stomach sinks when Willow's face isn't the first thing I see the next morning.

I'm alone in bed in the house next door to where she's staying. It's like we're back at home instead of in matching Malibu rentals. The place is so quiet that I can hear the soft sound of crashing waves in the distance, but in another hour or so, the other guests will be up and rattling around. Though, considering how late the reception raged into the night, there's a strong chance most of them won't be up until noon.

Less than thrilled to be awake this early, I lie on my back and stare at the ceiling as my thoughts drift back to last night. Willow and I no longer have to keep our relationship a secret from our friends and family, and that thought alone fills me with more joy than I felt even when signing with Mascort yesterday. But I don't want to take things *too* public yet. Not until she's been working with Reid for a while. That should ensure that she escapes any damage to her reputation, because I don't want anything overshadowing the career she's building.

Eventually it'll come out, of course. And when it does, I'll be shouting from the rooftops how much I adore that girl.

Still, there's a gaping pit in my stomach over how the unexpected conversation with Oakley went down. We were wrong to hide from him, I can see that now. But what's done is done, and all I can do is hope that he'll find it in his heart to forgive us.

I'd love for that day to come sooner rather than later. If I want that to happen, though, I'll have to make an effort to repair things. Since he's going back to Chicago at the end of the week, my timeline is limited, but there's no way I can let him leave without at least attempting to get our friendship back on track. And since there's no time like the present . . .

I shove back the sheets and haul myself out of bed, determined to get this show on the road. I pull on a pair of board shorts and tuck my wet suit under my arm, then head out into the hall.

I'm ready to barrel into Oakley's room and demand he come down to the beach with me, but I stop short when I reach his open door. The bedroom is empty. The bed is made. There's no sign of him.

I'm hit with a punch of disappointment that's quickly followed by a surge of panic. Did he leave already? I know he at least came back last night, since I spotted him slinking into his room just as I made it up the stairs. But maybe he woke up even earlier than me, packed up his shit, and got the hell out of here. I wouldn't blame him if he did.

Sighing, I turn away from the doorway and start for the stairs. I might as well let the waves pummel the anxiety out of me, even if I'd hoped to have company. If Oakley is gone, if he wants space, I can respect that. I'll refrain from blowing up his phone or stalking him . . . for now. I'll give him a day, but then there'll be no escaping me.

The path down to the beach is deserted, and I almost regret not waking Chava or Mark and forcing them to surf with me when I see how perfect the waves are. But when I spot the figure sitting by the edge of the water, I know I made the right choice.

I toss my board down when I reach Oakley and plant my ass on the sand a foot away—close enough that we can talk, but far enough that I can dodge if he swings at me. Just because he didn't last night doesn't mean he won't now without Willow here to protect me.

Neither of us speaks. I'm not sure what to say anyway. *I'm sorry* feels useless, and it won't fix what I did. It doesn't take back the hurt. And I don't regret doing anything that led me to where I am with Willow, so what's the point of saying the words if they'll just ring hollow?

Oakley doesn't look at me and I don't look at him. We watch the waves, respective boards by our sides, but neither of us makes a move for the water. We might end up sitting here all day, but even if we do, it means something that he hasn't gotten up and walked away from me.

"I'm still pissed," he finally says.

It's a simple statement, but it makes the knife of guilt twist in my gut. "I know."

There's another long pause before he speaks again. "The more I thought about it," he goes on, "the angrier I got. You had so many opportunities to tell me how you felt about her. She did too. And yet you just . . . didn't. Then, come to find out, both Mark and Chava knew before me." He shakes his head, like he still can't believe it. "I *hate* being blindsided by shit. If you'd told me right off the bat you were interested in her—"

"What would you have done if I did?" I interrupt, though I'm careful not to make it sound too accusatory. Oakley has to know he would have warned me off Willow, just like he did the night of his birthday. "What would you have done if I came to you and said, 'Hey, man. I'm into your sister. Do you mind if I date her?'"

The way Oakley winces tells me everything I need to know. So does the way he dips his head and grips the back of his neck like he's trying to ward off a headache.

"Why would I have told you I was interested in her after you straight up said to never try anything?" I push on. "You made it perfectly clear that you didn't want me anywhere near her."

"I didn't have a problem with her working for you, did I?" he shoots back.

"Because you thought it was strictly professional," I counter. "And it was. At first."

His shoulders slump even farther. He knows I'm right, and he's probably realizing that any arguments he might have are weak in the face of what I'm saying.

"I didn't know any of this was going to happen, Oak," I tell him, my voice soft enough that it's almost lost in the roar of the breaking waves. "Willow didn't either. We tried to keep it platonic, but the way we feel about each other . . . there was no ignoring it."

He inhales deeply through his nose, his jaw working. "Do you love her?"

"Yeah," I answer, not a single ounce of doubt in the word. "I do."

More silence follows my confession. Beside me, Oakley is fighting with himself, obviously torn between wanting to be furious and wanting to let go of something he can't change.

But nothing he says is going to make me want to break up with Willow. If his previous warning wasn't enough to keep me away, he's got to know that there isn't a single threat that will work now.

"Fuck," he finally exhales, dropping his hands from his neck and into the sand. "This is messy, Dev. You know that."

I sure as shit do. But I've learned that life is better with a little chaos. Especially if that chaos has brought the warmest ray of sunshine with it.

I let the quiet linger, giving Oakley the time and space to get it all off his chest.

"I guess I can't blame you too much," he begins, and there's a sheepish note to it. "I used to have a massive crush on Alisha."

Used to. Okay. It's obvious those feelings are still alive and well, even after watching her marry another man yesterday, but I won't correct his wording. There's a part of me that hurts for him, knowing how much it sucks to want someone you can't have—or who doesn't want you back. But he'll survive the heartbreak, and one day find the person who's meant for him.

"Yeah, dude," I say, chuckling. "I know you did."

"We *all* knew you did," says another voice from behind us.

I turn to see Mark approaching, his own surfboard tucked under his arm.

Looks like we all had the same idea this morning, minus Chava, who's probably still nursing his hangover.

"It's smart that you never went after her," Mark continues as he drops down on Oakley's other side. "Alisha never would have given you the time of day."

Oakley scowls and kicks sand in Mark's direction. "Man, fuck you," he grumbles. But then he twists his lips to the side in acceptance. "But . . . yeah. Would have been a waste of time."

"But a hilarious waste of time," I add, elbowing him in the ribs. "She would have eaten you alive."

That pulls a scratchy laugh out of him. He quickly cuts it off, as if he doesn't want to find something I've said funny. But it's progress.

"I'm guessing I interrupted a conversation about being into each other's sisters," Mark says after a tense beat of quiet falls. "May I just state for the record that I have never once been interested in Alisha or Willow? Or any of Chava's *five* sisters?"

I roll my eyes, and even though Oakley's watching the waves crash onto the shore again, I can guarantee he does too. At least there's one thing we can still agree on—Mark's annoying sense of righteousness.

"But anyway," he goes on. "Oak, I know you're angry. Willow and Dev didn't handle this the best they could have, but what else were they supposed to do? Wills had her reputation to worry about, *and* she was terrified that she'd drive us all apart. Did you know she still blames herself for destroying our group after what happened with Jeremy?"

The reminder makes me bristle, and based on the way Oakley's hands ball into fists on the sand, he's unhappy too.

"She and I had a long talk about it." Mark blows out a breath, glancing out at the water before turning back to us. "It was obvious how much she was struggling with how she felt."

She spoke to Mark about her feelings? When did *that* happen? And what could he have said to make her want to run *to* me instead of *away*? He's been critical of this situation from the beginning, though this speech right now is proving that's changed.

"She didn't make the choice to be with Dev lightly," Mark says, his tone firm, leaving no room for Oakley to argue. "And I've seen how they are together. They make each other the best versions of themselves. You'd have to be a selfish asshole to not want them together."

Well, that's a direct dig if I've ever heard one.

Oakley's scowl says he knows it too. "Yeah, all right," he grumbles. "Can we talk about something else now?"

"Sure, like how much your dancing sucked last night?" Mark supplies.

"*Excuse* me? At least I know how to move on beat."

"*You're* the one who nearly took out a crowd of aunties with your elbows."

Oakley scoffs. "Oh yeah? I'll show you what kind of damage I can do with my elbows. Come here, you son of a—"

"Yeah, okay, no," I interrupt, reaching for Oakley so I can distract them from going after each other, but they're already tussling.

Shaking my head, I pull my hand back and wait it out. At least it's not me Oakley's fighting with. I wouldn't put it past Mark to have provoked him on purpose. I'll have to thank him later for taking one for the team.

When they finally break apart, Oakley has a seashell stuck to his forehead, and Mark has an angry red scratch down his shoulder from where Oakley got him with a piece of driftwood, but they're otherwise unscathed. And the general animosity has been turned down a notch as well.

"Just like old times," Mark says, leaning back on his elbows and surveying Oakley and me. "Us fighting on the beach and Chava still passed out, missing all the fun."

"But he'll have breakfast ready by the time we're back," Oakley reminds us, plucking the seashell off his face. "Him failing out of culinary school was our gain."

Mark leans around Oakley to shoot me a smirk. "And since it's summer break, I'll even let you eat French toast."

I let out a relieved groan. "Oh, thank *fuck*."

The tension between us cracks, and the old camaraderie falls back into place. It doesn't mean that Oakley has forgiven me or moved past my misdeeds, but it's evidence that we *can* work through it.

"Come on, get your asses up," Mark says, climbing to his feet. "These waves are too good to just sit and look at."

Following suit, I heave myself up and test my luck, extending a hand to Oakley. I hold my breath as he scrutinizes it, because we both know it's more than just an offer to help him stand. It's an olive branch. A peace offering. A question—*Will we be okay?*

When another second ticks by and he doesn't make a move, I nearly start to sweat. But then he slaps his palm against mine.

"I still hate you," he says once I've pulled him to his feet. "But I get it. I don't have to like it, but I get it. And it doesn't change anything between us, all right?"

"Except you hating me," I point out, but I'm grinning.

"That's nothing new, man." He slaps my shoulder and pushes around me. "I'll get over it. Like always."

I'm sure he will. We just have to see how long it's going to take.

▰▰▰▰▰

I'm bruised and battered by the time I make my way back toward the houses. As I climb up the pathway, I spot my mom on the patio sipping her morning cup of coffee. She raises a hand to beckon me over, and I don't dare ignore it.

Like an exhausted kid, I drop in front of her legs and lean back against her shins. My wet, sandy hair falls into her lap, yet she doesn't complain. No, like the incredible mother she is, she runs her fingers through the strands to detangle them.

"You look like you lost a fight," she says warmly. "I take it the ocean won?"

With a snort, I close my eyes and let her massage my scalp. It really is like childhood all over again. "I let her win."

"Smart boy." She hums, and I hear the clink of her coffee cup on the table before she speaks again. "Is everything okay with you and Oakley now?"

I freeze under her hand. The question is far too innocent, like she's playing it off as if she doesn't know exactly what's going on. But she does. She always does.

After a beat, I tilt my head back to look at her, but her expression gives nothing away. "Is that your way of asking if he's okay with Willow and me dating?"

The corner of her mouth quirks up a little, but it's the sparkle in her eyes that gives her away. "Maybe."

I groan as I sit up and pull back, turning to glare at her. It's weak, though. "So you know?"

"Oh, beta." The full smile spreads across her face. "I've had my suspicions, but I knew for sure when I saw you sneak into her house last week. You're lucky you didn't fall off that trellis, you bad boy."

My jaw goes slack. "You saw that?"

She scoffs and circles her wrist. "I see everything."

Yeah, no shit.

"I'm happy for you," she says gently, touching my cheek.

"I've always liked her. And she's always liked you. Glad you finally noticed."

I exhale a laugh, still embarrassed by how oblivious I was.

"How are you going to handle that relationship?" she continues. "Is Willow going back to New York? I know her contract with you is up."

My heart lifts a little at her question. Because Willow won't be leaving. I get to keep her near me, and she gets to keep following her dreams.

I take a deep breath. "About that . . ."

CHAPTER 33

<u>WILLOW</u>

After six hours of unemployment, I have a job again.

The contracts with Reid and Scuderia D'Ambrosi are all officially signed, and I'm sure Chantal and Grace are already tired of hearing me squeal over the new opportunity and my relationship with Dev. But they're happy for me. Chantal especially, since she won the bet she and Grace made concerning how long it would take Dev and me to get together. I'm so thrilled about how everything's going that I can't even begin to be upset with them about it.

"Do you think you'll come back to New York at all?" Grace asks, her face at the top of my phone screen. "Or should we pack up all your stuff and ship it off to Europe?"

I laugh. "I'll be back in December to figure things out. I agreed to finish the rest of the season with Reid, but who knows what will happen after that."

I'm excited to find out, though. Sticking around in the world of F1, even if it's only for a few more months, has me giddy. It's exactly where I want to be. Dev being there, too, certainly doesn't hurt.

"We won't sublet your room then," Chantal teases from the bottom of my screen. "Or throw out all your crap."

"Oh gee, thanks, you're so ki—" I'm cut short by a knock on my door.

But it's not just any knock. It's Oakley's knock. *Our* knock.

"Shit, I have to go," I hiss to the girls, panic shooting through me. "Oak's here."

Grace and Chantal quickly say their goodbyes—and good lucks—before we hang up. I toss my phone onto my pillow and scramble up from the bed, but I pause in front of the door and take a deep breath, wringing my hands. I'm not *afraid* to face my brother, but I don't want the guilt and the remorse to hit me hard again, especially on a day when all I want to do is celebrate.

But I owe him a conversation. Keeping things from him was wrong, and the way he found out only made the situation more painful. He deserves a big apology, but having to face the consequences of my own actions? Not my idea of a good time.

After drawing in another deep breath, I haul open the door and offer my brother what I hope is a bright smile. Sadly, it feels more like a grimace. "Hey, sorry, I was in the bathroom," I tell him.

Oakley rolls his eyes. "I literally heard you talking to your friends. You don't need to lie. Again."

"Okay, fine," I admit, my face going hot. "I was scared to open the door."

"You're ridiculous." He brushes past me and collapses on the bed, fingers lacing over his stomach as he stares up at the ceiling.

I stay rooted to the spot, waiting for the other shoe to drop. He's acting like all's well, though he's a little more subdued than I expected. There's a scrape on his forehead that definitely wasn't there last night, so maybe that has something to do with why he's so calm. Oh god, did he fight Dev? Is he here to tell me he killed my boyfriend and threw his body into the ocean?

"I talked to Dev," he says.

I'm not sure whether to be encouraged or worried by that statement. Scanning his body, I surreptitiously check him for bloodstains, but it looks like he's showered recently. Any chance of finding evidence is gone.

I swallow hard. "How did that go?"

He runs his hands over his close-cropped hair, then settles them behind his neck. Okay, maybe there wasn't a murder; I can't imagine he'd be this chill after he just killed a man.

"I'm still not happy about you two . . . being together." He has to force out the last words. "But there's nothing I can do about it. Or that I'm *going* to do about it."

Some of the tension eases from my shoulders.

"You're not going to make me break up with him?" I try to go for lighthearted, but in reality, my tone is a little too serious for it to be taken that way.

"You're an adult, Wills. You can do what you want." He finally turns his head to look at me, his dark brown eyes solemn. "But I'm like this because I don't want to see you get hurt. I don't care how old you get, I'll always want to protect you. I failed you when it came to Jeremy, and I don't ever want that to happen again. Not that I think Dev is anything like him, but I figured it was safer to keep you away altogether." He exhales a short, unamused laugh. "Looks like I failed there too."

My heart aches at his words. He's been trying to keep me safe in some way or another since day one. But he can't always break my fall, and that clearly bothers him. He's tried his best, though. That's more than I could have asked from him.

"You can't protect me from everything, Oak," I tell him softly. I make my way over to the edge of the bed and sit beside his knees. We're not quite touching, but close. "Sometimes I have to get hurt. That's just life. Especially mine. But I don't think Dev will hurt me, and I never want to hurt him either."

Here I've been blaming myself for tearing apart Oakley's friend group, and all the while, it looks as though he's been beating himself up over not protecting me from them. But I've begun to accept that it wasn't my fault, and I need him to realize it's not his either.

"I know," he says a few seconds later. It's grudging, but it's something. "Won't stop me from trying to protect you, though."

I bump his knee with my elbow. "Feel free to tone it down a little."

He lifts his head enough to shoot me a narrow-eyed look, but his upper lip twitches, like he's trying not to smile. "Just don't fuck yourself up too badly."

I snort. "I'll do my best." Across the room, my laptop dings with a new email. From the preview on the screen, it looks like it's from D'Ambrosi. Probably the welcome package Reid mentioned they'd be sending. "Hey, did Dev tell you about my new job?"

"New job?" This time, he sits up. "Didn't your contract with him just end?"

"Yep. But he helped line up a new one. I'll be working with Reid Coleman and D'Ambrosi starting at the end of the break. I signed the contracts earlier."

He blinks a couple of times, almost speechless, I think, but then he's grinning. "Holy shit, Wills. Congratulations."

"Thanks." I mirror his expression. "This wouldn't have happened if you hadn't pushed me to work for Dev."

"You wouldn't be dating him either," Oakley mutters, but the delight on his face doesn't dim. "I may hate your guts right now, but I'm proud of you. That shit you did for Dev wasn't easy, and it looks like it made an impression on more than just him. Takes talent."

I give a mock bow. "I did my best."

My brother rolls his eyes at my dramatics before shoving up from the bed and striding for the door, our heart-to-heart over.

"Now get your ass up," he calls over his shoulder. "Chava made breakfast. And if you want French toast, you better get down there before Dev eats it all."

▞▚▞▚▞

Chava deserves an award for saving me a piece of French toast, because Oakley was right—Dev is a carb fiend when left to his own devices.

"Come on, you know you don't want to eat all of that," he wheedles from the other side of the table, his fork poised over my plate. "You should eat more protein anyway. Go ahead and finish off that omelet instead."

I knock his fork away with my own, the clang echoing through the dining room. "Don't you dare." I shoot a glare at Mark next. "You created this monster."

Mark puts his hands up in front of him, but he doesn't look remotely sorry. "This is his one week to eat whatever he wants. I'm not stopping him until Friday, so either get used to it or get out."

In that case . . .

I scoot my chair away from the table and grab my plate,

taking in Dev's disappointed face and my brother's snicker as I do. "I'm going to keep Chava company in the kitchen. Eat somebody else's food."

"But you're my girlfriend," Dev calls to my retreating back. "You're supposed to share!"

I'm glad to be turned away from him so he can't see the smile I'm fighting. I'm pleased and relieved by how well he and my brother are getting along despite the changes that last night brought. Oakley's going to need time to adjust, and yet he's sitting beside Dev, laughing. I don't know whether to believe his words or his actions, so for now, I'm taking this as a win.

In the kitchen, I settle at the breakfast bar, where I can watch Chava at the stove and eat my food in peace. He shoots me a knowing look over his shoulder, like he's not surprised to find me in here with him, but before he can say anything, a pair of arms slide around my shoulders.

"I'll buy you all the macarons you want if you let me eat that," Dev murmurs against my ear.

Despite the distraction, I don't miss the way his fork is headed for my plate again. Hmm. It's a tempting offer. And as delicious as Chava's French toast is, I'd much rather be eating macarons right now.

I nudge my plate closer to him. "Fine. But we're going to get them as soon as you're finished eating."

"Deal," he says, already spearing a piece. "I'm taking you on another date too."

"Oh yeah?" I ask, my heart doing a silly little tumble in my chest. "What do you have in mind this time? Did you rent out another house for me?"

"Well, as luck would have it . . . I've rented out three."

I laugh and push him away as he shoves another piece of

French toast in his mouth. "That doesn't count, since you didn't do it specifically for me."

"Damn, all right, so picky." He finishes off what's left on my plate before sliding onto the barstool next to mine. "Since we're still trying to keep everything semisecret, doing too much in public isn't really an option. Are you okay with that?"

For now, I am. I don't mind our relationship staying private. All the important people already know, and that's what matters. But eventually, I'm going to want more. I'm going to want to show him off and gush about him to whoever will listen. Though while things are still new, we can keep this contained to our little world.

"I'm okay with it," I answer, leaning in to kiss a bit of syrup off his bottom lip. It's just as sweet as he is. "I don't mind you being my little secret."

His grin is sharp as he drops his fork and loops an arm around my waist, pulling me and my barstool closer. "Can I be your *dirty* little secret?"

"You can be whatever you—"

"Oh, come the fuck on," Chava groans from across the island, tossing his spatula down. "I love the two of you together, don't get me wrong, but I am too hungover to witness your gross shit this morning. Take it elsewhere."

There's a sly spark in Dev's eyes. "Should we take this upstairs then?" he murmurs.

"For a little while," I reply, grasping his T-shirt. "But you owe me macarons."

His lips find mine as Chava swears in the background, but I'm too lost in the kiss to bring myself to care. This moment is too perfect for anything to ruin it.

"Whatever you want, jaanu," Dev says when he pulls back, nothing but love in his eyes. "I'll give it all to you."

EPILOGUE

DEV

One month later, September
Singapore

As a city, I love Singapore. But its weather can get fucked.

"I hate to say that it's hot as balls out here," Chava says, panting as we make our way from the hospitality suite to the garage, "but my balls are *hot*, and I swear the air's the same temperature. I think I'm sweating through my pants. Shit, *am I* sweating through my pants?" He contorts his body, attempting to look over his shoulder so he can assess his backside in his navy Argonaut shorts.

"Until you're the one wearing the fireproof suit and sitting in a car for hours, you don't get to complain," I grumble, giving him a once-over without slowing. "And you don't have crack sweat."

He turns back around, beaming. "Thanks for checking out my ass."

"Please never say that again."

Once we're in the garage, he slaps me on the back and wishes me well in the race before sauntering to his designated spot in the back with the other nonengineering team members. Out of habit, my focus lingers on the space, even though

Willow isn't there. By now, she's standing in a similar spot in the Scuderia D'Ambrosi garage.

Even after two races of her working for them, it's still strange to see her in head-to-toe D'Ambrosi red, but there's no denying that she looks incredible in the color. She spent the last week of the summer break in Italy at the team's headquarters, getting things together so she could jump into working for Reid. She called me multiple times a day while we were apart with every new update that excited her, and I was more than happy to answer each time.

This is the form of long distance I can handle. Moving in the same sphere, being close enough that we can spend our nights and days off together. If I can't have her directly by my side, then being at opposite ends of the paddock is a compromise I'll take. The knowledge that she's only ever a few yards away brings me peace in the madness.

And said madness begins the second I climb into the car.

Thanks to some truly absurd penalties several drivers picked up in qualifying and a handful of cars starting from the pit lane due to needing modifications, I'm starting from sixth on the grid. It's still wild to sit in a third-row box, but next year, it won't be out of the norm. Unless Mascort absolutely tanks next season's car in development over the winter, it'll be rare for me to start farther back than where I am now. It's a fucking dream, and it's going to come true so, so soon.

I flex my fingers around the steering wheel as I wait for the drivers behind me to pull into their spots. Up ahead, Zaid is on pole with Axel next to him, the classic setup. Otto is directly in front of me in fourth, with Lorenzo to his left. Beside me sits Thomas in the McMorris, and behind is Reid. He took a penalty for impeding another driver on a flying lap, even though he really had no place on the track to go in order to get out of the way in time.

But he's behind me, and all that matters is staying ahead of him.

As the lights come on one by one, I inhale slowly. Waiting. Ready. And then it's lights out.

I'm off the line quick, close on Otto, but Thomas is squeezing me. I grit my teeth and hold tight through the first series of corners. When the second straight opens up in front of us, I edge ahead of Thomas, still defending from Reid in the back and watching for an opening to present itself.

When it does, I don't hesitate. I slot in just inches from Thomas's front wheel, forcing him to brake to avoid the collision into the next turn. It's shitty of me, sure, but it's legal.

Our encounter is nothing, though. The real drama is happening ahead in what appears to be a three-way battle among Zaid, Axel, and Lorenzo. I'm just far enough back to watch, knowing I need to react quickly if I'm going to stay out of it. And that's my plan, because Lorenzo is a terrorist on the track, and it looks like—

Fuck.

I blink. That's all it takes. A split second. A tagged back wheel. A 360-degree spin. A swerve.

A reaction just a hint too slow.

A flame. A blaze.

I see it all happen before I hit the wall.

My ears are ringing. My neck's aching like it's almost been snapped clear off. My hands are still on the wheel, shaking, adrenaline hitting in an attempt to help me block the pain.

I blink again, slower this time, my conscious brain trying to keep up with its subconscious actions. But it's the acrid smoke that has me turning my head to look in my one unbroken mirror.

I don't even need to see it. I can feel the heat of the fire. But I force myself to look. To count.

One. Two. Three.

Three cars. Mangled messes. The risk we take on full display.

"Dev."

There's a voice in my ear, calling my name. It takes a second to realize the person isn't beside me.

"Dev, are you okay?" Branny says, his tone urgent, like he's asked this question more than once already. But this is the first time I've truly heard him.

There's panic in his voice. There's never panic in Branny's voice. He's calm and cool and collected. He's my captain on these stormy seas.

"Dev, talk to me," he pleads. "I need to know if you're okay."

I swallow, tasting the smoke in the air, trying to remember how words work. "I'm fine," I choke out. "I'm okay."

And I am. Just rattled and disoriented from the force of the impact. My thoughts are jumbled as I try to get them out through my mouth. "But Zaid. And . . . and Axel. *Lorenzo.* Are they—what happened?"

The world around me spins. There's a track marshal leaning over me now, shouting, wanting to know if I'm hurt. I can't make out what my race engineer is saying. I tell the marshal I'm fine, to go help the others.

The fire burns brighter in my mirror.

"Branny, tell me what's happening," I demand again, the burn of acid creeping up into my mouth as I fight to undo my seat belt with trembling hands. "Is everyone—are they okay?" My voice cracks. "Branny, you've got to tell me. Please."

There's more silence as the smoke grows thicker. Cold horror settles over me.

"It doesn't look good, Dev," he finally says. "It doesn't look good."

WILLOW

I'm going to be sick.

I *want* to be sick. I want to let out the bile churning in my gut as I watch hell unfold in front of me. There's nothing but flames and twisted barriers and shattered carbon fiber. I want it gone. I want it scrubbed from my being. I don't want to remember this for as long as I live.

The smoke from the fire reached us in the pit lane just seconds after the crash. The flashing lights of emergency vehicles are muted by the dark plumes, but the sirens are deafening. Person after person runs toward the chaos to help the drivers involved in the worst of it. I wish I could do something—anything—but just like most of the D'Ambrosi garage, I'm frozen in place, knowing the worst has happened.

And Dev is somewhere in it.

I always thought I'd be more responsive in the face of an emergency. I didn't think cold shock would settle into my bones and nearly bring me to my knees. I thought I would run and scream and claw my way past anyone who tried to hold me back.

But I'm not. I'm just . . . numb.

I can't watch it transpire like this, but I'm stuck, rooted to the ground, mind whirring with the loudest, most painful white noise. I refuse to believe this. The boy I love can't be twisted up in those barriers. I can't lose him like this. I can't lose him *at all*. I can't, I can't, I can't—

My phone buzzes in my white-knuckled hand. The far-away sensation cuts into my spiral and snags my attention. Words flash across the screen. It takes a few seconds for me to blink away the cobwebs.

Chava. A text. All capital letters.

HE'S OK. DEV IS OK.

〰〰〰

Dev is okay. But Zaid, Axel, and Lorenzo are not.

It's been hours since the crash, and all I know is that the three are in intensive care. That they're alive.

The D'Ambrosi garage was solemn and quiet before I slipped out. I made my exit the second I got the news that Dev was being discharged from the hospital after being evaluated out of an abundance of caution. The whole team was lost for words as we waited for news on Lorenzo's condition. But all we heard were terrible whispers. Of the drivers involved, he was in the worst shape when the helicopter took him away from the circuit.

And it seems he still is.

"I've got some updates," Dev says from where he's stretched out on his hotel bed. He's got an ice pack pressed to the back of his neck with one hand, and his phone in the other. He walked away with bruises and whiplash, but that was the worst of it. "Zaid's wrists are fractured. Axel's pretty badly burned. And Lorenzo is . . . They're saying he might be paralyzed from the waist down."

I don't know what to say. Past sobbing into his chest when

we were reunited and telling him how much I loved him and how glad I was that he was okay—how glad I was that he swerved just in time—I've barely spoken a word to Dev. Because that could have been him. It could have *so easily* been him.

Now, though, in the privacy of his hotel room, I'm back to being numb and speechless. I sit in the armchair in the corner, legs drawn up to my chest, arms clutched around them, trying to hold myself together.

I've seen crashes before. Bad ones. Ones that resulted in just as many injuries, some even worse. I was there for the last F3 race that Oakley participated in before retiring. Was there when a boy nearly died that day. It was Oakley's final reason for leaving the sport. Back then, I thought I'd understood his decision, but I carried around a hint of resentment, too, because he'd chosen to give up such a promising future. One I'd never come close to having.

Now, I wish I'd never felt that resentment. There's no shame in not wanting to put your life on the line for the sake of entertaining others. I may have never told him how I really felt, but I still apologized when he called earlier to check on Dev and me, even if he had no idea what I was talking about.

But unlike my brother, Dev pushes harder when fear grows. He doesn't back out. Doesn't back down. He keeps going.

What happened today isn't going to stop him.

It's like he's reading my mind when he says, "We all know the risks when we get in the car."

I drag my gaze up from the spot on the carpet I've been absently staring at for god knows how long. His expression is solemnly determined, like he's ready to convince me of his choice to race—and keep racing—if he has to. Is he thinking of Oakley and his decision to leave? Does he think I'd pressure him to do the same?

Is it wrong for me to not want him to give up his dreams, no matter how dangerous for him and for my heart?

Silence hangs as we consider each other, a dare passing between us. But there's nothing to dare. Nothing to challenge. We're on the same page.

"I'm not going to tell you to stop racing, if that's what you're waiting for," I say, the words thick from the tears I'm still choking back. "And it's not because I don't care about you. God, Dev, I'm scared for you every time you climb into the car. But this is what you chose to do. What you love." I swallow past the lump in my throat, but my voice still cracks when I speak again. "All I can do is ask that you come back to me every time."

His expression immediately softens, the hard set of his jaw relaxing. "I'll always do my best. I promise." He sits up slowly, putting the ice pack and his phone on the bedside table. Then he extends his hands to me. "Come here, Willow."

I hesitate before unfolding myself from the chair, knees and hips and shoulders protesting with every move. The ache seeps through me as I crawl up the bed to Dev's awaiting embrace. I force myself to focus instead on his solid chest and strong arms and the coolness of his hands. His nose brushes against mine, luring my lips up and my head back, and I let him kiss me as the tears spill down my cheeks.

It's far from perfect, but it says everything we need it to. He understands and respects my fears. There are no guarantees that he'll leave every race alive and unscathed. And I accept that he's going to keep doing this until the day he can't or doesn't want to anymore.

As he clutches me to him, my shoulders droop, my body

coming down from the surge of adrenaline it's been running on for the past few hours. I'm safe here in Dev's arms, and he's safe in mine.

That's all I can ask for, even if it can't always be like this.

DEV

"What do you *mean* they're not canceling the race?"

I track Willow's every move, words failing me. She's livid because this upcoming weekend's race at Suzuka is going on as scheduled. The FIA announced it a few minutes ago, and I thought telling her over morning coffee in bed would be just another part of our conversation. I didn't expect to start my Monday watching her pace the room in her strawberry-print pajamas, curls flying in every direction as she shakes her head in pure disbelief, but here we are.

"Three drivers are still in the hospital!" she rants. "Yes, they're alive, but they may never race again! How can they not cancel it?"

The only answer I can come up with is a weak "The show must go on."

That comment has her whipping around and clenching her fingers at her sides, like she's ready to scream again.

Before she can, I put my hands up. "I know it's shitty. But that's why teams have reserve drivers. Other sports have substitutes too. They get called up if a player gets hurt. It's the norm."

"It's all fucking *ridiculous*."

She's furious, but she burns so brilliantly. And this passion is because of me. Last night, she told me she'd never stop me from following my racing dreams, but her concern is the trade-off, and today it's manifesting in the form of anger.

She'd probably kick my ass if I said it out loud, but she looks so goddamn sexy as she huffs and stomps over to the balcony and throws the doors open. She pauses and draws in a deep breath, though it does little to dull the flame still scorching within her.

"What if you all refuse to race?" she suggests, whirling back around to look at me. "If the entire Drivers' Association bands together on this, maybe they'll call it off."

I try not to scoff. "That'll never happen. No one even brought it up in our WhatsApp group after the announcement was made. Honestly . . . I think most of us want to do this."

"*Most of you* are thrill-seeking hooligans who need to pull your heads out of your—" She cuts herself short, drawing in yet another shuddering breath. "I'm sorry. I'm just . . ."

"The hottest thing I've ever seen?" I supply, flashing a lop-sided grin that manages to pry a laugh out of her, even through her anger. "Keep yelling, baby. You're making me hard."

"You're the worst." She's scolding me, but she's mostly mad at herself for giving me that beautiful sound.

I'm about to get out of bed and convince her to come back and calm down—and, all right, maybe do a little more than that—when my phone buzzes on the bedside table. I freeze when I see the name on the screen.

"It's Howard."

My eyes dart to Willow again, and I watch as her own go wide, her wild hands motioning to the phone.

"Answer it," she hisses, like she's worried that Howard can hear her. "It could be important."

She's right. But what if it's bad news? That's the last thing

I need after the shit show of yesterday. Still, at her insistence, I scoop up the device and answer on speakerphone.

"Hello?"

"Mascort has been in touch," Howard says, skipping over the pleasantries.

My stomach drops straight to the floor. Shit. His tone is impossible to read, and it's left me fearing the worst.

"Zaid won't be returning for the rest of the season," he continues.

Even though I had a feeling that would be the case for my future teammate, I hate to hear it. "Shit." I suck in a breath, ready to ask if he's heard anything about Axel's condition, or even Lorenzo's, but he speaks before I can.

"Mascort wants you to take his seat for the rest of the season."

My heart lurches as I lock eyes with Willow. Did I hear him correctly?

From the way she mouths, *Oh my god*, I know I'm not hallucinating.

"You're kidding me," I blurt.

As usual, he doesn't entertain my shock. "You'll finish out the season alongside Kivinen," he explains, "and you'll take Kivinen's seat when Zaid returns next year."

I take a little comfort in that. They're assuming Zaid will be well enough to make a return, and judging from Willow's soft exhale, she feels the same. But it doesn't temper my shock otherwise.

"And Argonaut is going to *let me*?"

"Argonaut will get paid a pretty penny to let you leave early. In fact, there was a bit of a war over you. D'Ambrosi wanted you to replace Lorenzo—claimed they had the rights to you because of the engine agreement Argonaut has with them. But money talks, and Mascort is offering more."

I'd be a little more flattered if I wasn't pissed that Howard did all of this behind my back. "You didn't think to ask what I wanted or involve me in these talks before now?"

"They were happening when you were getting scans to make sure your brain was still intact."

Well, fuck.

"You're being looped in now," Howard goes on. "Obviously the choice is up to you, but you now have an opportunity to go to Mascort earlier than planned."

I blow out a breath, taking in the way Willow has pressed her lips into a thin line. She's clearly stunned by the mad moves these guys have been making too. "They didn't waste any time, did they?"

"There can be no empathy where millions of dollars are involved. You know that."

He's not wrong, no matter how sick that idea makes me. "Does that mean the news about me going to Mascort next season is coming out soon too? They can't keep that a secret for long if they expect me to be in their car by Friday."

"I'd say in the next hour, if it's not out already. And I'm guessing this means you're willing to accept the agreement?"

I look at Willow, taking in her cautious expression. Obviously, I need to see the amended contract for myself, and I need both Howard and my lawyers to walk me through it, but . . . I want this. I really do.

And when I start to see a hint of Willow's dimples, I know she wants this for me too.

"Yeah," I tell Howard, amazed my voice sounds as strong as it does, because holy *shit*, this has me nearly shaking. "Send over the new contracts."

"They're already in your inbox for review." He pauses, letting me process everything. "Get ready, Dev. Your life's about to change."

WILLOW

Unsurprisingly, I feel pretty comfortable in hospitals. Same goes for urgent care centers and doctors' offices. It's all thanks to how much time I spent in them as a kid, having tests run and my joints put back into place. Dev, however, is beyond uncomfortable. And I can't blame him. For him, hospitals mean the worst.

"I hate it here," he grumbles, sticking close to my side as we make our way down the hall toward the patient rooms. "Why does disinfectant have to smell like that? It's so *gross*."

"You'll be fine," I soothe. I have to bite back a laugh at his whining. He's truly nervous. "Zaid wants to see you. And you don't say no to Zaid Yousef."

We can't stay long, considering our flight to Japan leaves in two hours, but when summoned by a seven-time world champion—and future teammate—Dev did exactly what he was told.

He straightens up a little, composing himself. "That's for sure."

I'm here for moral support, but knowing Zaid is well enough to receive visitors has lessened some of the weight on my chest. I still don't know much about Axel's or Lorenzo's conditions. I can only hope they're improving as well.

Dev was right, though. This is the world of Formula 1.

And I have to accept it. It's a high-risk, high-reward sport, and there's nothing I can do to change it. I can only stand behind the drivers I'm there to support and do my best to stay strong.

And I will. Because I'd do anything for Dev. Anything to stay in his world. Our world.

When we reach Zaid's room, he pauses outside the door and squeezes my hand, a question in his eyes. "Will you come in with me?"

I'm pretty sure this is a conversation for just the two of them, but if he wants me in there and Zaid's okay with it, I'll happily stick by his side. "Of course."

It takes him several seconds to hype himself up. After a couple of deep breaths and a few shoulder rolls, he gives me a nod. Then he knocks on the door and pushes it open when a voice calls for us to come in. His hand is still wrapped tightly around mine as he guides me inside, and I file in behind him, peeking around his shoulder to see into the room.

The machines, wires, and tubes are the first things I spot, and I trace them over to the bed where Zaid is resting. Before today, I never would have thought he was nearly forty—good genes and an even better skincare routine probably help—yet here, in his hospital gown and with dark circles under his eyes, he looks every one of his years. But when he spots Dev and he starts to smile, a decade instantly vanishes. Dev is absolutely the most attractive guy on the grid, but Zaid . . . let's just say he's a very close second.

"Anderson," he greets, his voice surprisingly strong. "Thanks for coming to see me."

Dev nods, gently pulling me to stand by his side. "Of course, man. Is it okay that my girlfriend's here?"

"Absolutely." Zaid's attention shifts to me, and I'm suddenly on the receiving end of the world's most intense—but surprisingly kind—stare. "Lovely to finally meet you, Willow."

The shock of him knowing my name must show on my face, because he chuckles lightly.

"I've seen you around the paddock," he explains. "I'd shake your hand but . . ." He glances wryly down at where his arms rest in casts on a pillow in his lap. "Little injured at the moment."

"We'll save it for another time," I reply, relaxing when he huffs a laugh. "How are you feeling?"

"Like I got hit by a car going two hundred kilometers per hour and then exploded."

A surprised snort escapes me at his dry answer, and I immediately clap a hand over my mouth in embarrassment, but Zaid's replying grin makes me a little less mortified.

"I'll recover," he reassures, his dark eyes assessing me before shifting to Dev. "So will Axel. We'll be back."

There's no mention of Lorenzo. And I don't miss the flash of weariness in his eyes at the mention of his own return.

"But not until next season," Dev adds for him, getting to what we assume is the point of this meeting—Dev taking Zaid's place at Mascort, the contracts for which he signed just before we left to come here.

Zaid nods, black hair falling against his forehead. "First off, I wanted to welcome you to the team. Taking my place obviously wasn't the way you were meant to start with Mascort, but I'm glad it's you keeping my seat warm for me."

Dev dips his head, and I tamp down a grin when a hint of pink colors his cheeks.

Too cute.

"You deserve this spot." Zaid pauses, waiting for Dev to

look up again. His expression is serious now. "I've watched you drive over the years. In the right car, I think you can do well. Very well."

I keep my eyes on Dev as he takes in the praise from his idol. These words mean more than anything anyone else in the business has ever said to him, and Zaid seems to truly mean them.

"Thank you," Dev says after a beat. "I'll do my best to live up to that."

Zaid's smile shifts more into smirk territory as he relaxes into the pillows propping him up. "You better. If Mascort loses the Constructors' Championship this year to Specter Energy because of you, I'll have them rip up your contract. You understand?"

While I'm pretty sure Zaid is joking, he probably does have the power and sway to make that happen. And I wouldn't put it past him. He's clearly a good person, but championships aren't won with kindness.

Dev clears his throat and nods, and I swear he stands a little straighter. "Yeah, completely understood."

"Good." Zaid gives him an assessing once-over. "All right, go on. Drive my car this weekend. You have my blessing. And don't wreck it, yeah? It's seen enough trauma."

"I'll do my best."

With that, we wish Zaid a speedy recovery before we slip back into the hallway. We're quiet as we walk down the corridor, each processing that one-of-a-kind interaction. I'm certainly starstruck. And, okay, maybe developing the tiniest crush that I will *never* tell Dev about.

Eventually, my boyfriend wraps his arm around my shoulders and tugs me close, pressing a kiss to my temple. "I'm

driving for Mascort this weekend," he mumbles in pure disbelief, as if it's just hit him.

A giddy wave of butterflies swarms my stomach. I'm so
proud of him I could scream. "You are."

"I'm taking Zaid's seat until he's better."

"That's right."

"I have to fill Zaid fucking Yousef's shoes."

It's definitely a big deal, but the way he says it sends crushing pressure down on me too. I wouldn't blame him for being
anxious about it. "I'm sure you're gonna be—"

"I'm so fucking excited."

Sucking in a breath, I study his face, surprised by that
gushing confession. "Really? You're not nervous?"

He shrugs. "I mean, if the semi I'm rocking is anything to
go by—"

"I'm sorry," I splutter, coming to a stop in the middle of
the hallway. "Are you saying *Zaid Yousef* makes you hard?"

He grins cheekily down at me. "Okay, correction: knowing I get to drive for a team I've always dreamed of being part
of makes me *really* hard."

"Oh, ew, Dev."

He backs me against a wall, just around the corner and out
of sight of the main hallway. And yep, I can feel just how *excited* he is.

"But it's knowing that I get to have you with me through
all of this that really takes the cake," he murmurs, dipping his
head so his lips ghost over mine. "I couldn't do this without
you, Willow. Any of it. Not after I discovered what it feels like
to love you and be loved by you in return. It's what gives me
strength. *You* are my strength."

A lump grows in my throat, and happy tears prick at the

backs of my eyes. Yesterday was easily one of the worst days of my life. That fear and anguish when I didn't know whether Dev was involved, as quickly as it came and went, nearly broke me. But his return built me up again. It hardened my bones and strengthened every muscle and ligament within me. It made me stronger than I ever thought I could be, and I've done the same for him.

I never want to live without that power.

I want to live with him right beside me. Always.

I'd tell him as much, but Dev goes on, that grin of his slowly spreading.

"Seriously," he says. "How lucky am I that I not only get to travel the world and drive fast cars, but I get to do it with the woman I love by my side?"

"Very lucky," I agree, resting my hand over his racing heart. Mine is beating just as fast. "I think it might even be fate."

"Written in the stars, huh?"

I tip my chin up in open invitation. "Do you think the stars could write a future where you kiss me in the next five seconds?"

"I think they could make that happen."

And what do you know—the stars give me exactly what I want. They always do.

WILLOW

One year later
New York City

"Can I *please* take the blindfold off now?"

I swear I've had the scrap of silk over my eyes for at least a half hour, and the sounds of New York City are heightened because of it. Everything's so loud, and I'm terrified of tripping as Dev leads me down the sidewalk. He'll probably have permanent nail marks in his forearm from how tightly I'm gripping him.

"Not yet," he answers cryptically. It's the same tone he's been using since he interrupted my visit with Chantal and Grace to herd me into a waiting SUV. "We're almost there."

We better be, or I'm going to say to hell with whatever this surprise is and ditch the blindfold.

This was the last thing I expected today, especially since Dev wasn't even supposed to be in the city. We agreed to spend the two-week gap between races apart, not because we needed a break from each other, but because our schedules conflicted. I needed to be in New York with Reid while he did a mini press tour, and Dev needed to be in the UK at Mascort headquarters to test new car upgrades on the simulator.

So his appearance in itself was a surprise. But when he showed up to kidnap me for some kind of date? An even bigger shock.

"Five more steps," he announces. "And . . . stop."

An air-conditioned breeze hits me as a door opens, and bells tinkle above my head. It only takes one step inside to know where I am. The scent is a dead giveaway.

"You brought me to Stella Margaux's?" I ask, laughing. "You didn't have to blindfold me for this."

"Maybe not," Dev concedes, untying the knot at the back of my head. "But I did want this part to be a surprise."

Before he pulls the silk from my eyes, it dawns on me how quiet it is in the building, which never happens. I would know—I've been here every afternoon since I arrived three days ago. Each time, the line has been down and around the block. My suspicions are confirmed when the blindfold falls away to reveal that Dev and I and another man in chef's whites are the only people in the store.

Wide-eyed and stomach flip-flopping, I turn to Dev. "Did you rent out the entire place?"

"I did." He grins, rocking back on his heels in smug pleasure. "I figured you didn't want witnesses when you attempted to make macarons again."

I groan, but my excitement bubbles up and takes over. A macaron-baking date is truly the most *me* thing he could have planned. "I fully regret ever telling you about my baking failures."

"We'll make sure they turn out perfectly," the chef promises.

"Don't underestimate her," Dev says, earning an elbow to the gut from me. It only makes him grin wider.

The other man steps forward with his hand outstretched. "I'm Antoine. Stella's sorry she can't make it, but she said she'll see you in the paddock next week. You ready to get baking?"

I nod and shake his hand. "Please teach me your ways. I've been trying to replicate these for *years*."

I can't believe I'm more excited about these than I am about seeing Stella next week. But if there's one perk to having a boyfriend in F1, it's getting to meet the celebrities I always dreamed of interacting with.

Antoine waves us back to the kitchen. "Come on. I'll show you all our secrets."

▰▰▰▰▰

An hour later, I've achieved the impossible. I've made a perfect macaron.

Actually, I've made *several*. There's a whole array of vanilla-peach masterpieces laid out in front of me. I might be prouder of these than anything else I've ever done.

As a testament to Antoine's amazing teaching skills, even Dev has made a tray full of gorgeous and uniform macarons. The man is a decent cook, but I didn't know baking was in his wheelhouse. I swear, there's nothing he can't do. It's just another reason why I love him with all my heart.

"Here," Dev says, handing me a classic Stella Margaux's box. "Add your creations in with mine."

I take the box from him, focused on making sure I pick out the most perfect ones to bring home. When I have my ten selected, I pull the sunset-orange lid off the box and grab the first macaron to place gently inside next to his.

And then I freeze. The macaron slips from my fingers and onto the floor.

Tucked between two stunning strawberry macarons is a ring. A diamond ring. The biggest, sparkliest, most beautiful diamond ring I've ever seen.

When I look up again, heart lodged in my throat and lips parted in surprise, Dev isn't standing in front of me anymore. He's down on one knee and gazing up.

"Willow Williams," he begins. He's going for serious, but he's fighting what's bound to be the world's widest grin. "My sunshine girl. My macaron-loving menace. Absolute love of my life. Will you marry me?"

Holy shit, this is happening. This is *actually happening*. We've been together for over a year, and I couldn't imagine living my life with anyone else, but *still*. I'm in shock.

"Oh my god," I splutter, my eyes darting between his expectant face and the massive diamond. "Oh my god, Dev, *yes*. Yes, yes, yes!"

The box clatters onto the stainless-steel worktop, and Dev's laughter serves as the soundtrack to the moment I throw myself at him.

"Is this why Chantal told me my nails looked ugly and forced me to get them done today?" I sob, clinging to him. I'm so happy I could explode. "Did she know?"

He holds me to him, his arms strong and warm. "Yeah, I gave her and Grace a heads-up. I had to get their approval anyway."

"And is that why Oakley called this morning?" I demand. All the pieces are falling into place. God, how did I not see this coming? "He was all sappy and sweet! I just thought he was trying to butter me up to get passes to the D'Ambrosi garage!"

"It's a miracle he didn't give it away," Dev says. "I told him weeks ago what I was planning, and made him promise not to ruin the surprise. Never seen a man so stressed about keeping a secret."

It's amazing how far we've come since the day Oakley found out about us. I was worried he'd never get over it, but instead, he's become one of our biggest supporters. Dev and Oakley are partners in crime once again—the only difference now is that I'm not the unwanted hanger-on. I'm part of the group. Never thought I'd see the day when that happened.

I press my face to Dev's chest, not caring that my tears will ruin my makeup and stain his shirt. "I can't believe you did this!"

"Figured it was about time," he murmurs against the top of my head. "I would have done it sooner, but we're so damn busy all the time."

I pull back again, something else dawning on me. "Wait, did Reid know too? Is that why he kept pushing for me to take today off? Who *didn't* know?"

Dev's grin is sly. "Let's just say there were a lot of people in on this." He dips his head once more and murmurs in my ear. "By the way, Reid's not expecting you to work tomorrow either. Or until we're back on the road again. You're all mine, Willow."

I stare up at him, my heart near bursting. He's right. I'm all his. Just like he's all mine.

Guess that's fate for you.

ACKNOWLEDGMENTS

It's mind-blowing how many people it takes to make a book come to life, but I couldn't have done this without any of them.

My amazing agent, Silé Edwards, who replied to my first frantic email thirty minutes after I sent it on a Saturday night, and stayed up late to field my panicked calls. You've held my (very sweaty) hand through what has been such a whirlwind experience, and I couldn't be more grateful.

My Pan Macmillan editor, Kinza Azira, for believing in this story and helping to make it so much stronger. I love how our visions for the book aligned, and working together has been an absolute dream. My Berkley editor, Mary Baker. I knew from our first conversation about Danny Ric that this book was going to be in good hands. And the teams from both publishers—you all keep everything running so smoothly, and you've made my debut experience so lovely.

Beth Lawton, for taking the first draft of this book and helping to turn it into something coherent with your magical line edits. Leni Kauffman, for creating the most stunning

402   Acknowledgments

cover. You brought my ideas to life better than I could have
ever imagined.

Soraya and Mahbuba, for laying the groundwork so this
book could reach more people. You two did so much to help
make my publishing dreams come true. Your kindness has
meant the absolute world to me, and I'll never be able to thank
you enough for it.

The readers who have followed me across pen names and
platforms and genres. Thank you for sticking with me and for
growing with me. We've come a long, long way.

All the CTL beta readers who took the time to help shape
the story. Your feedback was invaluable! Jenna, Deidre,
Norhan, Aaliyah, Ruqi, Bei, Naorès, Moon, Ann, Tiyasa, Viv-
ian, Nat, Teigan, Zarin, and Chloe, for being the biggest cheer-
leaders and shouting about this book. You're all superstars.

The A-Team, for putting up with me at karaoke and simply
being there through some of the toughest moments. This
time, I won't ask if you enjoyed that.

Kate, I quite literally wouldn't have gotten through this
without you. Thank you for taking such good care of the
shared brain cell when I couldn't, for listening so patiently to
all my wild ideas, and for sitting beside me in Palm Springs
while I whined over what I thought was going to be the last
edit of this book. I, too, hope we keep writing accidental com-
panion books for decades.

Kell, I'm so glad we managed to escape from You-Know-
Where, but meeting you there was the best thing that could
have happened. Thank you for all your encouragement to just
keep writing, and for being the coolest ever. Time to plan our
next Vancouver trip.

Marlene, for being my third mom and pushing me to keep
following my dreams even when I felt held back. You got me

through some of the worst minutes and hours and days of my life, and I will never forget that.

Sammy, for being the sister I honestly never asked for but got stuck with anyway. There's no one else I'd want to share a creepy roadside motel room with.

My grandmother, for bringing me chai, calling to wake me up for early F1 races, and babysitting my dogs so I can actually get some work done.

Mom D, if you're reading this, it means I've finally let you read one of my books. Congratulations! Let's never talk about it again! But thank you for respecting my privacy throughout my childhood and teenage years, because that allowed me space to become the writer I am today. Thank you for being my chef, my chauffeur, and my therapist. Love you more than words can say.

And Mom J. I know you didn't like romance, but I like to think you would have enjoyed this one (only because I wrote it). Miss you. Thanks for getting me here.

ABOUT THE AUTHOR

Simone Soltani is a romance author and former ghost-writer for a serialized fiction platform. Born and raised in Washington, DC, she holds a BA in geography from the George Washington University, which she likes to think comes in handy for world-building in her novels. When she's not writing, she spends most of her time planning vacations she'll probably never get to go on, reorganizing her many bookshelves, and watching sports while cuddling with her dogs.

VISIT SIMONE SOLTANI ONLINE

SimoneSoltani.com
SimoneSoltani
SimoneSoltani
AuthorSimoneSoltani